DEATHLESS BEAST

DEATHLESS BEAST

THE KALLATTIAN SAGA
VOLUME ONE

Andrew D Meredith

Games Afoot, LLC

Copyright © 2022 by Andrew D Meredith

All rights reserved. No part of this book may be reproduced in any manner whatsoever without written permission except in the case of brief quotations embodied in critical articles and reviews.

Second Edition, 2024

Books by Andrew D Meredith

NEEDLE AND LEAF SERIES

THRICE

FOUR-SCORED

FIFE AND DRUM (*UPCOMING*)

SWEAR BY THE SIXTH (*UPCOMING*)

THE KALLATTIAN SAGA

DEATHLESS BEAST

BONE SHROUD

GLOVES OF EONS

DREAD KNIGHT

SIDEWAYS TALES

QUAINT CREATURES: MAGICAL & MUNDANE

*To my parents, Scotte and Renae,
for raising me as a proper nerd
A Meredith is never on time.
We arrive when we mean to.
Early.*

FORWARD

I've a tender place in my heart for impossible heroes. Not the underdog that rises to greatness, but the one who just wants to go back to his normal life, yet is thrust onto the road instead. Not the warrior who glories in battle, but the one who questions what anyone would see in him. Not the woman who seeks to carve a name for herself, but the one who would just be contented knowing she had choice for her life.

The Kallattian Saga is replete with characters such as these—those that recognize that more often than not, the hero falls, and they'd rather not be the example others learn from. It's the age-old tale of the Call and Refusal, followed by the Threshold Guardian. Only, the Threshold is not one gate and its gate keeper, but a series. Every day we must rise from bed and choose to continue on our quest. Each of us is The Traveler, each of us living out our own epic poem. We can learn from others or learn by experience. The true lesson learned is finding that both of these are valid, and that the heroic cycle is not made up of one path, but many.

For some it is a quest. Others, a road deeper into faith. Yet The road to Faith is never ended, and the reward is never won on this side of forever. Yet the friends and treasures gathered on the way are gleanings richer than gold.

I look forward to taking you down these many paths carving their way through *The Kallattian Saga*. Together let's examine ourselves in the lives of the Clouws, Jined and the twins, Katiam, Seriah, and many more to come. These names mean nothing to you now, but in time, they will.

Thank you for joining me on this journey.

—Andrew D Meredith

WESTERN GANTHIC

PART 1

PROLOGUE

"It would have been better if I had made it here before the Prima Pater and his entourage arrived."

Though a Paladin, he wore a short black traveler's cloak, trying to cover up his armored frame, though it was a futile attempt. Gold cordons intentionally displayed on his shoulder marked him a Pater Minoris. It was an unnecessary show of rank, though, since they had all known each other for a long time.

"I disagree," the other Pater Minoris said. He had a thin nose, close-set, beady, childish eyes, and road-weary wrinkles showing lighter against the tanned skin of most Paladins stationed in the south.

"Excuse me?" the first Paladin asked, his rage seemed always a hair's breadth away, and offense was easily taken.

"Vanguard," the second said. "If the Prima Pater had been visited by you, or myself, he would have questioned why two Paladins in leadership, from far-off fortresses and citadels—ones not on his itinerary—made such a trek to see him. That is why it is better that we arrived later than we did. Better that Dusk here moves them along their path and deeper into the turmoil that awaits them."

"I agree, Bell," the third said. He had bright blonde eyebrows and a short stubble of matching blonde hair which was quickly growing in, despite his regular ritual of shaving. "It will be easy enough to keep things civil, with the pretense that all is well to the north. Any and all calls for aid from Bortali and Boroni came to my desk, and were easily disposed of. No one at St. Hamul even knows there are issues in those countries. Even the Konig of Nemen has remained in the dark, as the brother stationed there has been intercepting any messages from the north."

"What turmoil do you speak of?" Vanguard asked.

"Not only are Bortali and Boroni on the verge of all-out war, the vül are acting up. There is even rumor of one of the cursed who has taken matters into his own hands. If it's who I think it is, then the Prima Pater and his followers are walking into a death-trap as soon as they leave Nemen."

"If they all die, what good will that do our cause?"

"If they live, then they walk into deeper political intrigue. It will give us ripe fruit to harvest for our cause—strengthening our numbers. If they die, the power vacuum left by the majority of the Order's leadership simply disappearing will give the three of us plenty of power in our own rights."

"What of the Aerie?" Bell said, turning to Vanguard.

"What about it?"

"You came all this way. What news do you have?"

"It was merely my hope to come and pull additional wool over the Prima Pater's eyes. But the fact is, we suspect that we've found who holds the Plate, and expect to have it in our control soon."

"Very good," Bell said. "Shroud has implied that he wants me to travel to Bulwark soon. I'll see if I can convince a number of them to travel in the direction of the Aerie. You can do what you like with them."

"Why do that?" Vanguard asked. "I have no need to see them destroyed. They are not part of my plans."

"Shroud could care less about your plans. He needs the Bulwark emptied and you're the best man to take care of it."

"Tell Shroud I do as I please. If he wants to be so demanding, he should have come himself."

"Don't be fools," Dusk said.

The other two balked, Bell in surprise and Vanguard with barely contained rage.

"I am no fool, Primus," Vanguard growled. "You know the Motean tenets. We each walk our own path to glean for ourselves what power the gods let fall to the wayside. I have grown tired of being ordered about by a man I've never met. If he doesn't want to share his plans, I'll make my own."

Vanguard stood abruptly and walked out of the inn.

"Ignore him, Dusk," Bell said.

"I've already forgotten him," he said, smiling.

"But you're considering his words."

"Of course I am. He's right; we each have our own plans. But I also understand why we must work together. Otherwise, everything is vanity."

"What plans do you have in place? Shroud will want to know."

"I haven't had to make plans, to be honest," Dusk said with a smirk. "The political climate is toxic in the north. The Pater Minoris at St. Rämmon is an ignorant fool and he's making a mess of everything. When the Prima Pater arrives in Garrou, it's going to ignite a wildfire of problems."

"And this Pater at Rämmon has been the perfect pawn?"

"An ignorant pawn. He doesn't know a thing about our Motean sect. He certainly knows nothing of international diplomacy. He's been scrambling back and forth from St. Rämmon to Garrou all year and thinks he's fixing things, but he's making it worse. I don't know how he even made the rank of Pater, but he did. It's going to topple around him in a gentle breeze and I won't have to lift a finger. My move will be to pick up the pieces. Tell that to Shroud when you see him."

"Tell him yourself," Bell said. He pulled open a leather-bound book from its place at his elbow to the center of the table.

"What do you mean?"

Well done, Dusk. The words flowered on the page in a deep red, nearly black, ink. *A war between Bortali and Boroni is exactly what is needed.*

"How? A shadebook?" Dusk asked, pulling his hands off the table.

You should know. You're the furthest into the secrets of the Feather.

"Shroud? Did you die?"

No. I'm very much alive. I've long known how to make a shadebook.

"Of course," Dusk said. "But how so, if you still live?"

It's simpler than you think.

"I want to know."

That is not why you're meeting. You were here to make sure that Brother Vanguard and his people were aligned with our plans. It seems they have taken matters into their own hands, and no longer feel their plans align with ours. That makes Limae dangerous for all Paladins—Moteans or otherwise. It also tells me he's lying, and they've long had the Plate in their possession.

"How do you come to that conclusion?" Dusk asked.

Because they wouldn't be scrambling if it were otherwise. We knew they had the Plate at one point, but they must have lied to us about having lost it. It belongs to me by right. I should have taken it while I had the chance.

"Shroud, if you suspect Vanguard has ill-intent, then you should make your way north."

I intend to. Make sure the Prima Pater is stalled from arriving in Mahn Fulhar. Mid-winter should suffice.

"I will do that."

Brother Dusk rose and left the inn without another word.

Why have you gone silent? The ink read.

"Dusk left."

Do you think Dusk is for or against us?

"I believe he is for us, but I think he also has it in him to go too far, or to go his own way entirely."

Very well. Please proceed to Birin. As suggested, see that the Pater there rides to the apparent rescue of The Aerie.

"That will be an easy task. Pater Kocl is a man of action, given little to do in Birin."

More the reason I need him and his followers away; I don't need him underfoot when I arrive.

"You'll be in Birin?"

Soon.

"You'd best conserve your energy. I'm sure this has cost you much blood."

This is true. You are a faithful friend to the cause. I will meet you in Birin. I look forward to being reunited with my shade.

"The promise your predecessors made with us is coming close to an end," Bell said.

Final words bloomed: *We are only just beginning.*

I

Bortali Border

A long road ahead, and straight

Its eddies as the sea.

The curves wind like wind and wave

The lands a tapestry.

Take now your life, be free

—FROM THE TRAVELER, THE EPIC POEM BY JUREN LEIFSEN OF BORTALI

The trees and shrubs grew smaller, fewer, and farther between as the caravan approached the treeline. The gray-green carpet of griefdark grew in patches of sunlight, and it would soon be all the eye could see as they broke out onto the plain that ascended to the ridge far above.

Twelve wagons lumbered along the gently steepening road. Some merchants walked alongside their wagons, leading their yokes of massive bovine aurochs whose horns curled down along thick jaws, hunched shoulders and heads lowered. Other merchants drove smaller wagons pulled by one or two six-legged sleipnir horses. Some merchants rode in the comfort of their wagons, while their apprentices or sons held the reins.

Ten Black Sentinels took guard positions around the caravan, their faces obscured by widow's peaked hood-lines and pointed tops rising off their heads. The Clouw Caravan Detail, though unique for Black Sentinels who usually worked alone or in pairs, had become a fairly common sight along the road from Garrou to Edi City. Their larger numbers of experienced guards dissuaded brigands and opportunists from taking advantage of the merchants in their care.

The Clouws took the lead that morning, walking out front of the line of wagons.

Hanen, older than his sister by four years, and standing just as many inches taller, bore sharper features, and had his black hair tied up loosely on the top of his head, tussled by the hood he kept off his head and on his shoulders.

Rallia kept her cloak open and moved with a short staff in one hand, a club mounted to each end and bound with single bands of metal—a signature of Black Sentinels of lower ranks. Rallia wore heavy leather pads over broad shoulders gifted to her by her father, and two hand axes hung from the belt across her waist. She had sun-bleached blonde hair bound across her scalp in two braids, the tips of which didn't quite grace her shoulders and ended in two polished brass caps.

"You should close your cloak," Hanen said. "Everyone else does. With your clubs on display, it looks like you're a lower rank than you are."

"The axes on my belt say otherwise," Rallia replied. "If anyone underestimates me, that's their own fault."

"The merchants were quick to rise this morning."

"Half of them were up all night," Rallia continued, "unless I'm wrong and they got up before me to start drinking early."

"I don't know how you do that," Hanen said.

"Do what?"

"Wake before the sun. For one, why would you? And two, how do you know to rise when the sun isn't even up?"

"And three?" Rallia asked.

"Three?"

"You always make lists of three."

"No, I don't. That's you," Hanen said.

"Not true. I don't like three; three is uneven."

They arrived at the tree line. The path was well cared for across the long meadow before the border crossing. It needed to be. Rocks no taller than knee high had been erected in a short, makeshift wall to keep the invasive griefdark from growing over the path. Lumps covered over in griefdark lay in the meadow, more than likely the remains of animals fallen numbed by the touch of the leaves rather than rocks. While griefdark made for a good salve, many a traveler had gotten a leaf into their boot that left them with a leg that wouldn't work for hours.

A Sentinel standing nearly as tall as Hanen, but built of firmer grit, came up next to them. Eunia Halla lowered her hood. She had the deeper sun-browned skin of a Morriegan, with the angular features of the Northern Scapes. Her hair was a plain brown and had been shaved along the sides by Rallia, the company's resident barber.

"I will range ahead to the border station."

"Do you want us to join you?" Rallia asked.

"No. A few of the men there owe me a drink. I'd like to make sure they pay up before these merchants get in my way."

Eunia was a firmly stubborn woman. Hanen found it best to leave her to her own business. She never caused trouble for others as long as they kept out of her way, and if it came to a fight, he wanted her as a trusted ally, not a begrudging one.

Another Sentinel approached as Eunia walked away. He too lowered his hood and walked in silence between the Clouws. He had pale skin and a heavy jaw. His thick hair grew long and upright, and down the back of his neck disappearing into the collar of his shirt. He was the only man from the Oruche Marches, south of Œron, that Hanen had met. Hanen understood why so many people insulted Oruche calling them horse-people, even if the people of Œron and Sidierata grew the same wild mane. Thadar Saliss's crossbow, the mark of his captain's rank, edged its way out of his cloak every few steps.

"What is she doing?" he asked in a gravelly voice.

"She said some of the border guards still owe her a drink or two from our last journey through," Rallia said, uncorking a bottle of ale, tipping the contents into her dry mouth, and offering a swig to Hanen.

"You're not going to go with her? Make sure she doesn't mess up any arrangements you have with the guards?"

"What does it matter to you?" Hanen asked.

"I'm the ranking Sentinel on this caravan, I have a right to know."

"That doesn't mean anything. Sentinel or not, I hired you, and I'm paying you captain's wages. You know rank is just your pay grade."

Thadar scowled and slowed down, letting the Clouws gain a lead.

"Why did you let Eunia go up there on her own?" Rallia inquired.

"I trust her. She's good at what she does, and if she gets in any trouble, she gets herself out of it."

"Then why not just say that to Thadar?"

"Because I don't trust him. He says he was never in military service, but I think that's false. Either he insists on our acknowledging his rank because he's had rank before, or perhaps he was jealous of those with rank. If I had to guess, I'd wager he was a deserter. I can't prove it, so we live with it. We can't negotiate higher pay from merchants without a captain in the caravan."

Some of the merchants started to lag in front of the caravan, causing others to pile up and curse those before them. One Sentinel pushed his way up past the wagons and gave each pack animal a slap, urging them on. When merchants opened their mouths to protest, he just waved them along.

Aurín Mateau was a charming man, though he never smiled. His black hair was thick, kept cropped short on top of his polished pale face. The waxed mustache under his nose might have been out of place if he had not been from Œron. The dark hair that grew on his neck had been shaved off, but was coming in quickly.

"I saw Eunia take off," Aurín said, having jogged up to them. "Is she planning to cause trouble?"

"The guards owe her money," Hanen said.

"Damn," Aurín said.

"What?"

"I won't be able to gamble any money out of them myself if she spoils their moods."

Hanen heaved a sigh as he admitted to himself that Aurín was right. It would make their inspection harsh and the guards sour.

Eunia had stopped one hundred yards ahead, just before entering a group of twelve pillar-like stones, known as the Pantheon's Council—each granite slab named for a different member of the two families of gods. Merchants made signs of faith or cursed against bad omens near the stones of the fallen gods.

"Why is she stopping?" Aurín asked. "I never took her for a superstitious woman."

"Perfect distance from the border guard barracks for an ambush," Rallia said, squinting toward the lone, black-cloaked

Sentinel.

"What do you mean?" Hanen asked.

"Look past the two tallest stones of the Brother-Kings, Aben and Wyv."

Hanen imitated his younger sister's squints and saw the movement.

"Ambush? But the griefdark is across the entire meadow."

"Not amidst the Pantheon's Council," Rallia said. "We've still got a mile to the border. Even then, that's around the final curve and rise. You can only make out the back side of the stones from there. The guards won't even know an ambush has happened, and you know Barrack Captain Grodzi—he lets the griefdark guard the eastern flank. He just watches west and the road leading up to his barracks.

"You Clouws ought to go and check it out," Thadar said, having approached from behind.

The caravan came to a halt fifty yards from Eunia, as they watched the lone woman standing in the narrow road.

Hanen gave Thadar a glare. "So now you're not a captain?"

Thadar scowled and led the way forward. Hanen and Rallia moved to follow with Aurín and the rest of the Sentinels close behind.

Thadar strode confidently down the road and walked up next to Eunia. They passed the single stone known as the Sword of Rionne, fallen over twenty-five yards before the rest, like a huge sword blade lying in the griefdark which kept the weeds from growing any farther. Hanen could see someone trying to remain unseen behind the darker granite stone of Wyv, Judge of Noccitan.

"See?" Rallia muttered.

"Yes. I saw it. Ambush. Eunia?" Hanen said as they came to stand next to her. Thadar stood ten feet in front of them now. Though his cloak remained closed, Hanen could tell from his posture that he brandished his crossbow underneath.

"They have three arrows trained on me," Eunia said. "I thought it wise to wait for you."

A man came out from behind the second pillar. He wore brown leathers, though portions were dyed a ruddy red. Like Thadar, he had a coarse mane of hair. Unlike Thadar, he had a large number of tight wrinkles across his pale face. Three additional men came out to stand next to him. One didn't wear a shirt, showing off hair that grew all the way down his spine. These were Üterk, distant cousins to the Oruche of south Œron, and like them, ostracized by most cultures.

"Three more just came up out of the griefdark behind the caravan," Rallia said to Hanen as they all continued to look forward.

"Inna gon sout wih de wagns?" the first man said.

The broken speech of the Üterk had always been hard for Hanen, though he was generally able to understand them. He had heard it plenty on the streets of Garrou growing up. He pushed forward to stand beside Thadar, who remained silent.

"Yes. South," Hanen said.

"Yih gon pai golud."

Hanen shook his head and lowered his hood and tousled his own black hair free from the leather thong.

"Yih Üterk?"

"My mother died in childbirth, But yes, Üterk. So we'll be passing. You have to let the blood of the forest pass. This is my caravan."

"Wih kenna. Vulboss sai nah."

Thadar looked back over his shoulder. "They sound worse than my grandmother. I can't understand a word these mongrels say."

A large figure stalked out from between the stone cloven in two, representing the two fallen gods Kos-Yran and the Deceiver, Achanerüt. It had long, massive arms that hung low from its shoulders, with hands that reached just above the ground. The majority of its mass was held up by bulky, double-jointed legs. It had a barrel of a torso, with a powerful neck holding up its almost canine face.

Its jaws were built to crush, and its beady eyes shifted over a small, wet nose, sniffing at the air. Its entire frame was covered in a short but thick gray fur, which was longer on its arms and on the sleek mane that grew over its neck. Blackened leather over its body and legs sat in banded straps, framing its massive hunched back.

Atop the armored back lay a sword too heavy for a man to wield comfortably. It was a vül. This was not the scary image of a slavering beast that Hanen had come to imagine a vül might be, taken from the stories told to scare children.

This was worse, for this was real.

The intelligence flashing in the creature's eyes told Hanen he had much more to fear than simply being killed by such a monster. It stalked forward to stand at its full height in front of Thadar, who had slowly turned around, looking up at the fang-filled maw that smiled down at him.

"Your forest blood means nothing," the vül said with a low voice with more gravel in it than Thadar's. "Just the gold I take to my pack leader, and your lives."

The first move was sudden. The vül didn't wait for pleasantries. It swung with its massive arm across Thadar's middle, throwing him to the side of the road.

Hanen opened his cloak with his short hunting bow in his hands. The vül drew the sword off its back as he loped sideways. Hanen's arrow shot wide, taking the Üterk leader in the arm.

Rallia stepped in front of Hanen, her staff planted firmly on the ground, challenging anyone to come forward. Hanen nocked another arrow and let it fly. One of the bandits threw themselves to the ground as the arrow flew wide, and stayed down as Aurín charged over him. Eunia, keeping to Aurín's side, gave the man on the ground a swift kick, then threw herself onto the bandit leader, who sat cradling the arrow protruding from his arm.

"Look out!" Rallia shouted as Aurín and Eunia raised their weapons to deliver a killing blow to the Üterk leader.

Aurín spun to see the vül turning back to charge them. Rallia backed up into Hanen, shoving him away from the center of the road. Hanen's back bumped up against the remaining Sentinels, all gathered and facing additional brigands now coming up from behind. Beyond them, the merchants were frozen in a panic, unable to leave the griefdark-bordered road.

The vül raised its sword to strike Eunia, who still hadn't turned to look at it. She held a bloody axe in her hand. The two bandits on the ground were no longer moving.

Aurín gave a quick flick of his wrist, his axe just missing the creature's sword elbow. It responded by swatting at Aurín, who dodged deftly away.

Rallia started toward the beast.

"Rallia!" Hanen shouted. "Stop. Stay out of their way."

The vül advanced toward Aurín, who lept backward again and again, pulling the creature away from Eunia and her fallen opponents.

"It's what we're paid to do, Hanen," Rallia said, ignoring her brother and charging forward.

She lunged out with her staff, the banded club attached to the end striking the vül in the shoulder. The vül turned to face the young woman, swatting backward at Aurín to warn him off.

"Keep them back!" the vül shouted to the Üterk.

The beast stalked forward and Rallia backed up quickly in response. Hanen cast his bow aside and drew both hand axes from his belt, crying out as the heel of Rallia's boot caught dirt, causing her to trip backward.

As she hit the ground, the vül lunged forward. Rallia continued to roll, her legs coming over her head. She landed in a crouch on one knee, staff in hand. She looked up at the monster over her. The vül advanced.

Rallia's staff swung up under the creature's jaw, the force clamping the vül's mouth shut, producing a yelp. Caught off guard by the sound that came from its own maw, the vül paused, touching its bleeding lip. Rallia stood, spun the staff over her head, and set herself into position, readying herself for the monster.

A holler came from behind as Eunia flew at the vül in a rage. The creature ducked and took the assault with its shoulder, lifting her up over its head and throwing her away. She landed lightly on her feet next to an Üterk who stood gawking at the fight between the vül and Rallia. He crumpled to the ground as her axe bit into his shoulder.

Hanen glanced around once more to see the Sentinels behind him making quick work of the brigands at the rear. The vül broke forward and tackled Rallia before she could move out of the way. As Rallia dropped, she pulled a knife and repeatedly thrust it into the monster's side, shouting as she did. The vül took hold of Rallia's throat, holding her down in the dirt at arm's length. Rallia couldn't reach the monster's torso past its long arm, so she tried slicing at the heavy leather across the creature's wrists. Hanen stood locked in fear, watching his sister die—unable to help her.

"Hanen...," Rallia croaked, glancing over.

The vül looked over and smiled.

"Yours?" it asked.

"S-sister," Hanen replied.

The vül lifted Rallia bodily off the ground and held her out.

"Swear fealty to me and to my god, Kos-Yran. I might spare you and give your sister a quick death."

Rallia looked imploringly at Hanen and mouthed the single word, "No."

The axes in Hanen's hands grew heavy.

The vül's fang-filled smile watched as Hanen thought through the offer. He wagged Rallia in his hand like a rag doll. Rallia continued to struggle.

"My god is a gift-giver. I can be just as giving as he. You bear the blood of the Üterk. Follow your mother's blood. They make good servants. I would make you my..."

Blood shot out of the monster's right eye as it disappeared. He dropped Rallia to the ground and grabbed the bloody eye socket, the bolt shaft from a crossbow sticking out. The vül's tongue lashed out, became heavy, and seemed to pull it forward onto the ground where it slammed down into the dirt, dead.

Thadar stood behind the monster's dead body, his crossbow in his arms.

"I think you owe me more gold."

2

Deld

Oruche, Oruche, go away.

Take your dreams past bright Umay.

Your silly hair

and cursed nightmare,

We do not want them on this day.

—CHILDREN'S VERSE FROM ŒRON

"How did you make it past the vül," Captain Grodzi asked.

"We didn't," Hanen said. "We killed him."

"I killed him," Thadar said. "Let's not forget that."

"That monster has been harassing me and my men for the past week," Grodzi said. "I've not let anyone from Düran into Bortali, nor seen anyone make it past the Pantheon's Council until now."

"Isn't it your job to clear the way of brigands like those?" Hanen asked.

Grodzi turned and motioned towards the men with him. "It's me and five guards. Not one of us has been more than city guards before being stationed here. You think I can fight a vül?"

"I'd like to hope that we can make our inspection quick," Hanen said. "Unless you're going to offer us a bath."

"We ran out of wood for our fire three days ago."

"Then a quick inspection?" Hanen countered.

"Of course," Grodzi said.

Hanen led Rallia over to a wall, where his sister slumped down against the cool stone.

Hanen applied the contents of a jar of griefdark ointment to her sprained wrist, then lightly applied more of the greasy balm on his sister's throat. Eunia looked worse, though upon inspection, the blood covering her was not her own.

"That was close," Rallia said in a hoarse whisper.

"Don't talk too much. You need to preserve your voice while your throat heals."

"Hanen, the border guard captain wants to see you," Aurín said over his shoulder. "Thadar is getting pushy with him."

"What's the trouble?" Hanen asked, approaching the two captains.

"Nothing at all," Thadar said, his crossbow over his shoulder. "I was just speaking captain-to-captain with Grodzi here."

"You promised a quick inspection, Captain Grodzi," Hanen said. "All the merchants came from Garrou and have their papers."

The captain looked at the ledger in front of him. "Two of these merchants came from Boroni. It says they're moving barrels of ale. We need to inspect their wagons."

"Captain," Hanen said, "I paid you quite handsomely last time we came through, and we just took care of your Üterk problem at the Pantheon's Council."

Grodzi turned to look Hanen in the eye. "I'm not asking you for more money, Clouw. We have orders to check and double-check all travelers from Boroni. You know the borders have been closed between our two nations now for some time."

"I hadn't heard that."

"If it's just ale they're moving, I'll turn a blind eye, but I have orders."

They came to the wagon in question while the merchants wrung their hands.

"If there is trouble...," one said.

"No trouble," Grodzi said. "We'll just be giving your wagon a once over."

One of the merchants tripped and dropped a small sack of coins onto the ground. Reaching to grab it, the merchant un-subtly kicked it toward one of the guards, who picked it up.

Captain Grodzi eyed the guard suspiciously and looked over at the merchants. "If you're so keen to keep us from looking over your wagon, perhaps there is more to this than meets the eye. The borders between Boroni and Bortali have been closed now for longer than I'd wager you've been in the country. I shouldn't let you go through to Düran at all, but I won't betray the arrangement I have with the Clouws."

The merchants dropped their heads and let the inspection continue without complaint. After a time, the captain came back to Hanen.

"All appears to be in order," the captain said.

"See? Nothing to worry about," Thadar said slapping the side of the wagon in a show of confidence. A panel fell free next to him, revealing a glint of metal hiding within.

Captain Grodzi scowled at Hanen. "You told me they were clean. Now I see they're smuggling good Boroni steel into Düran when it should be going to Bortali blacksmiths!"

Hanen lifted his hands up in a show of innocence. "Grodzi, I swear, we looked the wagon over ourselves. I'm as taken aback by this as you."

"Captain Grodzi," Rallia croaked as she came to stand next to Hanen, "you know we're clean."

"What will it take for us to move along and forget this whole thing happened?" Hanen offered.

The captain looked around sullenly, considering his options.

"We're confiscating this illegal metal. We'll also be keeping these merchants here for further questioning. Whether they can bribe their way out of this will be up to them."

Hanen nodded and turned to begin moving the merchants along.

"Clouw," Grodzi called out.

Hanen turned back.

"I owe you for the vül. But with tensions rising between us and Boroni, I can't just look the other way next time. Vet those you escort, or else you may end up being dragged back to Garrou in chains as an accomplice."

The captain held out his palm.

"Then we're good?" Hanen asked.

"The crossing agreement was a gold coin."

"You said when we arrived that it wasn't necessary. And that you owed us for the vül."

"I said that, yes, but I assumed you'd still pay. Now, with these men I'm detaining, I need something to show my superiors."

"Grodzi," Hanen implored.

Rallia stepped forward, shaking her head in disappointment as she handed the man a gold royal.

Grodzi took it, nodding, and barked orders for the guards to take the smugglers into custody and move the caravan along. The remaining merchants didn't need goading.

Captain Thadar marched ahead of the caravan, head held high, as they trundled through the threshold and onto the easy slope down into the Dürani highland plain.

Hanen pulled his hood up over his shoulders and walked sullenly behind the last merchant wagon as it left.

"I don't understand why we even bring these Sentinels along," the merchant atop the wagon grumbled. "They make arrangements for us at the border and then don't stand up for us when the guards get pushy."

"That's true," his companion grunted.

"That head Sentinel says brigands don't bother us because their numbers scare 'em off. Didn't help today, and we still got held up at the border."

"Keep your mounts moving steadily down the incline," Rallia croaked from the side of the road as she let the caravan pass. "This is the third route you've traveled with us, so you know it's a long slope. Best to take your time.

"Don't mind them," she said as Hanen approached. "You know those two have always complained about everything."

"If they're voicing it then they aren't the only ones thinking it."

Rallia shrugged. "They've paid us. We do our job. They come back or they don't."

"Try not to talk too much," Hanen said. "I bet by Deld you'll be much better."

"Thadar is bragging about how much gold he found in the vül's stash," Rallia said, ignoring Hanen's suggestion.

"And he's not planning on sharing it."

"I doubt it," Rallia uncorked a bottle of travelers beer, took a sip and handed it to Hanen. "Does he share anything?"

"Ghoré Dziony will find a way to get a coin or two out of him," Hanen said, eyeing the man who walked near Thadar, hanging on his every word.

"Ghoré is always shouldering in to get what scraps Thadar will leave him. Little we can do about that. Should we inform the Dürani authorities what happened?" Rallia asked. "It'll be some time before Bortali gets around to doing so, especially if what they say is true about war with Boroni on the horizon."

"Let's have Thadar tell them," Hanen said. "It ought to give him something to do."

"That," Rallia said, "and you expect they'll confiscate some of the stolen gold he acquired."

Hanen chuckled. "Perhaps."

Deld sat like a pat of dung in a dry field. None of the buildings stood very tall, and roads ran through them like cracks upon its sun-dried surface. The main thoroughfare ran wide, but by no means straight. After passing through the mile-long stretch of outlying farms and collections of villages not yet absorbed into the city, they came to the gates, and just beyond them, the Auroch Yoke inn.

An oversized yoke, twice too big for even the largest auroch to shoulder, hung as a sign above the entrance to a large courtyard. Hanen ushered the merchants in, and porters ran out to take them to stalls where they could feed and water the pack animals.

As they entered, each merchant's contract with the Sentinels terminated. Some would continued on for the longer leg, south through the rest of Düran, and onto Edi City. Many had already expressed their intent to travel west to Birin, or east to Morriegan port cities. Most would stay at least one night at the Auroch Yoke. Many did not know where to find cheaper inns, and those who did still stayed for the simple reason that they were already there.

Hanen walked into the inn's common room and approached the bar, taking a stool across from the proprietor. Rallia followed close behind and took the one next to him.

"Ah, Clouws!" the innkeeper said as he placed mugs of ale before them. "How many customers did you bring me today?"

"Twenty-one, I think," Hanen said.

"Fine by me. Fine by me. You're welcome to stay the night. Seems a good trade to me."

Hanen took a long pull from the mug. The gingery punch of foreign spices with a hint of some unknown tropical fruit washed down the dust in his throat.

"I do appreciate the business you bring," the owner of the inn said as he came back to fill their drinks.

He had the light brown hair of most Dürani people, and his sun-darkened skin told of an early life on one of the ranches that dotted the area. "At least three of the Sentinels you brought along are staying here, too. Perhaps they sleep in a bed, perhaps they drink themselves into a stupor on a bench. Doesn't bother me, as long as their coin is good."

"If it's not," Hanen said, "tell me. I'll make sure they pay."

"I would. Needn't you worry."

Hanen looked back over his shoulder. A single Paladin sat at a table. He had dull metal circles the size of coins out, and had a file in his hand as he played at the edges, working on some side craft of his own as he traveled. Across the tower gorget around his neck, a black traveler's cloak lay over one shoulder. The Paladin looked up under heavy brows and gave Hanen a glare. Then he scooped the metal pieces off the table and dropped them into a bag, before standing up and tromping out.

"What's the trouble?" Rallia asked.

"What do you mean?"

"You keep looking over your shoulder."

"There was a suspicious Paladin sitting there a moment ago."

"Oh?" Rallia turned quickly to look. "I don't see him."

"He left."

Rallia pursed her lips in disappointment.

"Why do you care?" Hanen asked.

"You never know if you'll see someone you know," Rallia said.

"They're nothing but trouble," Hanen replied.

"Trouble? Paladins?"

"Yes. Passing judgment. Acting high and mighty."

"Hanen, they're Paladins. They protect humanity. They serve humanity. They aren't judging anyone. Grandpa was a Paladin."

"Your grandfather was a Paladin."

"He would have accepted you, too, if you had let him."

"But I didn't. I got enough looks from everyone, with an Üterk mother. Half the men who came into the poorkitchen knew her."

"Dad never minded," Rallia said.

"Our father was luckless and a fool. If anything didn't go wrong in a day he was happy."

Rallia shook her head. "Father wasn't luckless. Things just never went his way. It didn't keep him from feeding us."

"Do you have any plans to make contacts here?" Hanen changed the subject. "It couldn't hurt to pick up a few more contracts, even with most of the caravan staying on with us during the next leg of the journey."

"The day is young," Rallia said. "I'll see what I can do."

"Your voice is feeling alright?"

"I'm fine, big brother. It's been five days. Stop worrying."

Rallia left the inn, leaving Hanen to finish his ale.

Deld had always been Rallia's city. She fit in there comfortably since their first visit seven years prior as apprentices to the cheesemonger, Master Verith. Rallia had been good at keeping in touch with their late master's contacts up and down the length of Düran and Bortali.

If those Rallia sought were out and about, then by the following morning they would likely have another five wagons joining them, and they'd also have an idea of any trouble forming to the south.

"You have any problems on the way here?" the innkeeper asked as he passed by with a cloth to wipe down the bar.

"Yes. Had a run-in with a vül."

The man across from him stopped and whistled. "You lose anything?"

"Just some dignity."

The barkeep laughed. "Nothing shakes you, does it, Clouw?"

"Why should it? In the end, I still have it better than my father."

"Improving yourself, eh?"

"No. Just staying away from his bad luck."

The merchants filtered in, filling the tables. One of the city's musicians found their way in and started pandering to the crowd. Once it got too loud, Hanen retired to the small room he and Rallia had been provided and fell asleep. The sun woke him and Hanen rolled over to see Rallia's bed untouched but her pack gone. Hanen double-checked his own bag and shouldered it before descending to the common room and walking out onto the street.

The cobbled thoroughfare started off wide, but narrowed at times with fenced pens erected for ranchers to paddock animals overnight. The High Summer Fair wouldn't come for another month, so most sat empty, as locals had not yet been about their errands.

Most of the merchants that planned to continue on would conduct their business in town and arrive at the south end by nightfall where the next contract began—at the Burnt Bridge Inn.

He passed a brightly colored stall of reds and purples. A figure stepped out of the shadows into view and the green face of a hrelgren looked up at Hanen. The hrelgren merchant had large eyes and a soft, shallow beak of a mouth. He wore dun-colored robes, with a vivid blue and purple sash. His head was covered by a tall green hat. He gestured toward Hanen with a hand. It had a thumb on each side with two fingers between.

From within the merchant's tent, Hanen saw the bright eyes of a younger hrelgren watching its father work. The little one held a basket of fruit in its arms.

"Azho! Sint-hati-oi-zidil-moni-palitan," the merchant said in the courteous hrelgren greeting.

Hanen nodded and said in response, "Ashini! Eti-bo-sha'shina-zidil-palitan."

"Ah, a man of the road. A Black Sentinel, I understand you're called."

"Yes. Hanen Clouw."

"Well met. I am Terlit ni Teth, purveyor of many odds and ends. Perhaps you seek something. Perhaps I have it."

"No. Nothing in particular. I'm escorting a caravan south to Edi."

"Ah! The famous Sentinel Caravan! You must work for the two who run it."

"Actually," Hanen said, "I am one of them."

"I have just met your sister last night, then! I can't say I see the resemblance."

"It's a common mistake. We have different mothers."

"Very well. I already spoke with your sister. I will not be joining you, but I have asked that she take a package with her to the south to Edi and then on to Yqapa in Minor Hrelgreens. I would like to know it has arrived safely."

"If you have my sister's word, you have my word."

"I thank you," the hrelgren said. He took Hanen's hand in both of his, all four thumbs wrapping tightly around his hand and wrist and squeezed.

By midday Hanen came to the Fresh District of Deld. He crossed over a bridge built only sixty years prior.

The entire neighborhood took pride in its white-washed newness, rebuilt after the fire that had consumed a third of the city so many decades ago.

He came down the other side of the bridge and immediately came upon the entrance to the Burnt Bridge Inn's courtyard being swept clean by several stablehands. Rallia stood off to the side, speaking to a merchant inspecting his wagon. She looked up, saw Hanen approaching, and excused herself.

"Successful evening?" Hanen asked.

Rallia smiled broadly. "Six more wagons, a couple of people on foot."

"How are you doing?"

"I'm only standing upright because I'm holding a kyllyt nut in my cheek. I can feel its effects starting to wear off, though. I want to introduce you to a few merchants before I fall asleep right where I stand."

Rallia led the way into the inn, with tables filling the large room, some with wood frames and curtains to provide privacy. Waving to a few people as she made her way through, Rallia stopped at a table against the wall with two figures taking pints with one another.

They both had broad shoulders, hunched over from years of labor. The older looking of the two was shaved bald and had a mouth full of teeth he could barely close his lips around. His nose had been broken so many times it seemed shoved into his skull. The other had a full head of hair growing in every direction with a wild beard to match. He looked out from under heavily furrowed brows covered in thick lashes.

"This is Nair and his brother Kash," Rallia said as an introduction. She indicated to Hanen. "And this is my brother, Hanen Clouw."

"I can't express how pleased I am to finally meet you," the bald one said.

"Likewise," Hanen said. "Do you have a wagon?"

"No. No wagon. Kash and I are traveling south, though. We met good Rallia here, and she said we could join your caravan."

"What are you peddling?"

"Straightforward. I like it," Nair said. "We're on important errands, though nothing urgent."

"I heard they tell good stories," Rallia said. "So I thought a little entertainment on the way might help."

"Well, yes. That might be good," Hanen said. "But taking on a merchant without goods might seem odd to the others."

"We won't burden you. We pay just as well as the next man."

Kash, who had remained silent, pulled out a coin purse and set it on the table.

"We need only go as far as Amstonhotten," Nair said.

"So not far," Hanen said.

"No. Just far enough. We gladly accept the company."

Hanen took the purse. It wasn't heavy, but full of enough silver to satisfy him.

"Hanen," Rallia said, putting a hand on his shoulder. "I'm going to go to sleep."

Hanen nodded and watched her go up the stairs and disappear. He moved from table to table, speaking with merchants from the first leg, and meeting new members of the caravan. Once the main room was engaged in revelry, Hanen went up to the room and fell asleep in the other bed. When he awoke, Rallia was gone again, though she had somehow managed to repack their bags as Hanen slept. Hanen left them for the time being and walked down to the courtyard.

Thadar was standing in the center of the yard, shouting at Rallia, who ignored him as she helped a merchant brush the coats of his two draft sleipnirs who were waiting to be harnessed into the wagon straps.

Rallia looked up at Hanen and shrugged. Thadar stopped and turned to see Hanen standing there.

"You filthy shunt!" he said, marching toward Hanen. It wasn't the first time Thadar had called him that. Usually, it was after he was too far drunk. "I went to the town guard to report the incident we had with the bandits. They took the money we found!"

"Why did you mention it? Of course they took it. Probably said they were going to return it to those it was stolen from."

Thadar crossed his arms and scowled. "You knew they would take it!"

"No. I didn't. I counted on you being too stupid to keep your mouth shut about the gold you found. What happened with the gold was your own business. It's kind of funny that you let them take all of it."

"Funny?! I'm going to destroy your face!"

The first punch he threw swung wildly past. Hanen could smell stale ale on his breath.

"You're drunk," Hanen said.

"Doesn't mean I can't kill you. I'm still your better."

Thadar threw one fist, then another. His swings were reckless and his whole body lurched forward with each one. Hanen easily stepped out of the way and backed up to provide another easy target. It did the trick, taunting the man forward one lunge at a time.

Thadar took the bait and attacked with several wild swings in a row. Hanen leapt sideways with each punch, and Thadar turned to face him. After four more punches, he swung wildly around, forcing himself into a spin.

As Thadar turned to look at him, Hanen slapped him across the face and shoved with both hands against his chest. Thadar fell on his rear. Hanen took two firm steps toward him and pushed him over with a foot. He was dazed and looked up at Hanen with blank eyes.

Hanen looked over at Aurín and another Sentinel. "Find a merchant willing to carry this sorry excuse of a Sentinel in their wagon until he sobers up. We'll pay the merchant back from Thadar's own purse."

He started to stalk away, then thought better and turned back.

"Listen up!" he said. "We're leaving soon. We're taking Thadar Saliss with us. He's the captain on this caravan. The Sentinels watch their own, and they fulfill their contracts. No more trouble from anyone. We're making for Edi."

"We don't have to take Thadar with us," Rallia muttered. "We could terminate his contract now."

"I know. And we should. But even though you're the one who faced down that vül, he's the one who killed it. You're not one to brag, but he is. We'll put up with him until Edi and then let rumors of his killing a vül start growing. We won't hire him again, but our caravan will gain prestige for having killed a vül. Eventually, they'll be saying there were seven of them."

"Alright. But know that I would have backed you up if you had sent him on his way."

"I know. Thank you. I think we've almost got this caravan route to where it needs to be."

"For what?"

"For us to move on."

"Move on? We have a good thing going here."

They arrived at their room and shouldered their bags. Rallia turned back to her brother and shut the door with one foot.

"We're doing well, Hanen; we're making a lot of money. We're paying the other Sentinels a gold royal a month. That's four times more than dad used to make in a year. What are you and I paying ourselves?"

"Three royals a month between the two of us," Hanen said.

"Exactly. We have plenty of money and no time to spend it. Why move on?"

"I don't know. Maybe we can do more. Set up other routes."

"Let's finish this trip and get back to Edi. I met a hrelgren merchant who hired me to take a package on to Minor Hrelgreens. It's not urgent. I can wait and line up some other work and then continue down to Yqapa. That should give us both time to think about this. Alright?"

Hanen nodded.

The wagons were lined up in a circle and ready to roll out. Hanen nodded to each Sentinel, who returned the look. All save Thadar, who lay passed out in one of the wagons.

At the entrance to the courtyard Hanen came to a stop and turned around. Several merchants had followed him to the entrance on foot, almost forgetting their carts where they stood.

"I've made this trip plenty of times. If we make good time, we'll reach our usual campsite. If we make haste, then we can send word to a nearby farmer near there who is always obliged to bring out a cart of ale that rivals Zhigavan black beer."

"Then please let me take the lead and set the pace," a hrelgren merchant said. He motioned to a cart pulled by six tall horned drul, the stag-like common work animal of their people.

"Zhanur Obliau, is it?" Hanen asked.

The hrelgren shook his head. "Zhanur bh Obilau. My vhrenouah, er…middle name, 'bh' means Great Wind. Let me live up to that name my mother gave me. We shall make the stop in time for one to fetch this ale."

"Very well," Hanen said. "Lead on."

The hrelgren almost ran over to his cart and mounted it, giving the six shaggy animals a tug of the reins. The next merchants soon followed. Hanen started walking along the side of the road as the carts pulled past him in a long procession. The plains of Düran spread out before them once more.

The cart bearing the still-unconscious Thadar trundled past, and Hanen considered the coward he had been when he was too fearful to act and save Rallia's life—something Thadar didn't hesitate to do.

He owed Thadar that much at least. He would let him finish off his contract, even if he hated the shunt.

3

Amston Forest

How fortunate are we that the Judge created the wyvern and his smaller cousins, the savern, the wyloth, and the fury. Had he not created such vile creatures, bent on harassing travelers, stealing hot foods left out in windows to cool, and random screeches in the night to startle us awake, we might not have the daily reminder of what we have to look forward to for all time if we should end up in Noccitan.

—BEADRO VLYNN, PLAYWRIGHT OF NEMEN

They were nasty creatures, wyloths: simian, gangly, destructive. They usually hunted across plains, gliding above the ground by means of the taut skin between their arms and legs. Their screams could startle a grown man, though more often it was used to startle their rodent prey as they glided overhead. They were small—known to disappear into saddlebags and come out full and fat. Fortunately, they weren't as large as their much larger cousins the saverns, or the wyverns; but they caused enough trouble hunting in troupes of twos, threes, even tens, within cities.

The first morning out from Deld, a small pack of wyloths decided to harass the merchants. The following day, their numbers doubled. The Sentinels attempted at first to scare them off with torches, but they only returned the next morning with a larger troupe. At first, accusations were laid against the hapless butcher, his wagon drawing the vile creatures with the aroma of the hung meats within. To draw off the creatures, several Sentinels and merchants pitched in and purchased a hank of meat from the butcher and left it out near the road in the morning as the caravan moved on.

Sentinel Ghoré had volunteered to stay behind and observe the little raiders. He caught up later and reported that the wyloths had set upon the meat and were squabbling over it, showing no inclination to pursue the caravan.

As dusk settled, they came to the northern edge of Amston forest. They pushed into the woods, and before dark fell they had their tents pitched amidst the relative silence of the trees. Whether out of fear that the creatures might return, or from irritability caused by the scratches the wyloths left, no one talked.

A single fire burned with wagons situated to block sight of it to the road, while the two brothers, Nair and Kash, plied half their trade in the cooking of stew, while their other half, the telling of tales, remained unsaid.

Kash stood over his pot of stew and minded the contents within. Nair took bits of meat not yet spoiled, roots dug up along the road, and herbs from stands of bushes across the plains and placed them into the bubbling liquid. Any who brought enough to add to the soup would gain a share and their bowl would be filled.

Hanen awoke the next morning to further silence. He turned over and saw Rallia sitting cross-legged on her bedroll, staring intently to the north. As Hanen sat up, Rallia motioned for him to lay still.

Sitting on a rock by Hanen's feet, a wyloth cautiously watched them as it picked at the remains of a dead rodent in its hands. Wyloths weren't often seen in forests—the webs of Hunting Zvölders caught them in the low underbrush, and the Ælernes in the upper branches hunted them to extinction. Yet the troupe of wyloths had found them.

"Wyv judge it!" Hanen whispered harshly.

"What are we going to do?" Rallia asked. "We can't take these pests with us. Edi City will never let us in the gates."

"We've been pushing hard," Hanen said, "trying to lose them, hoping they'd get bored. Maybe we do the opposite: slow down and make a focused effort to eradicate them."

"We should probably offer a reward," Rallia said.

"We already have—a silver baro for each one."

"Then we double it: a silver conta each."

Hanen nodded as Rallia thrust out the end of her heavy-ended staff. The wyloth crumpled to the ground.

There was a silence for a moment before wyloths on nearby branches raised an alarming cacophony to mourn their lost brother.

The merchants groaned, rising from their bedrolls. Hanen and Rallia stood near the embers of Kash and Nair's dying fire as the two of them dished the remains of the evening's stew into jars for the next night's pot.

Merchants gathered along with Sentinels, anger plain across their faces. Thadar opened his mouth to protest, but Hanen held up his hand to silence the throng.

"It's a bit of bad luck we've come across here," he said.

"Bad luck?" a merchant called. "More like a curse!"

"I understand your frustration," Hanen said, "and we're going to take care of the problem."

"How?!"

"Despite these fiends accosting us, we've made good time. I'd say we're a day ahead of schedule, actually. So I'm proposing we move slower. We're going to let these shunts come. Rallia and I will offer a silver conta for each dead wyloth any one of you brings to us. Tonight we'll chase off any remnants with torches, as we always do, and do the same tomorrow, to ensure these creatures go away for good."

"Why are they harassing us?" another merchant asked. "Wyloths are never seen in these woods."

"I don't know why, but we'll find out."

The entire company was happy to give into their anger, tramping through the woods, bringing back a fair share of dead wyloth corpses.

"We'll take five dukt for the lot of them," Ghoré said. He was a reedy man, with a scraggly beard that grew mostly on his neck but hadn't been brave enough to climb up onto his chin. He held out several dead wyloths by their tails. Thadar stood behind him in sullen silence. He hadn't said a word to Hanen since Deld.

"There are seven here," Hanen said. "You get seven conta. I'm not going to pay you more than I promised."

Ghoré sucked his crooked, rodent-like teeth, baring them slightly. "We put a lot of effort into this."

"And so did the two young merchant apprentices that spent an hour trying to catch one. I'm not going to pay more than I promised and that's final."

Ghoré sneered as he turned. Thadar joined him, muttering something. The smaller man laughed a thin, weak laugh in response.

Over the course of the afternoon, the wyloths lost their courage, and watched from higher branches, out of the reach of their sticks and stones.

"It seems to be working," Rallia said.

"Yes. I think so. But what keeps drawing them?" Hanen asked.

"The constant smell of the soup is what I first thought," Rallia said.

"I did, too," Hanen said, "but when Kash left out someone morning, they wouldn't touch the stuff."

"I didn't know that."

"Wasn't important until now."

The sun began its final descent toward the horizon. They came to a large clearing and called for camp. The Sentinels started a fire, lit torches, and circled out into the woods, chasing away the wyloths with their natural aversion to flame.

By the time Hanen and Rallia had returned, the merchants had begun cooking over a few shared fires, the biggest of which was tended by Nair and Kash.

Hanen wrinkled his nose.

"What's the trouble?" Rallia asked, looking over at him.

"They're throwing wyloths whole into the stew. I'm not sure what I think about that."

"Remember the first time we had those small fish in Edi?"

"Yes. Silvertip."

"Right. You wouldn't touch them the first time you saw them. I think you order it every time it's being offered, now."

"True," Hanen replied.

"You want a story, do you?" Kash responded to several men muttering around the fire. He produced a bowl and passed it to the first man. "You want a story, you pay for my skills. If you pay for my skills, you pay for my brother's skills."

A few groaned, but everyone put at least two silver in the bowl, one for each brother. It came back to Kash, who looked in and nodded.

"That'll buy you a tale, and an old one at that."

"We've all heard the old tales," an old merchant spat. "Tell us a new one."

"I'll tell you an old one that none of you has heard. If you have, you split the contents of this bowl with my brother and I."

"Bah," the old merchant said. "I've heard them all. You might as well give me back my coin."

"You paid, you listen. You know it, I split it. Fair as fair."

"Stop scaring off the game and get to hunting," the old man said.

"Very well," Kash said. He took a seat, while Nair continued to stir and dole out the stew.

> *This takes place around the same time as that old tale of tales, that all people call their own, Vevomenia. There was another man who went off to fight that same war. Though he didn't fight for some maiden. He fought for greater glory.*
>
> *It was there, in that time of war, that he saw the futility and madness of the battle. He alone survived and cried out to the gods in his frustration, 'How long will you make us suffer? How long will you demand our worship and give us nothing in return?'*
>
> *A figure watched nearby, leaning against a dying tree from which moss clung like broken webs. He wore a cloak of tattered grays, and looked on with a grin upon his face. 'What cry is this? Do you rail against the gods who gave you breath?'*
>
> *"Why give us breath only to have us suffer? Was it not their own feud that brought us all low?"*
>
> *"Indeed that was the first, and yet, it was mortals who created the Deceiver. It was by their actions the children of Wyv were betrayed and torn asunder."*
>
> *"Then I shall seek the destruction of the Deceiver."*
>
> *"That you shall not accomplish. Only a god may slay a god."*
>
> *Secretly to himself thought he, that he would seek to become a deity, and thus kill the Deceiver, that Thirteen-Limbed one, to tear down the web that he hath spun.*
>
> *He traveled through many lands until he found a blacksmith who could craft the most exquisite armor. "Good smith," said he. "How can I become as a god? Will your resplendent armor make me so?"*

    And said the smith, "I can make armor to be made as beautiful as Kea'Rinoul, the beautiful god to the East.
    So he indentured himself while the smith made him the armor, and when it was finished, the man donned the armor with details immaculate. The lessons he learned while serving as an apprentice gave him skills with which he could one day slay the gods. He was told to go to the goldsmith who lived yonder, who would give him a shield that the gods could not breach. Thus he sought the goldsmith out.
    The goldsmith was a grizzled, hunched figure, who leaned over his bench and slaved away over the prized works he crafted.
    "Wilt thou make me a shield to keep the trepidations of the gods from falling upon me?"
    "I can make for you a shield so resplendent, the gods shall be too distracted to place their will upon thee.
    And so he indentured himself those many long years it took to make the shield, and it indeed was glorious—as heavy as the armor on his frame. The shield shone and sparkled. Any who looked upon it trembled with delight.
    Said the goldsmith, "You must seek out the tailor in the village yonder. There he shall craft a mighty tunic with which you shall walk in silence, with the rustle of a bat's wing as your friend, just as Wyv, the father of the outcast gods."
    The armor was heavy and the dazzling shield blinded him. He traveled then to the tailor, who worked with only a single needle, and slowly, surely plied his wares.
    "I wish for a tunic that shall be more resplendent than the gods, to be like a god."
    The tailor chuckled. "I shall make you this tunic. Indeed, in its folds and delicate features you shall feel as wise as they."
    And so he indentured himself the years it took to make the tunic, thread by thread, until at last it was finished. The man put it on and all that saw him gave him honor and respect.
    "Travel now a final time, to a graveyard dark, where moldering bodies lie. There one waits with a blade so fine that all who touch it know it is death."

And thus the man went forth. The armor was heavy upon his shoulders, the shield glittered until he was blinded, and the tunic, like a fine parchment, softly rustled and he had to move most carefully so that it would not tear. All who saw him gave him wide berth and bowed in respect. He came to the graveyard, and one was there who dug an empty tomb.

"I understand that I must meet you. You are to give me Death, the sword that kills any whom it touches, for with it I shall slay the gods."

"I see you wear an armor most resplendent. Who would cause harm to one burdened as you are? I see you bear a shield as shining as the sun, O how it blinds. I see you wear that delicate tunic, which tells me you are wise. Yet, you come to me and seek Death? Come therefore forward and I shall help you to visit the gods."

The man took the gravedigger's hand and stepped down into the grave beside him. The gravedigger came up out of the tomb and began to heap dirt upon the man, who dared not struggle for he knew this must be the ritual that would usher him into the presence of the gods whom he would slay.

"Tell me the name of the blacksmith who made your armor?"

"He never told me his name," the man said.

"You met Rionne, the god of destruction, and he crafted for you the burden of your healthy years of work. You wear no armor, only the days of your youth. Tell me the name of he who made your shield."

"He never told me his name," the man said.

"It was Kos-Yran, the Gift-Giver. Yet all his gifts come with a curse. You knew then how to craft with metal and with gold, and yet, you cannot craft, for you are now blinded and hunched, such as what happens in old age. Tell me the name of the one who crafted such a tunic."

"He never told me his name," the man said.

"It was Kea'Rinoul. He once was beautiful, and all the gods envied him, and yet now he is cracked and destroyed. Your tunic is simply your own skin, which hangs on you as parchment. Were you not blind you would see that people respected you for you are elderly.

DEATHLESS BEAST

You have cast your years away in regret and thoughts of vengeance. You are now nothing but an old man. All I can offer you is death. My shovel is my sword, and now you leave this mortal realm."

"And what is your name?" the man asked.

"I am he who sent you on this fool's errand. I am Achanerüt, known as the Deceiver. And I defeated you the first day you set out to destroy me. Who are you to think you can do more than any other mortal? Your death overtakes you and you die in futility."

And thus the final clod of dirt covered him over and he was no more.

Those around the campfire sat in silence. The only sound was the bubbling of the stew and the crackle of fire.

"That's a terrible story," the old merchant said. "But, I'll admit, true."

He stood and shuffled off into the night. Others awkwardly stood and left the firelight, leaving only the two sets of siblings sitting there.

"Why are all the stories of would-be heroes tragedies?" Rallia asked.

"Because heroes are only what they make themselves to be," Kash said. "The gods are not fools, as many of the stories make them. They know a hero's intentions much more than the hero themselves. It is by the will of the gods that heroes become great, and it is by the will of the gods that the heroes fall."

"But why are they so petty?" Hanen asked.

"The gods are not petty. They simply have greater plans, and mortals are only subtly a part of it."

"You said the story was from long ago, where you hail from. Where is that exactly?" Rallia asked.

"It is not something we like to share, exiled as we are," Nair said.

"What did you do?"

"You certainly are straightforward, aren't you?" Kash chuckled.

"We left of our own free will, to tell you the truth," Nair said. "You might call us princes of the realm. Two families rule there, though our uncle and his children brandish more power than our family. Our two older brothers are powerless to take any kind of control, so we're out to make our fortunes."

"What will that do for you?" Hanen asked. "Besides make you

rich?"

"Perhaps we'll march an army back and take the place by force."

"How will you do that?" Hanen asked.

"I have a servant who does not know a great debt he owes me," Nair said. "When the time comes, I'll call in his debt and he will answer."

"That's rather vague."

"It is vague. Rumors travel fast. If I said any more than that, a rumor could, over time, travel where I do not wish it to fly. I'd hate to see my servant find a way to wiggle himself out of the debt before I call it in."

"Well," Rallia said, "I hope you find not what you're looking for, as the man in your story did, but what you need most in order to succeed."

Nair smiled a broad grin of gnarled teeth. "I thank you, young lady."

Rallia excused herself. "I'm going to start the patrol."

Hanen made to rise.

"What of you?" Kash asked. "What goals do you have?"

"I am satisfied with what I do as a Sentinel. The responsibilities grow naturally over time. I'm happy."

"Are you, though?" Nair asked. "I could give you a few pieces of advice to improve yourself."

"Yes, but at what cost?" Hanen asked, smiling. "I've already been paid by you to join this caravan. Paying you back for advice I can learn on my own just doesn't work for me."

"No need to be rude," Kash said as he poured the contents of the cooling stew into jars for the next day.

"Please, I meant no disrespect," Hanen replied, bowing his head, "but if the myths and stories of the past have taught anything, it is to not accept a free gift, especially if you don't fully know the gift-giver."

"Wise words," said Kash. "Words that are worthy of defeating Kos-Yran at his own game."

4

Wyloth Problem

"Let not the Wyloth in," spake Ælerne. "He is no bird."

"What of his brother, the Savern, or sister the Fury?"

"Dear Gryph. Do not fear their wrath. Simply fly higher."

"But what of their king, the Wyvern?"

"You speak true. Their wrath is nothing compared to he. Let us not invite his rage."

—COUNCIL OF THE BIRDS, ACT 4, SCENE 7

The camp was quiet as Hanen and Rallia walked the perimeter. For Hanen, it was too silent. Rallia moved slowly, her staff prodding the underbrush. The silver light of Umay was two days past full and cast plenty of light to see by.

"Do you enjoy being a Sentinel?" Hanen asked.

"Why do you ask that?" Rallia replied.

"Why should it matter why I asked?"

"Because you obviously have a reason for asking. I'd rather know that first."

"Something Nair said."

"What did that storyteller say?"

"He asked what goals I have."

"And what did you tell him?"

"That I'm satisfied."

"Hanen, you're never satisfied."

Hanen stopped and glared at Rallia's back. "Now it's my turn to ask: Why do you say that?"

"Because neither of us ever are. I'm never satisfied with myself, and you're never satisfied with your situation—it's why we set up this caravan."

"But what if this caravan is as far as we go?"

"So what if it is?" Rallia stopped, crouched down, then, finding nothing, stood back up. "What more would you want past this kind of responsibility? It's not like we'd ever be kings."

"I'd set up more caravan routes. We could live like kings, barely lifting a finger."

"For one, I'd never settle down, no matter how much coin there was in it. And two, neither would you." Rallia stopped, looking back at her brother through the darkness.

"And three?"

"What?"

"There's always three when you make a list. You don't think we can set up multiple routes?"

"I don't doubt we can. It just might take time. Besides, you're the one who always makes lists of three."

"Not true. What would you do if you weren't a Sentinel?"

"I don't know. Maybe go east and join the Paladames of the Rose?"

Hanen stopped. "No. You're not becoming one of those fools."

"Why not? Grandpa was a Paladin. As a girl, that's not an opportunity for me. But the Paladames are a little different."

"Your grandfather," Hanen corrected. "I don't even want to think about you joining the ranks of a holy order."

"It was just an idle comment. Honestly, I've never given it any thought. I spend each day improving on the last. I don't think ahead like you do."

Rallia came to a larger tree and quickly ducked up against it. She motioned Hanen to join him.

As Hanen drew close, Rallia whispered, "Did you assign any Sentinels to patrol tonight?"

"No. Everyone should be in camp now. It's just you and I."

Rallia nodded, then gestured with her head.

Hanen leaned out and saw a lone Sentinel moving around the woods. He had a bundle of sticks in his arms and he was taking them out one by one and planting them firmly in the ground.

"What is he doing?" Hanen asked.

"I don't know."

"Let's wait until he's gone farther and we'll follow."

After a few minutes, the Sentinel faded into the night. Rallia took off through the woods and came to the nearest stick in the underbrush and pulled it up. She made a jerking motion with her head and ran back to Hanen and gave him the stick. He lifted and sniffed warily at the sticky substance glistening on the tip. He quickly regretted having done so, retching at the awful smell.

"What is that?"

"I don't know," she replied. "It smells like wyloth."

"That's what I thought," Hanen said. "I think it also has honey on it, too. Looks like bits of fat."

"So why is he putting this out? And who is it?"

"I don't know. Why don't you follow him, Rallia. I'll follow behind and pull up all the sticks."

Rallia nodded, turned, and disappeared into the woods.

Hanen followed his nose to seek out each rank stick, which made the search considerably easier than wandering aimlessly in the dark. There were over fifty stakes, spaced out evenly and circling the entire caravan. After gathering them he dropped the stinking bundle on a log pile near one of the fires and went in search of a brook to wash.

There was a sudden tumult as the sounds of fighting came from between two wagons. Hanen took off toward the sound and came around to see Sentinels and a few merchants in a circle around two people sitting at a makeshift table.

They cheered the two on, then went quiet as someone shushed them, seeing Hanen approach.

"What is going on?" Hanen asked as the man at the table suddenly swung out with an open hand and took Eunia across the face.

"What?!" Hanen shouted, pushing his way in. The side of Eunia's face was swelling around the broad grin she wore. She glanced up at him for only a moment before her hand went out, sending her opponent's head spinning. His eyes glazed over as he toppled off his seat.

Hanen rolled his eyes as a merchant's son stepped forward and took a seat, placing two silver baro in the bowl with a trove already collected there. It was a common enough tavern game in Garrou, and just another reason why Hanen was glad he no longer lived there.

"I didn't hear this pofonarc game from the perimeter," he said to Aurín, who stood nearby with a bottle of wine in his hand.

"Everyone kept quiet until Eunia took down a fourth man."

"Is everyone here?" he asked, looking around. Thadar and Rallia were nowhere to be seen. "That shunt," Hanen cursed.

"Who?"

"Thadar. If he's not here, then Rallia might be in serious trouble."

"I doubt that," Aurín said.

"Why?" Hanen asked.

Aurín pushed past two merchants to a wagon and shoved something with his foot. The black-cloaked figure of Thadar rolled over.

"Eunia's first opponent," Aurín said. "It was his suggestion we start the pofonarc. He was drunk before he even took his seat. It helped a bit, I think. He made it through four strikes from Eunia."

"And she's still going?"

"Yeah. I have my suspicions why, but I'm not going to say just yet. She's making me a lot of money on a side bet right now."

Another black-cloaked figure joined the circle, sidling in to appear as though they had always been there. Rallia appeared out of the darkness behind the figure, standing a head taller than the short Sentinel. Only one of their company stood that short. Rallia gave a nod to Hanen and reached out and tugged the hood off the Sentinel, revealing the face of the rodent-like Ghoré Dziony, who watched the fight with a gleam in his eyes, unaware anyone had even touched his hood.

"What's with the face?" Aurín asked. "You look like someone just insulted your mother's cooking."

"I'll tell you later," Hanen said, turning to walk into the night.

The night rolled on slowly, and dawn broke on Hanen's second watch. Hanen had moved to a fire nearer to Ghoré's tent and kept the fire stoked. Before the sun came over the horizon, Rallia joined Hanen, and not long after that Ghoré rose. He stood and stretched, looking around, and saw the stick Hanen had left lying next to the entrance to his tent. Ghoré lunged for it, taking it in his hand, and looked around suspiciously. Then he chucked it far into the woods and ran to the nearby brook to wash his hands. As he returned to his tent, Hanen called out.

"Ghoré. Good morning."

Ghoré spun and looked at the two Sentinel's sitting there. His sharp nose twitched.

"You did good with those wyloths," Hanen said.

"Wyloths?" Ghoré replied not moving from where he stood.

"Come on over and share the fire."

Ghoré inched toward them.

"I hope Thadar didn't take the credit."

"What?" Ghoré said. "He had nothing to do with it. It was my idea."

"You still split the silver with him?"

"Silver? Oh! You mean the wyloths you paid us for."

"Well, yes. Of course." Hanen stirred the fire. "Could you and Rallia bring some of those sticks over there to feed the fire?"

He approached the haphazard pile of sticks Hanen had indicated and reached out for one. He recognized them and froze.

Standing slowly from his crouch he turned.

Rallia grabbed him by the shoulders and shoved him to the ground. Ghoré started screaming. His voice broke and his cries alerted the entire camp. People who hadn't yet risen came scrambling as Rallia flipped the weaker Sentinel over onto his face and tied his hands behind his back.

"Stop hollering," Rallia said, forcing him to stand.

"What's the commotion?" Thadar said shoving his way to the center of the quickly forming circle. His face was purple with the bruises Eunia had given him. "What did you do, Ghoré?"

"That's what we're going to find out," Hanen said. "Given how eager Ghoré here was to escape once we found him out, I suspect we'll be finding it's nothing good."

After Hanen explained what had happened, a few examined the pile of sticks. Kash took hold of one stick and had the courage to give one a lick, grimacing as he did.

"Wyloth brains. And honey," the storyteller said.

"If I may," a voice said next to Hanen. He turned to see the hrelgren merchant, Zhanur bh Obliau. "For a time before I took up this calling of being a humble wool merchant, I served as a Templar, specifically an Ihtash of the 3rd Responsibility."

"Does this help us?" Hanen asked.

"Templars enforce hrelgren law," Rallia responded. "You were a law enforcer, then?"

Zhanur shook his head. "As a member of the Ihtash branch of

the Templars, it was my responsibility to protect, rather than enforce. As I had risen to the 3rd Responsibility, it was my privilege to assist those of higher authority to sit in judgment."

"You mean you offer yourself as arbitrator," Hanen said.

"I could not have said it better if my first language was your own."

Hanen turned to Rallia.

"He's not human," Hanen said. "The merchants may just take matters into their own hands, regardless of whether he helps."

"Since he's not human," Rallia responded, "who better to act as a mediator?"

Hanen nodded and turned around.

"Everyone," Hanen said. "I'd like to be on the road as much as the next person, but if our own Sentinel, Ghoré Dziony has done something illegal, then it is important we deal with it immediately. Please go and prepare your things to leave. Once everyone is ready, we'll conduct a public trial, which our good friend, the merchant Zhanur bh Obliau has agreed to act as arbitrator. The sooner you're ready the sooner we can be done."

The merchants leapt to their work, harnessing their pack animals, and pulling their wagons into a long line on the forest-shaded road.

The hrelgren paced back and forth, speaking to himself or to his druls as he hooked them up to his own wagon.

"Will you be ready?" Hanen asked, walking past the hrelgren as he inspected the line of wagons.

"Yes," the hrelgren said. "Although I would like the proceedings to occur up there, a hundred yards, at the crossroads."

"I had forgotten," the storyteller, Nair, said from nearby, "that hrelgren law recognizes the old law of the world. Decisions made at cross-roads are very old indeed."

The hrelgren nodded. "Indeed. It is why no hrelgren home touches another, and paths available to the public are made to pass between each home, so that all decisions made, even in the home itself, are at a crossroads."

Hanen approached Rallia, who was standing next to the smoldering fire. Her now-shackled prisoner, Ghoré, sat on a log staring wildly at the bundle of stinking stakes nearby.

"We'll be moving to conduct this trial at the crossroads."

Rallia nodded, and prodded Ghoré at her feet.

"Hanen," Rallia said. "I'm hesitant to do this."

"Why?" Hanen asked.

"We are not the law," she said. "Nor are we above it. Conducting a trial seems wrong."

"We're doing this for the merchants, more than anything. It should reestablish our clout with them, and it will strengthen the respect we have lost through Ghoré's actions."

Rallia chewed her lip and said nothing more.

The hrelgren merchant and the storytellers stood at the crossroads, by the sign that led off towards the larger town of Amstonhotten. A carved pillar stood behind it with older markings upon its weather-worn surface.

Rallia took Ghoré to stand next to the pillar as Thadar stalked up.

He looked around to see that there were no other merchants nearby, ignoring the storytellers altogether.

"I don't like this," Thadar said. "And I don't like you."

"Noted," Hanen said.

"I'm the captain on this venture, and Ghoré has been seen with me far too often. If this goes poorly, it will reflect on me."

Hanen turned.

"The first words you've said to me since we've left Deld are an insult, and now you're asking me to do as you say because of your reputation? What about the reputation of all Black Sentinels?"

"I could care less what happens to you or the others after we reach Edi."

"I could have left you in Deld," Hanen said, "but I chose to keep you on out of respect for what you did to that vül. By showing you respect you do not deserve, I've preserved all of our honor, and hopefully ensured that some merchants travel with us again. What are you going to do in return?"

Thadar stared at him blankly as realization dawned in his eyes.

"I could act as accuser," he said. "That would distance me from Ghoré's actions, and reinforce my position of authority."

"It sounds like your mind is made up."

Thadar grinned evilly. "I'll see him swinging from a rope."

"You'll show respect to the hrelgren as judge," Hanen said.

Thadar nodded. "I know better than to piss off a hrelgren. Their silver is too good, and that merchant is a lousy gambler."

He laughed to himself as he walked off.

"Why did you do that?" Rallia asked.

"I realized that Thadar only cares about perceived authority.

But he's so mindless to what is actually occurring around him that just by suggesting that any action will earn him respect, he believes it. Now, as the accuser, if things go well, the Sentinels will look good. If things go poorly, it'll be because of his own anger, and it'll fall on his head."

"You seem fairly confident."

"I hope that's how I appear," Hanen said, his smile dropping from his face. "Because I don't feel it."

The merchants had gathered in a crowd again, standing opposite the road to Amstonhotten, where the hrelgren stood. He had exchanged the white woolen cap on his head with a silver ringlet. The sapphire embedded in the center glittered in what little sun broke down through the leaves. Rallia stood with Ghoré next to the pillar, and across the Amstonhotten road stood the two storytellers.

"Hear you all, I am Zhanur bh Obilau, tamlor'fala of the ihtash horn of the tamlor'shawa. I shall act as arbiter in this matter we meet for, and the storytellers Kash and Nair shall act as ozan, or bard, to tell of what has occurred, to a higher authority, or to the gods themselves."

Hanen stepped forward.

"Zhanur," he said, "thank you for agreeing to do this."

He turned to the company. "It is our goal this day, to investigate whether Ghoré Dziony, the man I hired to protect this caravan, has instead brought harm to us all, through ways nefarious or in ignorance, by inciting the wyloth to harass us."

The merchants murmured to themselves.

The hrelgren held up his four fingered hand to silence them.

"Please let it be known, I am not a high enough authority to exact a punishment on this man," Zhanur said, indicating towards Ghoré. "My aim shall be to establish whether what this man has done should be taken to higher authorities, or whether what was done can be treated by all present as harmless. For we should all seek to live together in peace, but should one seek to break the peace, then let him be accursed as the dark gods, walking forever in their own damnation."

Thadar pushed forward through the merchants.

"I accuse that man of treasonous acts," he shouted, pointing an accusatory finger at Ghoré. "He baited those wyloths to attack, just to spite us."

"You were my friend!" Ghoré screamed.

"Halsha!" Zhanur hissed. He looked calmly at Thadar. "If you shall accuse this man, make your statement."

"That man," Thadar said, now refusing to look Ghoré in the eye, "was always sneaking around. Always finding wyloths hiding in bushes and then telling others where they were so they could kill them. In Deld I even saw him stop and watch a troupe of them."

He turned to the merchants.

"He even spoke to them!"

The merchants muttered to themselves, their faces darkening.

"Let someone speak for the accused," Zhanur said.

No one moved.

"If no one will speak for him," Zhanur said, "then we cannot pass any judgment."

Rallia stepped forward. "I'll speak for him."

Hanen sighed.

"I think we're acting too hastily," she said.

She looked around at the crowd.

"We've all done things. Some of us have let our anger get the best of us. Some of us aren't even peddling what we say we are. We tolerate that because it isn't harming others. But when someone does something, intentional or not, that offends us? Then we turn to righteous indignation. Even more so when the man in question is, perhaps, not the most attractive man. Let's be honest, Ghoré is downright ugly."

This produced a laugh from the merchants.

"We all have a member of our families who we still accept, despite their looks, or bad luck, because we know them. Who has gotten to know Ghoré? Or have we all written him off as someone lesser than ourselves? I would hear his side and see what he has to say. Then we can decide whether what he did was wrong."

"Very well, and well said," Zhanur said. "The accuser states that Ghoré Dziony has communed with wyloths, obsessed over them, and baited them to harass our company for means yet unknown. While his defender asks that we hear the testimony of the accuser. This is just and right, and shall be."

He turned to Ghoré, who now sneered at the crowd, his eyes snapping at the hrelgren, and to Thadar and Rallia.

"I shouldn't have to explain myself," Ghoré hissed. "First you call me traitor," he said to Thadar, "then you call me ugly," he snarled at Rallia through his crooked teeth. "What I say won't matter. You've already made your judgment of me. You can all go to Noccitan, for all I care."

"Explain whether you baited the wyloths to come to our camp," Zhanur said.

"Of course I did!"

"Tell us why."

"At first," Ghoré said, "it was to create a problem for us Sentinels to solve. To make us great in the merchants' eyes. But it...got out of hand."

"Because the Sentinels couldn't make the wyloths leave," Zhanur stated.

"And because the merchants didn't even notice when the wyloths were gone. So I did it the next night too. Using the honey to draw them to camp, and the wyloth brains to enrage them. You should see what a brain-mad wyloth does if it's locked in a cage and set in a trap for a œlik. They'll do all the work for you and make it look like the œlik died from an animal attack. Authorities don't consider it poaching if you find a carcass and take it."

"And then it continued to get worse."

"No," Ghoré said. "Then it became humorous. And those fool Clouws started paying for the wyloth bodies. Thadar suggested we could make some extra coin if we could convince others to pool the bodies and take off the top, from here to Edi."

"Liar!" Thadar shouted.

"Halsha," the hrelgren said again. "Explain the humor to me. Perhaps it is a human thing I do not understand."

"You all looked down on me, ever since I joined the Sentinels. Treated me as someone who would do the dirty work. To watch those wyloths scratch, tear, and ruin? It filled me with...satisfaction."

Even Rallia now stared in astonishment. She glanced at Hanen, her eyes filled with shame for having stepped up for this man.

The merchants started murmuring to each other, as the hrelgren put a hand to his chin and thought long and hard. After several long minutes, he held up a hand to silence them.

"This is a case of the accused admitting their fault, and admitting that their justification for their actions came from their spite toward their fellows. It would be to the disadvantage of both this company and to Ghoré Dziony to set him at large or acquit him. For if acquitted, our company may react violently. If set at large, then the accused may continue down his own road to destruction. Thus, this is beyond me, and the accused should be escorted to the nearest municipal authority and turned over to them for judgment."

Nair stepped forward. "If a single Sentinel could be spared, my brother and I would be happy to escort Ghoré to Amstonhotten, where we could give witness and turn him over. We were planning on leaving off here anyway."

"While you're welcome to join whoever takes him," Hanen said, "I won't allow you to take responsibility for him."

"Then I'll take him to Amstonhotten," Rallia said.

"What about the caravan?" Hanen said.

"My name is on it, too. One of us should take him to town."

"And the package you need to deliver to Minor Hrelgreens?"

"I'll take it," Aurín said. "I've never been."

"Works for me. Thank you, Aurín," Rallia said. "How about I stay back with Ghoré and those two storytellers. We'll take our time and move on to Amstonhotten. I'll meet up with you in Edi once business is concluded there."

"Aurín," Hanen said, "perhaps you and Rallia should also help me relieve Ghoré of his Sentinel cloak. He won't part with it peaceably."

The caravan was soon on its way, continuing south. Hanen took up the rear and looked back toward his little sister, who was driving the sticks into the ground in a small circle, setting what would be the last trap for the wyloths, before continuing on. The two storytellers stood nearby with Ghoré, who was still tied up.

"Rallia will be fine," Aurín said, walking alongside him.

"I know. I trust her, she's my little sister. It's the others I don't trust."

"We all walk our roads," Aurín replied. "If Rallia's road leads back to yours, none but the gods can know."

"That would only be reassuring if I thought the gods actually cared."

5

St. Hamul

He found his way
  Across the plain.
And there he stood
  Upon the road.

Give me entrance
  to humility.
I seek a pittance,
  I give now all of me.

—THE HUMBLE PALADIN

The Fortress of St. Hamul appeared to look like a large hammer dropped in a field. It was not as large as the original it was built to emulate, but it was impressive, nonetheless. If the Fortress-Monastery of Pariantür could house nearly ten thousand Paladins, and a third as many Paladames, St. Hamul could keep a tenth of that total number. Where Pariantür had twenty-two domes atop its massive frame, St. Hamul had a single dome over its chapel.

What St. Hamul had, that its father chapel did not, was a well-planned landholding. Pariantür's surrounding land was a chaotic patchwork of farms, groves, and houses.

The three Paladins of the Hammer came up over the rise and stopped to look at the miles'-wide valley, admiring the perfect grid of farms set around the citadel in a beautiful display.

Jined Brazstein sat atop his six-legged sleipnir horse in full regalia. As all Paladins, Jined's head was shaved. Where he contrasted from others was in his sheer size, height, heavy brow, and broken nose.

Over the chain mail that covered his body, heavy leather armor provided a foundation for overlapping metal plates on his arms, shoulders, and stomach. Atop that, a heavy breastplate and tower gorget that nearly obscured his prominent chin. Most notably of all was the hammer—namesake of the Paladins—held at attention against his right shoulder, the butt of the haft chained to his belt by twenty-two links. The head of the hammer, mirrored on each side, was topped by the aquiline head of a four-winged ælerne eagle.

Alongside Jined rode Killian Glass, and ahead of them both rode the elderly standard bearer Valér Queton. He held steady in his stirrup the standard of Grissone. The image of the four-winged Anka—twin-soul to Grissone—perched atop a hammer. Ribbons embroidered with scriptures trailed out from the pole they were tied to in the breeze.

They trotted along at a brisk pace, the heavily shod feet of their six-footed mounts pounding the road filling Jined's ears with a steady clip, clip, clop, clip, clip, clop. Behind him, a caravan of twenty-six Paladins stretched along a hundred yards of road. Ten guards, commanded by Pater Segundus Nichal Guess, made up the advance and rear guard, as well as outriders.

Of the four carriages, each had its purpose. One contained provisioners and their supplies, another the scribes documenting the expedition, the next held the leaders and administrators, and the fourth carried the Prima Pater Dorian Mür himself—head of the order and the leader of the Grissoni church.

A rider matched pace and fell in alongside Killian's right. The rider leaned forward and glared at Jined, who knew it was Dane Marric without glancing over.

"I'm very thankful that Pater Segundus assigned me as outrider today," he said in a forced, reedy voice. "I need to breathe fresh air after traveling through that city. There were far too many women out and about."

Dane had a sour smile on his face. He was a severe-looking Paladin, though he had loose jowls under his chin—a relic of a previous life of excess and gluttony.

"I'd be remiss if I didn't point out that half of the humans on the surface of Kallattai are women," Killian said, "being in a city means we're going to be around them."

"They could be staying within the confines of their homes. They saw us and they must know some of us are vowed not to interact with them. The Paladames at Pariantür do well to keep to themselves after all."

"The Paladames of the Crysalas Integritas may keep to their own, but they are about the monastery," Killian said. "They just know you and avoid your company at all costs."

"You could have stayed at Pariantür, studying your extreme view of your Vow of Chastity," Jined said, "if you thought this was going to be a problem."

"Our vow, Brother Brazstein," Dane corrected. "You would be wise to remember that."

Jined growled to himself. Not about Dane being right, but by Dane's need to use the Vow of Chastity as a crutch to benefit himself. Jined had, on countless times, seen Dane escape requisite work or responsibilities at the notification that a Paladame of the Rose would be present.

The Orders of the Rose and the Hammer had long shared the same citadel after the Crysalas Integritas sought refuge there centuries before. Those brothers and sisters who had taken vows and aspects that did not forbid contact with each other had allowances to marry members of the opposite order.

Only a select few, such as Dane, had sought refuge in extremist philosophies containing abhorrence of and abstinence from contact with the opposite sex.

"Why did the Prima Pater have to invite him?" Jined asked.

Killian chuckled, while Dane seemed not to hear what he had asked.

They passed a group of peasants on their way to fieldwork who stopped and gave a bow to the standard bearer and then the three of them. Dane lifted his chin and paid them no heed, while Jined and Killian each gave the peasants a swift salute.

"Brother Marric," Killian said, "your cordons are out of place."

Dane frantically looked down to the green cords across each of their breastplates, which denoted each of them as the rank of Brother Excelsior. Contrary to Killian's suggestion, they were not out of order.

"Having a laugh, are we, Glass?" Dane asked, sarcastic venom in his voice.

"Just lightening your mood. Your contempt for the people we are sworn to protect is showing. It's not fitting, given that the Paladins were founded to give them protection and hope, not hatred."

Dane scoffed and pulled at the reins, leaving off.

"Don't let Brother Marric bother you so much, Jined. He's a fool. I don't let him get to me."

"I honestly can't help but be bothered. He's a hollering wyloth. I can't believe they haven't given him permanent duty cleaning the washrooms instead of allowing him to continue as a soldier." Jined's mood, which had started out well that morning, had turned sour.

"He has an exceptional eye. He's spotted danger a mile away— I've seen it. I would suppose that the Pater Segundus is willing to suffer through Brother Marric's personality defects to gain access to that kind of talent. You know as well as I do how capable he is in battle."

Jined didn't bother responding. He hated when Killian was right, because it meant not only that Jined was wrong, but that Jined knew he was wrong in the first place.

They came over the second, lower rise. The road descended the last half mile to the gates of the citadel. At the appearance of the quiet standard bearer, the bells sounded, ending work and calling those nearby toward the walls. Lines of peasants moved toward the citadel and into the end of the haft of the hammer-shaped edifice. At Pater Segundus Guess's command, the entire entourage stopped.

They fell into a pre-drilled formation, flanking the carriages, and started the long ceremonial march down the road to the entrance. The bells of the chapel pealed wildly, and everyone inside filed out to create a large throng of cheering people, parting to provide a path for the entourage. Paladins from St. Hamul were interspersed within the crowd, each looking just as excited as the people indebted to the citadel. Thrown bramthistle flowers flew through the air. Jined could only imagine the trouble they had gone to, gathering the flowers from thorny hedges for the event.

The entrance was more than large enough to allow the carriages to enter. The façade was simple: an image of a four-winged ælerne with wings not outstretched, but huddled over to suggest protection would be found within. The philosophy of St. Hamul the Insightful, founder of the Vow of Prayer, had always aimed toward symbolism found in the Anka.

Jined could not see past the carriages as they continued on ahead, leaving the guards to enter last. The six-beat clop of their sleipnirs echoed in the long tunnel that led into a small courtyard where the passengers of the carriages and the guards would dismount and find washing and food available.

The crowd gave little attention to the Paladin guards as they filed last into the stable yard, and the care of their mounts were taken over by stablehands.

Jined took a tankard of light ale offered to him by a brother and took a seat on a bench along a retaining wall.

Nearby, the twin brothers Loïc and Cävian stood speaking with their hands. Both had taken the Vow of Silence. A provisioner from the entourage walked up to them and nimbly moved his own fingers as he joined the conversation.

Jined found it interesting that those who took similar vows usually congregated together. The silent Paladins huddled near the twins in silent, yet public conversation. The scribes and provisioners who had taken the Vow of Pacifism kindly deferred to each other as they kept out of each other's ways. The brothers of Poverty all talked jovially while they worked rust out of armor. Those who had taken the Vow of Prayer had gathered in the center of the courtyard and held hands in a circle as they sang a hymn of gratefulness together. Jined found himself thankful that Dane had gone over to preach his own humility to others of their vow, leaving Jined to his own thoughts.

He took a long drink of the cool ale and sighed. It had been a long road already, across the plain from Pariantür to the port in Macena, then stopping in each major port as they circled the Pyracene Sea to Poray a week before, and now, finally, to St. Hamul. Yet nothing had happened. All of the bastions' reports and ledgers had been accurate to the copper penny spent on boot oil.

"The thoughts of the holy weigh heavily on the shoulders," a Paladin standing next to him said.

"Ah," Jined said looking up. He did not recognize the man, and so assumed he must be stationed at St. Hamul. "I was considering how uneventful the trip had been so far, and wondered if it would continue to be so."

"It is in the small things that strife causes harm. Yet in the minutiae wisdom grows."

Jined furrowed his eyebrows. "You're speaking in scripture. From the Hammer of Faith."

The Paladin said nothing, but looked at him intently.

"The chapter defining wisdom. Chapter 32?" Jined guessed.

"Know ye your scripture. Know ye your soul."

Jined chuckled and stood up to stand eye-to-eye with the Paladin, welcoming the challenge. "Speak thus the words of wisdom, and plant a seed that will flourish in a parched land."

The other Paladin smiled. "Much was hidden, and the stars themselves felt darkness beckon. But all will be revealed."

"Interesting choice," Jined said. He turned to take water from an urn, to offer it to the other. "That is from Saint Nocci's commentary of the Book of the Precalamity."

Jined took a deep breath and turned to find the Paladin was gone.

The side door to the bastion opened, and the Pater Segundus Nichal Guess stepped out, followed first by the other, more elderly Pater Segundus, Gallahan Pír, the senior scribe for the entourage and, in fact, the entire order. They each flanked the door shortly before the Prima Pater emerged, a perpetual smile on his face.

Dorian Mür was a short, slight man. When standing next to others, most men stood head and shoulders above him. Despite being ninety-five years old, he almost leapt out of the entryway. Dorian's armor was in most ways similar to other paladinial armor. However, his was crafted from the original worn by Hamul the Insightful, founder of Dorian's Vow of Prayer.

On his shoulders aquiline eagle heads looked to his right and left. His gorget was styled like eagle wings, and an ornamental tail of metal sat embossed across his chest plate. He wore a red cloak cut to resemble the four wings of the ælerne eagle. Instead of the normal paladinial hammer, he held a scepter made of two slabs of metal, wide and thick, both hammer and axe, once more in the appearance of the four wings of an ælerne outstretched, representing the Anka twin soul to Grissone, god of Faith.

"It always surprises me what he can do at his age," Killian said as he sidled up next to Jined.

"Grissone strengthens him," Jined offered, "how else would you explain it?"

"I cannot." Killian smiled.

"Please gather around," Dorian announced.

Jined and Killian came to stand only a few paces from the small man, who looked up and around at each of their faces.

"I've spoken with Pater Minoris Gage, and his seneschal, Primus Zoumerik. The Matriarch Superioris of the Crysalas Honoris passed through here three days ago, as I expected they would, and traveled on to their destination of the Crysalas College in Thementhu. The Matriarch was in high spirits, and made sure they knew of my favorite meal, which they've prepared for our feast tonight."

The Prima Pater's smile broadened as he said this. The Matriarch Superioris was his wife, which was rare, but not unheard of—even more unusual since they were both in their late nineties and still very much functioning in their roles as the heads of two different religions.

"St. Hamul," Dorian continued, "was due to gather up the reports from the farms swearing fealty to them, so I have suggested that our own scribes do so. That being said, tomorrow we go to work. Please make sure you get enough sleep to rise at the usual bell to begin duty."

The Prima Pater turned without another word to leave.

"The feast is to begin in one hour, when the bell chimes," Pater Segundus Guess announced as he turned to join the Prima Pater, who now spoke to Pater Minoris Gage, head of the citadel. Guess and Pír followed the two men into the citadel while Jined and the others were shown comfortable cells before making ready for the feast.

6

PROTECTION AND FEALTY

Sing we now, of family and tide,

　Gather together in cheer and pride.

Water away, and blood up dried.

　But all come together where we shall abide.

　　　　　　　　　　　　　—BRONUAN TAVERN SONG

The feast was simple, with little pomp. The head table was deep in conversation, while the brothers spoke amongst themselves. It was a welcome reprieve from feasts thrown for the Prima Pater by the leaders of the cities and towns they had stopped at along the edge of the Pyracene Sea. Several of the local brothers took advantage of the additional barrels of cider and mead opened for the entourage, and the plates of meat and thick bread roiled steam across the tables.

　Several of the brothers under the Vow of Poverty took remainders away to give to the sick and ailing, and soon the choirmaster called for the clearing of the plates. Hymns were sung, followed by Pater Segundus Gallahan Pír reading the nightly scripture.

　Given the masked chortles by several of the local Paladins,

when Pater Segundus Pír got to St. Sternovis's Laud 87, it was obvious whoever chose the nightly reading thought to play a harmless prank on the high-ranking Paladin. The longest single entry in the holy scriptures of the Paladins began. The Pater Segundus looked as though he might stop a quarter of the way through. Instead, he reached for a glass of mead and read on, stopping at times to give his own commentary on the hour-long text, extending the reading well into the night—turning the prank back on the Paladins of St. Hamul. The smile on the Prima Pater's face broadened, allowing the reading to continue.

As the evening came to an end, Jined tumbled towards his cell, shared with Killian Glass, who struggled through the effects of the flagon of mead he had partaken of during the feast. Killian finished working his way into his own bed long after Jined had pulled his own covers up and turned to face the wall.

The snoring from the other bed came soon after, keeping Jined from sleep until only just before the first bells of morning rang.

Jined groaned as he rolled over to dress himself, despite the nearly free morning he had before his first order of duty.

He should not have been surprised when he arrived at the dawn service and found only a handful of Paladins present. Even those looked the worse for wear, and those not present were likely unable to rise after so long a feast and sermon the night before.

He finished his prayers and stood to leave when a Paladin approached.

"You're a member of the Prima Pater's entourage, aren't you?" the Brother Paladin asked. The red cordons across his breastplate indicated his station as a recently officiated member of the order.

"Yes, Brother. Jined Brazstein."

"You're from Brahz? In Boroni?"

"I hail from there, yes."

"I'm from Clehm, myself."

Jined nodded at the younger man, bearing the weathered look of a fellow Boronii. The younger man held out an envelope, sealed with cheap red wax.

"I received this at the guesthouse. I understand there are two in your company named Loïc and Cävian?"

"This is true," Jined said, taking the letter.

"If you know them by sight, will you please take it to them?"

"Of course."

He turned and walked toward the offices the Prima Pater and

the two Pater Segundii had requisitioned. The door to Nichal's office stood open. He looked up and smiled wearily to Jined.

"What is it, Brother Brazstein?"

"A letter has arrived at the guesthouse for the twins. Have you seen them?"

"Ah," Nichal said. "That letter has been expected. May I?"

Jined handed the letter over and Nichal broke the seal. Had it been anyone else, Jined would have been appalled, but as one of the four Pater Segundii, second in status to the Prima Pater himself, it was within his right.

"Good," Nichal said. "Jined, I will go and deliver this to the twins myself. Please return to the guesthouse and receive the elderly couple this letter comes from. See to their needs, and I'll see that the twins come and meet them."

Jined gave a salute and turned to find the guesthouse. He saw the Boronii Paladin walking quickly from the kitchens with a tray, and approached.

"Can I help you, Brother?" Jined asked.

The brother stopped and watched him approach. "I was taking this to the couple that brought the letter."

"And I've been sent by the Pater Segundus to see that they are made comfortable."

"Very well," the Paladin said.

Jined took the two bottles balanced under both of the other Paladin's arms and followed him.

The guesthouse faced southwest, not far from the haft-end entrance to the citadel. The common room was comfortably adorned, with three open doors leading off to guest halls. Plain white tapestries embroidered with a light gray thread visible only on close inspection lined the walls, as they did many walls in St. Hamul.

Sitting in two plush seats, an old couple looked uncomfortable in their surroundings. The man had long white hair, pulled back off his receding hairline in a tail. A leather apron, nearly the same color as his dark Seteran skin, covered up a white linen shirt with evidence of stains from grapes or some other fruit barely visible.

The woman wore a simple frock of plain linen, but the ribbons that hemmed the edges had been spared no expense. Though by Jined's discerning eye, the ribbons had some wear and had perhaps been moved from outfit to outfit as she worked the linen to dust with toil and happy labor. She had a full head of hair still, and bore the angular, pale features of an Ikhalan or Zhigavan.

As Jined approached, the woman looked up in anticipation then relaxed into her seat before fidgeting to an upright position. The Paladin placed the tray in front of them, then took the bottles from Jined and popped their corks, pouring each a flagon of mead.

Jined and his companion stepped back just as Loïc and Cävian entered, Pater Segundus Guess just behind them. They were not in full regalia, wearing only their gorgets over top of their brown habits. They each smiled broadly, the mirror image of one another as the two older guests stood from their seats.

They silently rushed up to them and took one each in their arms, giving them a warm embrace.

"Little Lo!" the woman said with a smile, pushing back the one who held her to look at him. "I'd know you even after all these years."

Cävian and the older man held each other at arm's length, examining one another.

"Cäv," the woman said, touching Cävian's arm. The other twin turned and gave the woman a strong embrace.

Loïc turned to look at his brother, signing something to him, and receiving a response.

"We," the woman said, "can understand you. And yes, you can speak freely."

Both brothers looked at the woman in astonishment.

"Your father has not spoken a word since you took your vows those many years ago. He wanted to show respect by emulating your vow."

Suddenly Loïc, Cävian, and their father began moving their hands in rapid succession—the floodgates of conversation opened.

"Shall we leave them to their peace?" Nichal asked Jined, as he stepped next to him.

"Yes," Jined said. "We should respect their privacy. They must have a lot to catch up on."

"They haven't seen their parents since they left for Pariantür at the age of ten."

"They were ten?" Jined asked, holding the door open for Nichal. They walked side-by-side back into the citadel.

"Their father owned a vineyard near the border of Zhigava, alongside the Zhig river. It was struck by vineblight, along with many others in that area, what, twenty years ago now? They were left destitute, and fled towards Düran, hoping to find a new life there. They only got as far as St. Hamul. The twins saw the Paladins here and decided to dedicate their lives to Grissone, if only to reduce the number of mouths to feed by two."

"Noble," Jined said.

"It was. I've known those two boys since they still had their surnames. I almost convinced them to take the Vow of Poverty. But Loïc convinced Cävian to join him in the Vow of Silence instead."

"So, did they send a message ahead to their parents?"

"No," Nichal said, smiling. "I'll admit to a bit of subterfuge on my part. I sent a message to their parents, Jüdoc and Oaniss. Apparently, they now have a small vineyard of their own, bearing wine that graces the table of the Seteran monarch. They brought a cask of very fine wine for the Prima Pater, and another one for the twins."

Nichal left Jined to continue with his work, while Jined took a walk through the citadel. He saw the entourage scribes in a debate with the Paladins in the citadel scriptorium, while the smell of hot metal came from the large smithy. Killian Glass stood watching the glassworkers assembling a piece of fine stained glass as Jined walked by.

"Your father is a glazier for Pariantür," Jined asked as he sidled up next to the other Paladin. "Is he not?"

"Yes," Killian said. "Although he works mostly in glassblowing, rather than panes."

"Did you know Loïc and Cävian are from here?"

"Yes, their parents own a vineyard, I believe. They pay a tithe to supplement the twins' income. If I remember correctly, they're two of the wealthiest Paladins at Pariantür because of it."

"The wealthiest?"

"Well, yes. The stipend most Paladins receive from the coffer, not myself of course, with the Vow of Poverty—I forfeited that—is enough to survive on. But Loïc and Cävian never spend a penny of their coin, and their parents still send them a stipend from their vineyard, despite their debt to St. Hamul being paid off years ago. Don't you receive a pension from your family? I thought you came from nobility."

"For several years," Jined said, "I hadn't even realized I was being paid. I came as a penitent, so my coin went to pay the weregild of the man I killed."

"I'd imagine after all this time that the weregild is paid off."

"He was the son of the high Duke of Boroni."

Killian whistled.

"How did you know about the twins' parents?" Jined asked, changing the subject as the two of them turned to walk toward the refectory.

"Because they're always talking about it."

"You speak the silent language?"

Killian laughed and held up his thick-fingered hands. "Speak? No. But I understand it quite well. My sister and I were raised around Pariantür. It's mandatory to learn it in school. You must know some."

Jined held his own hands up. "I suffer the same problem. I know enough to get by for hand signals in the field, and to ask for the salt bowl to be passed to me."

A commotion came down the hall leading outside to the stable yard.

"Come on," Killian said.

"The citadel has its own guards," Jined said.

"Doesn't change the fact that I'm nosey," Killian laughed.

At they came blinking out into the light, a man knelt on the ground, his hands held up, pleading with the Paladin before him. His thick, heavy, black hair grew wild, and the red-dyed leathers he wore looked damp with sweat.

"Eh gom wih de childs. Take, please!"

The Paladin who stood above him looked around, unsure of what to do.

Before Jined could open his mouth, a Paladin wearing the black cordons of a Primus marched out of a side door and up to the Paladin. Jined saw two children with hair as wild as their father, up against a wall, their eyes averted to the ground.

"What is the trouble here?" the Primus asked.

"Primus Zoumerik, this man pushed his way in here and has been shouting at me for several minutes. I can't understand a word he says."

Jined watched the Primus turn and look at the man kneeling before them, and remembered the feeling he had when he had knelt before Zoumerik ten years prior. The Primus was only a Brother Adjutant then, traveling through Boroni from Mahndür, and had relented to escort Jined, threatened by a mob who wanted his head for killing the High Duke's son, to Pariantür to take his vows.

"Pelees, pelees," the man begged.

"What language is he speaking?" Killian whispered.

"The man is an Üterk," Jined said. "They live outside of society across the Northern Scapes, often marginalized to lives of brigandry and bare survival."

Zoumerik was now kneeling by the man, speaking softly with him as the man cried.

"She cannot be here!" a voice shouted from across the stable yard.

Jined sighed and turned to see Dane charging across the space toward the two children.

Killian leaped to intercept him, Jined hot on his heels.

"What are you doing?" Dane shouted, trying to push past Killian. "That is a girl! She is not allowed in the citadel."

"Dane," Jined said. "It appears they are seeking sanctuary. Please leave off and allow the Paladins of St. Hamul to take care of their own business."

"There is a guesthouse for places like that," Dane hissed. "No woman is to set foot on citadel grounds outside of the guesthouse."

"And what of sisters of the Crysalas?" Jined asked.

"Allowances may be made in that case," Dane admitted, "but that is not the case now."

"Brothers Excelsior," a voice said. Jined turned to see Primus Zoumerik standing beside them. "What is the trouble here?"

"Primus," Jined said, bowing his head.

"Brother Brazstein and I were aiming to allow you the privacy you needed to speak to the man over there," Killian said. "An interruption from Brother Marric felt like it might interfere with your work."

"I was merely passing by," Dane said, ignoring propriety, "and I saw that there was a girl in the courtyard. Parianti Law stipulates that women are not allowed on the hallowed ground of lands owned by the Hammer."

"And what of members of the Crysalas Honoris?" Zoumerik asked.

"That was brought up," Killian offered.

"I believe I understand," the Primus said. "Brother Marric, I see you keeping a close eye on the children that stand along that wall over there. Can I have your attention for a few moments so I can dispel the accusation of heresy you have for them?"

Dane looked at the Primus, then back at the children, before looking back and nodding with a sigh.

"First, I imagine the three of you are rather weary, both from your long journey, and perhaps with one another. The road can do that to the fastest friends."

Killian chuckled, while Jined and Dane both grunted, giving each other a look.

"I would encourage you to, aside from required duties, take time to rest here at our citadel. You still have, I understand, a long road ahead of you. I'd rather know that the Prima Pater has three trusted individuals who were not at one another's throats while protecting him and his cause.

"Furthermore, while you are in most respects correct, Brother Marric, I'm afraid that you are basing your accusation off Minu the Gentle's Book of Common Life. It stipulates propriety at the base level in the lives of our brotherhood. But it was only that—broad outlines for life in these hallowed halls. Within one hundred years, a twenty-year project went underway by those Paladins of legal mind, to prepare and propose adoption of the larger Code of Commons, which elaborated on Minu's treatise.

"As a student of these laws, I am familiar with your claim, but also with the allowances. After all, if we lived by Minu's book, then that encompasses all land under control of the Hammer, which means that only men could serve as peasants beholden to our cause, and their wives and daughters would be forbidden from working the land."

Dane gave a shrug of indifference.

"Brother Marric," the Primus said, leveling his gaze at the Paladin, "without women serving as peasants, within only a few decades we'd have no one farming our lands. We do not have thousands of people coming to submit themselves here on a regular basis. Reproduction is necessary."

"The courtyard is still part of the citadel," Dane said.

"Yes, it is. However, it is a cobbled courtyard. The Code of Commons states that within walls, that which is flagstoned with the same material as the walls is designated hallowed. Thus, the cobbled stable yard allows women merchants to enter to sell their goods to the Hammer's holdings. The guesthouse is floored with a different stone, and the nave of the chapels up to the transept is also marked as good for use by those not part of the brotherhood."

He turned and looked back over his shoulder.

"Now, if you are satisfied...?" He stopped and stared at the three of them.

Jined and Killian nodded, but it took some time for Dane to give in and bow his head in acquiescence.

"Good. I shall return to hear this man's request. Apparently, his tribe has been subjugated by vül. He has been on the road for many months to bring his children, whom he intends to give to the Order of the Hammer."

"And the girl?" Killian asked.

"She'll be given the option to stay here in the lands owned by St. Hamul, along with her father."

"What of the Order of the Rose?" Jined asked.

"That may be a possibility," Zoumerik said, "but we have no Paladames here at present. I'll consider this, and speak with the Prima Pater. Perhaps he'd be willing to take her with him towards Nemen, to rendezvous with the Matriarch Superioris."

The Primus walked away from them and helped the man to his feet, moving him over to a bench to speak. Killian touched Dane's arm and started walking off.

"I can see why he made Primus," Jined said.

Dane said nothing as they walked to the door into the citadel.

"He has charisma, and he knows his law. He saved my life ten years ago. Listen to his words, Marric, and maybe he'll save yours, too."

"What makes you think I need saving? What makes you think I haven't already been given relief by Grissone himself?"

"We all need saving," Jined said. "Some of us need saving from the brink, some of us need saving by being reminded why we do what we do."

"A rather smug statement," Dane said.

"I'm not going to reply to that."

"Why? Because I'm right?" Dane said, spinning to glare at Jined.

"Because you're hostile, and angry, and I know better than most what anger can do to a man."

Dane turned and stormed away without another word.

7

Accounting

Lastly, one shall choose prayer. Let the words I give to him pour continually from his lips, let him mutter under his breath consolation for the souls of others, and to him I shall turn an ear at all times, that his faith be a bastion and a mighty thing. But they shall not deny all of their humanity, for they are a guide.

—INSTRUCTI GRISSONI 5:9-12

The sun lent a soft glow to the room. Killian was tapping the wood of the bed frame in an even rhythm to wake Jined, who rolled over, grunting.

"Give me a moment," Jined said, sitting up.

Killian sat back down on his bed. He was already in full armor. He toyed with the weapon in his hand while Jined donned his own.

"I hope we can get the accounting done quickly, so that we can move along," Jined said.

"Why are you in a hurry?" Killian asked.

"I'm not in a hurry, but it feels like we're just making a show. It will be good to get back to Pariantür; back to fighting T'Akai."

"Jined, I doubt we've scratched the surface of this trip. It's not going to be a month away and a month home. The Prima Pater has business to conduct. He's looking over the figures at each bastion we stop at, comparing notes. Didn't you read the dossier for our journey?"

"Of course I read it," Jined said, "but I think I expected more trouble. The Prima Pater goes on one of these every ten years? And there are usually reports of trouble."

"Yes," Killian responded, "but that's why we're heading north. The Northern Scapes have shown figures of solid growth for the past fifty years, and no conflict, and so the Prima Pater has been able to let the bastions, under the leadership of the Citadel of St. Hamul, go without his supervision. That's a long time to go without the Prima Pater visiting. It won't be simply a matter of his seeing how they're resolving the conflicts around them, but making sure their reports line up."

"I suppose," Jined said. "But then why did he take several of the best warriors away from Pariantür?"

"No need to be humble," Killian said, laughing.

Jined scowled. "I guess I'm just wondering why I was asked to come along. It feels like a waste."

They walked together toward the eating hall. It was still very early, even for Paladins. Ten guards sat at a table together, breaking bread.

"Jined, Killian," the Pater Segundus Guess said, greeting them. He had a map out on the table, with Primus Jamis Zoumerik next to him.

"We understand that the lands to the north are primarily platted for ranching," Nichal said to Primus Zoumerik.

"Yes. We have an impressive herd of œlik. Farther north in a wild nut grove we keep a large heard of urswine."

"Jined, Etienne, Dane, " Nichal said, "ride north through those ranches. You'll be escorting the scribe, Brother Adjutant Azermo Donton."

As Nichal continued to give out assignations they left, and soon after rode toward the ranch and forest Primus Zoumerik had mentioned. Jined took the lead with the younger Etienne, while Dane and Azermo took the rear. Dane yammered incessantly at Azermo, hoping to find a like-minded brother in the Vow of Chastity.

"Chastity isn't just about not performing the sins of the flesh." When Dane started to preach, he elongated his use of s's, which always grated on Jined. "Grissone asked that we abstain, yes, but also for us to abstain from interacting with those tempters of the flesh."

"What verses are you referring to, Marric?" Jined asked.

"You know what I speak of, Brazstein."

"As well-read as I am, I don't. Please, enlighten me."

Dane scoffed. "In the Anvil of Faith, Justyn the Pure, our vow's founder, said, 'Look not upon her. Lest her gaze scathe you.'"

"That quote is incorrect," Jined responded.

"Excuse me?"

"The passage you refer to is Anvil of Faith, chapter 12, verses 12 and 13.

"'Know ye wisdom?' spake Ikhail.

"'Yea, I know her, for her visage is pure,' Justyn replied, 'she cannot speak wrong.'

"'Ye may know her, but do not look upon her without knowing she will burn away your impurities with a cleansing fire.'

"Note then that it was Ikhail, and referred to wisdom, not woman. It is often misquoted due to the paraphrase written by Pater Ügin three hundred years ago. He may have misled more than he saved through his work."

Dane scoffed again but said nothing.

"Brother Brazstein is correct," Azermo said. "He knows his scripture."

"Adjutant Donton," Jined said. "I'm sure you've heard all the speeches by those of Dane's persuasion within our vow's community."

"Indeed I have," Azermo said. "You'll find I'm not one to change my mind easily, Brother Marric. I subscribe to the Upward Path."

"Upward Path?" Etienne asked.

"Yes. I believe the path of chastity is about focusing on Grissone and his wisdom. We forego the pleasures of this world to better focus on him. I feel your Chaste Mind philosophy hampers you, Brother Marric. It keeps you from exploring the pleasures Grissone has to offer, and instead trades it out for a miserable existence here in the world."

Dane muttered to himself and pulled back from the rest to ride alone.

"Why does the Vow of Chastity have these different philosophies?" Etienne asked. "Why not just follow the originally intended purpose of the vow? Chastity would be hard enough a vow, I'm sure. Why complicate things?"

"Brother Etienne," Azermo said, "you speak as though only the Vow of Chastity has these variegated philosophies."

DEATHLESS BEAST

"Well, yes."

"You are a Brother Excelsior. You have been with the order for how long?"

"Since I was fourteen."

"I see. And what of the members of your own Vow of Poverty? What of those that ascribe to the Wisdom of Stringency?"

"You mean those that have given up all but bread and water? I wouldn't call it a philosophy. It is meant to bring them closer to Grissone through asceticism."

"And that is why there is the Upward Path and the Chaste Mind. Each of these are meant to delve deeper into faith, but in different ways."

They neared the first ranch. It sat along its own long valley, which rose steeply to the west and rose gently into hills to the east. Across the open fields of the valley floor animals grouped together.

The bovine aurochs—both larger meat and smaller milking aurochs—moved slowly across the grass, seeking out the choicest clumps. Their heavy brows were topped with horns that curved down and along their cheeks. The white and brown wooly coats of capricör stood out on the grassy green plain. One young boy was attempting to herd a group of them with his ynfald hound. The spry creature, covered in pinecone-like scales, sniffed the air with its sharp nose. At the boy's command, it took off like an arrow from a bow, quickly circling a capricör that had strayed from the herd.

Jined sat atop his sleipnir and watched for the hour it took for Azermo to approach a few of the farmers and take their accounts. They continued to ride north and soon reached the forest. It had a sturdy fence around the circumference. They came to a gate made of wicker, through which a farmer watched out for passersby. Beyond that, the forest was devoid of most ground cover. Figures almost as large as the sleipnirs rummaged in the shadows.

"We understand you farm urswine here?" Azermo asked.

"We do. Not many are willing."

"Worth the trouble?"

"I'd say so. Better than the trouble of hunting them down."

Etienne had dismounted and walked toward the edge of the forest.

"You oughta stop him," the farmer said.

Jined had tied his own mount off and approached Etienne. They both froze before the urswine hidden at first from view.

It stood as tall as a sleipnir but at twice the weight. Coarse fur covered its entire body, and its legs were muscled and powerful. A spine of fur ran the length of its body. It turned toward them, but continued to shovel through the leaves on the ground, disinterested in them. Its head was huge, with small beady eyes and a flat snout that combed the ground for anything it could find. Apparently it had found something. It lifted its head to scarf down a mouthful of mushrooms.

Large tusks, which had been hidden in the foliage, now flashed, impressing Jined. Rows of teeth chomped at the find. It took another glance at Jined and Etienne before it lumbered away into the woods.

"They make good meat," the young farmer said, now standing with them. "You were smart to stay still. They don't like sudden movement."

Etienne exhaled. He had been holding his breath for longer than Jined realized. Jined turned along with the farmer and Etienne and they walked back to where the other two Paladins stood with the head rancher.

"Have you boys eaten?" the older farmer asked.

They were led into the home through the kitchen. The rancher's wife was busy at the hearth, keeping an eye on a bread within while a roast of some sort turned on a spit. The rancher walked up to a huge hock that hung from the ceiling— almost reaching the floor.

"I hung this leg here a good three years ago," he said.

With a large knife he cut away pieces and handed one to each of them. The salty piece of meat melted like butter in Jined's mouth. Even Dane was smiling broadly.

"If I may be so bold," Etienne asked, "may we take a piece of this back for the Prima Pater?"

"That might be a long journey. The Prima Pater is far off in the lands of Pariantür. You must be a new Paladin, if you don't know that. But if it means a lot to you, you can."

"But the Prima Pater is at the citadel," Etienne said.

"Is he now?" the farmer said. He quickly cut down a larger piece, wrapped it up in some cloth, and gave it to Etienne. "The meat won't spoil, regardless of the distance."

They were soon sitting at the long table. A display of herbs dried overhead. Strips of meat, fried and hot, were set atop hunks of soft cheese. A nut paste was laid out, as well as bowls of dried apples from the season before.

Before they ate, Brother Azermo stood and spoke a prayer to Grissone. As they sat, the farmer's two daughters entered with bottles of wine. They moved from place to place and poured the white vintage into their cups. When the younger of the two came to Dane, though, he held up a hand, not daring look at her.

Jined sighed, knowing he wouldn't just leave it at that.

"'I shall not take sin from a sin-maker's hand.'"

Jined shook his head in disappointment, knowing well the oft-misquoted scripture.

The girl stood with a confused look on her face. She was perhaps only ten, young enough still to be wearing a child's frock.

"Is something wrong, Brother?" the rancher asked. He sat next to Jined, who sat across from Dane.

"I will not accept wine from her hands."

The rancher stood up. "Let me offer the hospitality of pouring it myself, then."

Jined stood, too. "Goodman farmer," Jined said, "please allow me. It is beneath you."

"Beneath him?!" Dane shouted. "To suggest I am beneath a peasant farmer. Do you know who I am? What I am?"

Jined stared at Dane. Anger roared in his ears.

Azermo placed a hand on Dane's arm, who shook it off.

Jined opened his mouth to speak. Instead, the very quiet Azermo raised his voice with authority.

"Excelsior Marric," he said, "you will leave this place at once and wait by the gate for us to join you."

Dane turned and looked incredulously at the Paladin next to him. The young girl now stood against the wall, tears streaming down her face as she whimpered. Dane rose and stomped out of the home into the night.

Azermo reached over and took the entirety of Dane's portion and placed it on his own plate. He turned to the rancher while he spread nut paste on a piece of bread. "Goodman Wen, I appreciate your hospitality today. I look forward to tasting this fine wine you made."

After a few minutes, a quiet normalcy returned. Azermo worked hard to clear the double portion on his plate, not letting a single bite of hospitality nor a drop of wine from the host go to waste.

Jined and Etienne left the farmhouse in silence while Azermo thanked the farmer quietly, made apologies for the actions of Dane, and purchased the large leg of meat they'd tasted, for more gold than it was worth as recompense.

The sun had fully set, and they rode with only the sliver of Umay, the silver moon, rising to the east. Jined thanked Grissone that the ruddy and eerie red of Norlok did not add its haunting glow to the silent ride.

After several long minutes, Dane spoke.

"You embarrassed me, Brazstein," he said coldly. "You embarrassed me, you made a mockery of our vow, and you insulted the order."

The anger once more ran hot in Jined's ears.

"That you dare shame me and my personal beliefs," Dane began again. "That you dare to speak ill of me, telling a simple farmer, and one that is subservient to the church no less, that it is beneath him to serve me? I will be writing a report on you and submitting it immediately."

Jined pulled his mount to a stop. Dane and Azermo did the same. Etienne was up ahead and had turned his horse around, staring in silence.

Jined felt a hand on his arm. He turned to see Azermo reaching out to get his attention. In the moonlight, he could see the Paladin indicating he look down. Jined had his hand on his hammer, gripped tightly.

Dane opened his mouth to speak again.

"Actually, Brother Marric," the Brother Adjutant said, stopping him, "you've said your piece. Before I say anything else, though, I'd like to hear what Brother Brazstein has to say. He deserves the opportunity to respond to your accusations."

Dane clamped his mouth shut tightly in a scowl.

Azermo turned to Jined. "Count to twenty-two first, Brother Brazstein."

Jined took a deep breath and did as he was told before he spoke.

"Brother Marric," Jined started, "in the nation of Setera, just as it is in Morriego, it is proper for one showing hospitality to put out food and ready a bed, but the food and drink does not come from his hand directly. His family places the food before you and pours the drinks. It shows he has a certain control over his household, and that all in his house have shared responsibility. When you indicated you would not be served by his daughter, you insulted her. You insulted her father. When he moved to stand, he was taking your insult in stride—humbling himself. I indicated I would take his place because, as a Paladin, I am a servant of man.

"Therefore, I did not embarrass you. I intended to save your face. You instead embarrassed yourself, and insulted the farmer and his family. You called his ten-year-old daughter a cheap whore by likening her to a sin. You have now sown seeds of doubt, and have shaken any faith she had. It may very well send her into the sins you so readily heaped upon her head. Thus, you are the sin-maker and make a mockery of our vow. And lastly, you insulted our order by potentially destroying any bonds of loyalty we had to a farm that provides one of our primary citadels with meat.

"I can say this now, with full clarity of mind––I will not demand recompense for the insults you've heaped on me. But if this happens again, you can be sure I'll break your nose."

Etienne laughed out loud and immediately covered his mouth to stop himself from going any further.

"Are you finally done, Brazstein?" Dane said wickedly.

Jined remained silent.

Dane's face contorted into a sneer and he opened his mouth to speak.

Azermo lifted his own hammer and leveled it at Dane. "That is enough, Marric!" he snapped. "You will not say another word. You will be moved to a penance cell when we return, and in the morning, you'll kneel before the Pillory and face a court of your leaders."

They continued in silence, arriving back at the citadel several hours after dark. Etienne was given the reins of the mounts to take to the stable, while Jined and Azermo escorted Dane to the penance cells. The jailer there, a young and sharp-featured Paladin, received orders to bring him to the Pillory in the morning.

As they left the penitentiary area, Azermo pulled Jined aside to sit on a bench nook cut into the wall.

"You handled yourself well, Brother Brazstein. I want you to know I intend to speak highly of you when I go and visit the Prima Pater now."

"I'll admit, I wanted to hit him, Brother Donton."

"So did I. Now get some sleep."

8

PILLORY

Lord of Faith and god of man,
Two parts in one,
Grissone and Anka, with Pariantür
Your guidance is sure—firm I stand.
Grant me faith, fill my cup with you;
Grant me a winged mind, soaring above the turmoil;
Grant me strength of iron and a will of bronze.
I will protect the helpless, and serve the weak,
I will honor your name, and uphold your tenets;
I will praise you in chant, in prayer, in daily ritual,
I will be truthful, and will not over-indulge;
I will not harm those that harm my honor,
I will show mercy to those who attack my pride;
I will bestow grace on those I find unworthy;
I will take a vow and keep it:
Chastity, Blind-Introspection, Pacifism,
Poverty, Prayer, Silence.
Your will is mine to deliver;
Your way is mine to follow;
Your faith is mine to have;
Your grace is mine to give;
Grissone, Lord of Faith, let me not falter.

— THE TWENTY-TWO LINKS

DEATHLESS BEAST

Jined found his way back to his cell, where Killian already snored in the neighboring bed. Throwing himself down on his mattress, he stared at the ceiling. The morning took its time coming and sleep never arrived.

Jined rose before the other Paladin, who would likely wonder why he never came to their shared cell. Jined passed by a few others in the halls on their way to complete the morning chores, and found himself finally at the citadel chapel.

It was smaller than the chapel at Pariantür and also served St. Hamul as the judgement seat. Someone had already set up a wooden pillory with iron chain links hanging from it in the center of the room. The judgement seat for the Prima Pater had been placed at the front. Jined walked the nave, found a bench halfway up the aisle, and took a seat. A set of windows looked to the east, heavy glass set into their frames. Jined thought he saw a bird of prey circling high in the sky. He always liked to think that a bird so high might be the Anka, circling the world, watching over the followers of Grissone.

To center himself, he began reciting The Twenty-Two Links:
"Lord of Faith and god of man,
"Two parts in one,
"Grissone and Anka, with Pariantür..."
"'The words of the scriptures are a source of comfort.'"

Jined turned to see the Paladin from the courtyard sitting at the other end of the bench.

"Anvil of Faith, Chapter 9." Jined smiled.

"'Know ye the way of Grissone?'" the other Paladin continued. "'Know ye his patterns? Look then to your heart and be silent.'"

Jined almost opened his mouth to speak. He knew the verse. It was one of his favorites. Then he realized the other brother was encouraging him with the words. He closed his mouth. The other man responded with a smile.

"'The way of the hammer is not a path, but a guided walk of active faith.'" The other Paladin indicated toward Jined, inviting him to speak.

Jined thought for a moment, choosing his words carefully.

"'From the heights he raises me up,'" Jined started, "'from the depths he grounds me.' Sacred Words, Minu the Gentle, verse 34."

"'Seek ye now to enter a deeper faith. Seek ye now the way to the heart of a true servant.'"

Jined was about to speak when the other Paladin looked over

his shoulder as others began to enter. He held up a pausing hand and said, "'She sees now a rose whose petals wilt. She sees now a vine that has been cut. Prepare, then, a hedge of thorns, and be vigilant as a dwov watches over her nest.'"

Jined turned to watch the others enter and when he looked back, the other Paladin faded into the crowd and out of sight.

Azermo entered and indicated for Jined to join him near the front, where the two Pater Segundii had already come to stand at attention.

Prima Pater Dorian Mür entered from a side room, wearing his full armor with a white robe draped over it. He sat in the judgment throne, his sigil of office held in one arm. He was trying to look stoic, but a playful smile crept onto his lips, as it always did when the mood became too serious.

The back door opened and Dane Marric was led in by two Paladins. He wore only his habit and belt. They brought him to the tall post, ceremoniously unchained the hammer from his belt, and shackled the chain to the pillory. Then one of them handed Dane his hammer. He lowered himself onto his knees and held his hammer up in front of him toward the Prima Pater. Jined had been brought to the Pillory only once before he was a full Paladin. Holding the hammer in that way had been a painful lesson in endurance. His arms ached thinking about it.

Nichal Guess addressed the group.

"Brother Excelsior Dane Marric, under the leadership of myself, Pater Segundus Nichal Guess, has been brought up against the Pillory for the following offenses:

"Public conduct unbecoming of a Paladin.

"Unwarranted disrespect and verbal abuse of a fellow Paladin.

"Minor blasphemy by misquoting scripture for personal gain."

At the last one, Dane's eyes popped in disbelief.

"How do you plead to these charges, Brother?" Nichal asked.

Dane said nothing for a long while.

"May I face each charge in their full accusation before stating comply or opposition?"

The Prima Pater waved a hand.

"On the account of Improper Conduct, let Primus Azermo Donton state for the record."

Azermo retold the story in full, of the farmer's daughter offering wine, Dane refusing her service, and the escalation caused by his social gaffe, through to Azermo asking Dane to leave the house.

"And please explain the grievance to those not from this part of the world," the Prima Pater said.

"In Setera and Morriego, the host does not themselves serve, implying that they've already made arrangements, and are privy to enjoy their own celebration. Thus, the farmer's daughters were to serve. Excelsior Marric brushed these attempts at proper hospitality aside. Excelsior Brazstein attempted to assuage the situation as it occurred, but previous irritations prevented Excelsior Marric from recognizing this was the case."

The Prima Pater turned to Dane. "What do you have to say in your defense?"

A bead of sweat ran down Dane's temple, but the heavy hammer held in his hands did not yet tremble.

"While I allowed discontent between myself and Brazstein to blind me to the good he attempted to do, I implied that I was being insulted based on Parianti tradition."

"And which tradition was that?"

"That those under subservience to the Hammer did so for their own good, and for the honor of the brotherhood."

"Do you believe yourself not subservient to the Hammer?" the Prima Pater asked. The question did not sound admonishing, but genuinely curious.

"I...," Dane spluttered.

"We are all a common brotherhood," the Prima Pater said. "In actuality, a peoplehood, if you take into consideration the Paladames and the wives and daughters of those who submit themselves under our laws. You ought to, therefore, consider yourself a servant to those who are servants to us. We do, after all, exist by their toil, and they by our protection. Do you wish to say anything else?"

"I accept guilt to this charge," Dane said. "Pleading ignorance."

The Prima Pater stood. "Very well. On the charge of Improper Conduct, what is the punishment?"

Pater Segundus Gallahan Pír held a large book open on his lap. "The charge for Improper Conduct can be anything from a lashing to an extended service."

"Pater Segundus Guess? As his acting commander, I will let you choose the punishment."

Nichal cleared his throat. "An apology issued to the farmer and his daughter, and a one week penitentiary Vow of Compliance— Excelsior Dane will comply to any request made of him, so long as it is not immoral."

The Prima Pater nodded and made a hand signal. Shortly after, a tower bell pealed once to seal the verdict.

The Prima Pater took his seat again and waved his hand toward Pater Segundus Pír. "Regarding the second offense: Unwarranted Disrespect. What are the details?"

"Nichal Guess states that he holds the guards he selected for this entourage to the highest observances," Pater Segundus Pír said. "According to the testimony of Primus Azermo, after leaving the farm, Dane accosted Excelsior Brazstein, who remained calm under the assault, and attempted, once more, to assuage the situation by deliberate explanation, to which Excelsior Marric continued to find and offer offense.

"Pater Segundus Nichal Guess stipulated to each guard, before leaving Pariantür, that they were to avoid such conflicts, and if they do take place, to ensure that no one but members of your entourage were present, so as to ensure a show of solidarity."

"Nichal?" the Prima Pater said, turning to the other Pater Segundus.

"I know that a long time on the road can cause irritations among companions. I hoped to head off strife caused by such sentiments ahead of time. But it seems they still came out."

"Marric," the Prima Pater turned to Dane, "do you have anything to say to this?"

"I shall admit I let my better nature get the best of me. I have nothing to say to the contrary."

"Brother Brazstein?" the Prima Pater turn to Jined. "As you and Brother Donton are the offended parties. Do you wish to select a punishment of recompense to you?"

"My Prima Pater," Jined said, standing. "I am reminded of the 13th link of the chain. 'I will show mercy to those that attack my pride.' I wish to forego asking for anything in compensation."

A surprised look, then a smile, played across Dorian Mür's face.

"Primus Donton?"

Azermo shook his head.

"Very well. The offended parties do not wish to exact any compensation. However, Nichal, you've something further to add?"

"After Excelsior Marric has apologized to the farmer and his daughter, I would like to ask that he take a penitentiary Vow of Silence."

Dorian slouched back in his chair, nodded, and waved a hand.

The bell tolled again.

"Now, before I allow Marric to respond to the allegations of Minor Blasphemy, Gallahan, will you please specify the difference between a minor and major offense?"

"A major blasphemy is rather encompassing of that which makes insult or mockery of deity or holy scripture, the fomenting of heresy, or the attempt at dissent for dissent's sake. Minor blasphemy can run the gamut of either speaking the name of a holy figure in vain, or misquoting a scripture for personal gain, negligently or otherwise."

Dane was shaking his head as violently as his arms shook under the duress of the hammer in his hands.

"You wish to challenge these claims?" the Prima Pater asked him.

"I am no blasphemer," Dane said confidently.

"To what length do punishments go for minor blasphemy?"

"Swift penance is given to those who speak ill, and study of scriptures is added to the penance quite often," Pír said.

"I will face these charges with a stiff chin," Dane said.

"Very well. Know that if I decide you're guilty, I will set a new precedence with the punishment."

Dane nodded weakly, and stared straining at the hammer before him.

"Brother Donton, would you please explain the scripture that was misquoted?"

Azermo stood. "The scripture quoted, as can be verified by two Paladin witnesses—'I shall not take sin from a sin-maker's hand.'"

"And this was in regards to…?"

"Excelsior Marric refused to take hospitality wine being offered by the ten-year-old girl."

"I see. Marric, care to explain? And also where this passage of scripture is found?"

Marric pushed his shoulders back and lifted the hammer even higher. "That proverb was spoken by St. Hamul to King Entabe of Ancient Zhíg."

"I can see the problem. It seems Dane Marric here believes, because of this scripture, that a simple glass of wine is a sin, and it was offered by a girl who would lead him into the temptation of drunkenness by doing so. We have what, five brothers here who have taken the Vow of Chastity? Brother Primus Beltran Cautese." He turned to the man who had planned the expedition. "Do you, a

Primus, find that you have felt your vow shaken by being offered a single glass of wine from a young girl?"

"No, Prima Pater," Beltran said with a smile playing on his face.

"Neither do I. But I suppose that's not the point. The point is, the verse had nothing to do with wine nor women seducing St. Hamul."

Dorian turned back to Dane.

"That verse you quoted was not even spoken by St. Hamul. It was spoken by St. Negen, two hundred years after St. Hamul, and it referred to bribery from other countries. It was a warning not to side with a nation in a treaty hearing. I believe it would be found in the Historical Codices rather than scriptures. It is also not the first time I've heard this spoken as scripture."

Marric was sweating profusely under the strain of the hammer.

"I think it's a simple matter. You felt the need to show your own piety to the farmer and misused a verse, or I should say a supposed verse, to achieve that agenda. It is important that any punishment exacted is fitting.

"Since you have thus stated that wine is a sin that would lead you astray from your vow, I hereby sentence you to a penitentiary Vow of Temperance. Your diet is restricted to bread and water.

"Please note, Excelsior Marric, that if you are going to quote scripture, then you must know it in its accuracy. Thus, in addition to your penitentiary vows of Temperance, Silence, and Compliance, you are to report to Pater Segundus Gallahan Pír, or the scribe of his choosing, before each midday meal, where you will instead be assigned to the reading of a portion of scripture. I should not like this to occur again. Do I make myself clear?"

"Yes, Prima Pater," Dane said, now barely able to speak under the strain of the weight in his hands.

"Then this Pillory is adjourned," he said. The bell pealed in reply, and soon after a different bell began to ring wildly, calling the assembly to morning meal.

The hammer in Dane's hand dropped as the Prima Pater dismissed everyone. The right-hand man to Gallahan Pír, the silent Primus Aeger, came and knelt next to Dane and offered him water from a skin. He put his mouth to it, but could not lift his hands to take it.

Jined stared at Dane, feeling more sorry for him than smug that he had earned his punishments.

"I hope he will learn and grow from this." Jined turned to see

Primus Jamis Zoumerik standing next to him. "Someone of his zeal, if he could see outside of his own shame, could be an asset."

"That may be true," Jined replied.

"Grissone will use a man like him either as an example, or as a leader."

"I think we can all hope to be either of those," Jined said. "Although, I'd like to hope that if I am used as an example it is not at the expense of my soul."

"Too true," Zoumerik said. "Jined Brazstein of Brahz, isn't it?"

Jined nodded.

"I believe I owe you an apology, for not showing recognition of you these last few days. Admittedly, I had recognized your face, and even your name, but had not been able to place where I knew you from. I do now."

"I'll admit, I had wondered if perhaps you had forgotten."

"I often think of the journey the two of us made together," Zoumerik said, "but you were a very different person then."

"My hair was longer, and my nose was less broken."

"Yes!" Zoumerik said, laughing. "That's what threw me off. It appears that the order suits you. You must be twice the size of the tall and much skinnier boy I took from Boroni."

Jined smiled. "Many lessons have been hammered into me since then. I have so much to thank you for. I wish there was a way to show my thanks."

"In fact," Zoumerik said, "there is a favor I could ask of you. You may not think it equal to the thanks you wish to give me, but it would be."

"How may I serve, Primus?"

"I have a parcel I hope you might deliver to a Paladin in Mahn Fulhar, if you'd be so kind."

"Of course. I would be honored."

He held out a small square wrapped in red silk and tied up securely with ribbon that was, curiously, redder than the silk packaging. Jined took the package in his hand. The shape spoke of a small handbook, but the weight was leaden.

"Please keep this on your person. It needs to be delivered to Primus Melit."

Jined nodded and opened up the satchel hanging off his belt. The burden of the responsibility carried a weight he did not expect. The serious look in Zoumerik's eyes spoke volumes.

"I will see it done."

9

Interludes

"Have the copies of the reports been prepared in triplicate?" Hiram van Höllebon looked up from the desk to the scribe standing before him.

Aeger, silent assistant to Pater Segundus Pír, nodded and placed a ribbon-tied parcel on the desk.

Höllebon looked back down to his own work.

"Brother Upona," Höllebon said to the other man sitting at the desk, "see to it that the parcel is sent in the next ship back to Pariantür."

"I'll make sure one of fortress scribes sends it off."

Höllebon looked up with a glare.

Upona gave him a look and sighed. "Pater Minoris."

"Thank you." Hiram smiled. "It is important to acknowledge our ranks and authority. Order is the best form of protection against chaos."

Upona stood and took the parcel, leaving the two men alone in the room.

As the door closed, Höllebon looked up.

"Have you made contact with the brotherhood here?" Höllebon asked.

Aeger shook his head.

"I find it odd. I would have thought the Piedala and the Aerie might at least send a representative to welcome me."

Aeger held his fingers up and began speaking in the silent language. *You once said you feared they no longer respected*

Pariantür.

"Yes, and that they might decide to go their own way. Together or separate."

It may also be that they do not know that you hold the title of Fidelity now. They don't know who to approach.

"This is also true."

I believe I have identified the best place to leave a message for them. If you would like me to do so, I will ask for them to send message after us. Perhaps warning us of any dangers to the secret brotherhood.

"No need," Höllebon said. "If there are dangers, it is something they themselves have set up, to entrap either us or the Prima Pater. So let us be wary. If we spot them, be discerning on whether we ought to simply let them play out."

I worry that if we act paranoid, we shall only draw attention to ourselves.

"Then don't be paranoid. Merely expect the worst to happen, and be surprised when it doesn't."

Aeger gave a bow and turned to leave.

"Brother Adjutant," Höllebon said, "the time may be nearing, where the motes of power bequeathed to us shall be used for the good of many."

For the good of the truth we have come to know, Aeger replied.

The orchard owner's wife was the only one to see Seriah off as the sun edged up over the farm buildings and warmed the courtyard. The woman's servant brought a tray of goods from her cellar, and the woman gently placed a cheese and two jars of preserves into her satchel.

"May the gods bless you for the judgment you make," the woman said.

She had been kind to Seriah, offering her a place to stay despite the decision she had made in favor of the man claiming the orchard owner had built his wall into the property belonging to the man's dead grandfather.

Seriah touched the satchel at her side, ensuring it was closed, her other hand holding the tall staff of her office. Rings mounted at the top jingled in the breeze. She forced a smile. It was always an awkward thing to say goodbye to those who had given her a place to stay. Despite all the years she had served, to not pay for her bed was still foreign to her.

"Thank you for your hospitality," she said.

Seriah could not see the woman through the blinder bound over her eyes, but she could sense the woman and her servant making a holy gesture. Not the touching of the head and pointing to the sky, as a follower of Aben might, but instead the enwreathing gesture of someone familiar with the Vaults of Crysania. That the woman and her servant were bold enough to do that in broad daylight must mean there were no men around.

"Glœra," the lady said to her servant. "Please see the Holy Nefer to the end of the road."

Seriah felt the servant come up on her left and put her arm under hers. Most did not realize she did not need assistance, but it was an easy assumption to overlook. Most did not help her along out of pity, but out of respect for her order, as one did out of respect for an elder.

The girl took her to the end of the lane, past the stone wall, and indicated the way north. The orchard was a long one, and the stone wall that ran the length of its border provided an easy means to avoid leaving the road and falling into a ditch. Seriah found, with the help of her staff, the stone marker where the wall ended, and where the road she walked met with the road north out of the nearby town of Suel.

She soon entered a short length of forest, and began the long ascent to the chapel that topped the hill.

She heard the humming of the priest in his garden and smelled cooking coming from his kitchen. She hoped Father Diono had not once more negligently left food burning on the hearth. The two other trips she had made from Birin to Temblin had both taken her this way, and the old priest had certainly become increasingly forgetful.

"Father Diono," the voice of a woman called from the chapel. "The food is almost ready, and it appears you have a guest."

The older priest grunted, and Seriah heard him waddle through his garden to the wall.

"Holy Nefer!" he said. "Greetings, fellow dedicate!"

"It is good to see you, Father Diono," Seriah said.

She felt the old priest come up to her and wrap her in his arms.

"I feel I should know your name. You've been to my table

before," he said.

"Yes, Father. Seriah Yaledít. I came by last fall on my way to Temblin."

"Of course, of course. Come inside. The table is being set."

He turned and led the way toward the front door of the chapel.

"Who is cooking?" Seriah asked. "Did your order finally send someone to re...share your workload?"

"Another priest?" Diono said. "No. I don't think so. Just a young woman who came to visit me. She comes by often."

She could feel the name of the young woman escaping Diono's memory as he pulled open the door to his small chapel and stepped inside.

There were few places Seriah had been that were as serene and silent as Diono's chapel.

The sun had risen high enough that it now streamed warmth and light into the place, toying at the edge of Seriah's vision behind her blinder. The priest hurried on his way into his back rooms and kitchen, leaving her a moment to herself.

She found herself a seat on one of the benches and took in the timelessness of the place. The sound of her own breathing was her only companion, as even the constant jingling rings on her staff had fallen still.

A moment later and the silence was broken as Diono came back into the chapel.

"Ah! A fellow dedicate! Just in time. I was about to eat. Come! Come!"

She stood and offered a smile, following the old priest into the kitchen.

Someone moved around deftly, placing down a bowl in front of her.

"Welcome, Holy Nefer," the woman said. "The bowl in front of you is wooden, but filled with hot soup. Be careful."

"Thank you," Seriah said.

She felt the priest lower himself down on the bench next to her with a heavy grunt. He reached across the table, brought back a loaf of bread, and placed it in her hands.

After Diono said the blessing, the other woman took her seat opposite them.

"We have not been introduced," Seriah said. "I understand you're one of Father Diono's common guests, as I am?"

"Yes," the woman said, with a smile in her voice. "My brother and I stop through here several times a year, as we travel north and south from Edi City to Garrou."

"That is a long trip to make so many times a year. Much more often than I, traveling to Temblin once a year."

"What takes you to Temblin so often?" she asked. "Although I suppose someone has to go and offer even those in Temblin the judgments of the Monks of Nifara."

"I would admonish you not to cast so quick a judgment on the hot-tempered people of Temblin. If you spent any amount of time there, you might come to respect them for who they are."

"My apologies, Holy Nefer."

"Since we are sharing a table, please just call me Seriah."

"Very well, Nefer Seriah," the woman said. "My name is Rallia Clouw."

"You mentioned you and your brother stop here, but I hear only you and Diono at the table?"

"I'm traveling south to catch up with him," Rallia said. "I had an errand to run in Amstonhotten."

"And what takes you north and south from Edi to Bortali so often?"

"My brother and I run a caravan detail, escorting merchants up and down the length of Düran and Bortali."

"With that much walking, you must stay fit."

"A Black Sentinel who doesn't stay fit doesn't find work."

"I've not heard of Black Sentinels traveling so much," Seriah said.

"We're a different pair of birds," Rallia said. "You're on your way back to Birin then?"

"How did you guess?"

"You said you were coming from Temblin, and you appear to be heading north, so I assumed you were heading back to your order's Templum in Birin."

"You're observant."

"I'm paid to be."

"Young Rallia here has come for my blessing," Diono said.

"You give me a blessing every time I'm here, regardless of whether I ask for one," Rallia said.

"If you're to sit at my table, I'll give you one. Perhaps our fellow dedicate has one she can offer, herself."

Seriah coughed as she tore off the bread in her mouth and moved the wad to her cheek. "I know few blessings," she said.

"Do you not bless someone after you give them a judgment?"

"We make our decisions and then encourage those nearby to just be themselves."

"You are a monk, an adjudicator of Nifara. Bless the girl after I have. It is our sacred duty."

"Of course, brother," she said. "I'm not saying I can't. But in the few years since I bound my eyes, I have not been asked to do so."

Diono grunted as he rose and shuffled around the table.

"Kneel down," he said.

She heard Rallia scramble to rise and then drop to her knees.

"Do right and seek the path. Do not listen to the words of the Web-Weaver, Achanerüt the Deceiver. Listen to your heart, for this blessing will tell you what is true and right. If you stray, return to the path. If you cannot find it, seek aid, and you shall find your way."

Seriah rose and circled the table herself. Diono took her hand and held it out, assuming she could not find her way. Her hand came to rest on the top of Rallia's head.

"I...," she began.

"Go on, sister," Diono urged.

She took a deep breath and sighed, silently praying to Nifara that she be granted the words to say. The words of the proverb her long-dead parents had spoken to her as a child came to her.

"Cold touch of chaos and deceit, melt away in the light of the path of righteousness. Look not left, look not right, but stay true to truth, and even servants of darkness shall walk free of the chains that hold them."

"Thank you, Nefer," Rallia said, rising. She turned to the priest. "I do need to continue on my road, Father Diono. I can see the Nefer out."

The priest muttered his goodbyes and tottered out a side door.

"Should we help clean up?" Seriah asked.

"No, he'll nibble at the food over the course of the day," Rallia said. "Any other travelers who come along will be invited to help themselves. Thank you for joining us."

"A meal is always welcome. You're heading south?" she said as they came to the gate outside the chapel door.

"To Edi City. North to Birin?"

"Yes," Seriah replied.

"Thank you for your blessing. I don't know that I've ever heard of a Nifaran giving one."

"You've interacted with my order?"

"I've been present for a few judgments. I was raised among Paladins in Garrou, so Nifarans were often guests at my father's poorkitchen attached to the bastion there."

Rallia said her goodbyes, and left, and Seriah began the walk north, thinking on the words she had said, and trying to recollect why she had never given a blessing before, and wondering why she had never heard one ever given by a Nifaran.

Part 2

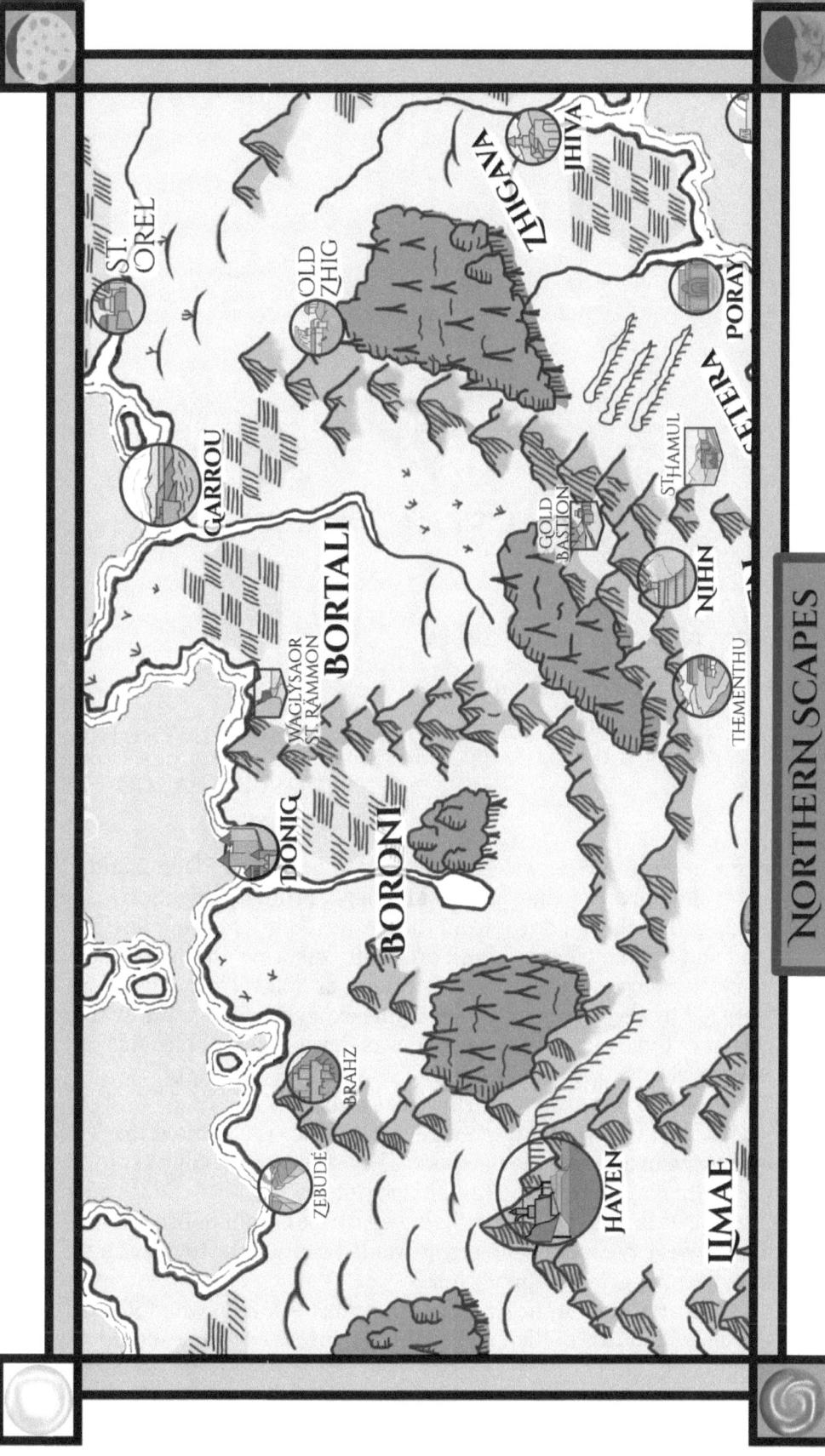

10

Thementhu College

Sister, Mother, Daughter, Bride.

Lift your chin up, hold it high.

— FOUND EMBROIDERED IN THE HEM

OF MOST BRIDAL GOWNS

The Emthu river was the lifeblood of portions of Düran and the northern vineyards of Morriego. From it, irrigation canals flowed down from the western border of that fertile land and fed the vineyards and orchards, ensuring another season would see harvest, regardless of drought or flood. The headwaters were fed by seven springs in the alpine expanse of the southwest corner of the country of Nemen. It was there, where thousands of flowers bloomed, each in their due season, that the city of Thementhu grew around the Crysalas College.

The land was verdant, but meager. Wildflowers painted the landscape in a multitude of colors. They stood out in contrast to the white marble buildings and black slate roofs of the college and the houses in between. Every living space had room to breathe, and in every personal field a long-wooled capricör or two roamed free, keeping grass cropped short.

The sisterhood of the Crysalas Integritas—women who followed Crysania, goddess of life, purity, and the future-tapestry—could claim their college in Nemen as their oldest, still-standing, institution. In Nemen, they had never suffered under the religious persecution seen in other nations, and had long ago built the college as a place where any could come and study botany, medicine, and the sciences. Students in white robes shuffled along well-kept paths, discussing their studies and philosophies.

Some were formal members of the sub-branch of the Crysalas Integritas and had taken on aspects of purity, such as the shaven heads of the aspect of cleanliness, or the gold rose circlet denoting an aspect of virginity. There were hrelgrens and qaylli, and even fewer and far between, men in black robes, standing out in stark contrast.

A starker contrast still came from those who wore the polished breast plates of the Paladames: the Crysalas Honoris hailing from Pariantür itself. There, the Crysalas had found solace over nine hundred years prior. Their close vicinity, and Pariantür's purpose—to protect the borders to the east—had quickly seen armor crafted for the women who had taken up residence there. Even those who had taken on aspects that would forbid them from violence wore a symbolic woolen mantle, reminiscent of the armor, and had undergone some training in the martial arts of defense.

Katiam Borreau felt self-conscious with the elderly Matriarch Superioris on her arm. How she had come to be the caring physician for the ancient leader of their church, without the formal training of the college, escaped her. The woolen armor that hung from her frame brought further attention to her as an outsider—as a member of the entourage that had come to visit as the Matriarch's attendants. She was already looking forward to the journey back to Nihn, where they would meet up with the Paladins of the Hammer after they concluded their assessment of their own holdings in Setera and St. Hamul.

The Matriarch Superioris, Maeda Mür, wore a white robe and a tall headdress meant to convey the appearance of a rose bloom. Over her frail frame she wore a chasuble mantle resembling Paladame armor, but made of blocked wool. She shuffled along slowly. It was nothing new to Katiam, though the glances of attention they both received walking along the path continued to send anxiety coursing through her stomach and spine.

"Do calm down, dear," the Matriarch said.

"I'm sorry, Auntie," Katiam said. The Matriarch was, in fact, her great-aunt, and she had been under strict orders to refer to her as

Auntie when they were alone. Maeda and her husband, Dorian Mür, the Prima Pater of the Paladins of the Hammer, had never had children of their own, and often doted on Katiam because of it.

"I can't help but feel the stares of those from the college."

"Nonsense. Everyone stares at us as we walk the halls of Pariantür."

"Those are looks of deference. Here they look as though we are intruding."

"I think you are mistaken. They are looking to one they only thought a myth. I'm ninety-four years old, after all, and I haven't made it back over the Pyracene Sea since I was a young girl leaving my home to become a Paladame in the first place."

They arrived at the greenhouse college. It was by far the largest building on the sizable campus. Six separate greenhouses ran off the south-facing side. They came to the door, which was opened by two attendants. Stepping into the vestibule, the outer doors were pulled shut. They were quickly admitted into the inner hall and hit with a blast of humidity.

"It seems the greenhouses are getting enough sun these days," the Matriarch commented.

They started down the well-lit, white-tiled hall. The wall to their left was decorated by images and figures of flora studied and diagrammed. Doors regularly broke up the long wall, opening to classrooms and laboratories.

One room was full of greenery requiring shade while someone inspected the fronds. In another, a noxious smell wafted out as two women and a hrelgren maiden leaned over a boiling pot.

"I suppose that is where we're going," the Matriarch said.

Katiam's attention snapped back from looking into each room, and she saw several sisters standing outside a single office ahead, watching their approach.

All of the women bowed, bringing their cupped hands up to their noses in the formal greeting.

The women parted and another came out of the room. She was a black-skinned Sidieratan, head shaved bare, and wearing brown rather than white robes, denoting her as a follower of the Aspect of Charity. Her long, thin features bordered on severe angularity, making Katiam all the more aware of her own short, curvy frame. The woman touched her cupped hands to her nose, bowing.

"Matriarch Superioris, thank you for coming to visit me here."

"The honor is mine, Esenath Chloïse," the Matriarch said. She indicated to Katiam, who reached into the satchel hanging at her side and pulled out a package wrapped in silk.

"Please," Esenath said, taking the package, "follow me into my laboratory."

They entered the door after her, the other sisters close behind. It was a larger room, with rare glass phials and tubes over small flames. The other sisters moved to return to their stations, continuing their work, albeit distractedly. Esenath walked over to her own desk, which was strewn with papers. She set the package down and opened it. Inside, there were two books. She lifted one to her nose and smelled it. "It is good to have you back," she whispered, placing it down carefully. She opened the other one, glancing through a few pages. Then she turned back to the Matriarch.

"I cannot thank you enough for returning this to me. What a risk it was to send you my only copy. If anything had happened to it, I cannot imagine what I would have done."

"Well, we've brought with us over a dozen fresh copies of the book. The Chloïse Book of Flowers and Their Uses is sure to be very informative to new botanists over the coming generations."

"More than twelve copies? The scribes of Pariantür outdid themselves. We had hoped you might make three for the college and one for Pariantür."

"When my advisors and I finally saw what you had accomplished, with your instructions for care, gathering, and the extensive diagrams, we turned the entire scriptorium onto it, and even brought in some of the more capable illuminators from the Paladins to help. We brought five copies for the college. Those twelve I mentioned are just the ones we're continuing on with, to make sure the vaults have access to it, too. And that's not including the five we kept at Pariantür."

"Twenty-two copies?" Esenath said, astonished.

"Twenty-three if you include your own."

The broad smile on Esenath's face beamed wider.

"What are we working on here?" the Matriarch asked.

"Ah, yes!" Esenath said. "We are working with feren root. Perhaps you know, it is used for the creation of both the ferenard green dye, as well as ferann, the toxin used to keep many pests at bay. Ferenard makes for a soft green dye, but it fades all too easily. We know that the closer ferenard gets to converting into ferann, the green dye becomes very strong, and retains its dye strength much longer."

"And so you seek to see just how far you can go before conversion?" Katiam asked.

"Yes," Esenath said.

"Much like steeping a cruth tea," Katiam said. "If you are not careful, preparing cruth for aching elderly bones, it will convert into a sleeping agent, and knock someone out for several days."

"Esenath, this is Katiam Borreau. She is my constant companion and a physician."

"You hold a prestigious position," Esenath said. "Many a physician here at the college would give their left leg to have apprenticed under the Matriarch Superioris's last physician, the Matriarch Minoris Pallan."

"I was very fortunate indeed," Katiam said. It was a practiced phrase she had come to say often.

"How long do you expect this experiment to take?" the Matriarch asked.

"We will not present any findings for at least a full year."

"Then, if you have the time, perhaps you would be willing to give us a tour of the rest of the building?"

For the next several hours they were taken in and out of labs, and into each of the greenhouses. Each had its own function and ran under the tutelage of a master botanist.

They came to the last greenhouse.

"Ah, before we go in there," Esenath said, "let me introduce you to Sister Felli Tagge. She's studying the Beardfrost toxins that have come to such common use in the vendettas of Redot."

Though it was a small study, the walls were covered in shelves, upon which sat dome-covered plants, each looking more dangerous than the last. Most had white paper cards alongside them, loudly marking them as toxic, and then the uses—for scent, or for spices in small amounts. Others bore pink, red, and finally black cards. The last group of plants had heavy leather gloves placed next to them, and a full warning to the reader to tread lightly.

The Matriarch spoke with Esenath and the recently introduced Sister Tagge as she showed them a display of minuscule plants, each bearing a frosty fuzz across the leaves.

Katiam wandered by herself around the room, reading the placards and considering what she knew of many of them when their compounds were found in her own apothecary chest. She came around to the botanist's personal desk, and spotted an odd fist-sized pod holding down a stack of papers. It was shaped like a walnut shell, but smooth like an unopened rosebud. It was mottled with flecks of blue and purple across the green.

"What is this?" Katiam asked.

The three women all turned to her.

"Ah, the mystery pod," Sister Tagge said.

"It is sad to see it reduced to a paperweight," Esenath responded. "It has quite a history behind it. I suppose many a student who has attended has at one time or another considered ways to get it to bloom."

"I recall," the Matriarch Superioris said, "it being mentioned in books I studied as a young girl when I first journeyed to Pariantür to join the sisterhood."

"But what is it?" Katiam repeated, holding it up. She could not close her hand around it, but it fit comfortably as she cupped it in both.

Esenath approached. "It is called the Rotha. No one knows its origin, just that it has been around for centuries. Many have tried to make it bloom. It has been planted and forgotten until it was tilled up again. It has been exposed to flames and charred black, only to slough off the ash to return to how it looks now. It has soaked in water for a decade, to no avail. It is a quandary that no one has ever solved."

"All these centuries, shouldn't it have turned to a dry wood or something like a gourd?" Katiam asked.

"Her interest is piqued," Sister Tagge said.

Katiam held it up. It had a waxy surface that was almost supple in her hands. She smelled it, and it gave off a sappy, sweet fragrance.

"Perhaps it ought to be allowed to leave the college," Sister Tagge continued. "Maybe the women of Pariantür can try to bring it to life."

"That's probably a good idea," Esenath said. "Katiam, would you take care of it?"

"Me? I wouldn't know what to do. I killed a pot of porumarias given to me last year, and those are hardy."

"You could teach her botany," the Matriarch said to Esenath.

"Oh?" Esenath replied.

"I was hoping that perhaps you'd join us on our journey toward Mahn Fulhar. That way you can see the copies of your book placed into the hands of those who will find a use for it."

"It has been a while since I've visited the vaults in Garrou," Esenath said to herself.

"Very well, it is settled. We'll be leaving for Nihn in five days. I expect you to be ready to go by then." The Matriarch took Katiam's arm. "We should return to the Paladame guard. They'll be expecting us."

The two of them made their way down the hall toward the door and heard a commotion outside.

"Give me a moment to see what is going on, Auntie."

"Of course, dear."

Katiam stepped up to the door and peeked out.

Four Paladames sat atop lean gray sleipnirs. They each wore a full suit of functional armor, from the breastplate down to the cuisses upon their upper legs. More so than paladinial armor, it was built for ease of movement rather than resilience. Joints were covered only in a very fine chain mail, and the chain mail skirt provided modesty to the women. Rose motifs of silver and gold embossed the entirety of the armor, and pierced-out haloes were mounted to the backs of their shoulder. Upon their heads they had hair cropped above their shoulders or shorter, and a tiara made of silver rose leaves and a single gold rose blossom on their forehead.

Captain Sigri Smith, a tall woman with an imperious demeanor, looked forward, ignoring the crowd that was forming beyond them. There were several hundred students waiting, holding fresh roses in their hands.

Katiam closed the door behind her and approached the captain's mount.

"Captain?" Katiam said.

Sigri looked down sternly. "I take it she is ready to come out?"

"Yes. What is this crowd?"

"It seems that the students were kept unaware that we were visiting the campus. Rumors of our arrival struck a tinder and now the surprise is spoiled and everyone wishes to see her. I sent Sabine Upona, as the Matriarch's assistant, to go and speak with the headmaster, but she has not returned."

Katiam slipped back into the building and explained the situation.

"Very well," Maeda Mür said. "There is nothing to be done. We were supposed to hold a large banquet to let the students know I was here. I suppose we'll need to go and face them."

She turned to the door without another word. Katiam held the door open and the Matriarch Superioris stepped out.

The crowd outside erupted in a cheer.

They pushed forward, and in response, Sigri Smith, in unison with the other three guards, nudged their sleipnirs forward a step. The crowd halted and fell silent.

Katiam felt the Matriarch's arm fall from hers as she stepped forward between the mounts.

"Be still, Captain Smith. These are students, not T'Akai come to assault Pariantür."

Katiam watched Sigri's chin rise in defiance before she held her hand up. "Presenting the Matriarch Superioris," Captain Smith declared, "head of the Crysalas Integritas, Maeda Mür."

The crowd broke free of their emotional confines and cheered again. They did not quickly move toward the stairs now, but kept their distance. The intimidating challenge set by the Paladame captain was clear.

The Matriarch approached the top of the stairs and held a frail hand up to silence the throng.

"Thank you for coming to welcome me and my Paladames from Pariantür. I suppose this comes as a surprise to you, one that we'd hoped might be maintained until dinner in the great hall tonight. Needless to say, I am here, and we shall see to greeting and meeting with you over the course of the next several days. I look forward to seeing what projects you are working on, and what lessons you are learning. I have no doubt that a few of your brilliant minds might be invited to join us in our studies at Pariantür after this is all said and done."

"Where will you go after your visit?" a voice shouted out.

"We should like to continue our journey from here to Mahn Fulhar and the Oracle at Crysania's Massif. It was where my own journey started, after all. Fitting I should make the journey as I near the end of my life."

The crowd groaned in protest.

"Now, now, don't get worked up. I'm not dying, but I'm ninety-four years old. No need for dramatics, but I'll be joining Crysania sometime soon. At least I should hope so."

She descended the steps carefully. Katiam rushed forward to offer her arm, but the Matriarch dismissed her with a wave of her hand and made her own way. The crowd parted and began throwing roses in front of her. She came to the rear of the crowd and turned around.

"Now," she said. The entire crowd grew silent. "Off with you. I need a rest from all this excitement before dinner tonight."

Almost as one, the entire crowd dispersed, running back to the chores and assignments they had neglected to greet the old woman. Katiam approached as a group of middle-aged women rushed across the green behind a single Paladame, the personal assistant to the Matriarch.

"Hello, Sister Upona," the Matriarch said, her arm now in Katiam's again. "A few minutes too late I should guess. It seems word got out of my arrival and an impromptu welcome was assembled."

Sabine Upona wore a brown robe the color of her skin. The small bells shaped like rose buds that hung from her ears tinkled as she shook her head.

"I am very sorry, Matriarch."

"No need to worry. Captain Smith has everything under control. Perhaps a bit too much control, but all is well, nevertheless."

II

Higher Callings

Frost to Flowers,

Bud and vine.

Flourishes in all due time.

—A PROVERB OF ABBESS PATIENCE OF NIHN

Katiam roused the Matriarch from her short respite with a cup of tea just before the dinner bells summoned the college to the dining hall. They made their way in the early evening summer sun along with Sabine Upona, who quietly brought her up to speed with the events at the college administration level.

Students rushed along paths toward the continually pealing bell tower. Others cut through the green grass before they spotted the Matriarch making her stately way toward the central building, and they sheepishly rejoined the designated paths to take their time.

Halfway to their destination, two Paladames approached who were as different from each other as they were from most other members of the Crysalas. Lutea Calimbrise was a sun-darkened Morriegan who stood almost as tall as the stately Captain Sigri Smith. Unlike Sigri, she was heavier, somber, and had the apt ability to memorize anything said to her.

Next to her walked Narah Wevan, one of the Veiled Sisters, and yet from a more severe minority within that self-secluding sect. She had taken on all three of the isolating aspects—Stillness,

Sanctity, and Solitude, indicated respectively by the veil, gloves, and hood she wore. To add to that, like Katiam, she had taken on the dietary Aspect of St. Klare, dictating a strictly ascetic diet, and thus, though Katiam had never seen her face, she had come to know the girl through the whispered conversations she was allowed to partake of during meals and other designated times of community.

"Sister Wevan, Sister Calimbrise," the Matriarch said, "your trip to the library was fruitful?"

Neither smiled. At least, Lutea did not, her Aspect of Solemnity, marked by the lacquered black circlet in her hair, allowed no outward emotion. That, or her naturally solemn homeland of Morriego had bred it into her. If Narah smiled, none could say. She did, however, nod fervently.

Lutea leaned toward Narah and nodded along with her. "Their library is impressive. We have not requested access to the restricted books yet. We have time still."

"Very well. The Prima Pater asked we read through the restricted section in an attempt to glean more recent testimonies. Especially regarding interactions with the women of Limae. He wishes to understand their work within the Northern Scapes."

"Of course, Matriarch Superioris."

"Why are there no Paladins here?" Katiam asked.

"What, dear?" Maeda Mür replied.

"Paladins. There are none here studying that I've seen."

"There have been a few who have come to study, but that is a good observation. There are not many."

"But why?"

"Oh, you know how Paladins are. They are very caught up in their mission. It is important to have them field-ready, armed for battle and prayer. Then they can study. And even then, it's the study of trade, taught from master to apprentice."

"But we sisters?"

"We sisters have a different calling. To study the creations of our goddess—life, purity, medicine, and, most importantly, history and the future. Studying this is how we come to know her."

"I should have liked to study here. I might better understand my medicine."

"I'm still alive. So that's a testament to your abilities. Nevertheless, I'm sorry you did not find the time to come and study here. Perhaps someday. In the meantime, take solace in the acquisition of Esenath Chloïse as your tutor for the remainder of our journey. Consider the Rotha pod you have in your satchel. You will have much to learn from that, even if you fail, as everyone else has over the centuries."

"Sister Chloïse is joining us?" Lutea asked. She almost broke her composure as excitement tried to bubble out of her.

The work of Esenath Chloïse had been all the Paladames of Pariantür had spoken of for many months as the copies of her book were created.

"She will. I'm sorry, your own journey to deliver copies of the book will be taking you on a different road."

"Her company will be one more thing to look forward to when you return, and we meet again," Lutea said, regaining her composure.

"I'll see to it you are able to meet her before we all leave for Nemen, if you'd like."

Both women nodded adamantly.

As they walked together toward the hall, Katiam reached down into her satchel and touched the pod there, stroking it gently and thinking upon the road that lay ahead.

The following morning, the entire college collected in a great hall, with the Matriarch Superioris taking loan of the throne from the college chancellor, who sat beside her. Along the center nave of the room stood fifty women. Among their number, three hrelmaidens.

Once the pomp and initial ceremony was concluded, each stepped forward to present their body of work. The Matriarch Superioris had spent time well into the previous evening preparing for each of them, to observe their character, and decide whether she would choose any of them to journey to Pariantür and contribute to the community there. For each scholar she selected, a Paladame off the waiting list in Sabine Upona's ledger would be given permission to travel to the college and begin their own era of study.

The women presenting themselves to the Matriarch hailed from each of the major schools. The Matriarch quietly consulted the chancellor, and Sabine sat at the Matriarch's other arm, checking the needs of Pariantür against the chancellor's preferences of who she wished to keep at the college to further their fields of study.

From the botany school, three were selected, including one of sister Tagge's own apprentices. From the chiurgeons, the Matriarch needed little consultation to take back Sister Gara Ablein, a Paladame of some renown, and whom the Paladames had been reluctant to part with five years prior. She would be very welcome back with her new knowledge of human anatomy.

From among the apothecaries a single woman was chosen for her intimate knowledge of both botany and the chemical compounds of the earth. Katiam recalled the Matriarch noting her the night before, as one who would be able to best replenish the apothecariate at Pariantür, supplemented with her mineral knowledge.

But it was with astonishment to all gathered when the Matriarch Superioris took not only a handful, but all fifteen applicants from the school of medicae—including the three hrelmaidens, who would be the first hrelgrens to be invited to become Paladames in the past twelve years.

As the women of the college cheered, Sabine whispered the names of those that would be sent to the college when the chosen applicants arrived at Pariantür, and Katiam's heart sank, knowing her name would not be read.

Tables and chairs had been moved out to the lawn by younger students, and throngs of college servants carried troughs full of food before the attendees as they came out of the hall. The smell of freshly baked bread and the colorful vegetables grown in the botanical greenhouses dazzled Katiam's senses. Even the meat smelled wonderful, even if her diet forbade her from eating it.

Astrid Glass, one of Captain Sigri Smith's Paladame guards, tore a shank off of a roast capricör as it was carried by, and threw herself down into the seat next to Katiam.

"Did you want some?" she asked, drawing her dagger, and preparing to cut some of the meat off for her before hesitating. "I'm sorry Katiam. Aspect of St. Klare, right?"

Katiam nodded, touching the stylized thorn-necklace sitting around her throat.

Astrid reached out and took hold of a large piece of seed bread. "You may be restricted to bread, water, and those nasty bugs, but you can at least have some of the best bread any baker has ever made."

Katiam smiled. "It's nice to see them making Sower Bread here." She tore open the bread, and various seeds seemed to pour out onto her platter. "I thought it was only made at Pariantür."

"I almost became a baker when I took my vows," Astrid said with a large smile. "It turns out I'm as terrible in the kitchen as my brother was at blowing glass for our father."

"Your brother? Killian?"

Astrid nodded.

"Do you miss him?"

"I go weeks without seeing him at Pariantür," Astrid offered, "but yes, I do miss him, even while we're here with the Matriarch Superioris."

"I thought as much. The two of you have been inseparable since we left the Fortress Monastery."

"He keeps me centered when we aren't at home, near our mother and father."

"I often forget you were raised in the shadow of the Hammer."

"If one can say anything is in shadow there."

"Too true."

"More bread? Water?"

"At times of feast, I'm allowed to cut the water with some mead."

Astrid took a large jug and poured out a helping of the golden liquid for herself, then put a splash of it into Katiam's own cup.

"To the college," Astrid said.

Katiam and several others nearby lifted their cups to join her.

The women who had been selected to journey to Pariantür sat at the head table with the Matriarch well into the night, while Katiam sat and listened to Astrid continue to tell stories of her brother's exploits against T'Akian raiders, and equally humorous stories of sleipnir throwing shoes and riders.

"What seems to be troubling you, girl?" the Matriarch said as Katiam helped her out of her woolen chasubles that evening.

"Nothing, Auntie," Katiam said. She stepped away and mixed up a draught of the Matriarch's evening medicine.

"You know that lying to the highest authority of your religion is a sin."

"I am not lying, Auntie. I'm merely avoiding speaking words that will hold no meaning or sway over my future."

"Katiam," the Matriarch said.

"Yes Auntie?"

"Stop being petulant, and tell me what is on your mind."

Katiam stopped and turned, the glass of medicine in her hands. "Only if you agree to take this without complaint."

Maeda Mür sighed. "Very well."

She took up the cup, drank it down, and then handed it back.

"See?" Katiam said. "It's not so bad if you just take what I tell you to. Complaining only prolongs the discomfort."

"I'm fighting hard not to make a face of disgust right now, child."

Katiam turned and put the cup back in the apothecary cabinet.

"Now, what is the trouble?" the Matriarch asked.

"The trouble is, my name has, for years, been on the list of Paladames wishing to come here to the college and study. And once more, I am passed by."

"I see. You truly are uneasy, taking care of an old woman like myself?"

"Auntie," Katiam said, coming to sit next to her on the bed. "I enjoy my time serving you. You're the mother I never had."

"Then why are you discontent?"

"'Cause…because I feel like I never had a choice."

"Katiam," the Matriarch said, "do you not recall that you get in this mood every couple of years?"

"What do you mean?"

"You came to us with your brother, may his soul rest, when you were but twelve years old. I ought not to have, but I pampered you. You flitted from study to study, never settling. I tried, during those formative years, to nudge you toward this field of medicine, because it was where you naturally flourished. You were like I was at that age. Feisty. Stubborn."

"You still are," Katiam said, smiling.

"This is true." She took Katiam's hand in hers. "Do you know what I realized about you? I realized that what you needed was to feel a part of a group. To have a family. It was about that time that you first put your name in the ledger, to come to the college. And do you know, I thought to send you? But then I made a decision.

"You were at a point in your life where if I were to send you here, you would feel abandoned. Your brother had just died, and I was all the family you had. So I sent a letter to the college and requested they send Matriarch Minoris Pallan. Rather than allow you to feel abandoned, sent to the college, I brought the college to you."

"Auntie," Katiam said, "why have you never told me this?"

"Please do not be angry, dear."

"I'm not angry," Katiam said, tears coming to her eyes, and her hands began to shake.

"Katiam."

She suddenly burst out, hot tears streaming down her face. "You never told me. You let me continue to put my name on that list every year. And you never gave me a choice."

"I admit my fault," Maeda said, "and I admit that what at first I meant as a means to protect you slowly became my own selfishness, to keep you near me."

"Why?" Katiam said.

"Because I love you, dear. I do not say it flippantly when I say you are the daughter Crysania never gifted Dorian and I with."

Katiam threw herself gently into the arms of the old woman.

The Matriarch held her, and let the tears fall on her linen evening blouse, and gently stroked the younger woman's hair, softly whispering her care for her.

Eventually, the tears subsided to long, deep breaths, and Katiam sat up, sniffing, and looked over at the old woman, seeing tears on her face, too.

"My dear," Maeda said. "What is the first prophecy we follow?"

"The flowers of the mother shall be a balm," Katiam sniffed. "A healing touch to the world."

"How do we interpret this?"

"By tending her garden. By serving the needy. By healing. By teaching."

"Yes. I cannot part with you now. But when this journey has come to its end, I will make every arrangement for you to come to the college. I hope that through that action, I can be a balm for you. Would you like that?"

"Very much, Auntie."

"Very well. In the meantime, please accept my arrangement with Esenath Chloïse to be an interim college, if you will. You have much you can learn from her botany. It will set you apart when you do come to join the ranks of the scholars here."

Katiam nodded.

"Did you ever question your choice?" Katiam asked. "To become a Paladame?"

"At first, no. Afterall, I had visited the Oracle at Precipice, in Mahndür, and the Worldrose spoke and told me to journey to Pariantür. But there was a time that I doubted."

"What made you doubt?"
"Dorian."
"The Prima Pater?!"
"Yes. See, we grew up together. When I disappeared, my brother, Nethendel Unteel, went after me with Dorian in tow. They came to Pariantür to convince me to return home. Instead, they both became Paladins, and Dorian and I fell in love. When the Protectorate Wars ended, and Dorian had become the Prima Pater at so young an age, I thought to abandon my vows and support him. But I didn't."

"What made you change your mind?"

"The Oracle that sent me to become a Paladame told me of my future, and where it would end. It told me that if I remained faithful, my journey toward true purity would usher in the rebirth of the original intent of the Worldrose."

"A rebirth?"

"I thought perhaps that it might mean any number of things. Perhaps I'd have a child who would be some sort of legendary hero. Perhaps it meant I should rise to leadership in the ranks of the Crysalas Integritas. Perhaps I was always meant to be a foil to my husband, who in his younger years always answered with might and a strong arm."

"If my understanding of the past century is correct," Katiam said. "Perhaps all of those are true."

"Perhaps," Maeda said. "Perhaps I am meant simply to continue down the path that has been set for me, to do all I can to fulfill the will of Crysania, and allow that prophecy to flourish like a rose in the desert. Perhaps all I can do is try to be a good mother to a beautiful twenty-four-year-old woman, and when the timing is right, let her leave my nine decades old frail nest."

Katiam smiled, gave her great aunt another embrace, and they both cried and laughed a little longer before turning in for the night.

12

Nihn

The prayer of an honest man resounds blessings in the Halls of Aben in Lomïn. And despair to the depths of Noccitan.

—GHULLIBEN 12:9

The city of Nihn struck the senses in broad strokes that all seemed to complement one another as a single chord. The people of the city wore various shades of yellow, white, and beige to match the yellow stones that made up the walls and most houses. The bell towers, announcing the arrival of the Matriarch Superioris, did not have the discordance of many cities, but instead had been harmonized to one another perfectly—a testament to the bell forge that was the city's pride. The smells that came from the bakery on every corner spoke of the gariff seed powdered and sprinkled on the bakes—the yellow-dyed bread colored with the flower the seeds came from.

The Matriarch's carriage trundled through the city toward the palace in the center. A large, squat edifice that, to Katiam, looked like a loaf of bread itself.

A row of Paladins who sat atop their sleipnirs at attention and watched their approach should have been what drew the eye. It was the Konig of Nemen that she could not help but notice.

Perhaps it was the strict lifestyle of those that lived together in community at Pariantür, but Katiam knew no one as corpulent as Konig Bermach Gelbliht. He sat upon a throne, the spotted white fur lining his outspread robe surrounding his throat and framing the wide smile plastered across his face.

DEATHLESS BEAST

Stories of large men were often rife with morality lessons, and the corruption of those men was made obvious by the storyteller with details of warts, pimples, and sores. This man was different. The pleasant joy he took in from everything around him was almost as singularly noted as his city. At a distance, Katiam had judged the man too quickly, but her criticism was washed away as he stood, stepping down from the throne and holding his arms open in greeting.

The Matriarch's carriage came to a stop, and the door was opened for her by one of the Paladames. She came down to the beige cobbles, and looked up to face the Konig.

"Matriarch Superioris Mür! Hullo, hullo!" He roared with laughter. "Welcome to my city. A small country we may be, embraced by mountains and smothered by surrounding countries, but let me welcome you into my own arms!"

Katiam could see her auntie almost flinch as the man hefted his way across the courtyard to her, to gather the frail old woman in his embrace. His long train stretched out behind him.

"Your husband!" he announced, turning, and the small Prima Pater stepped down, as equally glad to see his wife as she had been to see him, talking about it the entire ride from Thementhu to Nihn.

He approached her and gave her a simple touch on her arm, his armor preventing him from giving her anything more.

The fanfare continued, as it often did in cities showing hospitality to their entourage. Katiam watched Astrid urge her own mount forward. Her brother, Killian Glass, fell in beside her. By their small movements Katiam could tell they were already lost in conversation.

"They know one another?" Esenath asked, riding alongside Katiam.

"Brother and sister," Katiam replied, looking to the woman next to her. "Their parents are glaziers for Pariantür."

"And you?"

"I had a brother," Katiam said.

"I meant where did you hail from, before joining the Crysalas."

"I followed my brother Hemaine from Varea. He journeyed to Pariantür to become a Paladin, and I was sent after him to ensure he didn't become distracted on the way."

"And what became of him?"

"He died."

"I'm very sorry to hear that."

"The T'Akai took him."

"Katiam," Sabine Upona said, turning back to look at the two of them. "The Matriarch Superioris has asked she be given privacy once she is settled in her rooms."

"Of course."

"The Prima Pater will be visiting, and she mentioned that they have not had a moment's peace since we left Pariantür."

"I understand," Katiam said, smiling. "Will you take a moment to see your husband?"

Sabine blushed. "Perhaps. Let us see to the Matriarch and Prima Pater first." She turned forward toward the gates that swallowed them up as they entered a manicured courtyard.

"Sabine and her husband, Jurgon, are two of the most admired members of society at Pariantür," Katiam explained to Esenath. "That the Prima Pater is married to the head of our own church is one thing, but the Uponas, as attendants to the two of them, are loved by all who know them and see them together."

"Why is that?"

"Have you ever seen a pair of lovers that make you both jealous, and perhaps a bit disgusted?"

"My brother and his wife," Esenath said, rolling her eyes.

"Watch the Uponas at dinner tonight. At first you will probably roll your eyes, as you do now. As this night wears on, it will turn to appreciation. I've never known two people whose love is so genuine—almost chaste. You'll feel ashamed you started the night bearing almost ill-will toward their love."

"I doubt that," Esenath said.

"You'll see," Katiam said, smiling.

Katiam prepared the Matriarch a basin of rose water and set clean linen by it.

"Hello, Katiam," the cheerful older Prima Pater said as he entered.

"Dorian," she said, giving him an awkward hug over his armor.

"Is Jurgon here to help you in and out of your armor?" she asked.

"I think for now I'll only have a short time to sit and enjoy a rest with Maeda," he said. "I've given Jurgon some time with his wife, and the queen of Nemen has requested to speak with the Matriarch."

"I had hoped we might have more than a few minutes," Maeda said. The look of discouragement on her face was obvious.

"We will find time," Dorian said. "Konig Gelbliht was fairly insistent that his wife come and visit you. You haven't had more than a few moments in the courtyard to know him. He's not a stern man, but he was about your seeing her."

"Very well," the Matriarch sighed.

"I'll give the two of you some privacy," Katiam said.

"Thank you, dear," Maeda said. "Please let us know when she arrives."

Katiam left the room and took a seat on a bench down the hall. Further down, the twin Paladins Loïc and Cävian stood guard with Captain Sigri Smith. The latter stood as stoic as ever, while the twins spoke with one another casually with their fingers.

The clack of wooden-soled shoes soon rang down the tiled halls, and the twins came to attention. The figure approached, just out of Katiam's sight.

"The Matriarch Superioris is expecting me." While her voice was commanding, she deferred to Captain Smith.

Sigri turned and looked at Katiam, who stood, nodding.

Sigri indicated for the woman to follow her.

The queen was the opposite of her husband. She was tall, slender, and severely regal. She wore yellow that verged on burnished gold, which stood in defiant contrast to her raven black hair, which was pulled into an elaborate headdress attempting to contain it.

"Queen Malla of Nemen," Captain Smith said.

"The Matriarch Superioris is expecting you," Katiam said, turning down the hall. "I'll let her know you've arrived."

She came to the door and gave a light rap.

"Come in, Katiam," the voice of the Matriarch said.

She pushed in as Dorian rose from the lounge next to his wife. He had taken off the elaborate shoulder-pads, though he still had his metal breastplate on. The Matriarch had a pillow in her arms, and was rearranging lounges.

"I'll leave by way of the second chamber," Dorian said, giving Katiam a smile.

He hefted his armor pieces and went out the door by the hearth, closing it behind him.

"Please show the queen in," the Matriarch said, rising from the lounge herself.

It was late afternoon, and nearly time for the feast to begin, when the queen left the room. Katiam prepared her auntie's evening tonic, while Sabine dressed her.

"They married very young," the Matriarch said, "and they have been happy. But she has not bore the king a son in the twenty years they've been together."

"That would explain the continual donations she's made to the college," Sabine said.

"She brought that up, as though she was confessing some sin. I calmed her fears. That she would seek remedies for her condition from the college is no sin. If her funding were to discover a breakthrough, and find a means to ensuring an heir, it would be a gift to many."

"There are many reasons a woman might not bear," Katiam said. "There would be no one cure-all."

"I know, dear."

"It could even be the king's own size that prevents it," Sabine offered hesitantly.

"I asked her that," Maeda said, then laughed. "You ought to have seen her blush when a little old lady like me asked her that question, though."

Katiam caught Sabine blushing, too.

"It is something to take into consideration. It is a constant discussion of she and her husband. The whole kingdom, in fact, is worried that with no heir, other nations might decide to take a portion of Nemen for themselves."

In the large feast hall Katiam found a seat with Narah Wevan and Lutea Calimbrise. She had trouble, as most did, paying attention to her food while the jovial king and his stern, demure wife engaged in conversation with the Prima Pater and Matriarch seated next to them.

At a long table staged above the rest of them, sat twenty-five other men and their wives. Each wore deep ochre robes, differentiated by various colored sashes and headdresses. They didn't wear coats of arms, but were instead denoted by stripes and chequers. When accompanied by a woman, she wore the colors of her companion boldly.

"Esteemed members of my council, and titled nobility," the Konig said, struggling to stand from his chair. The murmuring in the room fell silent. "I thank you all for coming. Not one of you is missing, and for that I am greatly honored. I find myself in a rare position to have your attention without having to wait for me to move my fat belly all the way across the palace to the council hall."

To this, the Nemenese nobles laughed. The Paladins and Paladames offered a few awkward chuckles.

"We have with us here the heads of two holy orders and their attendants. Both churches have long held respect in our country, as our loyalty to them is stronger than any other nation. Whether each of you holds faith in their gods or in one of the various sects of the Church of Aben makes no difference, but Nemen is, and shall be, continually loyal to the Grissoni Paladins. Long have we given protection to the usually hidden vaults of the Crysalas Integritas.

"I wish to extend my hand once more, and renew our bonds of promise to them and theirs. May the White Pantheon continue to bless the Holy Orders they have established."

He lifted a glass into the air and looked around. Katiam caught a moment of regret in his posture, choked down by a smile. Then he took and drank the entire goblet down. Others followed suit.

"I have arranged special entertainment for tonight, by my own hand. Please enjoy the performance of this short dramatic interpretation, played by Kelemere of Zhigava and his troupe, and written, as I have suggested, by myself!"

Two figures took the center of the room in masks. The first wore a white robe, and from the mask flowed a white beard. He took up from one of the other actors a crown and placed it on his head and stepped forth. The second wore black robes, and his mask had three eyes set into it. Together the collection of actors chimed in harmony the word, *"BEGIN!"*

The actor in white stepped forward, his voice booming over the chorus.

"I am brought forth by word 'Begin,'
  to bright shine like the fallen snow.
From sun I came called forth by day,
  His word the measure of the All."

The black-robed figure took center next to the first.

"Lo, brother, by that word so spake,
  He gave us both our power,
From deepest well of blackest star,
  I Wyv, you Aben, brothers."

It followed the story all knew since their early toddler years. Separately, the sisters, Crysania and Sakharn, were spoken into the All by the Existence, and together the four of them took hold of a large silken blanket and unfolded it.

"By power given to rule and weigh,
  Four corners taut on Kallattai,
White light of soft silver Umay,
  Norlok that ruddy glow stands by.

"Forth now the world, encircled in,
  Our pow'r together buck and bend,
The water surge and grain grow forth,
  For all who come from south and north."

Streamers of green and gray flew across the blue silken sheet, and soon it was laid down, to settle on the floor. Wyv became a plowman and began to sow seeds. Soon after, both sisters produced bundles, presenting their firstborns. From the troupe, two took their roles as Lae'Zeq and Rionne.

Lae'Zeq held a book in his hand and proclaimed the birth of Wisdom, while Rionne wore a helm with a red plume. The others came to the stage until all eleven gods stood in a long line, from Aben down to Kasenet, and after the gap, proceeded back from Kos-Yran to his father Wyv.

Together they spoke in unison.

"All hail Existence, who hath borne,
  Our force of life upon this firm.

DEATHLESS BEAST

To us he gives all rule and hon'r,
    In turn breathe the same."

Wyv stepped forward and his brother joined him. They took each other's hand. Wyv spoke first.

"My brother, let me show you now,
    This thing which I hath wrought,
Let now we tie that thread of life,
    To Gigantes over yonder.
What shall you make to match his weight,
    And will they do thy bid.
For I hath made as Existence had,
    A thing with graceful stride."
Then Aben spoke.

"I see this now, the Titan there,
    But see these graceful things,
The Watcher who shall flit and fly,
    Upon angelic wing.
Come now my kin, my son, my girl,
    Let all now find thy way,
To make a peoples to admire,
    And teach unto the others their ken."

Each god brought forth a symbol of the people they made. And soon a panoply sat in the center of the fabric. The gods all turned and removed their masks and placed them to face the center, in a circle. The company turned to face the Konig's guests and conclude in unison.

"Consider now Existence will,
    That power be shared for good or ill.
Glory brought to Him on high,
    By pantheon, man, woman, and child."

Everyone rose and offered claps and cheers to the troupe as they took their bows. The Matriarch Superioris had a large smile on her face, and Katiam remembered her saying as they sailed into Poray that she hoped to see proper plays, since it had been so long since a troupe had journeyed to Pariantür. The moral plays put on by members of their orders were often too dry, or masked scripture readings that turned quickly to sermons on obscure passages.

"Now!" the Konig said, holding both hands up. "I pray you all take heart to the lesson this play has given, for it shall matter in the coming years."

Everyone took their seats and turned to listen.

"As you know, I am rarely serious, nor wish to go on for any length of time greater than six hours."

A few chuckles came from the head of the table.

"But I find myself in the very rare occasion to be in the full council of my lords, and under the auspices of the two churches I most respect. Thus I find I am able to ask you all to bear witness to a proclamation I have considered, and now wish to make.

"I found myself in the position I am in, albeit slightly smaller than I am now, nearly twenty years ago. My father died only a few short months after I wedded my beloved bride, of the same ailment I expect will take me sooner, rather than later." He looked at his wife, who smiled up at him, nodding for him to continue.

"For twenty years you have watched and obsessed over whether I should have an heir. Indeed, while we have had our differences, all have in one way or another conveyed their desire to ensure the line continues. Perhaps it was out of care for the well-being of our small nation, or perhaps it is because I've allowed certain allowances of authority to go unchecked. Perhaps we all wish my line to continue in order to avoid being swallowed up by Düran, Setera, Morriego, or, pantheon forbid, Bortali, who would, at the very least, enjoy the untaxed use of our mountain mines. Nevertheless, my life, and the lives of my unconceived heirs, is a glue that binds our nation together.

"Thus, as the Existence said, 'Let our power multiply by means of common rule.' I wish to proclaim this day that with my death, my power is not dissolved, nor passed to one who seizes it, but rather disseminated to you all. I have already chosen the members of this council, who shall act as chairs at my table as we focus the remaining years of my life to pre-establishing how my proposed parliament shall rule."

He pointed to one of the lords, who had been fidgeting.

"Lord Wensla, I know your mind. And you would ask what should happen if I sired an heir in that time. Should that happen, then they would take my ancestral title, and become yet another member of the parliament. Should no heir be born, then my brother continues to hold the title."

"What of Thementhu?" the Matriarch asked, pulling herself up from her own seat. "The city of Thementhu surely continues to remain independent, under my authority and its own."

"So it shall remain," Konig Gelbliht said, "and I should like to extend a seat in parliament to a representative from Thementhu, whom they may select. All this shall be decided by the council, but I wish to have the blessing of the Church of Grissone and of Crysania if we are to proceed."

"This is certainly more than the Boroni jarls did when they broke away from Bortali," the Prima Pater said. "The ties you have with Crysania's church are stronger still than those with Pariantür. If the Crysalas gives their blessing, then the Grissoni church shall, too."

"When your council has decided everything," the Matriarch said, "bring it to the leadership of the Crysalas. You can have the College of Thementhu deliver it, and we shall look it over with Pariantür's best lawyers and theologians, to ensure a satisfactory reply."

"That is all I ask," the Konig said, smiling broadly.

"To the future of Nemen!" someone shouted.

The room roared in reply, and fell into the chaos of loud conversation that lasted well into the night.

13

Sentinel Office

A wretched creature joined him,

They traveled 'long the road.

Lost their way despite the

many wonders it showed.

They lighten'd each other's load.

—THE TRAVELER

The city of Edi was built upon eleven hills—each hill visible from its own harbor, and each hill's face pointed out to sea. The top of each wall-like sheer cliff sat crowned with white marble homes upon the estate of the controlling family.

Below each estate, a tight tier of lesser noble families lived in the shadow of the Master Estate walls. Like beetles feeding on the droppings of some greater beast—clinging, clamoring, grasping up the side of each hill—the merchant class's homes and places of work sought the attention of those above. Below the merchant tier, man-made wharfs jutted out into the calm sea. Upon those wharfs clung the warehouses and homes of workers and sailors, precariously balanced shoulder to shoulder, as they attempted to shove their neighbors into the sea.

Edi City was a city of possibility, and possibility was all Hanen and Rallia Clouw had sought when they had first arrived five years prior. Their office was located in one of the lesser traveled side streets of the merchant tier, upon the Aritelo Hill. Outside their door hung a shield, painted black, marking it as an office of the Black Sentinels.

Hanen sat at his desk with his back to the wall. One of the two secretaries worked at a writing desk with his back to Hanen. Arelt Yakin made a terrible Sentinel, but his strength had been found in details, so Hanen had been quick to find ways to keep him sequestered at the office doing the menial tasks no other Sentinel would dare sully themselves with.

The northbound caravan they passed as they approached Edi City wouldn't be seen for a handful of months. Hanen hoped to leave town with the next caravan in three week's time, to begin the return journey before winter started groping its way down south.

Arelt stood as he pulled on his cloak. "I'm going to go down to the Blue Canal for food."

As he approached the door, there came a tight rap. The secretary opened the door, nodding to the person on the other side, excused himself, and disappeared. Hanen took some of the papers he had across his desk and moved them out of sight.

Long fingers held the side of the door, and into the room stepped an alien and elegant figure. The qavyl merchant was of obvious means. He carried a tall staff with a leather cover bound over the top two feet of wood. From the staff hung various pouches, tied by leather thongs.

He stood a hand taller than Hanen in stature, and was elegant, with a stretched out and powerful neck. His legs were hinged like a horse, and he bore long arms that reached to his knees, with slender fingers, and a thumb set in the center of the palm that posed left or right as needed. Behind him a long, flat, and prehensile tail moved.

He wore form-fitting robes, with layer upon layer of finely woven silk that moved around him like the branches of a weeping sill tree. His head was round in the front and tapered in the back. The face bore large eyes full of years, and a flat leathery nose with long slits for nostrils with two tendrils drooping below as a sort mustache, or like the whiskers of any number of bottom-feeding fish. From his forehead rose two short, soft, round horns, covered in skin—thus he seemed young for a qavyl, perhaps no more than eighty. His very long ears fell down and out from his skull.

"Leqaw y dis!" he said.

Hanen rose and walked up to the qavyl and gave the formal

qavylli bow. "Kith ylas wiran."

When the qavyl spoke, his lips pulled back to reveal a full grin of teeth, like a house manticör hissing, but with no hint of hatred. "I am Ymbrys Veronia, a merchant by trade, and wanderer by habit, from the Qavylli Republic, across the Kandar Sea, and now here. If you would extend your hospitality, strangers though we may be, I would be obliged."

Hanen indicated a comfortable stool by a meager fire, which Ymbrys took. Hanen poured the guest a glass of brandy and took a seat next to him. The qavyl held the brandy in one hand and sipped at it occasionally. His staff lay across his lap.

"Allow me to make introductions," Hanen said. "I am Hanen Clouw and this is my office."

"Yes. It's an odd thing too, to have a Black Sentinel office. I came by way of Œron, and in the cities there I saw no offices. Black Sentinels, yes, but no offices."

"It was my own idea," Hanen said. "We set it up by necessity. We've met no small success escorting merchants up and down the road from here to Garrou in Bortali. Merchants needed a place to find us, as you have."

"It does seem impressive what you've done. To be frank with you; I am not looking for a bodyguard."

"What can I do for you then?" Hanen asked.

"I need to abuse your connections."

"Abuse?" Hanen asked, cocking his eyebrow.

"I'm sorry. That is perhaps the wrong word." The qavyl sipped at the brandy while he thought. "Take advantage of, I should say."

The qavyl took a pouch from the staff and laid it out on the table. It rattled when he placed it down. He waved his hand for Hanen to take it. Hanen reached out and poured several nuts into his hand.

"Those kyllyt nuts are a gift from me to you. Perhaps it will entice you to hear me out." While not an overly rare import, kyllyt were not cheap. "I understand there is a certain gala happening in a few nights. I do not have an invitation, and I should like to attend."

"We don't crash parties," Hanen said. "We are invited."

"Exactly. I'm not asking you to help me 'crash the party' so to speak. I understand you may know members of the upper class here and can see to it I receive an invitation. I have only just arrived in town, and wish to make some connections with other merchants. The market is a good place to do it, but not for the trade I wish to involve myself with."

"And what trade is that?"

"Exotic spices. Spices most common people cannot afford. I should like to meet the upper echelons of society in Edi, and by way of giving them samples of my wares, they will be in demand, and their kitchens will then desire them."

"I see," Hanen said, pursing his lips. "The gala you're talking about takes place at the Boraño estate. It is not easy to get an invitation."

"Very well," Ymbrys said as he stood. He held out a hand, which Hanen took. As their grips parted a single gold coin was left behind. It filled Hanen's palm. The stamp upon it marked it as a qavylli gild-pound. A year of gold royals from the north could not be exchanged for one.

Hanen looked up at the qavyl in surprise.

"You're very trusting, and quick to spend money." He looked at the piece of gold in his hand. "Quick to spend a lot of money."

"I have more money than I know what to do with—it is nothing to me to give you that. If it makes you feel better, think of it as buying your loyalty."

"Thank you," Hanen said. "I will think about how I can do what you ask."

Ymbrys rose and bowed his head. "I am staying at the Windlass. If you'll send a message to me there when you've met success, I would appreciate it."

Hanen sat back down at his desk, setting the gold medallion in front of him with a heavy tap on the wood. He stared at it for a long time, wondering what he would do with it. People might try to kill him for that kind of wealth. He heard heavy footsteps approach the door, and quickly took up the medallion of gold and shoved it down into his boot.

Thadar came into the office and walked around the room to an oak barrel that stood on a stand. He grabbed a tankard from a nearby shelf and filled it with beer from the tap.

"That's for clients," Hanen said. "If you want some, you have to pay."

Thadar turned and glared at Hanen while drinking deeply.

"It's still cheaper than paying at the bar," Hanen said. "The least you can do is pay for the drink so I can keep it full."

Thadar turned and filled the tankard again, walked across the room and sat on the corner of Hanen's desk.

"I saved you and your sister's asses."

He leaned forward toward Hanen, glaring into his eyes.

"Do you know what they're calling me at all the taverns now? The vül-slayer. But I don't feel like it's enough." He stood, having drained the tankard a second time. He walked over to the tap and filled two tankards, bringing one to Hanen. Hanen glanced at it but didn't touch it.

"I think you still owe me," Thadar said. "It is nice to have a reputation. It'll be nice for your caravan to have so illustrious a Black Sentinel on the job. But that's a few weeks off now, isn't it?"

"Three weeks," Hanen said.

"Three weeks. I gotta stay busy. I'm going to need some work if I'm going to pay for the attentions of some of the ladies I've met since we returned."

"And you want me to do what about it?"

"Isn't that obvious?" Thadar asked.

Hanen shook his head.

"You're going to find me work."

"That's not my job," Hanen said.

"Well, it is now."

"It's not," Hanen said. "Every Sentinel finds their own work. I've hired you for work on the caravans. It's a steady job and pays well. You can find your own work in the meantime."

"No. I shouldn't be spending my free time having to grovel and beg for work from nobles, when merchants are coming straight here and hiring you in the off-time. I saw the tail-wag that just left here. He looked to have means, and I suspect you took money from him."

The heavy gold medallion in Hanen's boot scratched at his conscience.

"You and your sister," Thadar continued, "have plenty of standing offers to guard merchants. You give me one or two of those, and for now, we're even."

"That's what it will take to get you out of this office?"

"You send work my way, and I won't step foot in this office again. I'll escort your beloved caravans, I'll call myself the vül-slayer, and you'll pay me. I could have let your sister die back on the road. But I didn't. I guess I'm just too kind."

Hanen scoffed.

"Don't!" Thadar slammed his tankard down on the desk. "I own you, boy. You don't have your sister around. And I know how sound a sleeper she is, too. I'll kill her if you give me reason and

DEATHLESS BEAST

then I'll kill you."

Hanen said nothing.

"So, give me a job. Or you pay me for work you aren't providing me."

Hanen touched his boot, thinking it might buy the man off. But if he gave him that he'd only be bled for more. He touched his pouch. It had a few coins. Reaching in he pulled out the first three he touched—three Edian silver lír.

Thadar snatched them out of his hands. "Pleasure doing business with you."

He turned and stormed out of the room without another word.

Hanen sat in the silence for a while, his heart rapping in his chest. He stood up, pulled on his cloak, and walked out into the city. The sun was high overhead, gleaming against the white walls of the Aritelo hill above. Hanen kept his hood over his head as he walked by the Blue Canal tavern. He could hear plenty of noise in the cool space, and with a glance saw a group of Sentinels standing around Thadar who was telling some tale.

Hanen circled the hill and came to the gate that led to the next hill over. House Narvon had once been a small one. It had purchased the smallest hill in the city, between Aritelo and Seritue, centuries before. Once it had been second string to House Aritelo, but success with growing and harvesting zvölder silk launched it into the richest, albeit the smallest, landownership of all the houses.

The walls were whitewashed, and the streets were cleaner and less populated. Light purple house colors flew on every home. Hanen had first argued at setting up their office there, but Rallia had won out, putting it on the more populated and cheaper Aritelo Hill.

But the clean streets and everyone politely walking by one another could not rid Hanen's mind of the threats made by Thadar.

Hanen took the long way around the city, from hill to hill, coming back around to Aritelo Hill, turning the last three corners, and arriving at the entryway to the street that terminated at the Black Sentinel office. Hanen stopped and stared down the lane. The other shops that shared the street with them would already be closed. Despite the silence that was normal for the street, something felt off. He took a cautious step forward. There was nowhere for someone to hide. No shadow to conceal someone looking to hold him at knife-point.

He took a deep breath and walked toward the office door. There were several voices inside, so he turned the latch and walked in. Nine Sentinels waited for him. Having nine Sentinels in the office was common enough, but usually only before a caravan departed. They fell silent. To his relief, Thadar wasn't present.

The secretary had returned and sat trying to ignore the noise around him. Hanen walked up to his desk and sat down.

"So, what's the trouble?" Hanen asked, folding his arms.

One of the Sentinels, goaded on by two others, walked up to the desk.

"We heard you're giving out guard work, and we were thinking we want some of it."

"Thadar lied to you."

"If you know it was Thadar then you know what we're talking about. He told us to come and see you. He said you'd be able to get us some work."

"I don't have any work," Hanen said.

"Sure you do. Rallia hasn't been here, and she's always got work. Give us some of her contracts since she's not here to fulfill them."

"That's not how it works," Hanen said.

"Says who?" another Sentinel asked. "Says the Sentinel leadership in Limae? That's a thousand miles away. They don't have any say here."

"Let me get this straight. You all became Sentinels, so you could wear a black cloak and get paid to stand around guarding whoever hires you, but you're too lazy to go out and find your own work? Your own contracts?"

A large Sentinel stepped up to Hanen's right. Hanen turned and looked up into the face of Ozri Baça. He was from Macena, with black hair bearing a hint of red when he walked in the sun. He had his arms folded to match Hanen. He was a giant of a man, though not too smart.

"Are you looking for work too?" Hanen said. He had never had any trouble with Ozri. But there could always be a first time.

Ozri looked down. He realized Hanen was addressing him.

"Work? Me? No. It just looked like there might be trouble, and I don't want you fighting," Ozri said.

Hanen turned back to the crowd. "Are we going to have trouble?" he asked, feeling a bit more confident with Ozri next to him.

Everyone stood silent.

"I didn't think so." Hanen stood up and leaned forward on the desk. "I'm going to ignore the fact that you all walked in here and started ordering me to give you my own hard work. Perhaps you forgot that I hire each of you to fill the ranks of my caravan and I can just as easily stop giving you that job."

Everyone broke eye contact with him.

"I'm leaving now."

Ozri followed him to the door.

"What do you want Ozri?" he said, spinning on him.

Ozri held his hands up. "You looked like you could use a hand."

Hanen sighed. "Thank you," he said reluctantly.

Ozri folded his arms again, turning back toward the the others. Over his shoulder he said, "Are you going to your room?"

"Yes."

"I'll stand here and make sure no one follows you."

Hanen made his way up to the wall that stood against and under the main estate. Apartments lined the way, clambering up the side. Hanen and Rallia's room was tucked back a ways, looking out toward the sea. Hanen opened the door and walked in. There was just enough light left from the sun going down in the east for Hanen to see by. He knelt down by the hearth and lit the tinder. Once the fire flared up he set the tip of a twig to flame and lit a few candles around the place. It was a small room, lightly furnished with two beds, a table, and a hearth. He shuttered the windows up and dragged his bed off the wall.

A heavy piece of cloth hung there. The intricate Üterk weave of blues and purples was the only color in the room. He peeled back the cloth to reveal a hidden alcove sparsely stacked with his and Rallia's personal possessions.

Hanen stuffed his blanket and gear into the bottom of his travel sack, with a few spare undergarments. Both of his Black Sentinel clubs went in. He stopped wearing them once he had earned his first axe, but they were good for pitching tents and driving spikes into the ground. His side bag came out next, in which he stashed spare bowstrings and his mending kit. Lastly, he reached in to pull out his bow, unstrung and hiding in the very back. He pulled out a cloth, oiled it, and set it on his bed.

From a shelf near the hearth he took the lid off the large vinegar jar a client had gifted him and filled his horn flask, and checked that his salt box still had enough of his favorite herbed salt.

Lastly, he riffled through papers that sat on his small writing desk, folding some of the more important figures he had been working on, and stuffed them into the side satchel.

He turned and looked at the place. He considered what he was thinking of doing, skipping town and hoping to meet his sister on the road. Perhaps at the chapel near Suel.

"The merchants won't appreciate it," he said to himself aloud. "Maybe the caravan will still run just fine without me. If it falls apart, I don't care anymore. I'm not dealing with Thadar, and I'm certainly not dealing with every Sentinel we know turning on us because they're too weak-willed to know what a fool Thadar is."

He turned back and looked at the hearth. His boot twisted on him, the gold medallion within biting his calf.

He reached down, pulling it out and crossed his legs in front of the fire. The gold in his hand seemed to speak both of what he might lose and what he might gain.

14

Edi-Fôz

Three hills squat,

Five hills tall,

Three more stuck between,

Eleven greedy, all.

—EDIAN CHILDREN'S RHYME

The fire had died long ago, and Hanen sat staring at the gold in his hand as the early light from the sun trickled through the cracks in the window. The door behind Hanen opened, but Hanen didn't bother turning. He could tell from the sounds, or lack thereof, who it was.

Rallia stepped into the room and dropped her sack on her bed, along with her staff, and turned.

"Oh! Hanen! What are you doing up this early?"

"This late," Hanen corrected, finally coming to, and turning to look at his sister.

He stood, his muscles aching from sitting all night in the same position. Rallia looked and saw Hanen's travel sack on his bed.

"Are we leaving?" Rallia asked.

"What?" Hanen said, looking over to the bed. "Oh, no. I'll put that back in a bit. Tell me how it went in Amstonhotten?"

"Traveling there went fine. The storytellers are a lot more quiet when you walk with them alone. The authorities took Ghoré in and shipped him off to Birin to figure out what to do with him."

"Well, I've had my own fair share of trouble," Hanen said.

"What kind of trouble?"

Hanen explained what had happened with Thadar, then the Sentinels who later confronted him.

"And what's that huge piece of gold you keep playing with?"

Hanen looked down and then handed the medallion to Rallia. "It's a qavylli gild-pound."

"Holy Pantheon," Rallia swore, "how did you come by that?"

Hanen went on to describe his meeting with the qavyl merchant and the promise he had made.

"That's why I didn't skip town and go looking for you last night," Hanen said. "I have to finish up my responsibilities here. That, and as long as Thadar doesn't kill us, which, let's be honest, we're his Golden Auroch right now, the worst thing that will happen to us is our egos will get bruised."

"We could get some other Sentinels together and convince him to leave town," Rallia offered. "If he puts up a fight, I bet I could take him."

"There are two problems with that," Hanen said. "He knows how heavy a sleeper you are. He threatened to kill you in your sleep if I did anything. If we did succeed and he just left town, then we'd never know where he was. When we leave town, he could just be waiting to do something to us."

"I suppose if we could figure out a way to get him to leave town for a while, we'd buy us some time to figure out what to do about him."

"Well, that's easy," Hanen said. "I don't know why I didn't think of that before. We could have Lord Ergen hire him."

Rallia laughed out loud. "That's a great idea. The last time Ergen hired a Sentinel, he took them on a chase all the way to Penoña, and almost on to Macena."

"Ergen's guards might even rough Thadar up a bit in the process."

"Why do you say that? It's just an old man's sport. His guards aren't that good. Thadar's much more likely to harm them."

"Not if we pay Thadar up front."

"What will that do?"

"Ergen pays good gold for these games. If we suggest that he lead the Sentinel he hires on a long chase, say to Ormach? He'll probably pay more than Thadar will see in two trips to Garrou. It's always suggested to hire a couple of other Sentinels to help out."

"But Thadar is greedy," Rallia offered, smirking. "He'll take all the coin for himself, and then be outnumbered."

"Exactly."

"That's a good idea. Once the sun comes up, I'll go round to Ergen's villa and set up the job."

"In the meantime, I need to figure out how to get an invitation to the gala."

"I've got that covered," Rallia said. "The reason I spent all of last night trying to get home is because I knew that the gala was coming up. Before we last left town, Derro Aritelo, son of Lord Aritelo, asked me to be his bodyguard to the gala if I returned in time. As long as he hasn't lost his money to his friends, the contract should still be good. Perhaps we can persuade him to let this qavyl in?"

"Alright. Where can we find Derro?"

"I usually don't have trouble finding him."

That evening, they found Derro Aritelo in a tavern on Baraño Hill, the Woolen Bale, sitting at a table with several friends playing the game Edi-Fo̊z.

Derro had a child's face, despite being as old as, if not older than, Hanen. And while most of house Aritelo bore the richer and deeper black skin of the Edian nobility, Derro bore a cream-dark skin—a gift of his late, and pale-skinned, Dürani mother. His brown hair was slicked back, and his green and black house brocade was well-kept.

One of the four Edi-Fo̊z players had already been eliminated, and was nursing his wounded ego with a large tankard of ale. Hanen stood with his hood off his head and arms folded. Rallia came behind Derro. A serving girl came by, and Rallia ordered another drink for the noble who was being ganged up on by his two remaining opponents. Within a few moves, he was ousted from the game.

The two friends stood up, laughing.

"I'm headed out back to feed the sea," one said.

The third friend followed them like a kicked dog. Rallia sat down next to the defeated Derro and handed him the beer.

"Lord Aritelo," Rallia said.

"I'm not a L..." The noble looked at Rallia, noticed Hanen, and said, "Oh. It's you, Rallia. Who is this?"

"My brother, Hanen Clouw."

"I don't know if tomorrow night is going to work," he said. "I may have just lost the money I was going to pay you."

Hanen shook his head. "It's good we found you tonight then. You've already got a contract with Rallia. So you'll need to pay us."

The man put his head on his arms folded across the table.

Rallia urged Hanen to speak.

"Lord Aritelo," Hanen said. "We may have a solution."

Derro perked up.

"Let us play your friends at this game. We'll win your money back."

"You can do that? I barely understand the game in the first place."

Hanen sighed. "Yes, but there are conditions."

"Whatever you need. Name it."

"You get both of us as guards tomorrow night, but we want our pay in advance. Also, you're going to see that another client of ours is on the guest list."

Derro smiled. "If you can trounce them at this game, I'll make sure all of that happens."

The two friends returned, the third no longer with them. They saw the Clouws sitting across from one another. Derro stood behind Rallia.

"Feris, Dilan," Derro said, "I found a couple more players who were looking to get in on some action."

Feris and Dilan sized the Clouws up and looked at each other, hesitation written across their faces. Feris's esteem was tied up in the approval of Dilan, as he watched the other man's reaction carefully. Dilan, on the other hand, had a cool look about him, and paid no attention to his sycophantic friend.

They both came closer to the table and saw the stack of five silver lír sitting on each of the Clouw's corners.

Hanen looked at Feris and smiled. "Lord Derro told us you two only played for real money. We thought a friendly game of five lír might be enough to start. If the game isn't to your taste, me and my friend here can move on."

Dilan sat down and Feris sat across from him. They both put a stack of five coins of their own on their corners. Hanen took a bag of flat glass pieces from Feris, and Rallia the same. They poured the contents out in shallow cups. Rallia had drawn red, while Hanen yellow. Feris had blue, and Dilan drew white, for the lead.

They each placed their token bowls out in their corner of the Edi-Foz board, and the game was underway. Hanen and Rallia rarely looked at one another. For all the other two knew, they had never met. Rallia feigned misunderstanding of the game, asking questions of moves she should take, occasionally touching Dilan's arm flirtatiously.

Hanen took that as an opportunity to move into Rallia's territories, capturing pieces. Hanen's own ham-fisted attacks quickly stretched him too thin, which gave Feris the opportunity to take the advantage. Meanwhile, Dilan seemed to be spending the entire game teaching Rallia how to play, which left him distracted. Feris booted Hanen from the game, and then turned his attention on Dilan. This aggravated the latter, who responded by stomping wildly over Rallia, leaving himself wide open to a wholesale win by Feris, who, as it turned out, had never actually beaten Dilan.

Dilan seemed ready to quit when Hanen pulled out a bag of coins. Rallia did, too. They both put down ten lír.

"I enjoyed being taught by you," Rallia said to Dilan, touching his arm. "I'd love to play again."

Greed glinted in Feris' eye.

Dilan remained cool. "I don't know. I'm feeling like the night is wearing out."

"How much would it take to get another game going?" Hanen asked.

"I was just playing for some sport, Coin Cloak," Dilan said.

"How much?"

Dilan scratched his chin. "Tell you what, you both put down fifty, and we have a deal."

Hanen pulled out a piece of paper, on which was a stamp minted one-hundred lír. "This ought to cover us," he said.

The game was reset. This time Rallia drew the white pieces and led. Within a few short turns, Hanen had seemed to stretch himself thin, while Rallia built up her pieces as a defense. Dilan and Feris worked together and started consuming Hanen's territories. In response, Rallia meticulously took territories from all three of them, which caused Dilan and Feris to turn back on her. Hanen feigned to work alongside the other two, to wrestle Rallia back to a manageable size, before Dilan realized the trap too late. Feris was ousted from the game almost immediately, while

Dilan was stretched too thin.

The game was almost over when Dilan stood. "I'm going to spring a leak in the alley."

"Not without paying," Hanen said.

"Excuse me?" Dilan looked at Hanen incredulously. "Do you even know who I am?"

"You're Dilan Hartwite, son of Danel Hartwite, a cloth merchant of some means. I've had the honor of escorting him north for trade. So, if you're not good for paying up a simple sum of fifty lír, I'm sure your father will be."

"You lied," Feris said, arms crossed. "You both know the game."

"We didn't lie," Hanen said. "We feigned. Edi-Foż is all about feigning. If you can't learn to read your opponents, you should find a new game."

Hanen took the hundred lír from Dilan and Feris and pocketed it. "I believe you owe Rallia and I our pay for tomorrow," he said to Derro as he held out a hand toward him.

"But those winnings from Dilan and Ferris, doesn't that pay you?"

"We used our own money to win that from them," Hanen said. "How much was the contract for, Rallia?"

"Thirty lír for my services."

"So you owe the two of us sixty," he said to Derro.

"I've got fifty," he said, pulling out a leather bill from inside his clothes.

"I think we can settle on fifty, since you're also getting our other guest in."

Aritelo sighed and handed him the piece of paper, then walked out into the night.

The Clouws rose and approached the bar, giving a spare coin to the barmaid before turning for the door.

Aurín sat nearby and waved them over to join him.

"How did he get back to town so fast?" Hanen said. "He parted with the caravan at Suel. But that was only twelve or thirteen days ago."

Aurín had a tall tankard of beer before him and a large citrus fruit next to him, cut open and sprinkled with salt.

"Clouws!" he said. "Join me. Sit down."

"You're back?" Hanen asked.

"Yes. I made good time. I got back none too soon, too." He played with his waxed mustache. "I think Temblin is on the verge of breaking."

"Breaking?" Rallia said. "As in, fall apart?"

"No. They are a wall of water trying to break open a dam. I heard the word from a friend of yours."

"What friend of ours is out east?" Hanen asked.

"Searn VeTurres. But he came into town with me. He and that apprentice of his. Did you know we Sentinels could have apprentices?"

"When did you arrive in town?" Hanen asked.

"This morning. I don't know where he was off to, but whatever business he had was urgent."

"Did the package get delivered to the hrelgrens?" Rallia asked.

"Yes, of course it did. I delivered it to the Teth family in Yqapa. I had hoped to see more of the city, but when I arrived at their place in the late evening they gave me enough drink to kill an auroch. Next thing I remember I was walking northward. I figured I had probably embarrassed myself enough the night before, even if I couldn't remember it, so I just kept walking."

Rallia laughed. "I don't know if I've ever seen you that deep in drink."

Aurín smiled. "Then you don't know me that well." He winked as he took another drink.

"And then you met Searn?"

"Soon after. In the woods north of Yqapa, I met a few Paladins who were riding northward toward their fortress. What was that one called? Padal?"

"Piedala," Rallia corrected.

Hanen glanced over in surprise.

"What? You know I poured over all those paladinial maps as a girl." She turned to Aurín. "Our grandfather had a nice collection of maps."

"Your grandfather," Hanen corrected.

"Anyway," Aurín continued, "they gave me a ride north to their fortress. Searn was heading out of Temblin and ran into me there. So I joined him heading this way. It was mutually beneficial."

"Oh?" Hanen asked.

"Yes. I guess he had a lot of questions about how the Black Sentinels were faring in Edi. He especially had a lot of questions about you two. It benefited me because his apprentice is something to look at."

"A girl then?" Rallia cocked an eyebrow.

"To say she's not bad on the eyes is an understatement, but I kept my thoughts to myself. I had to. She's got a biting tongue on her, too. What have I missed in town?"

"I only just arrived back this morning as well. But Hanen has been harassed by Thadar, who has taken it upon himself to start demanding work."

"What are you going to do about it?"

"I haven't really decided yet," Hanen said. "In the meantime, we sent word to Lord Ergen to see if he wants to employ Thadar on a chase."

"That probably won't work," Aurín said.

"Why not?"

"Old Lord Ergen died just before we all went north before the last caravan."

Hanen walked sullenly beside his sister as they returned home for what promised to be a restless night's sleep. Sending Thadar off on a chase for Lord Ergen had seemed the only option. Now he was back where he started.

A figure leaned inside the arch leading onto Aritelo Hill. As they shrugged themself off the wall, a second figure, smaller than the first came out of another shadow.

Hanen tensed, and Rallia stopped in place, her club-ended staff in both hands.

"It's good to see the two of you haven't lost your touch," the voice of the larger of the two figures said. It was a charming voice, and one Hanen hadn't heard in several years.

Rallia relaxed and stepped forward, a hand outstretched in the dark.

"Hello, Searn," Rallia said. "You scared me half the way to Noccitan."

"I can have that effect on people sometimes," Searn said. While Hanen couldn't fully make him out in the dark, he could tell the man was smiling.

"Earlier today I stopped by that office you set up," Searn said as he motioned for them to come and walk alongside him to the streets of Aritelo Hill. "Quite a space. Though it was a bit crowded."

"What were the Sentinels doing there?" Hanen asked.

"Ransacking my beer barrel?"

"I think they must have, yes. When I went to get some for myself, it was empty. They claimed they were waiting for you to show up and give them work."

"Dammit," Hanen swore.

"What are you doing giving out work?"

"I'm not. I've had some trouble with a local Sentinel captain who decided to try his hand at extorting work out of me. He's told the others I'd find work for them, too."

"We'll just have to see about that."

"Who's the girl?" Rallia muttered, leaning toward Searn and glancing behind them.

Hanen turned to look at the other figure as they passed under a torch and realized for the first time that it was a girl.

Searn nodded to the other person as he stopped up short by a torch, and the figure approached to join them in the light.

She was perhaps four years Rallia's junior. The tall wooden heels of her knee-high boots cracked on the cobblestone. The black leather trousers and the vest she wore over a white blouse tunic clung to her curves, though the loose belt that hung from her hips was as relaxed as her stance. Her forearms were covered by long fingerless gloves. The entire outfit looked uncomfortable and newly purchased. Her hair was long and raven black, though the guttering torchlight lit a redness that no doubt caught in any light. Her mouth was pursed in a permanent smirk under her sharp nose and cheekbones, and she lazily eyed the two of them under sharply arched eyebrows.

"This is Ophedia del Ishé. She's already earned her first club as a Sentinel. She's been traveling with me for about a year now since we met in Macena."

"I'm Hanen Clouw, and this is my sister Rallia," Hanen said, giving Ophedia a curt bow.

She looked them both up and down. "I know," she said with a rich contralto voice.

"We ran into Aurín earlier," Hanen said. "He mentioned the two of you were back in town."

"He said you just came from Temblin," Rallia said. "Are things as bad as everyone seems to think?"

"Yes," Searn said.

"If not worse," Ophedia interrupted.

Searn looked over at Ophedia and gave her a dismissive glare.

"Temblin is the same as always," Ophedia continued, "dreary and at war with everyone, including themselves, it seems. Their king was killed not two months ago, just after Searn and I arrived. It has effectively shut down the border and plunged them into another civil war."

"Seems like you could keep busy with contracts there if that is the case."

"Yes," Searn said. "But some important news came filtering into Temblin a week ago and I've been trying to work my way north ever since. I wondered if the news had arrived here yet."

"That depends on the news," Hanen replied.

"The head of the Paladins of the Hammer is touring the continent, as he does every ten years or so. This time, though, he went north across the Scapes."

"Makes me wish I was going north with the caravan half way to Bortali right now," Rallia said, smiling. "I'd love to have seen the head of the paladinial order marching through there. Maybe they'll resolve some of the issues forming between Bortali and Boroni."

"Why is that big news?" Hanen asked.

"It means I think I can pick up a big escort job. I just need a few more Sentinels to join me who have enough reserve money to go without pay for a bit."

"Paladins don't need escorting," Hanen said. "They're a walking army."

"They are. But the Nifaran Monks aren't. I intend to hoof it up to Birin and offer to escort the monks to meet with the Paladins in the far north before winter sets in."

"Winter is a long time coming," Hanen said.

"Yes, but we don't know if the monks have thought to go north on their own. By tradition they always travel on foot, so I hope to make it there quickly, before they leave. The sooner I start toward Birin, the sooner we can start out from there and begin the slow pace the monks will set through the Dead Pass from Düran to Mahndür."

"That's a long march," Rallia said, then paused, considering something. "It's several hundred miles to Birin. If we forced a march over sixteen days we could make it."

"Two weeks hard march?" Hanen said. "We'd kill ourselves doing it."

"We wouldn't kill ourselves," Rallia said. "Sleipnirs are an option."

"No," Searn replied. "Sleipnirs can only ride hard for a few hours a day. Knowing how well you two travel, we could march all day and then some, and make much better time. And we could travel light."

Hanen turned to Searn. "Why the rush? Why do you care about a bunch of monks?"

"Because I've noticed the world is getting a bit more dangerous. You mentioned Boroni and Bortali are on the verge of a conflict? It won't be long before Temblin decides to march to war. They've been itching to go to war with the Hrelgrens of Kar-Aghar, and if they don't think they can stand against the full might of the Hrelgren Empire, then they'll take out their frustration on Hraldor, or even Morriego if they're foolish enough. If all that is true, then the Dead Pass will be even more dangerous. Bortali and Boroni already contend for the pass with Limae.

"I suspect the naïve monks will send a mass of monks north—perhaps influential ones at that. If bandits got a whiff of that happening, they might take advantage of the situation. If Paladins have to stop their mission, whatever it is, to mount a rescue party to save a few robbed, blind monks, it could be trouble for everyone."

"So you're suggesting we travel north and suggest that to the monks, which may scare them enough to hire us for probably more than we're worth, just to look like we're keeping the peace?" Hanen said.

"Well, when you put it that way..."

"It would improve the image of the Sentinels," Rallia said.

"Not that the Sentinels need it. It looks like we're doing well here in Edi, and that's because of you Clouws."

"Let's say we go," Hanen said, brushing past the compliment. "What happens once we meet up with these Paladins? Where do we meet them?"

"Mahn Fulhar."

Rallia whistled. "That's a long way."

"Rallia," Hanen said. "This could be a chance to get away from here for a time. And on good terms."

Rallia nodded. "Just the four of us heading north?"

"I'd like you to select a few extra Sentinels you trust," Searn said.

"And if we land this contract with the monks, what's our cut?" Hanen asked.

"A quarter for me, a quarter for each of you. The rest we split between whoever you bring."

"And how soon do you want to leave?" Hanen asked.

"I've arranged to pick up a spare coin or two tomorrow night. There is a gala..."

"We'll be there, too," Hanen said.

"We could leave shortly after that."

"This is pretty sudden."

Searn flashed a smile. "Do you really care to stay another day when the road beckons?"

15

Difficulties

Seek not contempt for adversity. Instead befriend the lessons it seems to teach.

—SIDIERATAN PROVERB

With the lack of sleep the night before, and the upcoming nighttime travel, Hanen dropped onto his bed and fell asleep, although in the bed across the room his sister snored even before Hanen drifted off.

The sun streamed into their room at a high enough angle, Hanen knew it to be later than he expected. On the table by the hearth lay a message from Rallia, letting him know that she was off looking for Eunia Halla, the first person they had discussed would be best to ask along on their journey. The letter included locations Rallia thought Hanen might find the others, and mentioned that she would be back to ensure their bags were packed before they left for the gala.

Hanen pushed his axes into his belt and pulled his cloak over his shoulders. The gold medallion in his boot sat uncomfortably next to his ankle. He thought to stash it somewhere in their apartment, but didn't doubt that someone might find it.

As he turned to the door, a light rap caused him to jump.

"Who is it?" he said, his hand going to an axe.

"Ophedia," called the contralto voice of the girl they had met the night before.

Hanen pulled the door opened and she didn't wait to be asked in.

"Nice place," she said, looking around. She took a quick turn about the room and took a seat on Rallia's bed. "Although it smells like two men live here."

"I was just leaving," Hanen said.

"Probably a good idea," she said. "Not having a cloak yet has its advantages. I've spent the last hour down in the market stalls below watching your Coin Cloak captain, Thadar was it?"

"What about him?" Hanen asked.

"He's down there waiting for you to come out. You know, I don't think he actually knows which door is yours."

Hanen swore.

"You ought not to swear in front of lady, even if you are scared of the Nocc-damned shunt down there."

Hanen looked at Ophedia. "A lady, huh?"

"Well..."

"If you're going to be a Black Sentinel, you ought to expect it from any one of us. But if it bothers you," Hanen said, his ears burning.

"I was only joking," Ophedia said, laughing. "Searn sent me here to keep you company today. He figured Thadar might be looking for an advantage, and you being alone is the best time to take one."

"Well, like I said, I was just about to leave."

"Then I'll tell you what. Since you probably don't want him ransacking your room, or sending someone else to, I'll go down and give him a bit of a distraction, and you can pop out of the room and down to the streets before he notices. You and I can meet up at the end of the street, say outside that last tavern?"

"The Windlass?" Hanen asked.

"That one," Ophedia confirmed.

She stood and sauntered out the door. He heard the clicking of her wooden-heeled boots. He took a peek out the window and watched her move down into the crowd. Thadar wasn't hard to pick out. He was leaning against a wall, squinting up at the apartments, trying to guess which one Hanen would come out of.

Ophedia walked right up to Thadar and began talking to him. He tried to brush her off, which wasn't like him, since he was usually the first to get handsy with any woman around when the Sentinels stopped for the evening. She turned to go and Thadar gave in, watching her walk away. He whistled after her, which turned the heads of a few others. Hanen quickly popped out the door and took the stairs, bounding several at a time, so that when Thadar looked back, he might think Hanen came out on an entirely different level. He didn't go directly to the street, but instead jogged across the landings and stairs of the wall-clinging apartments. When he came to nearly the end, he took the final set of stairs down to the street, just outside the Windlass. Within, he could see the qavyl, Ymbrys, sitting at a table. He entered the inn and walked up to the foreign creature.

"Leqaw y dis!" he said.

The qavyl looked up and smiled. "It is good to see you," Ymbrys replied.

"I'm afraid I do not have time to spare," Hanen said. "But I want you to know that I've secured your place on the guest list for the gala tonight."

"Most excellent!" Ymbrys said. "Where shall I meet you beforehand?"

"I'll stop by here tonight, and we can walk there together."

"Very well. I shall make sure I am available."

The qavyl looked over Hanen's shoulder to the door.

"It appears you have someone looking for you."

"How do you know?"

"The girl wears one of your Sentinel clubs on her belt."

Hanen nodded.

"Tonight then," he said.

"Of course."

Hanen turned as Ophedia marched up to him.

"I think he saw you running along the wall," she said. "A black cloak flying along the white walls of the terraces was pretty obvious."

"What did you say to him to keep his eyes on you," Hanen said, walking toward the door.

"Not really your concern," she said as she stuck her head out into the street. "He's marching right towards us, though."

"Then let's go out the back. We need to get over to Irsonne Hill, anyway."

"What's there?" she said, following him through the kitchen and out the door into the alley.

Hanen flipped a coin to the kid who sat on a nearby stool peeling vegetables. "You see another Sentinel come this way looking for us, we didn't come by here."

"See who?" the boy said with a wink.

Hanen walked deeper into the alley and took the next turn out onto the thoroughfare.

"What is on Irsonne hill?" Ophedia asked again.

"Not what," Hanen replied. "Who. I need to find Ozri Baça."

The brutish Ozri was easy to find, sitting on a box outside a milliner, watching the tavern across the way.

"Good morning Ozri," Hanen said as they approached. The large Macenan glanced at him and back to the tavern. "Considering whether it's too early to go over there for a drink?"

"A man in there owes me money," Ozri said.

"You do some Sentinel work for him?"

"Mmm," Ozri muttered.

Hanen turned to Ophedia. "You'll not meet a man easier to convince that you've paid him, when you haven't."

"Speaking from experience?" Ophedia asked with a smirk.

"No, it was why I hired him, though. He's reliable. He rarely spends a coin, so he forgets who has paid him, since he used to keep all his money on him."

"And now what?" Ophedia asked.

"I keep it for him," Hanen said and turned to Ozri. "How much does he owe you?"

"I stood guard for his daughter while she tried on dresses for over five hours. When we returned to his estate, they shut me out."

"And so you've been waiting for him to pay you?"

"I approached him a couple of times, and he told me to wait. So I've kept waiting."

"What's his name?" Hanen asked.

"Ebão Nal."

Hanen laughed. "Ebão Nal has no daughter. But he does have a mistress. Three, actually. If he had you guarding one, then he was probably worried she was moving on to a new miser to cuckold."

"I don't understand," Ozri said.

"Where did you escort her to?"

"I took her to their home on Narvon Hill."

"He lives on Baraño. What did he say he'd pay you?"

"Normal five lír."

"You're not asking enough for your work again, Ozri. Ophedia here and I will get your money for you, if you agree to come with me on a trip north to Birin."

"I thought the caravan didn't leave for a few weeks."

"This is another job."

"Alright."

Hanen indicated toward the tavern and Ophedia followed. They walked past the bar and toward the private rooms.

"You can't go back there," the keep said.

"We're on the job," Hanen said, revealing the axes on his belt to the man. "Ophedia, wait here, and get us both a drink."

She stopped and approached the keep to place the order. Hanen walked back into the recesses of the private rooms. He heard the click of coins on a gambling table, and the hollering of someone still working off the night prior's drinks.

He walked up to one of the nicer doors, and the only one near the back that was latched, and rapped on the frame.

"'Nother drink?" he called out.

"Please," the man on the other side of the door said.

Hanen fiddled with the handle, intentionally jostling it.

"It appears you locked it from the inside," he said. He heard someone rise and walk toward the door and open it. A woman not much younger than Hanen peered out, a blanket pulled around her shoulders.

"Someone is here looking for Sir Nal," Hanen said. "A coin or two might keep prying eyes off you, Lady Narvon."

The woman's eyes bulged, and she shut the door in Hanen's face.

A few moments later, after the woman had stopped hissing orders at the man within, the door opened again, and Hanen found himself face to face with an older man with grease-slicked hair tousled, and awry.

"Sir Nal," Hanen said, reaching out and pulling the man out of the room. He pushed the man into the wall opposite the door.

"You agreed to pay one of my colleagues some money, and you've failed to pay him for several days."

"What are you doing?" the man squealed. "Don't you know who I am?"

"Not someone who will easily get another contract with the Sentinels, if you don't square up. If you haven't paid, then we don't owe you any silence. Maybe the lady's husband would like to know the cuckold you've made him into."

Ebão Nal suddenly bolted toward the front room. Hanen could see Ophedia leaning against the bar, a tankard raised to her lips.

She stuck her foot out behind herself as the man ran forward. He tripped over her heel and took a flying sprawl across the floor. Hanen walked out and lifted the man up and against the bar.

"Ophedia, would you mind going to see Lady Narvon out the back door?"

Ophedia laughed and walked to the back room.

"About the pay," Hanen said. "You now owe Ozri Baça twenty lír. I think a fee for the service my young friend is providing to your mistress is probably due."

"Of course," Nal said, sighing.

They waited a few minutes until Ophedia had returned to the common room, nodding. Nal led the two of them back to the room. Inside the bed was disheveled and the fire had run out to coals. He walked over to a pile of outer cloaks, and reached in, swinging suddenly round on them with a sword in his hands.

Hanen had expected him to do so, and already had both axes out in his hands. Ophedia quickly drew her club.

"You could just pay," Hanen said.

"After the insult you've given me?"

"Yes," Hanen said, "you signed a contract."

Someone entered the room behind them, and Ebão's face melted into defeat.

"What is taking so long?" Ozri asked, his two clubs in his own hands.

"Your contract here thinks perhaps he could fight the three of us, rather than pay you what is owed," Hanen said.

"That would be stupid," Ozri laughed. "He hired me because he told me he was a terrible duelist."

Ebão dropped his sword to the ground in defeat. "How much do I owe you?"

Ophedia left with Ozri, who had offered to buy her a drink for her help. Hanen declined the offer and began the walk home. He passed through one of the back passages from Seritue Hill into Aritelo, and came out not far from the Sentinel office. He turned toward the office, to see if there was anything he might need to gather there, and whether he should speak to Arelt about how to run the office while he was away, but thought better of it. A letter would suffice, and Hanen could make sure no point was missed from the list.

He turned toward home and felt a cold shiver run down his shoulder.

DEATHLESS BEAST

The sun was high, and warm, but the cold dread sat on his heart, and he looked around to see if something was amiss. There were plenty of people around, and none stood out. He shrugged, and began to walk.

"You're a difficult man to get alone, I'll grant you that."

The voice came from just behind Hanen's shoulder. He spun and watched the smeary shadow of Thadar peel itself out of a recess of a shop, closed with a notice of infestation.

Hanen kept his hands on his axes in his belt.

"Don't bother with that," the man sneered. "I'm not here to rough you up."

"Then why are you following me, Thadar," Hanen said, keeping several strides between them.

"I don't appreciate you trying to line me up with a job with Ergen. Not only is the man dead, I was one of the first to be hired by him for a chase. That's what landed me here in Edi."

"It's still good money, when he's lost the chase."

"You wanted me out of the city," Thadar barked. "You'd have been halfway through Düran with the next caravan, and without me, by the time I returned. Are you trying to be difficult? Trying to get rid of me?"

"You asked for work," Hanen said. "It was all I could think of—to make sure you got paid."

"You're going to that gala tonight."

"With a personal connection, who expects Rallia and I to be his only guards."

"Then you'll see to it that I join you. Introduce me to your job as the vül-slayer."

"I'm not in a position to do that."

"I'm asking you nicely," Thadar said, "to hold to the understanding we've come to. We can do this easily, or we can do it at crossbolt point."

Hanen stared at the man, an evil smirk playing across the other man's face.

"Let's go to the office," Hanen said, "and see if anyone else is expected to be at the gala, and we can see if you can't take their place."

Thadar nodded and followed Hanen as he turned toward the office and circled the hill to the back street.

Within the office, Arelt was struggling to hoist a new barrel of ale up onto the stand. Hanen rushed forward to help him situate it into place while Thadar watched them struggle.

"Thank you," Arelt said.

"No," Hanen said. "Thanks for replacing that without my asking."

"That captain friend of yours thought we ought to take the initiative ourselves and get it into place."

"Listen," Hanen said, leaning in. "Do you know of any Sentinels planning on going to the Baraño Gala tonight?"

"As guards?" Arelt asked.

"Yes, besides Rallia and myself."

"Why?"

"Thadar is looking for work, and I'm obliged to check and see."

Arelt glanced over Hanen's shoulder to Thadar, who was eyeing the two of them suspiciously.

"I don't have anyone in my records going as a guard."

"But you know of someone who is?" Hanen asked.

Arelt gave him a look. Then he turned towards his desk.

"Let's look at my ledger," he said to Hanen who followed him across the room.

Arelt turned back a page and began to run his finger over the lines, slowing to tap one of them as he passed by.

"As you can see," he said, preparing to turn the page. "I don't have any."

Hanen read the line Arelt had pointed to quickly.

Arelt was going to be attending, hired by Lord Baraño himself to take stock of the number of attendees.

"I'm sorry I couldn't help you with that," Arelt said.

Hanen turned to Thadar.

"It appears no one else is attending."

Thadar gave Hanen a look that could fell an Auroch.

"What are you going to do about it, then?" Thadar asked.

Hanen looked at the ground, then back at the angry man across the room.

"I have an idea," Hanen said, "but you're going to have to give me a moment."

"What do you mean?"

"I mean, if you'll go wait for me outside, I have an idea, but I need time to think without you staring at me."

"So that you can sneak out the back?"

"In the time you've been in Edi, employed by me as a captain, with time spent in this office, have you ever discovered a back door?"

Thadar pursed his lips, grunted, and walked out the door.

"Are you going to go out the trap door?" Arelt said. "Because if you are, I'm going with you. I don't want to be here when Thadar finds out you've slipped away."

"He's been following me all day long, it turns out. He's obviously desperate to get some work, for whatever reason, and he's pressing me to be the one to give it to him."

"What are you going to do about it?"

"Before we discuss that, I might as well tell you, I'm leaving town tonight after the gala. Rallia and I have an emergency job coming up."

"You'll be back in time for the caravan?"

"No," Hanen said. "We're going to Birin, then on to Mahndür."

Arelt whistled. "What do you want me to do in the meantime?"

"Pay our rent here. You can have my apartment if your own living situation isn't any better. And see that the caravans keep going."

"That's a tall order. What do I get in return? Besides a much better bed than the closet behind the Blue Canal?"

"You can have half the office cut we take from each caravan."

"And the other half? Keep that for you?"

"There are some expenses that usually come from our cut," Hanen said. "Spend what you need, even improve the office here if you want. But yes, keep the rest for us for when we return."

"If you disappear, others may rush to leave town, too. They might even want their share of coin from the vault."

"It's a good thing there is a stash we keep in our apartment then," Hanen said.

"I was wondering why the books never quite lined up," Arelt said.

"My office, my coin," Hanen said.

Arelt held his hands up. "I'm not questioning you. I'm just saying, I noticed."

"Your vault key will work in the box hidden under the floor boards in the back closet of the apartment. How much coin does Ozri have in the vault here?"

Arelt pulled out a ledger and flipped through it.

"Looks like he's got about ten crowns."

"Alright. He's journeying with us. I'll take those crowns from my own stash to take with us. You can replace those when you move into our place tomorrow."

"Thanks for trusting me with this," Arelt said.

"You've done well," Hanen said. "Even if you've skimmed a bit for yourself at times."

Arelt blushed.

"I'll overlook that if you do me one more favor."

"What's that?"

"One single night of discomfort."

"You want me to take Thadar with me as an assistant for the head count?"

Hanen nodded.

"He'll be useless."

"Once he's in, let him go free when he gets bored. He'll cause trouble, I don't doubt, but our hands are tied."

"What do you want to pay him for it? Because it's not coming out of mine."

"Pay him twenty lír. And if he gets pushy, promise him you'll turn a blind eye whenever he drinks the beer here at the office."

"He already takes what he wants and never pays."

"It's the gesture that'll count."

16

Gala

Like a crown cast upon the shore, the jewels of each house dazzled in the sun. And jealous were their enemies. For only by sea could they trade with they who held sway.

—THE EDIAN HILLS, BY KELLIUS, HISTORIAN OF VAREA

The gala was not the largest event the Clouws had seen, but it was well-attended. The house hall, adorned in the blue and silver of house Baraño, overlooked the sea and all the other house hills to the east. The house sentries, similarly attired, stood everywhere, keeping a cautionary eye on the crowd.

Derro Aritelo waved sentry after sentry away, holding in his hands his invitation rod and a document showing he had paid the fine for the Clouws to carry their weapons.

He moved with a practiced sophistication in his finest house colors. The black slashed doublet and green velvet cape caught torchlight with a shine that the dull black cloaks Hanen and Rallia wore could not.

Derro never stopped talking, and Rallia, comfortable with their arrangement, listened attentively.

"What is your secret to winning?" Derro asked.

"Winning?" Hanen replied.

"Edi-Fo'z. How do you win?"

"We played a lot as children," Rallia replied. "Our father was very good at it. He said he learned it from his grandfather."

"I thought it was a newer game," Derro commented.

"New in a relative sense. I think they started playing the newest iteration of it during the Protectorate Wars."

"There are many ways to play and win," Hanen circled back to Derro's question. "It's a matter of learning what type of game an opponent is playing, and then beat them at it."

"I'm only good at two major tactics," Rallia said.

"Yes, but you're better at feign and boiling than I am," Hanen replied.

"That may be true. But you're good at all fifteen." She leaned toward Derro. "That's why I won't play Hanen one-on-one anymore."

Derro laughed. "I ought to set you up to play against some of the better players in town and see if we can't make a tub full of coin for the three of us."

They neared the entrance to the ballroom. The qavyl Ymbrys Veronia had sauntered ahead and waited for them there. This time the layers of silks he wore were different shades of purple. He had his staff with him, and held a rod of invitation in his hand, provided by Hanen earlier that afternoon.

"Master Clouw," Ymbrys said. "I can't thank you enough for finding a way for me to attend."

"It was no trouble," Hanen said. "Ymbrys, please let me introduce you to Derro Aritelo."

Derro bowed and Ymbrys mirrored him.

"And who is this?" Ymbrys said, turning to Rallia.

"My sister, Rallia Clouw."

"Ah. Sister you say?"

"Same father, different mothers," Hanen said.

"That would explain the dissimilarities." Ymbrys bowed to Rallia. "Leqaw y dis."

Rallia respectfully bowed back. "Kith ylas wiran."

Ymbrys smiled, and looked around. "It would seem my money was well spent."

"Perhaps," Hanen said. "I cannot imagine how attending a gala would warrant your paying me such a king's ransom."

"Ah. Yes. Perhaps I did pay you too much. I'll admit, I was having trouble finding a moneylender in town who could exchange the piece. I forgot just how much they were worth in the lands of men."

The ballroom was larger than the temple of Aben located at the foot of Rigolé Hill. Off each side ran two additional ballrooms, and another room ran off the head toward the sea to the south. The marble pillars that held the roof aloft were a smooth gray with blue veining. The ceiling was painted like the night sky, with the constellations painted in a soft silver paint.

"Thank you again, Master Clouw," Ymbrys said. "I shall take my leave of you and mingle with the people here."

"You're welcome," Hanen said. "I hope you find what you're looking for."

Ymbrys excused himself and began moving through the crowd. He played to an audience of ladies who quickly made a gaggle around him. Hanen noted that Ymbrys was an odd one. Where most qavyl preferred their own kind, staying with their gydith and looking down on other peoples, Ymbrys ate up the attention, as though he had never talked to another being. Soon, Hanen saw him doling out pinches of some spice, and the ladies, tasting it, made ghastly faces and laughed at one another.

Derro chatted with Rallia when no one else was nearby to converse with, while Rallia was ever the consummate guard. Her own money had been well spent on private trainers, learning to fight, duel, and move. Hanen felt inadequate next to her.

Hanen was serviceable with a weapon, but he wasn't as capable as his little sister. His own strength lay in his ability to see the bigger picture and account for the costs. Perhaps that was why Hanen was the better Edi-Foż player, whereas Rallia was just the better soldier.

Two figures in black cloaks walked by, and Hanen turned away, noticing Thadar before the man, his eyes glazed with boredom, could noticed him. He followed Arelt, who walked with a ledger in his hand, making tally marks with a piece of charcoal.

A retinue of sentries stood in the center of the party, acting as a cordon. They were not wearing the silver and blue of Baraño, but the red of House Seritue. Derro Aritelo indicated Hanen and Rallia follow. Hanen placed his hands on the two hand axes on his belt, under his cloak. Rallia walked with her staff openly in her hand. Perhaps it was Rallia's feigning technique from Edi-Foż coming through.

They came to the edge of the circle, and Hanen and Rallia approached a sentry. The guard did not look them in the eyes, though Hanen noticed his knuckles whiten on his spear. Derro pushed through the Clouws.

"I am Derro Aritelo. May I pass through?"

The sentry adjusted his eyes to look at the lordling and stepped aside.

The Clouws entered behind Derro. Within the circle of sentries, three men sat on comfortable chairs around a portable brazier. They sat chatting as though they were in a private study, with no party going on around them outside the square of guards.

One man wore the silver and blue of House Baraño. Given his age, Hanen assumed he was the host, Eddal Baraño. He was a large, heavy man, with dark skin and thinning white hair. He sat with a plate of meat and cheese beside him, off of which his right-hand man fed him bites. Baraño's lips were wet, wide, and bore a bluish tint. Hanen disliked him immediately.

The second man wore the black and green of House Aritelo— Derro's father, Tergon Aritelo. His skin went well past being dark to purely black, as many Edian or Sidieratans. He had the sides of his head shaved like Rallia, but the hair on top that grew down the back of his neck was long and very thick, leaving him looking like some black warsleipnir. Derro went to stand next to him. His father looked up for a moment, and then back to the others. He leaned forward with intensity, as he gripped a goblet made of bone, which was filled with a blood red wine.

The last man wore the same colors as his sentries, in a red cloak, with plain, undyed clothes underneath. Hanen recognized him as Gell Seritue. He was young, no older than Rallia, with long blonde hair. He may have been an Edian, but he looked more like he had pure Œronzi blood, being paler even than Derro.

Hanen recalled when Gell's father, Lord Pruim Seritue the Good, died a week after the Clouws had arrived in Edi. While Pruim was known for his good nature, his son, thrust into power five years ago, was known to all as paranoid and overtly particular. The show of force with the sentries fit into his character. Behind him stood a Black Sentinel whom Hanen recognized immediately— Searn VeTurres.

Searn stepped forward to stand next to the seat of Lord Seritue. He knelt down and said something. Seritue nodded and took the bottle Searn pulled out of the folds of his cloak.

He stood, holding the bottle up for the others to see.

"Gentlemen, it seems my Black Sentinel bodyguard here has come across a rather rare vintage, that I was hoping I could share with you, Baraño, Aritelo." He turned and looked at Derro. "It's

Derro, right? A glass for you, as well."

"What is it?" Eddal Baraño asked.

"An Obaceñan Fuchsia, from 2212. It was my late father's favorite vintage and year. How my bodyguard came upon it, I cannot guess, and I'm sure I'll feel it when the bill comes in." He turned and faked a chuckle back at Searn. "I think there is no better gathering of powerful men in Edi to share in this fine bottle."

A steward appeared with four crystal glasses and set them down. He proceeded to pull the cork and run through the ceremony of checking the bottle and pouring out the contents into the goblets. The steward took a mouthful and tasted the wine before spitting out most of it onto the ground.

The color was indeed true fuchsia. Hanen had once watched his late master, the cheesemonger and gem smuggler Taben Verith, sit with a client and spend the evening contemplating the riches found in the glass. It had been a different vintage, but cost the client ten gold royals. Hanen had meant to steal the bottle from the alley after it was tossed out to taste the wine, but had slept in too late the following morning.

"The word is that Temblin is starting to writhe," Lord Baraño said. "If that drækis of a country sheds its skin, it'll come out fighting something nasty."

"It is good, then, that Hraldor stands between us and them," Lord Seritue said. "Best let them fight their vendetta and be done with it."

"And if Temblin wins?" Derro spoke up.

"Shut your mouth, son," Lord Aritelo said. "Let the adults do the talking."

"Come now, Tergon," Lord Seritue said. "He'll be sitting in that chair someday, and he's several years my elder."

"Then I'll just turn back when I get to Noccitan and come take care of things myself. This boy can't stop bleeding my coffers dry from his gambling and whoring around the city."

"He had enough spine to come and stand next to you even though he knew you'd say something like this," Lord Baraño said. "That counts for something. I wish I was still young and fit enough to whore around."

Seritue laughed at the corpulent lord next to him. "What do you have to say, Lordling Aritelo. You know you'll get a beating from your father later, so you might as well play your whole hand."

Derro stood there in shock.

"Wh-what about? My life choices? Or Temblin?"

"Ha!" Baraño laughed. "I'm happy to lend an ear. Defend yourself and let's hear what you think of Temblin."

Lord Aritelo sat back, fuming but silent.

"I...I don't wish to lose money. But it has a way of spending itself."

"Don't we all know it," Lord Seritue said.

"And I don't whore around." Derro looked at his feet.

"I can attest to that," Rallia said, speaking up.

"And who are you?" Lord Seritue said.

"Rallia Clouw, Black Sentinel. I've had the honor of guarding Lord Derro many times, and it's never to go chasing after any skirts. Those are probably lies spread by the poor company he chooses. They're the ones who usually chase skirts, and they aren't that good at it, either."

"There you go, Lord Aritelo. It seems your judgments passed on your son are unfounded."

Aritelo crossed his arms.

"Alright Derro, what do you think of the Tembii?"

"I think we ought to give them a voice. I've met them a few times. They aren't bad. Just... pushed down by everyone else."

"What, good boy, would you offer them? What in return would they offer us?" Baraño was delicately picking up the crumbs of various cheeses off a plate while his steward left off to find him more food.

"We won't know unless we ask," Derro offered. "It could be that we've been putting words in their mouths. The worst that could happen is they don't want our help, but at least they won't consider us the enemy."

"No," his father said, "the worst that could happen is everyone else assumes we're in league with them. When it turns out those foolish Tembii are just looking for a reason to go to war, everyone turns on us, too. Namely Tashar, right across the bloody sea."

"The boy has a point," Baraño said. "We could send a single house to meet with them. One of the less political ones. Kolaon perhaps. It won't look like Edi as a whole was looking to ally with them. Just an Edian House looking to advantage themselves."

Lord Aritelo grumbled something, but nodded.

Hanen saw a movement out of the corner of his eye and glanced over. Searn was pulling his crossbow out of his cloak and pointing it straight at Lord Aritelo. Hanen opened his mouth to raise his voice, but Rallia beat him to it and hollered out as the crossbow let loose its bolt. It sailed over all of their shoulders, just missing Aritelo's head and sailing past them into the chest of one of Seritue's sentries. The guard had drawn his sword and had moved toward the back of the Aritelos before Searn had responded. He doubled over and hit the ground as several others turned and advanced toward the inner circle.

Seritue's steward, holding the empty bottle of wine in his hand turned it over and swung it violently into the head of Baraño's steward as he approached with a new plate of meat, knocking him senseless.

"What in Noccitan?!" the fat lord shouted. The Seritue steward rushed toward Baraño, drawing a knife. Rallia shoved Derro to the ground and Hanen stood over the young man as Rallia flew over the table toward the attacker. Her staff shot out and met the man in the jaw. Searn had dropped to his knees with the crossbow over his head.

Seritue stood up, looked at Searn, then turned. "Stand down, sentries!" he shouted. Most of them immediately stood at attention, their spears hitting the ground. Three of them did not pay heed. They advanced toward Baraño, too large to get himself out of his chair, and Lord Aritelo, dueling sword now in his hand.

"In whose name?" Lord Aritelo demanded.

Those behind the three advancing assassins hesitantly raised their spears having trouble deciding if these sentries were traitors or following house orders.

Searn and the sentries nearest him were dragging Lord Seritue away to safety. Hanen had both axes in his hands and stood defiantly over the quavering Derro on the ground.

It was Lord Baraño who acted first. The plate of food next to him suddenly flew into the face of one assassin. Rallia took the advantage and charged the man, swinging her staff overhead, taking the attacker across the side of his helmet, knocking it off his head and sending a spray of blood and broken teeth across the floor. Rallia swung the staff repeatedly over her head in wide, sweeping arcs toward the second. The assassin stood his ground. Rallia threw the staff at the man and rushed him blindly as she pulled a dagger. They both went down in a tangle of arms. Rallia rolled over the other and sprang up, her hands now empty. The third assassin was coming far too close to Lord Aritelo. Rallia turned and quickly drew both axes. Hanen watched Rallia throw a dirty look at the sentries standing idly nearby and then advanced. She was a second too late.

The assassin charged toward Lord Tergon Aritelo. The black stallion of a man lowered his sword and raised his chin defiantly. The spear thrust met Aritelo directly in the heart, but the sound from the spearhead was the scratch of metal on metal. Aritelo smiled as he twisted, the spear tearing open his suit and scratching off to his left. The man staggered forward.

Aritelo struck the back of the man's head with the pommel of his sword, and he went down hard. Rallia was still advancing from behind and dove on top of the man. She dropped both axes, pulled out a cord, and quickly tied the would-be assassin's hands behind him. Everyone stood in shock as Rallia finished her brutal work and spun the man into a sitting position. She sat behind him, one of her blades held to the man's throat.

Aritelo walked over to crouch before the man. "Who sent you?" He gave the man a slap across the face. "I said, who sent you? Another house?"

Aritelo looked over at Baraño who was now drinking deeply from another goblet of wine and taking gasping breaths.

"Do we share any common enemies?" Aritelo asked the fat man.

Baraño shook his head. "No more than usual. I made peace with House Avedoi six months ago."

He turned back to the man, sniffed, and then asked Rallia for the razor and slashed the man's uniform open. Underneath he had a tattoo across his chest. It was a feather and a castle tower that almost looked like a gauntlet. A burn the shape of a coin sat in the palm of the gauntlet.

"Did Castenard send you? Are you Sidieratan?"

He looked up. Baraño's own guards had arrived.

"Eddal, perhaps you should interrogate him. I'd likely just string him up." Aritelo walked over to his seat and sat down. He glared over at Lord Seritue. "All evidence says you had nothing to do with this."

Seritue was shaking his head violently, shock across his face.

"If I ever find you did, then consider us enemies. For now, let us consider each other allies. If you are innocent of this, you had better see to it that you pick better house sentries, or you're going to wind up dead."

Seritue looked up at Searn. "You...you'll reconsider and stay here as a guard?"

Searn looked at him. "No. I'm afraid the errand I have to go on is more important. If you'd like, I'll give you my opinion of which of your sentries can be trusted."

Derro was standing once more by his father, who sat brooding over his cup of wine as he watched Baraño's servants rush to clean up the mess. Baraño gave a few short orders, but largely ignored them. He tried not to show how much he wished the party to return to normal.

"Shall I see you home?" Rallia said to Derro.

"No," Lord Aritelo said. "I need to have words with my son."

Derro flinched.

"Why wait until then," the man suddenly scoffed. "I'm sending you away to serve in the Edian Fleet Guard. If we have assassins coming after us, and war growing to our east, then I need you to grow up and be a man. Take Seritue's seat."

Derro did as he was told and sat down, taking a goblet from a passing servant.

Then Lord Aritelo stood and walked up to Rallia, motioning for Hanen to approach.

"It would seem I owe you both my gratitude. You both acted quickly to keep my son safe." He turned and squared himself off with Rallia and clapped both of her shoulders.

"You, young lady, were something to watch. If you'd consider becoming one of my own personal bodyguards, I'd pay you handsomely."

Rallia blushed and then glanced at Hanen.

"I belong at my brother's side. But I will consider it."

Aritelo motioned for his steward who had just arrived at the scene.

"Do you have a coin purse on you?"

The steward nodded.

"Show me?"

The steward lifted it and Aritelo looked within, nodding. He took it and handed it to Rallia.

"Consider it a meager gift and please consider my offer of employment a standing one."

Rallia took the purse and bowed. Baraño's guards were cleaning up the mess and bodies from around their lord who continued to eat despite, or perhaps because of, the excitement. Hanen and Rallia turned to leave. Ymbrys stood nearby, watching the scene quizzically. He shrugged and disappeared into the crowd.

17

BORDERLINE JUSTICE

Stood he now and took a step,

Approached he then his gate.

Friends and fam'ly called his name,

For fernweh they did hate,

And bid him for to wait.

—THE TRAVELER

"I saw Searn raise his crossbow, and I knew something was wrong," Rallia said excitedly. "I thought at first he was going to attack Lord Aritelo, but then I saw the steward move. I didn't even think to look at the sentries behind me."

"Who do you think sent them, though?" Hanen asked.

"They were after Lords Aritelo and Baraño, so I'd wager it was someone looking to keep them out of the conflict with Temblin."

"Except Baraño owns most of the fleet, and would prefer not to meddle in foreign affairs. Although he does have a huge pull with the rest of the Houses."

"What do you mean?" Rallia asked.

"If Tergon Aritelo decided to go to war, he'd need the backing of most of the other Edian Houses. Baraño has that pull."

"So if it was Castenard, like Lord Aritelo suspected, then Castenard wants Edi to keep out of the conflict and let it run itself out."

"Or," a voice from the shadow of an alley said, melting into the street to reveal Searn, and, shortly after, Ophedia, "or it was another country trying to dissuade Edi from joining a conflict."

"What makes you say that?" Hanen asked.

"Edi is perfectly situated. If they stay out of the political mess, they can continue to do what they've always done—trade. But if Edi marches west toward their longtime enemies in Castenard, that would be a good time for Temblin to fight their way through Hraldor, take Edi while their army is away, and secure two major western ports. If they were to go to war, supporting their ally Hraldor and fight against Temblin, then the city state of Tashar would quickly move in. If Edi is to thrive, they would do best to stay where they are."

"But will they?" Rallia asked.

"I suppose we'll have to wait and see," Searn said. "Regardless, we won't be here when it happens. We'll be halfway to winter by then. Speaking of which, who did you find to travel with us?"

They approached the Blue Canal tavern, where the others were already waiting.

Ozri Baça sat at a table with Eunia Halla and her companion, the short and tenacious-looking Chös Telmar. All three were reliable, and though a bit into their drink, they were ready to go. Aurín sat at another table, watching a barmaid move through the tables when his eye fell on the Clouws as they moved toward the other three. He stood and approached.

"What is with the travel bags so late in the evening?" Aurín asked, eyeing the rucksacks leaning against the legs of Ozri, Eunia, and Chös.

"I've been looking for you all day," Rallia replied. "We're making an unexpected trip to Birin."

"This late at night?" Aurín asked.

"We've got a long way to go," Hanen said, "and we want to do it in a short time. Are you interested?"

"What's the pay?"

"If you can keep up and we make Suel by nightfall tomorrow," Hanen said, lowering his voice, "I'll pay you each a gold crown. When we make it to Birin, I've got another ten gold crowns to split between whoever doesn't give up."

"Hanen," Rallia said, pulling on his arm. "That's a lot of money."

"Remember what I have in my boot?" Hanen whispered. "We can afford it. And while I don't know Chös as well as the others,

Eunia trusts him. These are the Sentinels we need with us."

"And who is this?" the usually quiet Chös Delmar asked, motioning to Searn.

"Searn VeTurres," Searn said with a curt bow, "and this is Ophedia del Ishé. She is hoping to earn her cloak soon."

"You seem familiar to me," Chös said. "Perhaps we've run into one another in Haven?"

"It is possible," Searn said. "I'm a Sentinel, after all."

Everyone gave a courteous chuckle.

"Is this everybody?" Searn asked.

"It is," Hanen said.

"Let's go before Thadar and his sycophants show up for some late-night drinking," Rallia said to Hanen.

"I didn't see him as we left the Baraño estate," Hanen said, "and I don't see Arelt around either, and he's often here around this time."

The streets were relatively quiet, and the guards at the gate didn't really care that a group of Sentinels were leaving. They half muttered something about going to join others, and cracked the door open wide enough to let them all pass through.

They spent the five miles walking to the border of Düran adjusting their packs and walking at an easy pace. Rallia found a few good apples that had fallen off the orchard trees that would be picked clean come morning, and stuffed them into her side pack. Ozri and Aurín followed suit, chatting about some lute-playing girl they both knew in Amstonhotten, and whether they'd both run into her on their way through there.

There were signs that the orchard owners had shifted their focus to their civic duty of repairing the roads from high summer travel; piles of cobblestone could be seen here and there. Edi City not only required the work be done before winter, but took pride in the work.

By the bright moonlight of Umay, Hanen thought he saw figures in long cloaks and tapered tops shadowing their movements and pace in the orchard. He thought at first it was their own shadows bouncing off some wall or mist he couldn't quite make out.

"Hanen," Rallia said.

"I saw them," Hanen said. "Searn?"

"Why are fellow Sentinels following us to the border?"

The figures came out of the orchard trees and came onto the

middle of the road.

"Leaving town, Clouw?" the gravelly voice of Thadar Saliss said from under one of the hoods. "Your now very black and blue friend from the office let the Cör out of the sack."

"Before or after you beat him?"

Thadar laughed. "Does it really matter? He understands where he sits with me now. And he'll be a good little ynfald and make sure I get my pay when I ask for it. Might be time you came to the same understanding. Now come back to town, and make us all some money, boy."

"I'm not going anywhere," Hanen said. "Certainly not with you."

"You owe me," he announced loudly to those nearby. "So what makes you think you can leave town with some of the best Sentinels to be found in Edi. Well, perhaps not the best. After all, you didn't invite me, and I'm the vül-slayer."

The men standing with Thadar offered up a forced laugh.

He pulled back his hood and eyed each of them. His eyes fell on Searn before he turned to ogle Ophedia.

"Who's this? New blood?"

Ophedia clenched the club in her hand.

"You're that girl that flirted with me in the market this morning," he said with a smirk.

"She's with me," Searn said, stepping out in front of her. "Who are you? We haven't met."

"Captain Thadar Saliss. What's your rank, Sentinel."

"That's not your concern," Searn said. "I'd like to hear more about this work that Hanen owes you. I can't think of how a Sentinel would owe another one work. We each find and fulfill our own contracts."

"It's nothing," Thadar said dismissively. "I saved these Clouws' lives. All I ask is they throw a few bones my way."

"The caravan detail isn't enough?"

"Those Clouws get asked by some of the choicest lords in town to do bodyguard work in their down time. Doesn't sit fair that they get those jobs when the rest of us are doing the actual work on the caravan."

"The guard jobs we take on," Hanen said, "sees to it that clientele will join us on a caravan one day."

"And they rarely come to us," Rallia said. "We have to go looking for that work."

"Doesn't help me, though. Doesn't help the boys here." He

indicated to the Sentinels next to him. "We heard you were packing up your home and leaving. Took some work to catch up with you."

He took out his crossbow and hefted it levelly at Hanen. "This'll be the last time I repeat myself. You're going to march back to town and keep business going, and see to it me and the boys here get more work coming our way."

"They're doing something more important for me," Searn said.

"Listen," Thadar said. "I don't know who you are, but I'm the captain in the office."

Thadar suddenly roared and held his right shoulder where a crossbow bolt had sprouted.

Searn's cloak was now open and the crossbow in his hand disappeared back into the black folds as fast as it appeared.

"What in bloody Noccitan was that for?!" Thadar screamed.

"You've overstretched your authority," Searn said.

"So did you! You can't take law into your own hands," Thadar screamed. "The Sentinels don't have jurisdiction to carry out justice in Edi. I'm going to have your head!"

He screamed in rage and ran forward, his own crossbow coming up again. Searn spun his cloak around wildly. Thadar's own shot pierced the cloak, but not Searn. Searn charged forward, brought his boot up, and met Thadar's chest with his heel. Thadar flew back, stumbling several yards.

The sudden brutal attack by Searn caused the other Sentinels around Thadar to dive out of the way. Rallia rushed forward with her staff, cracking one in the head and tripping another. Eunia and Chös struck at the next one together, and had him on the ground, held at the ends of their axes. Ozri ran at the fourth with the smaller Ophedia next to him. He tackled the opposing Sentinel and straddled him, boxing his ears as he cried out for mercy. Aurín had both axes out and flailed wildly until his opponent dropped his own weapons and fell to his knees and begged for mercy.

Thadar tried to rise, but Searn pressed him back in a scramble. Twenty feet, thirty feet, forty feet. Thadar's hands shone with blood from scraping across the dirt as he retreated. He was gasping for breath.

"You're mad! You can't just attack a man!"

"You mean like you tried to extort your egg-layer, Hanen? Like how you beat Arelt?"

Searn stopped, put his boot down into his crossbow, and cranked back. He lifted it, nocking a new bolt. Thadar was rising to his feet.

"What? Are you gonna kill me in cold blood? The Edian Houseguard will have a heyday. They'll chase you into Düran. They'll dissolve the Sentinel charters in Edi."

"For killing one Sentinel?" Searn asked.

"Yes. They know to watch if I don't return. We have an understanding."

"Well, it won't matter. Since they'll find your body in Düran."

"Kill me and drag my body across the border?"

"I won't need to drag it. You did that for me already."

Thadar looked around, and saw he had moved past the short wall marking the border.

"Sentinels have full jurisdiction in Düran to kill brigands," Searn said. He fired his crossbolt into Thadar's chest. Thadar fell to the ground. He didn't say another word.

"I don't appreciate being slowed down," Searn said. "And even more so I hate being betrayed by my own people."

He looked at the other Sentinels being held at the end of weapons.

"Should I take care of you, too?" he asked.

They all began to beg for their lives.

Searn turned and began walking down the road again. Hanen put his axes back into his belt and joined him. Rallia soon followed, then the others. Hanen could just make out the sniffs and scrapes of the other Sentinel's rising and heading back toward Edi, leaving Thadar lying dead in the road.

18

Mountain Pass

A hammer rings, on wood, on stone, on anvil, and on bell. A nail is driven true, and the crack is broadened. The blemish is beaten flat, and the toll announces the prayers. Greater than all of these is the hammer that strikes a note upon a string. For music resounds into the hearts of even the most deranged.

—INCUS GRISSONI, PART OF THE THIRD BOOK
OF THE QUATRODOX

The entourage came to the stretch of the High Pass Road that looked back over Nemen. Jined could easily make out Nihn, Nemen's capital, thousands of feet below and twenty miles behind them. The high yellow walls that enclosed it did not look so tall in the air. The white chalk road that ribboned to the mountains was as clear as the yellow dust road that led back toward the hills down into Setera to the east.

Two Paladames walked past Jined and broke off their own conversation as they stopped to take in the view. The Matriarch Superioris and her ten Crysalas had rejoined the entourage at Nihn, along with the newest addition to her attendants: the dark-skinned Sidieratan, Esenath Chloïse.

Esenath wore the armor of a Paladame guard, though she did not ride with the other guards. The Pater Segundus had explained that she was a botanist of some renown and a guest of honor. The Crysalas sisters seemed to hang on her every word. The other woman who walked alongside the botanist was the physician to both the Matriarch and her husband, the Prima Pater. Katiam

Borreau was shorter and curvier. If seen in her robes at Pariantür, one might think her simply round, but here on the road, in full Paladame regalia, this was decidedly not the case. She reminded Jined of the baker's daughter that brought the morning rolls to his father's castle each morning when he was a young boy.

Jined patted his heavily breathing sleipnir on the neck. All but the sleipnirs that pulled the wagons were being walked. The steep climb had lasted all day, and Jined looked forward to the checkpoint: a cave with running water, and stockpiled with supplies by Konig Bermach Gelbliht.

"You can almost make out the college," Esenath was saying, pointing to the west.

"Do you miss it already?" Katiam asked.

"No. The world is my school. I have much to learn away from that environment. In fact, I'm hoping we have arrived at the right time in the mountains."

"Why is that?"

"We shall see. Keep an eye out for gray-purple helunga flowers. If you don't know what they look like, look in my book."

Katiam nodded and the two continued on.

"What are you thinking about?" Killian Glass said, coming up alongside Jined.

"The view. It's breathtaking."

Killian smiled.

"Has it been good to see your sister again?" Jined asked.

Astrid Glass, a member of the Paladame guard, was a small woman, with shoulder-length wavy blonde hair. She smiled as often as Killian did.

"Of course. I have been missing her every day."

Killian smiled again. Jined laughed.

"What's so funny?"

"I'm sorry," Jined said. "I was suddenly picturing you with Astrid's hair. I can't imagine you with longer blonde hair before you were a Paladin."

Killian rolled his eyebrows. Then he smiled and started laughing, too. "I did have hair like hers. I thought very highly of it."

Jined started laughing harder.

"We were raised in the shadow of Pariantür. Our parents were glaziers, hence the name. One day my hair crisped in the glow of our fires. I was so mad when my mother told me I'd have to cut my hair that I threatened to just shave it off and become a Paladin. She took that for permission and within a month I was taking the first vows. Apparently, they had been hoping I would join—they never had the heart to tell me what an awful glazier I was."

Jined was howling with laughter.

Dane walked by with his mount in tow. He glanced at the two of them and scoffed.

They arrived at the small man-made cave and packed in. There was a sheltered paddock for the animals on the outside.

When Jined awoke the fire had gone out, leaving the cave cold and dark. Nichal stood over the old standard bearer, Valér Queton, who worked to ignite a fire.

"Let me try from this side brother," he offered.

Valér nodded, handing him the flint and knife.

"How far is it to the bastion?" Jined asked.

"We're expected to reach the top of this pass in two days," Nichal said. "There is an alpine lake there. That marks the change from Nemen to Bortali. Then it's a day down to the Gilded Bastion."

"I remember that bastion," Jined replied. "I was in awe when I passed through there on the way to Pariantür as a young man."

"It is known wide and far," Nichal replied.

"Even as far as Aunté," Valér said, "the Gilded Stone, as we call it, is spoken of in awe."

Both Paladins looked at the usually very quiet Valér who returned to his meager flame, feeding it more kindling.

"Will they be able to house us all?" Jined asked. "I recall only two Paladins being stationed there when I traveled through."

"The bastion benefits from a wealthy village nearby, given the gold mines in the area. I think we'll be able to find accommodations for all of us."

The road into the mountains was well-maintained, but at times quite steep. They passed herds of wild capricör that climbed sheer cliffs and bleated mockery at the entourage as it passed. The silent twins, Loïc and Cävian, both excellent hunters, failed to bring any of them back. At one point one of the guards swore he saw a rock manticör stalking through a boulder field. The entire entourage stopped to catch a glimpse, but it turned out only to be a long hour's rest.

By the middle of the second day, everyone trudged on stoically. They were all glad to have made the final push to the top of the pass by the end of the third night out from Nihn. Jined's heart had become a hammer in his chest that did not stop its pounding rhythm whether he moved or stood still. The thin, cold air burned his lungs from the inside, but it was fresh and clean. They reached the summit just before sunset. There were no trees at that height, and the alpine lake reflected the sky perfectly. The sun was heading toward its bed, and the sky was a splash of colors. To the north ran the long and now easy road that would take them out of Nemen and down into Bortali. A dark shadow of forest spilled across the lower lands, growing darker in the shadow of the mountains they now stood amidst.

The sun dropped behind the mountain line, plunging them into darkness. Jined turned, approached the fire, and took a bowl of porridge from a provisioner. Cold fell upon them as fast as the darkness, and everyone scrambled to set up their bedrolls close to one another near the fire. The Paladames were offered the carriages to sleep in while the Paladins, even those of rank, stayed under the elements, looking up at stars that were clearer here than anywhere else.

Jined woke early the next morning from a cold and restless night sleep. Packing up his bedroll quickly, he walked down to the alpine lake to take a drink. It was frigidly cold, but the cleanest, purest water he had every tasted. He splashed his face, regretted it, and turned back to begin warming his sleipnir's six legs.

The animals practically pranced down the hill. The three days of hard work it took to climb to the summit seemed to flee from Jined's memory, each breath coming easier than the last. Soon they came over a small crest, and knew they were only a few short hours from rest at the Gilded Bastion. Jined rode alongside the entourage as an outrider along with Loïc and Cävian. Looking out across a field, he saw purple-gray flowers dotting the space. As though his eyes deceived him, the color seemed to pulse and grow, as though every moment revealed more of the color than before.

The front of the entourage had reached them as they stood there; the botanist, Esenath Chloïse, passed by.

"Sister," Jined said, "are those the flowers you were mentioning?"

Esenath looked out over the field.

"Yes! Thank you, Brother!"

She turned to the captain of the Paladames. "We must call for a stop and gather these flowers."

"The Pater Segundus has said we're not but a few hours from the bastion," the captain said, "can't we come back and collect these once we're there?"

"No. They only bloom for one day. It is great luck that we came upon this meadow."

"What purpose do they serve?"

"They're quite important when performing surgeries. Helungar flower teas and incense influence a patient to allow any procedure to continue without complaint."

The captain pursed her lips.

"One pound of the flowers is worth as much in gold."

This seemed to convince the Paladame, who nodded. "I will tell the Matriarch Superioris. You can organize the sisters to begin collecting the flowers with you."

Soon the Paladames were working their way across the field in a line, gloves off, collecting flowers one by one. The entourage stopped to watch. After several long minutes the Prima Pater stepped down from his carriage, offering a hand to his wife who came out to stand next to him.

Jined watched him lean over to Pater Segundus Gallahan Pír. The other man nodded. At his command, the scribes came down from their carriage and were rolling up their sleeves to help. Then the provisioners took that as a challenge and took another nearby portion of the field.

Other higher-ranking Paladins soon joined, until all but the guards, the Prima Pater, and his wife, stood watching. After a long hour, they had barely made it twenty feet into the field.

"How long would you say we have, Sister Chloïse?" the Matriarch asked.

"How long?" Esenath asked. "You mean until we can't gather any more? The buds begin to close and recede as the sun begins to set."

"I'd give that five hours," Nichal said from the top of his sleipnir nearby.

"Then," the Prima Pater said, "I will continue on with the Matriarch to the bastion. Nichal, see that a few more hands help out from among your guards. If the gathering of this flower is so important, we'd best do what we can with the time given us."

DEATHLESS BEAST

Nichal nodded. "Brazstein, Marric, and Queton, continue on with the Prima Pater."

Pater Segundus Pír, along with the Prima Pater and his wife, reentered the carriage, while the Prima Pater's seneschal, Jurgon Upona, took the driver's seat and urged the sleipnirs forward. Jined looked back once at the thirty individuals gathering up the flowers. He saw a figure move in the woods beyond the field.

Pulling his mount up short, he looked again, but saw nothing. He turned back to follow the carriage.

"What are you balking at, Brazstein?" Dane asked. "I hope you're not looking at those Paladames. Why they needed to join us in the first place is beyond me. It is better at Pariantür where they keep to their own side of the monastery."

"Have you ever considered complete isolation?" Jined asked.

"What is that supposed to mean?" Dane replied.

"You're insufferable, you know that? A burr in everyone's boot."

"Be silent!" Dane whispered harshly.

"No, I'm not done."

"No," Dane looked directly into Jined's eyes. The look of disdain was gone, replaced by an urging sincerity. "I need you to shut your mouth. Listen."

He pulled his own mount to a halt, and Jined followed.

There was a low sound that rose to a howl, followed by shouting. Then screaming.

"What in Noccitan was that?" Jined asked. The carriage came to a halt. The Prima Pater stuck his head out.

"Vül!" he shouted. "Go!"

Jined and Dane wheeled their mounts around. Jined hesitated. "We need to protect you."

"We are not far behind you," the Prima Pater shouted. "Go!"

Jined kicked his mount into a gallop and they rushed back down the road. As they came back into sight of the field, large figures retreated into the woods. The Paladins and Paladames were grouping up against the wagons. Sleipnir that had been grazing freely were now rushing around in a blind panic.

Nichal was the only Paladin still mounted. He had chased the attackers into the woods and was circling back.

"Form up! Form up!" he shouted.

Captain Sigri Smith had called her own sleipnir to her and mounted. The other Paladame guards were scrambling to find their own. Two of the sisters were crouched on the ground over the still figure of another. The form of a dead vül lay not far from there.

Jined and Dane rode hard toward Nichal, who sat atop his destrier on the edge of the road. Paladins formed a rank to their right, while a couple of Paladames on sleipnir-back formed the left.

Scribes and administrators huddled behind the carts, though even they brandished their hammers.

"Brazstein, what are you doing here?" Nichal shouted. "Where is the Prima Pater."

"Turning around to come back. He demanded we join you."

Nichal grunted and turned back toward the woods.

"A vül came out of the woods and assaulted the now-fallen sister. I was able to run off the five vül that came after the first. Now it seems they are already forming back up. Sister Borreau!" Nichal shouted. "How does she fare?"

Katiam looked up at him, her face streaked with hot tears, the dead Paladame's head in her lap.

The Paladames screamed in rage.

Their own howl was drowned out by one that rose from the wood, raising the hackles on Jined's neck. A second voice joined the first, then a third, until the woods were filled with a cacophony of nasty howls.

"How many do you see?" Nichal asked the sharp-eyed Dane.

Dane scowled toward the trees. He shook his head. He held up a hand and showed all five fingers, then closed his fist and showed five again. Then again.

"Damn," Nichal said. The howl wavered and quit. Another set of howls came from much farther away. The vül on the edge of the woods began to chatter and snarl in response.

The first figure stepped out. It was covered in a thick, black fur. The lower legs were short and dog-legged, clothed in trousers. Its torso contained a bulk that outweighed an average man. Long, massive arms hung almost to its knees. In each hand it held a finely crafted axe. The shoulders stood as tall as a man. It lifted its head above its shoulders to howl at the sky. A short, slavering mouth gaped. Beady black eyes, and short ears from the side of its head cocked toward its enemy.

It was the first vül that Jined had ever seen in the flesh. If the T'Akai were something to fear for their angular severity and horns, the vül was something to fear for its sheer, massive power and brutality. It lowered its head, teeth now grinning toward the collected men and women before it. Other vül burst out of the forest, loping toward them on all fours.

The Paladame flank charged forward, the captain and her two mounted Paladame guards forming a vanguard.

"Captain Smith!" Nichal shouted. "Hold!"

He growled when she did not heed him, and then gave his own signal. He kicked his mount forward. Jined and Dane matched him, while the twins, Killian, and one of the new guards from St. Hamul, followed on foot. On the right flank, three mounted Paladins moved at a march, but did not yet commit to a charge.

The black vül who led the charge snarled something in its crude tongue, and the group of vül veered toward the Paladames.

"No!" Nichal shouted.

He reacted and the center of their line joined him, moving to counter the vüls' attack on the women. Jined glanced behind him to see the right flank continuing to pick up speed across the field, hoping to gain a flank or rear.

The black vül charged at Captain Sigri Smith, leaping up over her sleipnir and taking her to the ground. Jined watched the Paladame disappear, and the vül came up holding its side. Sigri staggered to her feet, holding a bloody dagger in her hand. The Paladame Esenath was behind the vül and struck it from behind with her rose-shaped mace. The vül turned to see what could have thought to hurt it, providing the opening Captain Smith needed. The tall Paladame surged forward, swinging her own mace with both hands. It took the vül across the jaw, its head spinning with a snap. Sigri kicked it over with a boot and turned back to the others not far behind the first. The other two mounted Paladames swung with their maces, striking another vül simultaneously on the top of the skull. It fell to the ground without taking another step.

Jined felt himself cheering and roaring as he pushed his sleipnir forward. He heard the clank of metal and spun his head back toward the treeline. Rocks sailed overhead. One struck a Paladin off his mount. Five more vül came out of the woods holding slings meant for fist-sized stones. Another vül came out from behind them and broke into a run toward the right flank's charge. Two vül stopped to fall upon a riderless sleipnir, slaughtering the animal. The Paladin who had fallen tried to rise as a vül stepped on top of him, taking his head off with the swift swing of an axe.

Nichal charged into the flank of the vül that went after the sisters. As two of them stepped out of the way of Nichal's charge,

Jined and Dane each swung their hammers underhanded, taking them under their jaws. They fell where they stood.

The slower wave of vül behind the first fell upon the herald Amal Yollis. He came off his mount and hit the ground. Four vül encircled him. One lunged forward, striking him with an axe and sending him spinning to the ground once more. They closed in. Suddenly, Amal stood up and began a frenzied series of blows, raining death on all four vül. Amal had a look of surprise in his eyes. When he stood amidst the massacre around him, he looked over to Cävian and Loïc who stood signing a prayer over and over again. He nodded his thanks and limped toward the Paladames.

Shouting drew Jined's attention, and he urged his mount toward the right flank, where the vül toyed with the two mounted Paladins, unable to urge their mounts away.

One of the vül rose up underneath Jined and lodged an axe in the chest of the sleipnir. The second vül began clawing at the mount's face. The sleipnir fell and Jined threw himself clear. He got his feet out from underneath him and stood, holding his hammer with both hands. One vül stepped up to him as the other tore into the sleipnir flesh with its fang-filled maw. The vül before Jined stood taller and looked down on the armored warrior.

"Perish, pup," the vül hissed. Its breath stank of foul meat, and it held in one hand a femur with a sword blade mounted atop it. The bone was intricately inlaid with silver runes.

Jined did not hesitate. He threw himself forward, inside the monster's reach.

The vül stepped back, swinging its blade around with both arms. The hit caught Jined across the gut. His armor stopped the swing, but it stole his breath away.

He gasped for air and threw himself at the creature once more with several follow-throughs. The vül danced back each time, swinging again and again across Jined's armor.

Jined thrust his hammer and the vül struck down across the top of the hammer's haft, pinning it to the ground. The vül cut at Jined's face with its elbow. Jined dropped his hammer, pulling his head back so the vül's elbow struck his gorget. The face the vül made let Jined know it had hurt itself, though it sent Jined staggering with his hammer in tow by the chain on his belt. Jined caught his footing, stepped forward and took up his hammer. Lifting it, he spun around, swinging it with full force across the face of his foe. He felt the crack of the skull spinning on its neck as he knocked its jaw loose. The vül fell to the ground, dead before the dust exploded around its body.

Jined looked around. Sleipnir lay dead around the battlefield. The vül had targeted the horse-flesh, leveling the field, and likely providing food for their clan.

"To the road!" Nichal shouted. "Fall back and form up!"

Dorian Mür leapt out of his carriage as it pulled up next to the others. With his scepter in one hand he climbed up on top of one of the carriages and took a powerful stance.

"To me, Paladins! Paladames!"

Jined ran on foot to reach the road. He could hear sounds behind him but didn't dare look back.

The twins waved him on, but the look in their eyes told him he was safe. He caught his breath and turned around. A new line of vül were coming out of the woods. The field was now filled with the scattered remains of vül, sleipnirs, and at least one Paladame alongside several Paladins.

All but Nichal had been unhorsed. He sat at attention next to the carriage with the Prima Pater above him.

The vül continued to pour out of the woods, but they didn't advance. They just waited.

There were now twenty vül to the ten or eleven Paladins and Paladames still able to fight.

"Move the wounded behind the carts," the Prima Pater ordered, "and start praying. We're going to need it." He pointed his scepter toward the assembled vül. "They won't be reasoned with. And they won't leave us alive."

The vül beat their chests with their fists in rhythm with one another. Their growls rose into a deep rumble of a cadence. The vül in the center of their line parted. A shadow within the forest behind them moved. The shadow stepped out and into the sunlight.

It was covered in blonde fur that seemed to glint in the sun. Instead of a lean stomach though, it had a massive, engorged belly, juxtaposed to the well-built rest of its body. Its massive gut was covered by straps of finely crafted gold bands.

Jined knew the vül on sight from nightmarish tales told over fires and whispered to children who did not behave. This was a champion of Kos-Yran, the Cursed Gift-Giver god. This was the leader of the pack of vül that ranged across the Northern Scapes.

"Gold Eater," Jined whispered, his knuckles whitening around the haft of his hammer.

19

Gold Eater

Gar-Talosh had been born with an insatiable greed. And thus he sought out the company of his god, Kos-Yran, begging him to fulfill his desire for gold. "I shall grant your desire. Your hunger for gold shall be now all that fills you, for you shall no longer eat the flesh of your prey, but only their gold." And thus was Gold Eater born. It is said that even his bones are now made of the metal, and yet still his greed has not yet been sated.

— TALES OF OLDE

All of the legends of those who followed Kos-Yran were filled with cursed blessings. The appearance of Gold Eater was proof that legends were not myth, but history. It meant that the fear-inducing stories were not just allegories, but warnings. To Jined, the appearance of Gold Eater meant that they were facing the very heart of the local vül pack.

Gold Eater lifted a massive hammer and pointed it at the Paladins, shouting orders. The vül who stood behind the massive brute were working themselves into a frenzy.

Nichal called over to the herald. "Brother Yollis, Dirge of Oliman, if you will."

Brother Amal Yollis had a knack for memorization. Jined once listened to him recite the entire Book of Sternovis over the course of four hours. Yollis raised his voice and began to sing. It was a simple song, repeating many lines, but setting a solemn tone, telling the tale of the death of Oliman, a Paladin who gave his life as he stood alone against twenty-five T'Akai.

DEATHLESS BEAST

The Paladins began to march forward to the dirge's rhythm. Jined could hear the Paladames marching close behind. They began to sing a wordless harmony to Yollis's hymn.

Across the field the vüls' frenzy was building to savage levels. They foamed at the mouth, ready to be let off their leashes by their master. Gold Eater raised his own hammer—a slab of granite mounted atop a haft like a small tree—over his head and swung it down onto some field rock Jined could not see. The loud crack caused the vül to jump and leap forward, surging to feed upon man-flesh.

Nichal rode alongside the Paladins and Paladames. They did not pick up their speed. They marched. One of the vül broke free from the others and charged the Paladins' line. As the mad dog of a creature came at them, they cut it down with powerful, controlled swings to the beat of the dirge.

Jined felt the dirge take over. He entered a trance as it dictated his moves. He gave in and moved alongside the others with only the song in his head.

Two more vül charged ahead, and the same thing happened.

The two lines stood across from one another. The vül barked and roared their defiance. From behind, Jined heard a scream of rage rise. It was a Paladame. She came running through the Paladin ranks toward the vül line.

He heard Killian Glass nearby shout, "Astrid! No!" He took off running after his sister. She was filled with anger at the abominations that had stolen a fellow Paladame from her.

Killian was faster. He caught up with Astrid ten feet from the vül line and pulled her to the ground. Gold Eater held his hammer high once more, halting the vül advance.

"You had best take back your woman," the monster growled.

Astrid struggled to stand up as Killian tried to drag her away.

Gold Eater stepped forward, shoving Astrid out of the way, and kicking Killian in the chest, laying him flat on his back.

"Your sister, it smells like," the vül said, standing over the Paladin. "And back there I see the collected leadership of your order. I would see you die."

Astrid had risen once more and came at Gold Eater again.

She was not fast enough. The vül caught her by the throat and lifted her into the air, holding her at arm's length. Then he put a massive foot on top of Killian.

"I can keep my pack in line," the monster laughed. "Perhaps you should learn to keep yours under your authority, Dorian."

The vül was looking at the Prima Pater across the field.

"I recall the wars you fought so long ago. I have lived long enough to remember them as yesterday. You once were a great warrior. Let us see if you are such today."

"I will not give into your demands," Dorian shouted from atop the carriage.

"You will," the vül said. He put the full weight of his foot down on the breastplate of Killian until it crunched. Killian coughed. Blood flecked his face.

"You only send him to the bosom of our god," Dorian said.

"Yes. Along with his own sister."

He stepped down harder. Killian did not respond. Astrid screamed in the vül's hand. The vül tossed her toward the Paladin line. She fell still.

"If she can live through that," the vül said, smiling, "then she can live with the memory that her actions killed her own brother."

The vül turned to walk back to his line. He held his own hammer in the air to signal the charge from his pack.

"Gar-Talosh!" Jined heard the voice call out, and looked around to see everyone looking at him. The call had come from him. He swallowed his fear as the creature turned back around.

"I defy you," Jined shouted. "Gar-Talosh, Gold Eater."

"Ha! A champion then. Your own leader fears me and must resort to a champion. A big one, too."

Jined took a step forward, feeling his confidence rise, and walked past Astrid's still form. She was breathing. He made a hand signal in the silent tongue, one of the only ones he knew, "Go." He heard Paladins behind him rush forward to pull her to safety.

The vül began to laugh. The sound of footsteps rushed to meet stride with Jined. He turned to see the Prima Pater walking alongside him.

"You may stand down, Brother Brazstein," the Prima Pater said. "I must face this monster myself."

"No. I issued the challenge. I must go."

They stood together over the body of Killian Glass.

Gold Eater approached, standing just out of reach. Jined's head came to the monster's chest. Gar-Talosh reeked of stomach acid, and his bared teeth were made of solid gold.

"Go, Jined," the Prima Pater said again.

"No."

"Stop your squabbling," the monster said. "I'll fight you both. I am a chosen of Kos-Yran, infused with his holy anger."

"Unholy," Dorian corrected. "Your sentence in Noccitan begins today."

The vül lifted his head and laughed. He swung the granite slab hammer round his head and set it on his shoulder, confidently.

"Once I've destroyed these two pups," he said to the vül behind him, "hunt them all down, one by one."

He turned back to Dorian and Jined. Then he put his hammer down, having thought of something, and turned back to his vül once more.

"On second thought, keep the Paladame who came at us alive. I want to make sure she is reminded daily of her failure."

Jined heard Dorian next to him muttering a prayer.

"Prima Pater, thank you for accepting me into the Paladins."

"Be quiet, Jined. I'm talking to your god. You should be, too. If we die, we can all talk about it on our flight to Noccitan."

Dorian winked.

It was Dorian who made the first move. He closed the distance between himself and Gar-Talosh, giving the vül no time to react. The Prima Pater swung his ælerne-shaped scepter into the vül's knee. Gar-Talosh grunted and stepped back, hitting Dorian across the shoulders with the back of his hand. Dorian fell back while Gar-Talosh sucked at his hand. Grimacing, he raised his hammer and swung it round. Dorian leapt back, which took him toward the vül line. A vül stepped forward and took a swing. His hammer hit an invisible barrier and exploded, throwing the creature back through his own pack-mates. Dorian didn't seem to notice anything had happened, but Gar-Talosh had.

He barked at the vül. "He is mine! You stay out of this. Kos-Yran shall bless me for this."

Jined took the opening and charged the vül leader from behind. He swung down with his hammer on the creature's back. It struck with a clanking thump. It left a dent, but the vül seemed unmoved.

"My pelt is made of the gold I've consumed," Gar-Talosh said, turning back. "Your armor is nothing but a false faith."

"I have faith in Grissone. Your own god betrayed you."

The vül advanced toward Jined, who retreated cautiously. The vül paused and suddenly swung backward at Dorian, who was moving up from behind. Dorian dropped the head of his scepter to the ground behind him and held up his left hand. A flash of light blinded the vül and Jined as Gold Eater struck his own hammer down upon the raised hand of the old man. As Jined's vision came back to him, Dorian wasn't standing there anymore. He stood a hundred paces away, and was charging toward the vül, gaining speed. Jined ran toward the vül as it realized what was happening.

The monster swung wide in a sweeping arc but Dorian leapt up over the creature's head and landed gracefully, mouthing to Jined, "Now."

Dorian stepped in and delivered a flurry of blows. Chunks of gold flew off the monster as it backed away. Jined charged and felt a strength and speed building up in him alongside a peaceful serenity. The vül seemed to slow down as Jined brought his hammer down on its shoulder and head with the repeated hammering of a blacksmith. The vül slowly turned to look at Jined, and roared. The massive sound impacted Jined and brought him back to the world. Gold Eater kicked at Jined, knocking him ten feet away. He came down on his left arm and heard the crack of his bone breaking.

"Grissone, save your servant Dorian," he heard himself say.

The vül turned back to the old man. Dorian stood in defiance. The slab axe of metal ælerne wings in his right hand, and with his left hand, he reached down and picked up the hammer of Killian, who lay next to where he stood. With a twist, the old man snapped the chain that attached it to Killian and held up the hammer. He slowly lowered it, pointing it directly at the vül. The hammer glinted in the sun's light.

"All shadows are banished in the light of day," Dorian said.

The hammer leapt from Dorian's hand, glowing brighter with each passing moment, and shot across the field into the chest of the monster. As it struck the creature, the hammer disappeared, and rays of light exploded from his back.

Gar-Talosh fell to his knees. Jined stood and walked toward the creature now on its hands and knees. It looked up at Dorian.

"You were toying with me the entire time," it rasped.

Dorian nodded. "The battle was decided long before you accepted the challenge."

"Finish it. Before I give a command for my pack to devour you anyway."

Dorian nodded again. He lifted his scepter, took two steps to the side and brought it down over the neck of Gar-Talosh. The head fell with a heavy thud upon the dirt.

DEATHLESS BEAST

Dorian turned to look at the assembled vül who stood in awe and fear.

"Your cursed god is not with you. Now shoo!"

The final words were not the orator talking but simply an old man in armor kicking at mongrels. The vül turned one by one and loped off into the woods.

"They'll be back," Jined said, wincing at the pain in his arm.

"No. It'll take months for them to squabble over leadership of the pack. Did he break the bone?"

"Yes." Jined nodded. "I think so."

"Go and have it looked at. I'll have the twins collect the body."

"Collect?"

"Yes. If his bones are made of solid gold, it would be a waste to leave it here."

Dorian walked away toward the carts, his scepter over his shoulder.

Two Paladames had died, along with four Paladins. Each laid in the Prima Pater's own carriage. Of the war sleipnirs, only Nichal's remained. He offered it to Dorian, but the old man refused. He walked beside the sleipnir that pulled his own wagon, escorting the dead toward the bastion.

It took some work, but those well enough to help moved the body of Gold Eater on top of one of the carriages. His weight made the work hard for the draft sleipnirs, helped along by the slow dirge-pace set by Dorian Mür.

Jined tried to ignore the pain of his broken arm. He had agreed to let someone look at it, but not until they reached the haven of the bastion. If the pain in his arm was hard to ignore, harder still was trying not to think of the loss of his friend, Killian Glass.

They came out of the woods to the edge of the farmlands that would have surrounded the Gilded Bastion. When they came through the break in the woods, the land was burned and barren. There was no bastion, only ruins over a foundation.

"Where's the bastion?" someone voiced. "Where's the gold?"

"I suspect we're carrying it on the roof of that carriage," another said.

The Prima Pater, shoulders heavy, stopped at the edge of the fallen stone wall. The iron of the gate was entirely missing, save the hinges.

Everyone behind him waited in silence.

He turned. Tears streamed down his face.

"Gallahan, set your scribes to find a place we can set up camp. Amal, personally select a grave site, or if you can find the old graveyard, select plots there for the fallen. Nichal, you have fought well, but I need you to gather wood for fire. It seems there is nothing left here to burn. Provisioners, prepare food."

Everyone worked in silence. Night fell, graves continued to deepen. Food was brought to everyone and they ate without a word.

Just after midnight, the silver moon, Umay, passed by nearly full overhead. The red glow of Norlok was beginning to rise in the east. Six graves stood open with cloth-covered bodies of brothers and sisters beside them. The Paladins and sisters stood at the feet of the holes, while the Prima Pater and his wife stood at their heads.

The Matriarch solemnly performed her duties and saw the two women laid in their graves. Rose petals were thrown over their bodies, and the Crysalas Honoris sang a tear-filled hymn to lift their two dead sisters' souls to join Crysania.

Each Paladin was lowered into the grave, their hammers laid across their chests. Killian's hammer was no more, and so the Prima Pater had the heavy granite slab Gold Eater had used for a hammer laid across the fallen Paladin's chest.

A shadow flew across the moon above. As Jined glanced up, he thought it an ælerne, or perhaps the Anka himself, Twin-Soul of Grissone, come to see the fallen off. Dirt was heaped, and each left to sit at the nearby fire.

Too tired even to sleep, Jined remembered Killian's constant smile. Killian's sister wouldn't smile for weeks, if ever again. She sat across the fire, staring into the flames. Her tears had already dried up and left her eyes burning red.

"She sees now a rose whose petals wilt." He thought of the words that Paladin had said at St. Hamul. But something told him this was not the time nor the place to bring it up.

Loïc and Cävian both pulled out two boxes they had stored with the provisioners. Loïc opened his box first and pulled out the square-shaped, three-staved, stringed lyre. Then he pulled out the bow he would draw upon it as he held it upright on his knee. His brother, on the other hand, pulled out a small bowl-bodied mandolin. They each tuned their respective instruments.

Loïc began to pull a long note across the strings of his lute. He kept the note without breaking it as his brother began to pluck out a tune. It was a sad song. It had no words. It needed no words. It met Jined where he was as the sadness of the day filled him. It was a hopeless sadness as the reality of their trip consumed him. Even with their numbers, even with the head of their order with them, they would face, had faced, turmoil.

The song flew into the night sky, and the stars looked down upon them and sang along with them. A beat began low beyond a carriage. Jurgon Upona, the Prima Pater's seneschal came out from behind, having found his own stashed instrument, a wide hand drum that he could strike with a short stick in his other hand. He began to lay out a beat that with each drop filled in the despair, if only a bit.

Jined saw a few Paladins draw close to the fire, to gather around and mourn together. He saw Etienne with a small pipe in his hand. He would play when the time was right. One of the provisioners, Yan Dower, had his own wooden recorder in his hand. The song continued round and round between the two brothers. The drum beat pulsed. And then, it died out, suddenly.

The fire crackled. The wind blew. The trees answered. A gentle tune began to rise from a low instrument. Jined turned, along with everyone else, to find the source. Primus Beltran Cautese came out from the Prima Pater's own carriage with the instrument in his hands. The deep, rich dulcian he had been known to play at Pariantür began to sing an even more sorrowful song. The pipes in the hands of Yan Dower joined in and the woodwind chorus of lilted mourning lifted each person up even as it dropped them back down.

The twins joined in with the song. That was when Jined recognized the tune. It had been the song sung by the congregation of Paladins on their departure. It was the Hymn of Porumarias. It was said to have been written by St. Ikhail himself—the first Paladin.

He had written a song of the small, weak, orange flower that was said to have been found growing next to Pariantür shortly after its construction. Within a few short years, the porumaria flower had run wild, covering the landscape, spreading its orange petals across the grassy rises, and its soft, blushing scent through the air. The song had become, over time, a song of memory, taking many a Paladin back to Pariantür, even if they were parted for years. It was a song that would guide the fallen to a better place. It would have done its job that night.

Jined could swear he smelled the scent of porumarias on the wind now. He breathed deeply and looked up at the stars. They looked a little brighter as the song rose. Soon a voice rose from somewhere, and they each joined until a choir of Paladins and Paladames sang out the hymn together.

To some, the loss of six might be small. But when faced against a rising darkness, a loss of family, friends, and companions was always felt. It was a loss only a deep music could heal. And they sang to heal themselves long into the night.

20

Gates of Garrou

Saw he then the destination,

And walked up to the gate.

The guards looked down upon him,

And bid that he should wait.

And wait, and wait, and wait.

— THE TRAVELER

Prima Pater Dorian Mür stood outside the walls of Garrou with no one but the standard bearer Valér Queton next to him. When Jined had gone to his bedroll they were there, and in the pre-light dawn they still had not moved. Jined checked the binding on his arm. The break was setting well, but the dull ache persisted.

At first it was only the Prima Pater, who had insisted on standing alone. Valér had gone to stand next to him, refusing the Prima Pater's order to stand down. And thus their vigil continued. The city had barred their entrance, despite messengers having been sent ahead a year prior.

The provisioners prepared porridge again. It was all they had eaten for three weeks since the Gilded Bastion. A few people in the vicinity who had survived the destruction caused by Gold Eater's pack, had come to them starving, and the Prima Pater had ensured that they were fed.

After a week in the ruins, they began the two-week march on foot to Garrou. The road through Bédekvar, the halfway point from Nemen to Garrou, was barren. The market stalls were empty. Those few who remained spoke of vül to their south and military conscriptions in the capital in the north.

A pall of smoke hung over Garrou that the briny sea breeze could not seem to brush away. The smoke was under-lit by blue from starblush powder mined nearby and refined in the city, lighting street lamps throughout the night. While it was the city that never seemed to rest, its gates had been barred and the shadows of a doubling or tripling of the guard upon the walls made it obvious none would enter by night, and not during the day without express permission from the king himself.

The sun began its ascent into the eastern sky as the overly ripe silver moon of Umay made its bed far to the southwest. In response, the blue glow of starblush was replaced by a filthy orange haze. The morning breeze kicked up the smell of brine, dead fish, human waste, and tar pitch. Matching the stink came the brazen sounds of industry, sea birds, and people.

More guards now stood atop the sixty-foot wall. The second set of walls, twenty feet taller, were now occupied by higher ranking members of the guard, plumes atop their helmets, watching the two Paladins standing one hundred feet out in front of the entourage.

The herald, Amal Yollis came to stand next to the Prima Pater, and soon the two Pater Segundii joined them. Dorian did not turn his head, but from behind Jined could tell he was speaking to the others.

One of the plumed guards came to stand directly over the gate. He pulled up a cone to call out to the Paladins, but the voice of Amal Yollis spoke first. His voice echoed off the walls and all heard him.

"Prima Pater Dorian Miir, head of the Paladins of the Hammer and the Grissoni Church once more requests entry into Garrou."

The herald went silent.

"You claim to be the Prima Pater, but last night you approached our walls with a full compliment of armed knights."

"You shall send a message, as we requested last night, to the bastion within these walls, as well as to the king himself. Tell King Koffran we require entry. We will wait one hour."

The plumed guard disappeared.

DEATHLESS BEAST

Dorian turned and walked back to the entourage.

"How long ago did you send message of our arrival?" he asked Beltran Cautese, the Paladin charged with planning the trip.

"A year ago, Prima Pater, and we received a reply with signatures from the heads of each bastion, fortress, and of course, the citadel in Setera."

"That is what I thought. Why have we not seen a single Paladin since we left Nemen, then?"

"The vül may have prevented messengers from making their way through."

"I understand that. But by now the country should have responded. You'd think they prepared for war."

"With the vül, perhaps?" Nichal asked.

"I had thought of that. But if that were the case, we might have heard of that in Setera through Zhigavan ambassadors."

The gate opened. Ten riders came out, all wearing the green and yellow of the city. The man at the head wore a long robe and a fur-lined hat. His beard was braided in two cords. They approached and the leader dismounted, nodding curtly to the Prima Pater.

"I understand you go by the name Dorian Mür?" the man was looking at a ledger in his hands. "Prima Pater of the Paladins of the Hammer?"

"I am," Dorian said. Jined could hear an irritation in his voice.

"And you're requesting to enter our city?"

"I requested it over a year ago. I received a writ from your King Koffran granting that permission."

"I see. We don't have a record of that. It would have come to me."

"And you are?" the Prima Pater asked.

The man looked shocked. "Why, I'm the lord mayor of Garrou. I'm quite frankly surprised that you thought this ruse would work."

"Ruse? Who do you take me for?"

The mayor turned and walked away. "Your spies already entered the city two days ago from the west claiming to also be Paladins. To try to do the same from the south? Who do you take us for?"

"I take you for one who will go to the king so I can be acknowledged for who I am—head of a pantheon-ordained church, with more authority than you or your king can ever hope to muster."

The man scoffed, rolled his eyes and said, "We'll see," as he mounted up and rode back to the city.

"Why do they block entry to Paladins?" Etienne asked. "We're the protectors of humanity. What could we have done to offend them?"

"He raises a good question, Brazstein," Dane said. "You're from the north, or at least you always claim to know all there is to know about this gods-forsaken place."

"I don't know, and I've never claimed to know what goes on here," Jined said. "I haven't been here in ten years. Perhaps the political climate has changed."

An hour later the gates opened again. This time a complement of twenty knights rode out, two abreast. They split and lined the road. Above them, on the wall, it looked as though the entirety of the city guard had assembled, armed with crossbows. They came and stood in their own rank and file, crossbows on their shoulders.

The lord mayor rode out again, this time on his own. He came to the end of the line of knights and halted in the center of the road.

"Come. You are granted entrance. You are to be escorted to your bastion to be refreshed before you meet the king."

The Prima Pater grumbled something and pulled himself up onto Nichal's sleipnir. The carts drove forward, and the Paladins and Paladames marched behind them into the city under the watchful eyes of the guards and knights.

Guards stood at every street corner. Citizens had been ordered to the side.

At one point they were funneled through what seemed an alley that the carriages only just fit through in single file. The soldiers escorting the Prima Pater at the front dispersed to run around the block and meet them on the other side. At first glance it seemed like poor planning. Then Jined realized it was a show of force. The guards knew the city and could funnel an enemy into a tricky situation, if needed.

They came to a larger square, across which sat the bastion of Garrou—large enough to house five to ten Paladins, to host ten times as many, and, down the wall, he could see a poorhouse alcove, meant to supply food for the city's poor.

A single Paladin wearing the gold cordons of a Pater Minoris stood before the closed gate to the bastion.

"Greetings, Prima Pater," the Pater Minoris said. He was visibly exhausted and tried to force a weak smile.

"Greeting, Pater..." The Prima Pater left it hanging.

"Sarren Gui, Pater Minoris of St. Rämmon Fortress."

"St. Rämmon? We are not scheduled to see you for some time. What are you doing in Garrou?"

"I came of my own accord to see to your accommodations here in Garrou. I only arrived yesterday."

"Pater Minoris," Nichal spoke up. "We were expected over two weeks ago, the month Gryssyl has almost come to a close, and yet you have only just arrived? Why was no Paladin sent south to seek our whereabouts?"

The Paladin stood there, his mouth agape.

"Where is Primus Mason Derrig. Is he not here?" The Prima Pater waved at the street devoid of any people.

"Yes. He is. He has been assigned to preparing the bedding arrangements."

"Those have not been made?" The Prima Pater was now turning red with anger. "Open the gate, Pater Minoris. I've had enough stalling."

The Pater laughed weakly and did as he was told. Beyond, the sounds of Paladins and servants frantically scurrying about washed over them. Dorian rode into the gate and stood watching as the carriages and Paladins filtered in behind him.

"The bastion is not ready for us?" The Prima Pater came down off his mount, handing it to a Paladin nearby. "Brother Adjutant," he said, turning to his seneschal. "Clear the Primus's office for me. I will be meeting with Brother Gui and Brother Derrig in ten minutes."

In the two hours it took for the Prima Pater to meet with the two Paladins, the sisters disappeared off to their own destination. It was expected of them, and no one asked questions. Jined stood in the courtyard in silence with Loïc and Cävian.

They were summoned to the chapel, where the Prima Pater sat slouching in exhaustion in a seat. He looked as though the only thing keeping him awake was the anger that burned in his eyes.

"It seems we've walked into a bit of a situation. Bortali and Boroni have been in a trade dispute for several months now. The borders between the nations were officially closed in the middle of the month of Rone, on the eve of the Summer Solstice. Pater Gui has been put in a position of intercessor between the nations, since his fortress is located near the border. He is, however, not a diplomat. He's a choir director with enough talent to run the administration of a fortress, but apparently he doesn't have enough of a backbone to ask for help from St. Hamul nor Pariantür.

"Primus Derrig is less to blame. The bastion here is barely more than a soup kitchen for the poor and destitute. He had not heard of our coming until the messenger came to the bastion last night. He has been doing what he could to prepare the place for us in a day, what he should have been able to prepare for over the past year."

"Did Pater Gui know we were coming?" Nichal asked.

"I don't think so. I think our arrival last night was a surprise to everyone. Gui had arrived to continue his substandard diplomacy. Apparently, he has been traveling back and forth between St. Rämmon and Garrou for the past four months as things grew increasingly worse."

"So with Pater Gui arriving yesterday," Pater Segundus Pír said, "and our compliment of Paladins arriving from the south, the king thinks Pariantür is bringing a strong arm down on him?"

"Yes. I expect so. We need to send a message back to St. Hamul. We need them to send delegates and ambassadors."

Dane raised his hand. "Prima Pater, let me honor you by going."

"Very well. But not alone. Who else will go?"

Etienne Oren raised his hand.

"Gallahan," the Prima Pater said, turning to the old scribe. "Write up a message. I want a complement of ambassadors, administrators, and a historian who understands the Northern Scapes and their political turmoil. They are to ride to St. Rämmon and meet us there."

"Do you have that, Aeger?" the scholarly Pater Segundus asked his assistant.

The silent Paladin nodded.

"In the meantime," the Prima Pater said. "It seems your help will be needed, Eraim." He turned to Primus Glynn, Pariantür's chief ambassador. "You'll be staying here in Garrou to handle things in the city.

Then he turned to Beltran Cautese. "We have to change our agenda. We will not be going east to survey the Zhigavan coast. Arrange for some of our number to go there to do the work alone."

Beltran nodded.

"What about the remains of Gold Eater?" Nichal asked.

"I've already taken care of it. I'm keeping the skull safely hidden away. The rest of the gold we gathered has been given to the sisters.

I didn't want to be carrying around such a valuable treasure from here to Mahn Fulhar."

A knock came to the door.

The Prima Pater nodded and Loïc, who stood at the door, opened it. A Primus came in. He walked up with a cowed look in his eyes and handed the Prima Pater a letter before excusing himself.

Dorian broke the wax and read on.

"It seems the king has deigned to allow us to meet with him. Nichal, you'll be joining me. Bring two more guards."

Nichal turned and pointed to Amal and another before marching out of the room.

It was late into evening when they returned. The Prima Pater was angrier than he had been when he left, and paced the chapel as the guards stood near the doors. The leaders of the entourage watched their leader, worry across their faces.

King Koffran had died at the beginning of the year, and his son, King Vorso had taken his place. Years of resentment toward the wealthy jarls of Boroni had fomented into near-war and continual paranoia.

"That St. Hamul didn't even know is surprising. That Nemen said nothing is perturbing. The border between Bortali and Boroni is closed, and I can only imagine that means the canyons between Düran and Mahn Fulhar, their only access to Boroni and Bortali, are policed."

"Which may lead to further conflict," Nichal offered.

"And if Nemen is now considering trading their Monarchy for a form of Democracy...," Pater Segundus Pír offered.

"Then we must continue on our path, and assess just how bad things truly are," the Prima Pater said. He turned to the Primus in charge of the bastion.

"Derrig," Dorian said as he approached, "has this bastion ever received Parianti Mead?"

"We've been honored to receive it twice. We've never had the opportunity to open the casks though."

"Very well. I'm afraid I need to requisition them. I'll have Pariantür send you three in their place."

The Primus nodded. "Of course, Prima Pater. I can only continue to apologize that my bastion wasn't ready for you."

"This is not about you not being ready, but I expect our ambassadors may need it to entreat with the king. I fear that my overbearing authority may have been too much for this situation. We shall give the casks as gifts, and my leaving the city as another. Perhaps the jarls to the west can be better reasoned with."

He turned to Eraim. "Primus Glynn, tomorrow you're to go to the king with both casks and give them as a gift from me personally. I'll prepare a letter of apology to go with them. I need to make sure we're on equal ground before you start building relations between Bortali and Pariantür. I don't want the Northern Scapes turning into another Temblin-Hraldor fiasco."

The Prima Pater turned. Jined could see dark circles under his eyes. "Brazstein, find Upona. Tell him I need sleep. He can bring me food, parchment, and ink early tomorrow morning."

Jined sought out Upona and made his way to the refectory to eat. Amal Yollis sat next to him in silence. Several times he looked like he might become talkative but decided otherwise. Jined rose, his plate half-eaten.

"Are you feeling well?" Amal asked.

Jined shook his head. "I need some time to myself."

Amal looked around and said, "I'll handle anything asked of you."

Jined left and wandered the bastion. Most bastions consisted of a chapel-refectory, a dormitory, and stables. This one had several individual offices, the chapel separated from the refectory, and a subterranean dormitory.

Jined found his way to the chapel. A side room held a library with copies of each of the holy tomes. He touched the spines of each book and pulled down Anvil of Faith. He leafed to the ninth chapter. There he saw the proverb the Paladin at the citadel had quoted. "The words of the scriptures are a source of comfort."

Jined smiled. They were a comfort. More importantly, they reminded him of something that had nagged him since St. Hamul. He had not been able to place exactly each of the verses the other Paladin had quoted. He knew the quote from the Anvil of Faith. He had known the verse about silence. He even recognized the verse about being guided by the Anka. It was the last two verses the Paladin had quoted that seemed different. The first, about the deeper faith, and lastly, the reference to the rose.

He knew nothing of Crysanian scripture, but the deeper faith felt familiar, and all too personal, in a way. His hand was blindly feeling along the spines again as he breathed deeply of the smell of dusty leather. He came to a book with raised words on its spine. He recalled the sixth apostle of St. Ikhail, Ferruce Kalida. His followers took the sixth vow, the now-lost Vow of Blindness. It was told they had been greater scholars than others, able to memorize volumes of scripture, and they were even said to read a page by feel.

    He opened up the book. The title stood out in bold black letters: Deeper Faith. Below the words were marks, as though the words were set deep into the parchment. He realized then that the book only had a few dozen pages, each made of heavy, thick material. There was no ink, just imprints of a writing he did not recognize. He closed the book and held it to his chest. Somehow Grissone had spoken to Jined through that Paladin, and now he would need to seek out deeper secrets to deepen his faith.

21

Flower Vault

A rose and its thorn both grow from the same root. Be unto those that need our fragrance a welcomed scent. But keep thy thorns at the ready to protect those that need a briar about them.

—SAYINGS OF MATRIARCH DENSWYN

Katiam Borreau stood in the courtyard of the paladinial bastion of Garrou with the other sisters. The Matriarch sat on a bench in the shade of a wall, sipping water from a silver chalice as she watched the Paladins scurry around her. Katiam wanted nothing more than to find a wet cloth and wipe away the dry dust that clung to the sweat on her neck, but she knew the day's journey had only just begun.

A small woman appeared from the gateway and approached Captain Sigri Smith.

"Sister Paladame," she said, "I am Semivah, a simple tallow merchant. I understand the Paladames are in need of new candles for their journey west. I should like to show you my wares."

Sigri nodded and motioned for Katiam to retrieve the Matriarch. Her great-aunt was already standing when she approached, and quickly took Katiam's arm.

"A tallow merchant, she said?" Maeda Mür asked.

"Yes, Auntie," Katiam whispered.

As Katiam understood, the tallow trade in Bortali was one left for the lowest rungs of society, and thus one of the few trades where women could hold a shop.

They walked for some time through the streets of Garrou. They came to a series of warehouses, even filthier than the last. The final one stood at the end of a wide street full of refuse, yet all was swept clear from around the door they approached.

They entered through a side door into a spacious room beyond. Several women stood over vats, stirring hot tallow. Dried flowers and herbs hung in the rafters, providing a subtle scent to the air. At one vat, a woman with large arms continued to stir her cauldron with one hand while with the other she placed herbs and twigs into a metal case perforated with holes. She dropped the cage of herbs into the cauldron and stirred vigorously, drawing the scent out.

"Thank you for coming to look at my wares," Semivah said. "That the Matriarch Superioris herself should find me worthy is an honor I cannot repay."

"You are most kind," Maeda said. "Perhaps you can show all of us your finest goods? I have no doubt you keep them in a room separate from the rest."

"Yes, of course."

She escorted the sisters to a back room. Once they were in, the room was locked, and they all began to take off their armor, down to the simple white robes of the Crysalas Integritas. Semivah provided them with plain clothes to wear over top.

"What trade allies itself with tallow?" Sabine Upona asked. Sabine was a meticulous keeper of facts and information, and had produced a ledger and a charcoal pencil, ready for the tallow-wife's answer.

"In our level of society we are allied with the flower-wives. In the upper tiers the alewives are the most influential."

"And how does your trade fare?"

"Not as well as it used to," Semivah said. "Starblush powder lights so much of our city now. It's mostly in the streets, and near the wharves where fishermen can now clean and gut fish both day and night. Interestingly, the apiary chandlers have taken a harder hit. The nobility are enthralled with starblush light; they've all but stopped buying wax candles. The lower classes have begun to buy more tallow so they can work into the night and keep up with those able to afford starblush."

"And how are the women of the city?" the Matriarch asked.

"That is a question better asked of the flower-wives. You will be taken there soon. I have arranged for Ermani Wittal to take you to her shop. She is a flower-wife and has a plentiful garden."

They waited an hour after their host excused herself. Sabine and the scribes arranged for several boxes of candles to be delivered to the paladinial bastion in the meantime. Eventually, a diminutive woman entered. She had pale skin, and her head was covered with thick, coarse black hair that grew down the back of her neck. She wore a green frock with a brown long-vest over the top of it. She had overly large eyes and looked at each woman standing before her with a smile. She spoke with a heavy Oruchii accent. Katiam had assumed she was Oruchii by her appearance—her accent confirmed the fact.

"Matriarch," the woman said, falling to her knees, "I am honored you should visit us. I am Ermani Wittal."

"Please rise child. I am weary from our travel. I should like to visit your garden."

The small Ermani rose. She was older than she appeared—twice Katiam's own twenty-five years. She beckoned for them to leave with her. The Matriarch took Ermani's arm, so Katiam took the arm of Esenath.

They would walk in pairs, keeping space between each group. Some of the women of their party were better at looking inconspicuous, others chatted non-stop, keeping the eyes of passersby at bay. They took what seemed like random twists and turns, passing some shops twice. After an hour of walking, they finally approached their destination. Katiam and Esenath entered the shop last.

Fresh as well as dried flowers hung everywhere. Clusters of herbs sat out in nets in the rafters, and several jars and pots held flowers for sale. While the tallow factory had a subtle aroma of candles, herbs, and rendered fat, here there was an overwhelming garden of delight.

Katiam and Esenath found themselves alone in the shop. A young girl, no older than ten, appeared from a side room.

"Good evening, ma'ams," she said to each of them. "What are you looking for?"

"My sister has a hacking cough, I'm afraid," Katiam replied. "It always seems to come when the weather gets colder. Do you have any herbs that I might grow in my box garden to help her? I've heard porumarias might help with that."

"Yes," the young girl said. "I believe we have something in the back that might interest you."

She came out and handed them both a dried rose, symbolizing that they had said the right turn of phrase. Had there been others in the store not privy to the secret, they would have waited, roses in their hands.

They were led to a door that stood off the beautiful flower garden out back. As the door to the outer garden closed a closet door was revealed. The girl put her key into the keyhole at the back of the closet and turned, pushing back the door inset and revealing a long flight of stairs. They came to the bottom, which ran much deeper than a single story, and found themselves in a basement room. This cellar smelled even stronger of the herbs and flowers. A young Paladame stood guard in full regalia. She had satin gloves on her hands, and tiny bells jingled from her ears. She had a beaming smile.

"Greetings, sisters," she said. "You are visiting with the Matriarch Superioris?"

"We are," Katiam said.

"I am this Crysalas Societas guardian. The Garrou Flowerwife's Vault welcomes you. I am Maeda Salna."

"Maeda?" Katiam asked.

The girl blushed. She appeared no older than twenty, with an air of someone who hadn't aged more than a year or two since she came of age.

"Yes. I was named after the Matriarch, raised by the sisters in Düran."

"Not that we call the Matriarch by her name, but perhaps we can call you Sister Salna?" Katiam asked.

"Most know me as Little Maeda."

"Then we won't fight tradition."

The Paladame opened the vault door and let them in.

It was a long, vaulted room that sat under the very garden. Above, a keystone arched ceiling was held in place by a row of stone pillars. Doors off to the sides led to various storerooms and sleeping cells. Women gathered in small circles around the space, chatting. The pink glow of a chapel came from doors at the other end. Tables set against the walls were covered in goods as some women sold their crafts to one another. A few young girls ran around underfoot.

Standing out among the common women were the sisters. Many of Katiam's companions had already dropped their peasant frocks. Captain Sigri Smith was already back in her armor, speaking with two other Paladames Katiam did not recognize.

Of the women dressed in commoner's clothes, a few had bruises on their arms, shoulders, faces, one had her arm in a sling. Katiam's blood began to boil. Here in a secret Vault of Crysania the downtrodden and the harmed could find solitude away from husbands who had neither dignity nor self-control.

The Crysalas Integritas had always lived in these secret communities, hidden from the eyes of the authorities, and from men who sought to force their control over their wives through overpowering wills. Centuries prior, when the Crysalas made their diaspora to Pariantür, the Paladames were formed, and the then-ruthless church of Aben ceased to seek out these hidden communes, thinking they had dissolved. Instead, they grew stronger. From centuries of remaining in hiding, these communities had put controls in place to keep their locations secret.

Every country had a community embedded in trades where women could work without needing special accommodation, and in each country it differed. In Œron, the baker's guild was the secret commune of women. In Morriego, the salt-wives had grown to be the richest sisterhood in Ganthic, often offering financial help to other vaults and communities.

The Matriarch was already surrounded by members of the sisterhood. She looked even smaller without her headdress. Some asked her to bless them, others took her hand in theirs and simply smiled broadly, tears streaming down their faces.

A sister in white pushed through the group and stood before the elderly lady.

"Matriarch Superioris," she said, "you are here at the perfect time. We have a young girl who arrived last week. She is expecting a child and her husband has been gone for over a year. She is beginning the first stages of childbirth. She has asked for your blessing."

Katiam's great-aunt smiled. "I have not been asked to help with a birth for many years. I would be happy to." She turned and sought out Katiam's eyes.

Katiam shook her head. A physician she may be, but she had never excelled at childbirth, nor had she found the stomach for it. And so she left it to more capable hands. Her own strengths lay in nurturing the elderly—administering herbs and tinctures, and restoring their dignity.

Maeda nodded, understanding. As she left the room, the sister who walked alongside her said, "She wishes us to take the baby on as a charge, but our own coffers are rather thin."

"You shall no longer worry about money," the Matriarch replied.

As Katiam turned, the Matriarch's assistant, Sabine Upona, was turning herself to another sister who was awaiting her attention. The woman was tall, but hunched, and held a book in her hand. Her features were not attractive—more masculine than feminine, her lips large and heavy. Katiam felt sorry for her. She had no doubt joined the Crysalas because she could not find a husband.

"Sister Upona, I believe I've shared letters with you," she spoke with a voice that was low and rich, which leapt up into a broken falsetto as she emphasized words. "I am Sister Fedelmina Barba."

The diminutive Sabine grinned broadly. "You are Fedelmina? It is wonderful to meet you. Our letters have brought me more joy than you know."

The older woman towering over her smiled sweetly. "I agree. I'd like you to look over the figures I have prepared for the sisterhood's vault. It is far worse than I feared. No worse than the debt my late husband and I dug out of in our younger years before I joined the Crysalas as a widow."

Katiam felt a twinge of shame creep over her, and she bit her lip for the judgment she had cast over the towering woman.

"You have little to worry about now," Sister Upona said. "The Matriarch has a gift that I'll bestow to you and the vault. Shall we find someplace quiet to speak?"

The woman followed behind Upona as they found a private room to discuss the remains of Gold Eater. The Prima Pater had insisted the Matriarch take the remains and distribute the wealth to her church in secret.

Esenath was speaking with two women at a table along a wall. Katiam walked over and stood next to the botanist.

One of the women wore the white robes of a sister, while the other was dressed in ruddy brown, stained by work in the garden.

"Katiam, come and see these," Esenath said. She indicated to the woman in brown.

"This is Rinda. She helps Ermani out in the garden when her husband is too far into drink."

"You are well, though?" Katiam asked.

The woman looked unhurt.

"Oh yes. My mother introduced me to the vault here when I was newly married. When I was younger, my father insisted I marry the old man. He has not hurt me since I found I could flee here to avoid his drunken mood swings."

"He doesn't suspect you run away?"

"No. We have a large house. He thinks I run to hide in some other room, and he doesn't recall much of anything after he recovers from his rages." She spoke with a matter-of-fact way that likely hid the disappointment she found in her husband. Yet she had the spark of resolve Katiam saw in many of the women who had resigned to their lot in life, instead finding companionship and life in the hidden Crysalas Societas Vaults across the world.

"Then what can I do for you?"

The woman in white spoke up, "Sister Borreau, Rinda has proven to be a fine resource for odd plants." The woman, Katiam realized, was Ermani. She now wore the robes of the Crysalas, with the markings of an abbess.

"I thought you'd like to see some of the things these sisters have found," Esenath said, indicating for them to look at a table display against the wall.

"We do not have much to show here but our service," Ermani said. "And while this is a meager offering, we wanted the Matriarch Superioris to see this collection of interesting plants that she and her florists at Pariantür might have better luck with, being in a different climate."

The table had an assortment of bulbs and seeds upon it. Some were the usual bulbs used in every garden across Ganthic. Esenath pointed to a speckled erriph bulb.

"Ah, yes. We gathered this from a town to the south of here. The erriph grows in a stunning red that would make a rose blush."

There was a handful of seeds that were said to grow a grain less susceptible to sea-rot, which plagued the northern coastal lands of the Northern Scapes.

A dried fruit sat with a husk as hard as wood. It rattled when Katiam picked it up to look at it closer.

"That is a fruit that has fallen out of favor over the centuries," Rinda said. "The fact is that you can't plant it until it is as dry as this husk. Then the tree sprouts up and dies after five years. Most gardeners find it just too hard to cultivate. I've been waiting to find a place to plant it. The root system can cause havoc in the city."

"Do you recall the name of that plant, from that description?" Esenath had been working through her own botanical book with Katiam over the past few weeks.

Katiam had memorized more than a dozen herbs and their

qualities, but she had barely begun to study the fruit portion of the book.

"Felf?" Katiam guessed.

"Close," Esenath said. "Velif. Rinda, try starting it in a large pot with silt from the river mouth. Once it sprouts, pour a gallon of briny water over it once a day. It will grow quicker, and last ten years if you emulate the change of tide with brine water. You can suspend its root ball in a fishing net, changed once a year, and hang it over the river, and allow the tide to water it."

Rinda's eyes sparkled. "I had not thought of that. You're right; I've seen a few Velif grow near river mouths, though they are much shorter."

"Yes, but they will produce more fruit over the ten years they bear than they would for five as a tree, or worse yet, never grown at all."

"May I show you something of my own?" Katiam asked Rinda.

Rinda turned, nodding. Katiam pulled out the Rotha seed pod.

"What is this?" Rinda said, taking it in her hands.

"It had been at the college in Thementhu for generations, they say," Katiam replied.

"Generations?" Rinda said skeptically.

"Centuries, perhaps," Esenath added.

"It looks like it was just taken from the bush," Rinda said.

She held it in both hands, smelled it. Then, to Katiam's surprise, Rinda tested it with her tongue. Katiam inadvertently reached out to take it, but stopped herself.

"But what is it?" Rinda asked.

"It's always been known as the Rotha," Esenath said. "It is an unsolved mystery among scholars at the college."

"And now it travels with you?" Rinda asked Katiam.

"Yes. It intrigued me. Esenath suggested we might take it back with us to Pariantür. We can see if it will grow there instead."

"You might even find it would grow better here. We are near the sea, and not situated so high in the mountains as Thementhu."

Katiam could see Rinda becoming as interested in the pod as she had been at the college.

"I would rather not part with it," Katiam said. "I'm sorry."

Rinda offered back the pod with a nod. "I understand. I once transplanted a rose bush. I spent two years trying to nurse it back to health, but was failing. Ermani insisted I pull it up and let it be put on the burn pile, but I begged her to give me one more year.

That was five years ago. The bush shot up and took over most of our back wall. If you find yourself so attached to this Rotha, then you are no doubt the right woman to unfurl its secrets."

Katiam bowed her head. "Thank you for understanding."

She walked away, tucking the Rotha back into her satchel. She felt embarrassed for acting so protective. It reminded her of her childhood friend wanting to play with the rag doll that her grandfather had given her. She did not wish anyone else to play with it.

She wiped the sappy aroma of the pod that clung to her hands onto her skirt and then realized that it was the smell that had clung to the outer edge of her awareness since she had left Thementhu. She didn't mind it.

Several hours later, the Matriarch reappeared, holding a bundle in her arms. Women gathered around and the children pressed in to see the new baby girl. The mother was reported as doing fine.

"She has decided to give the girl over now. She fears becoming attached. Ermani, you'll find a wet nurse for her?"

Ermani was nearby and nodded. "And we shall find a home for her. She shall never be unloved."

The taller Fedelmina Barba, still holding her book in her hand, approached and stood alongside Sister Upona.

"Matriarch Superioris," she said, "I am Sister Fedelmina Barba. I was sent here a year ago from Precipice to take care of the vault's books."

"And how has the task gone?" the Matriarch asked.

"Not so well. I have been able to train a new purser in the meantime, though. She is able, but the vault does not have much money."

"I expect Sister Upona has given you the gift?"

"Yes. I thank you for that. There will be no trouble for some time now."

"What of the alewives? Have they not been able to help?"

"I have not had contact with them," Fedelmina said. "I have been sequestered here, given access to the books of this vault only."

"Very well. Thank you for traveling so far to see that this is done."

"Matriarch," Fedelmina said, "I should like to accompany you back to Precipice. My task is done here."

"Very well. Let us all rest. I expect that we'll be leaving

tomorrow."

"Why do you say that?" Sabine said.

"A feeling. I do not expect things are going well with the Prima Pater and the king. We will meet back up with them on the road to the west once our work here is done."

22

INTERLUDES

The chains on his wrists chaffed and rubbed, and the tree they had set him against was equally uncomfortable. Two men lay nearer to the warmth of the fire, leaving him to his cold misery in the nearby darkness. The sounds from the nearby lake and the trees along its shore filled his imagination with dark ideas. Without the chains binding him to the tree he might swim away. After he throttled the two men in their sleep.

"An interesting predicament to be in," a voice said. Cold shot up the man's back, and the hairs on his whole body stood on end.

"Where are you?" the man rasped from a parched throat. "Who?"

"I'll stay out in the dark for now. I'd hate for your friends by the fire to catch a glimpse."

"Do I know you?"

"I don't doubt that you do."

"Your voice. It feels familiar."

"Perhaps there is Üterk blood in your veins. They always seem to know me by my call."

He scrabbled and strained at the chains, trying to look around into the dark. The red light of Norlok didn't do more than cast evil shadows and spray the color of blood across the lake to the south.

"Not much you can do on those chains without a key," the voice in the dark said.

"Want to help me out?" he asked.

"That might be arranged."

"What do I have to do?"

"Tell me about yourself."

"I... Why?"

"I want to know who you are, and with whom I deal."

"Ghoré Dziony."

"No, tell me your full name."

"Ghoré Dzionka of Nasun. Son of Kirth Peshun. Son of Esh of the Üterk tribe of Wulig."

"And what put you in chains?"

The story spilled out of him. From his childhood as a trapper and a smuggler, and the time he spent as a Black Sentinel, to the baiting of wyloths and his being turned over to the authorities in Amstonhotten.

"All for using the skills your ancestors taught you? It hardly seems fair."

"It isn't!" Ghoré barked. "They dared to shackle me for doing nothing more than helping."

"I wouldn't have been so ungrateful if you had helped me."

"Nor would I, if you helped me," Ghoré offered.

"And all you want is to be free of those chains?"

"Not that I would expect you to help me take my revenge, but if I was free I could do that myself."

"And how would I free you? Those chains look strong."

"You could get the key," Ghoré said.

"What good would that do? It is a small thing to shake loose apples from a tree. Better to give the hungry man a pruning hook. That way your tree gets cared for, and they don't go hungry."

Ghoré saw movement near the fire. A single wyloth snuck into the light of the dying fire. It scrabbled around curiously, and then disappeared into the satchel of one of the guards. It came out holding something. It climbed up onto a log and considered the shiny object in its little hands. The ring had several keys on it.

"Nocc," Ghoré hissed. "Did you do that?"

"Do what?" the voice said.

"Cause that little shunt to pull out the one thing I needed?"

"How could I do that?"

"I'm imagining you're going to tell me."

"Why don't you try instead."

"My grandfather told me about you," Ghoré said. "About the Walker. The Tale Collector. I paid my due and gave you my story. Now you'll grant me one request."

"Presumptuous," the Walker chuckled. "That is all you know?"

"You'll offer me more, but at a cost."

"Only those who become too greedy are taxed a full cost."

"Then you do not deny who you are?"

"Are you not fearful of who I am?"

"You came to me, rather than me seeking you out. What have I to fear?"

"Much," the voice replied.

"Is that wyloth going to bring me the key?" Ghoré asked after a long silence.

"It might. That would be the simple way."

"But it wouldn't be giving me the pruning hook."

"As you say."

"Then what happens now?"

"I can tell that creature to give you what would free you. Or…"

"Or what?"

"You could tell it to come yourself."

"That's absurd."

"You commanded wyloths to harass your caravan. I thought that was humorous."

"I merely baited them. No man can command wyloths, nor any creature, to just do what they want."

"You're better than most men, though, aren't you, Ghoré?"

"I am. I'm smarter than most men."

"You just haven't been given the chance."

"And you're going to give me the chance?"

"If you'll go to Birin, where those two men were taking you, I'd hand-deliver you the chance to prove you are better than most men. That is all I offer. That is all I ask."

"How?"

"You need only give your commands to those lesser than you, and they will have no choice but to do as their king orders."

Ghoré looked back at the wyloth.

"Just tell it what to do?"

The voice was gone.

Ghoré and the wyloth considered each other for a long time.

"Come here," Ghoré said.

The wyloth stared back curiously.

"Come on," he whispered.

Nothing happened.

"Bring that!" he roared.

The wyloth jumped several feet into the air and disappeared into the dark. The men near the fire stirred but did not wake.

A set of small beady eyes glowed from a bush nearby, and from the shadows came the small figure of the wyloth. It approached and placed the keys at Ghoré's feet, in a mocking bow of supplication.

Ghoré laughed nervously, pulling the keys closer with his toe. He picked it up and fumbled through the ring until he found the right one to unshackle one wrist, then the other. The chain almost clattered noisily to the ground before he caught it. He gathered up the chain and quietly set it down as he turned to the lake. Norlok was starting to set now. He could swim away and they would never find him. The road was just out of sight to the north, leading to Birin.

A sound came from the trees and bushes behind him. He turned, and saw a small troupe of wyloths appear, all gathering near the fully prostrated first wyloth.

"Bow," Ghoré hissed.

They emulated the first wyloth.

Ghoré giggled hysterically to himself.

"He just asked I go to Birin and wait. In return for this?"

He turned north and started to walk. Behind him, the wyloths edged forward to follow. One stopped and considered the keys and chain by the tree. The sound of the jingling brought Ghoré's attention back to the men sleeping by the fire.

"Why just run?" Ghoré said. "He gave me this pruning hook to use for revenge."

He took up the chain in his hands and crept closer to the men sleeping by the fire.

The wyloths began to howl. Nearby troupes of wyloths could be heard far away howling and screeching in the night in reply, following the call of their new king.

He ran his finger over the text once more and closed his eyes, repeating the words.

"Faith can be made strongest through adversity. Only guard your heart from sin."

He repeated the verse several times until a knock came at the door.

"Come in," he said.

"Primus," the Brother Adjutant said. "We received two messengers from the Prima Pater. They rode hard from Garrou to deliver it."

"Very well," the Primus behind the desk said.

He stood and checked himself in the burnished brass hanging on the wall. Yesterday's shave was already sprouting strong across his face, scalp, and down his throat. He grimaced.

"Brother Pyle."

"Yes, Primus."

"See that a bath and shave is scheduled for me first thing tomorrow morning."

"Of course."

"Brother Damí was also starting to show signs of uncleanliness, and you know I don't like uncleanliness. Fighting against the gifts our hairier ancestors from Œron gave us seems to be increasing."

"They say that St. Hamul had the same problem."

"That was a story created by the Hairy Hermits to further their cause, back in the day." The Primus smiled as the two of them left the office.

They made their way down the candlelit hall. The silence across the citadel was thick, with most already asleep in their cells.

The two Paladins stood at attention in the guest courtyard. On a bench nearby sat two empty plates.

"Welcome back to St. Hamul," the Primus said. "I see you have been fed."

"Yes, Brother Primus," the older of the two said.

He recognized the hasty look in the man's eyes. It was the Brother Excelsior put to the Pillory by the Prima Pater for too much zeal.

"Brother Marric, is it?"

"Yes, Primus," the man said, a faint smile playing across his lips for the recognition.

"And I'm afraid I don't know the name of your companion."

"Brother Excelsior Etienne Oren, Primus."

"Welcome, both of you."

"We've ridden hard to reach you," Brother Marric said. "The Prima Pater and his company have experienced trials you would not believe just to reach Garrou, and the two of us have ridden to call for aid."

"Aid?"

"Yes, Primus," Brother Oren said, stepping forward, holding out a rolled leather message.

"Thank you, Brother," the Primus said as he took it. He turned to the Adjutant. "Brother Pyle, please see the brothers here are shown a guest bed and not disturbed until the midday meal."

"Very well."

"Brothers," the Primus said smiling to the two messengers, "please find solace. I am going to retire to read the message."

The two Paladins saluted as the Primus left and returned to his study. He unrolled the leather wrap and broke the seal made by the Prima Pater's own mark. The message was detailed and straightforward. It described an attack by vül, including a champion of Kos-Yran, the destruction of the riches of the Gilded Bastion, and the issues faced at Garrou. It specifically requested brothers from the citadel, detailing which ambassadors ought to be selected, to patch the cuts bleeding the northern states dry.

What caught the Primus's attention the most, however, was a small notation below the signature of both the Prima Pater, and the actual signatory, Pater Segundus Gallahan Pír. The small notation was made in black ink with a hint of red, and looked like a small chalice with a drip of some sort falling into it.

"You devious little man," the Primus said, smiling to himself.

He stood from his desk, walked to the door, dropped the bar in place, then returned to his desk. He took up a box from underneath, pulled out a small knife, and placed it beside a blotting cloth. He pinned the message open, then he took up the knife and with it a sharpened griffin feather quill.

He pressed the tip of the quill into his thumb and let a small bead well up, before squeezing the blood onto the small image of the cup. The blood pooled larger than the small icon, then contracted and disappeared into the cup, filling its empty lines with blood. Across the empty space at the bottom of the page words began to bloom.

Greetings, Dusk. I wish first to apologize that we were not able to meet face-to-face when the company traveled through St. Hamul. I am under scrutiny by one who has abandoned the Motean cause, and I would do well not to expose myself to him. Add to that, I was under the orders of Brother Fidelity to remain silent.

If you deem it within your purvey, please include yourself among the relief sent north, as Bortali and Boroni will most certainly go to war, and soon. Your help to bend the situation to the will of our brothers would be most welcomed. Once here, I expect we can find time to meet. I should like to inform you of what the Motean cause has accomplished within the walls of Pariantür, as Brother Fidelity has been, as of late, undiplomatic with the Moteans of the continent, namely those whom I once stood amongst as equal brothers, yourself, and those I need not name, for risk of their exposure should this message be unlocked by another. The Moteans sit on the verge of inheriting a greater wealth of power, should all our plans align.

Please note, the two messengers the Prima Pater sent are not members of the brotherhood. Marric, you may well remember from the Pillory, is a zealot, and the other, Oren, is naïve and knows little of the world outside of the Order of the Hammer. Both would do well under your guidance, if your oratory is still as sharp as it was when we were all taken under the tutelage of our former mentor.

—*Cup*

The words faded as he read the message, so he read quickly, and sat in silence, pondering the message long after. He took a deep breath, sighed, and then took his own journal off the black leather underneath. He untied the red ribbon that held it closed. He opened it up and took up the quill still damp with his blood. He pricked his thumb again and brought out another bead of blood. Then he put a single dot onto the page. It sat there, crimson. Then it faded into the paper. Black words began to form on their own.

That rest was too long, the words wrote.

"It was two days," Dusk said out loud.

It felt like a month. I have read through your notes in your journal, Dusk. I do not know how he did it. How he made a living shade. And he was my student. He must have learned it from someone else.

"If we can unlock the secret Shroud is keeping from us, imagine what we could accomplish?"

You could completely cheat death, and not be forced to end your life as I did.

"Speaking of Shroud and the other members of the order, I just received a message from Cup, who travels with the Prima Pater."

And what did Cup say?

"That Fidelity traveled among them."

Did he now? The newest member to bear that name, if you did not recognize him.

"Yes. But if the head of the Pariantür Motean Order chose to travel to the continent, they must have had a reason."

Or no choice. Perhaps he is one required to travel with the Prima Pater. If the head of that branch of the brotherhood has truly ascended to such heights, it will be hard to make a name for yourself. Those within the Father Fortress Monastery are notorious at keeping power to themselves. After all, I was the same in life.

"He sent a blood message. Something I believe you taught to those studying the Way of the Feather before you became a shade yourself."

What are you getting at, Dusk?

"The principles for creating both blood messages and giving your soul in its entirety to a shadebook are similar."

The thought had occurred to me. The question is...

"Where is the line where you will not lose your soul, but retain a connection to it?"

That is the correct question. One perhaps only Degan's Cloud can answer.

"Degan was a madman. I was haunted by nightmares for months while studying that one page you gave to me."

I expect the line we are feeling around for in the darkness lies somewhere close to madness. I have little to fear of madness, after all, as madness requires a mind, and all that is left of me is my soul.

The words faded from the page. He went to the shelf and opened a secret compartment, pulling out a moldering tome. He placed it on top of the black journal, bound the two together with the red ribbon, and put them both into the drawer of his desk. Two days' preparation ought to be enough time before leaving St. Hamul and still make good time to Waglÿsaor before snow closed the passes for the winter.

Part 3

23

Last Feast

The town faded from mem'ry

Gave way to fields of grain.

The stony build sat alone,

Its portal—sacred fane

—Shelter from coming rain.

—THE TRAVELER

The day turned out to be warmer than expected, making traveling uncomfortable as exhaustion set in. Really, Hanen had planned the fifty miles to test the others. After the second four-hour stint, Searn fell in alongside him.

"I said I wanted to get to Birin quickly, but I hope we aren't planning on doing fifty-mile marches every day."

"No. I figure we'll make about thirty-six a day. I wanted to see how hard we can press everyone."

"As long as no one gives up."

"The only person I figure will quit is your girl," Hanen said, looking at Ophedia. She was gasping for breath, but continued pushing herself. "She can barely breathe in that absurd vest."

"She's tougher than you think," Searn said, "and she'll figure out the vest herself. Let her make her own mistakes."

"Where did you find her?"

"In Macena. She was doing a dismal job of picking up bounties.

She owed debts to several collectors. But she helped me in a pinch, so I took on her debts and made her a Sentinel."

"Not quite the same way you introduced Rallia and I to the job."

"No. But you two came with heads on your shoulders. You made, what, two promotions before I left Edi?"

"You taught us the ropes," Hanen replied. "We owe you that."

"I hope you don't think you owe me the same way Thadar thought you owed him."

It was the first thing anyone had said about the dead Sentinel.

"No. Loyalty to someone we respect is different than being forced into extortion or a form of slavery."

Searn nodded. "I hoped that's what you thought."

"Thanks for helping out back there."

"I wasn't going to let him push around the two best Sentinels I know. How'd he save your lives?"

Hanen related the vül attack and how Thadar had finished the fight.

"Sounds like it was an easy opportunity for him," Searn said. "To think of the reputation he could have built if he hadn't gotten so greedy..."

"Just leaving town last night would have left the caravan in his hands," Hanen said, realizing the gravity of what he had done.

"Probably not the best idea," Searn replied. "But under the circumstances, I didn't leave you much choice."

They marched on in the midday sun for another hour.

"We should be nearing Suel soon," Hanen said.

"That's the village we all met near, isn't it?" Searn said. "Fitting."

They entered the village. While small, it benefited from being fairly close to Edi. Craftsmen could be seen building carts and wagons to take goods from the major trade city to the world beyond. Herdsmen stood in a pasture nearby watching large aurochs graze. Blacksmiths could be heard forging chains and brackets, while carpenters turned spokes and wagon axels.

They passed a village green that was overgrown with weeds. Ophedia stopped and stared at the space where a few burnt pieces of wood stuck up out of the soil.

Searn called back to her, and she brought herself to and joined them as they walked into the village inn's common room.

"The old inn was half the space," Rallia was explaining to Searn. "It wasn't small, but when a new proprietor moved into town and built this one, after the last one burnt down, it took a full year to build."

The man behind the bar was nodding and grinning widely. "Clouws!" he said, beckoning Hanen and Rallia toward him. "I didn't expect to see you for a few weeks. How many merchants this time?"

Hanen shook his head. "No merchants. We're traveling north on other business."

The innkeeper looked visibly disappointed.

"How did the old inn burn down?" Searn asked.

"Ah," the innkeeper said. "I've heard a couple stories from each member of the village since I moved here from Arbeswald. I heard one old man say he saw Nifara herself come and start the fire. Another said the innkeeper did it, for his past sins."

"Bah!" an old man nearby said. "It was the barmaids. They banded together and burnt the place down. Tired of the merchants pinching their rears; the innkeeper himself was guiltier than most others."

"The barmaids died in the fire," the innkeeper replied.

The old man looked them all over with a baleful eye. "I think they all went to live in the woods, descending on evil men as vengeful harpies, now."

"There was only that one girl who worked at the bar then," another patron said. "She likely died right alongside the innkeeper and his family."

"Will you be staying the night?" the innkeeper asked as he turned back to Hanen, rolling his eyes at the old men as they continued to improve their tale.

"No," Hanen replied. "We'll go up to the chapel. I hope you'll keep the arrangement with the caravan, even if we're not traveling with it."

"I always do. Your caravan is good for business."

Searn sat at the bar and clicked a coin down. "You're from Arbeswald?" he asked.

"I am."

"Then I can only assume you're serving arbwall ale."

The innkeeper winked and poured a tall tankard for him as the others sat around him. The foamy head rose high above the rim, and continued to rise, keeping its shape and never breaking.

"One for all of us," Searn said, taking his hand off the gold royal hiding underneath. The barkeep took it greedily and promised to send them along with some aged bottles in heavy travel jugs.

The long march made the amber-colored liquid go down smoothly. The dense bubbles danced down their throats. It tasted of a dusty orchard and the clean water of a mountain stream.

"It is rather fortuitous to meet you here," a light and airy voice said from behind them. Hanen turned in his seat to see Ymbrys Veronia standing before them.

He had his staff in his hand, the leather-covered top above his already taller head. Instead of the long flowing robes layered upon each other, he wore a bright red coat. It was closed in the front with an elaborate array of qavylli buttons and straps.

"What are you doing this far north?" Hanen asked. "Did you not find what you wanted at the gala last night?"

Ymbrys smiled. "I learned exactly what I needed. I left just after that little disruption you were at the center of and began the walk north. What takes eight Black Sentinels north? It seems you have traveled as much as I have in just as much time."

"We have a job we'll be picking up in Birin." Hanen turned to the others. "Everybody, this is Ymbrys Veronia, a spice merchant."

Everyone nodded and said their pleasantries.

"I would think a spice merchant would do well in Edi," Searn said. "Why head north?"

"Many of my spices were already readily available in Edi. I'm heading north to enlighten bakers and chefs there. That, and I am doing research into a piece of history that has a gap in qavylli history books."

"I'm a student of history myself," Searn said. "What are you researching?"

"The Alvarian Line," Ymbrys said.

Searn nodded knowingly. "A noble effort. But why Edi?"

"Because the two lines of Alvaria disappeared, and I am tracking them down. I first sought to speak with the Edian nobility and see if any of their pedigree matched. It did not. I am hoping to find more information in the north now."

"Why not start in southern Mahndür and Varea?" Aurín asked. "In the lands of old Alvaria?"

"One must start somewhere. I'll make my way there eventually."

Hanen stood up. "It was good to see you again, Ymbrys, but we probably ought to get going." He turned to the others. "We need to reach the chapel two miles down the road before dinner."

"Why go to a chapel?" Searn said. "The inn here is fine."

"The food and bedding at the chapel is free," Rallia said, "and we'll eat like kings and queens. Hanen and I know the priest there. He'll feed us very well."

"Oh?"

Rallia smiled. "As the saying goes: Always a table ready for a guest, and ne'er a soul with which to share. Nothing to waste, but instead to waist, for he cleaned his own plate bare."

The other Sentinels were already smiling broadly and nodding in agreement.

"As I said, I am heading north myself," Ymbrys said. "Perhaps I can join you? The company would be enjoyable, and Birin is where I am headed."

"That may not be the best idea," Searn said. "Hanen has a stringent marching schedule planned for us."

"You're a man of history, you say. I would find what information you know helpful. In return, I'll pay my way. Just how fast do you plan on making Birin?"

"Two weeks' march," Hanen said.

Ymbrys's eyes lit up. "You are most ambitious. Nearly five hundred miles in sixteen days. I'm impressed. But I can keep up, as evidenced by my appearance here. If I cannot, we part ways. You can decide how much you want me to pay before tomorrow morning."

Hanen looked at Searn and at Rallia.

"Alright. You can join us until we near the southern edge of Amston Forest. By then we should know if you can keep up with us."

Ymbrys smiled. "I thank you."

He walked over to a table and picked up his own pack. It was a shoulder-wide box, only a couple of inches deep. Below it hung two rolls. He pulled the straps over his shoulder. It didn't bear his posture down at all. He shrugged. "I am ready."

Rallia was out the door first, with Hanen just behind.

"Maybe we ought to have talked to Searn first," Rallia muttered.

"Perhaps, but it's free money."

"Yes. I know. I'll feel bad taking any money, if only because it's free."

"He offered," Hanen said.

Searn came and walked alongside them.

"That was enterprising of you," Searn said.

"Thank you," Hanen replied. "I figure, if we're going to walk from here to Birin with no pay, we might as well make something."

"That should help with the costs we've already promised to pay the others," Rallia added.

"True," Hanen said. "I'll ask him for four royals. If he agrees to that, great. If not, we'll still be doing better than we were this morning."

The two miles from Suel to the chapel were sloped and made for a trudging march. They slowed the closer they came to the chapel. Perhaps it was the realization that the first leg of their journey had come to an end, or that Hanen and Rallia, used to the walk, had slowed. It was still well before sundown.

Hanen could see Father Diono out back of the chapel, rummaging around in his garden. Even at a mile off, he stood, watching the nine of them walking up the hill. He gathered a few more things from the dirt and entered the side office of his chapel. As they came up the final rise, Father Diono was standing out front, watching them approach.

"Father Diono," Rallia said.

The Abecinian priest looked at them, seeking for a memory that would tell him who they were, and it dawned on him. "Clouws!" he shouted.

He opened the door to the chapel and ushered all of them in. He sized each one up, including the qavyl. Searn and Ophedia came last.

"As I live and breathe. It is good to see you!" His voice was old, and full of heavy breath.

"Father Diono," Rallia said, "I was only here three days ago, as I headed south to Edi?"

"Ah. Yes. Of course. I know that." The priest hesitated. "But it is still good to see you, regardless."

Ophedia stopped in front of Diono. "Hello, Father Diono," she said.

"Why, little Phedia? Is that you?"

She smiled and gave him a hug.

"I feel so old, seeing you all grown."

"I've seen the world now, that's what made me grow," she said, and continued into the chapel.

Everyone dropped their rucksacks on the bench pews and stretched.

"How long have you been traveling?" Diono asked.

"From Edi," Searn said, looking around with a critical eye.

"That's fifty miles south of here! How long have you been

walking?"

Hanen walked up and put a hand on his shoulder. "We've been walking since last night. Can we sleep here tonight?"

"Of course, of course! And you need food!"

Everyone heard what he said, and began opening up their packs, making space for themselves to sleep. Diono rushed out of the chapel and disappeared for a long time. Soon he returned with bread and apples and a wheel of cheese. He handed the cheese to Rallia to divvy between them.

"This will do for tonight. Tomorrow you'll feast before you leave."

As they settled into their places to sleep, Rallia walked over to Ophedia.

"I thought I recognized you. You're the girl who worked at the burnt-down inn in Suel."

Ophedia kept a straight face. "What of it?"

"Did you recognize us?"

"I'm not a fool. Of course I recognized you. Neither of you has changed."

"You've changed."

"Maybe I have. Maybe I haven't and I'm just older-looking now."

She pulled her bedroll over herself and rolled over to face the wall.

The qavyl did not immediately find a place to sleep, but disappeared into the back.

"Did you know?" Rallia asked Hanen.

"She looked familiar," Hanen said. "But no more than another face I've seen pass me in the street. Now that she says she's the barmaid from Suel, I can see it."

She had been a catalyst for their becoming Sentinels. The brigands they had overheard in the inn in Suel had been treating her poorly, and the Clouw siblings had worked to usurp their plans to rob and kill a duke. She had only been a fifteen-year-old girl then, but she had done what she could to distract the handful of the brigands the next day while Hanen and Rallia picked them off one by one. Searn had been involved, too, seeing their work, and invited them to travel south with him to Edi.

Hanen rolled toward the wall and closed his eyes, thinking about how little had changed, yet all the while everything had changed.

The next morning they all awoke to the smell of urswine bacon. Hanen walked into the kitchen behind Ozri and found Aurín cooking alongside Father Diono. Ymbrys sat at the table, while Rallia entered from the garden with fresh firewood for the Father's hearth.

One by one the Sentinels trickled in and sat down at a table spread with bacon, eggs, mushrooms, and other fresh vegetables from the garden. Ymbrys didn't have any of the vegetables, but helped himself to large portions of bacon, and some leftover cold meat the father had on hand.

"What brings you north?" Diono asked.

"We're traveling to Birin," Hanen said.

"It's a busy city, Birin." Diono dished out mushrooms to those who had already finished theirs. "And under the constant protection of Nifara. If I could choose a city to die in, it would be there. I'd wager she'd have an easier time finding me there before I'm ushered off to my judgment."

"What is that supposed to mean?" Chös asked.

"He's talking about the superstition that the goddess Nifara is important in deciding whether we go to Lomïn or Noccitan," Searn said. "Just another tale told to make children behave."

"Don't you believe in the gods, good man VeTurres?" Diono asked.

"Doesn't matter if I believe in them," Searn said, "I'm more concerned with wondering why there are stories talking about how they meddle in the affairs of honest people, instead of leaving us to do as we please."

"She finds each of us no matter where we are," Ymbrys said.

"Ah!" Diono said, his interest suddenly turned to the tall foreign creature in his kitchen. "So Nifara is part of the qavylli culture, too, then?"

"She is sister to Lae'zeq, god of the qavylli. So, yes. She judges the qavylli, too."

"She doesn't judge," Diono said. "She merely escorts souls to the gates of Noccitan, and makes a case for them to the Judge himself."

"Make a case, judge, it is the same thing," Ymbrys said. "She barely mounts a defense for those who don't deserve it."

"We need to be on the road," Hanen said.

Everyone stood up, cleared their places, and went to pack their bags. Hanen approached Diono. "Thank you for your hospitality."

"Did I tell you about the young man who came to visit me last week? I should have sent a letter to Mahn Fulhar; he might have been able to ask the High Priest to have me sent to Birin."

He stood and began to putter about with a look of confusion as he muttered to himself, "That young man—I can't remember his name. But I sent him north not long ago. He wished to become a priest."

Searn touched Hanen's shoulder, but Hanen turned, shaking his head. "Just let him tell his story."

"He was a spunk-filled young man. Hoped he might change the world. Said he left his home, his family. He could have been a duke or a lord. Instead he went off on his own, seeking to change it all."

"And he came by this chapel?" Rallia asked as the priest fell silent, reminiscing.

"Yes. Yes, he did stop here. He was given priestly encouragement. Enough to decide to take up the cloth and join the church of Aben."

He stood up and shuffled around.

"Ah!" Father Diono said. "Young man!" He came to stand before Rallia. "Kneel down so I may bless you before you go off to change the world."

"I'm a g... I'm not...," Rallia said before the priest interrupted.

"Nonsense, boy. Rise from your bench and kneel. Aben blesses those he blesses, and there is nothing you can do to stop it."

Rallia stood and went to her knees.

"Do right and seek your path. Do not listen to the words of the web-weaver, Achanerüt the Deceiver. Listen to your heart, for this blessing will tell you what is true and right. If you stray, return to the path. If you cannot find it, seek aid, and you shall find your way."

There was a long and awkward silence. Rallia left the kitchen last, giving the old man a long embrace.

"He's not right, is he?" Aurín asked.

"He slips more and more every time we stop through," Hanen offered. "That young priest he mentioned was himself. He tells the story every time."

"We tried to correct him once," Rallia said. "It aggravated him. He was very offended when we left. But the next time we came through he had no recollection of the conversation. That's when we knew. And I always wonder if he'll be here next time we come through."

"Before we go," Hanen said, changing the subject. "I believe I owe everyone some money." He opened up his purse and paid everyone what he had promised.

"I owe you some money myself," Ymbrys said. He handed Hanen four gold royals. "Will this be enough?"

Hanen looked up, astonished. "That's exactly what I was going to ask for," he said.

Ymbrys winked, though from a qavyl it looked odd or forced. "I have good hearing."

Each night they set up camp while Aurín prepared food over the fire. He and Ymbrys discussed which herbs and spices to add. Ymbrys listened intently as Aurín showed him herbs he had gathered along the road, while the qavyl added dashes and pinches of liquids and powders from his box of exotic spices.

Six days out from Suel, they came to the edge of the forest and set up camp as twilight set in. Ymbrys was preparing food and promised something special. Rallia came up to Hanen.

"My head is feeling scruffy. I really need to shave." The hair above her ears had grown in as rough stubble.

"Can I get one after you're done?"

Rallia nodded, turned, and set about her work. She soon had another fire going, with water boiling atop it.

The others ate when the food was ready, while Rallia spent the time to herself. She came over to the light, the sides of her head shining clean and shaved.

"Hanen, you ready?"

Hanen nodded, put his food down, and joined Rallia at the other fire.

"What is going on?" Ozri asked.

"It seems," Aurín said, "that Rallia has set up shop. I was hoping she'd be about her business soon." He left the fire, too, and walked over to the other to sit down and wait his turn.

Rallia had always been good with a razor. She soon had hot cloths in boiling water, and put them on each person in turn. She had a bar of soap to lather them up, pulled out her razor, and deftly cleared each man's face of unwanted whiskers. Ymbrys watched, fascinated by the whole procedure while Rallia shaved the sides of Eunia's head.

"You are very interesting creatures, you humans," Ymbrys said to Hanen.

"What do you mean?"

"We grow our little tendrils," he said, indicating to the two long tendrils that dropped down from his upper lip. "It would be a terrible thing to cut. We'd bleed all over. And then you humans grow hair everywhere. You cut, you trim, you make yourself unique with it. It's fascinating."

"You don't do anything like this?"

"I mean, we have our own traditions. We paint our bodies with dyes that last for a month. Then they fade away. Perhaps that is similar."

Rallia finished shaving Chös last. He stood up and took a deep breath of the night air, then put a silver lír in Rallia's outstretched hand and walked off toward the other side of the cooking fire.

Rallia dropped the coin into her purse before cleaning up.

"I have no need for a shave," Ymbrys said. "But I'm interested in what you're doing." He sat down and watched Rallia clean up, as though he was watching bread baking for the first time.

Hanen went back to his tent. As he climbed in, he saw Eunia sitting close to Chös by the cooking fire. They didn't think anyone was looking as she touched his freshly shaven face.

24

SWIFT AND TERRIBLE

Stay true my path, and protect me from eyes that peer from the bush.

—FROM *COMMON PRAYERS OF TRAVEL*

The next morning they began their trek through the Amston Forest. The road was just as well-kept as others, but the sun rarely shone on them between leaves that were turning but not yet fallen.

"Searn," Hanen asked. "Are we thinking we'll have a day or two in Birin?"

"Complaining already?"

"Not complaining. Just looking forward to this leg being over."

"I'm just joking with you, Hanen. Of course, we'll have a little time there. There'll be business, too."

"Do you expect it to take some work to gain the contract?"

"I do. I expect the monks will know all about the Paladins' arrival, but I doubt they'll have left Birin yet."

"How do you figure that?"

"Because they make decisions about as slow as a mountain moves. What do you know about the Nifarans?"

"They walk among the people and make decisions for those who can't afford to go to court."

"They meddle, and they take donations to pay for it. They say they resolve issues between parties, when really they're just getting in the way of people taking care of their own problems then calling it divine intervention."

"What would you have them do?" Hanen asked. "If they feel their faith called them to charitable service, let them feel good about themselves. I don't care for the priesthoods, but they do. Others do. They can have their way of life."

"That's fine, but not at the expense of others."

"What do you mean, 'at the expense of others'?" Hanen asked.

Searn sighed. "Listen, the gods have a history of abandoning us. So why can't they leave well enough alone and leave us be? Why do so-called 'holy people' need to force-feed us their moralities?"

"I guess I'm not understanding what you're getting at. Why even go offer our services to the monks if you don't believe in what they're doing?"

"Regardless of what I think, the monks are heading into what could be a momentous meeting, and it will be at the risk of their lives. If something were to happen to them, I don't doubt it would provide a means for the nations surrounding the Dead Pass the opportunity to go to war.

"I won't stand by and let monks martyr themselves on a trek into dangerous mountains when I can hand deliver them and perhaps provide some clout to the Black Sentinels while I'm at it. Imagine if the Black Sentinels were as organized across Ganthic as you were in Edi? We could be as powerful as the Paladins, but without all the stigma of some uncaring god ruling over us."

"I wouldn't call the gods uncaring," Ymbrys said from nearby. "The services your Paladins provide, and the Nifarans as well, can't be ignored."

"No offense, but the qavylli god has been largely silent on the matter for centuries."

"Ah. A historian as well as a scholar, I see," Ymbrys replied. "Lae'zeq loves his people in his own way. Just as a parent lets their child grow up and leave home, Lae'zeq lets the qavylli make their own decisions. It's not really for you to understand, not being a qavyl."

"You're right. It's not. But as a human it is in my experience to try to understand the gods that humanity follows. Grissone abandoned humanity for a select few and gave the rest over to his lording father, who can't even get his own church in order."

"It's obvious you both have an education on these matters,"

Hanen said, stepping in. "But we've still got to march alongside one another for the next week. Can we keep things civil?"

"Of course," Ymbrys said smiling. "I take no offense at this conversation."

Searn smiled and turned away, dropping the smile once his face was turned from the qavyl.

They soon came upon a stretch of road lined with bushes covered in white silken sheets. The look of it sent shivers down Hanen's spine.

"Not often you see a zvölver breeding nest," Searn was saying, stopping to look at the mass of webs.

"This is a nest of those awful creatures?" Eunia asked.

"This is a small one," Ymbrys said, stepping up. Everyone stopped, quickly gathering close. No one wanted to stray too near the edge of the road.

"We should move on," Hanen said.

"It is fine," Ymbrys said. "The adults gather together, build this nest, and move on. Inside are probably thousands of eggs. They'll hatch in a day or two and start devouring each other, then the few that survive eat the webbing, grow, and move on. Zvölders are small here in your country, aren't they?"

Searn held up a hand and grabbed his wrist halfway up to the elbow. "No longer than this."

Ymbrys nodded. He pulled out a knife. "You're welcome to continue. I'll only be a short while and I'll catch up."

He walked up to the edge of the web, slashed it open like a bed sheet, and disappeared within.

"I'm not sticking around for this," Eunia said. She turned and began walking down the road. Chös joined her.

"I'll wait for him," Rallia said.

"You've never liked zvölders," Hanen said.

"I didn't say I do like them, but he hired us to protect him. I'll wait for him."

"Fine."

"You're not going to stay with your sister?" Searn asked Hanen as they walked away together.

"I would," Hanen said. "But..."

"Zvölders."

"Exactly. You seem to know about them."

"I did some zoological studies when I was younger. Their pinchers. Twelve legs. Capturing prey. They fascinate me. But when you wake up and one is crawling across your pack? It made my appreciation cease quite rapidly."

After an hour Rallia and Ymbrys came jogging up behind them. Rallia had a mischievous look on her face.

"What?" Hanen asked.

"Nothing," Rallia said innocently.

Twilight set in and they found a place to set up camp. Ymbrys offered to make dinner, and soon had a pot boiling near the side of the road. He opened up a sack and dumped the contents into the water. A savory smell washed over them, and they quickly gathered round.

"What did you make?" Aurín asked. "I've never smelled something like that before."

Ymbrys stuck a spoon in and pulled out what appeared to be an egg. He set it on a cool rock.

"Please, try one," he said. More were being pulled out of the water. He sprinkled nothing but salt on them. He picked the first one up and popped it in his mouth, chewed, and swallowed.

Rallia stepped forward and took one, and did the same.

"Where did you find eggs?" Searn asked. "I don't recall you stopping to speak to a peasant."

Ymbrys shrugged.

Ozri picked one up, sniffed at it, then bit it in two.

"This is no bird egg," he said.

"No. Not from a bird," Rallia said, smiling.

Hanen was reaching for one when he realized where Ymbrys found them.

"I'm not eating that," Hanen said.

"Oh, come on," Rallia said. "They taste great! I had no idea you could eat zvölder eggs."

"You should taste a whole cooked zvölder," Ymbrys said. "Though not all are safe to eat."

The others visibly blanched, and refused to eat, while Rallia, Ozri, and Ymbrys ate their fill.

Eunia and Chös excused themselves and went walking farther down into the open field toward the pond just out of view before stopping abruptly.

"Everything alright?" Hanen called.

Chös slowly lifted a hand and closed it in a fist. Everyone grew silent and drew their weapons. They watched as Eunia began taking slow steps in retreat. Chös crouched down to the ground and started crawling backward. There was a high-pitched squeal like the sound of a monstrous stuck pig. They both spun and began running wildly toward the road. Something else crashed up from behind that stood much taller and weighed several tons. An urswine. It seemed to be charging directly toward the Sentinels, but then veered and ran off in another direction toward the woods.

A second sound began to rise. At first it was a low growl that rumbled through the woods, and rose slowly in crescendo, then sharply to an ear-piercing shriek. It was like wind screaming through a barn, like the sound of the dying on a battlefield, and even like a young woman mourning the loss of her husband to a foreign war. The hairs on everyone's necks stood on end.

Eunia had a head start and made it to the edge of the road, while Chös was twenty yards behind her. Something great and terrible leapt up out of the tall grass and over Chös, trapping him in the field. It was lithe and covered in dark stripes on a sleek coat the color of the dry grass it had been prowling in. On each paw it bore dagger-sized claws. Hackles rose along its spine, and within the hairs rose even longer, sharper quills. It bore a long tail that swished back and forth, a curved spike on the end oozing a deadly venom.

"Hey!" Rallia shouted out from just behind Hanen's shoulder.

The thing turned around to see what could be disturbing its hunt. It had red-lined eyes and a long mouth filled with rows of teeth, each wickedly sharp, like an evil grinning smile.

"Manticör," Aurín hissed.

This was no house cör that hunted vermin for farmers and city folk, but one of the great manticörs that hunted across the central lands of Ganthic, stealing herd animals, and causing the disappearances of lone travelers on the road.

The showing of teeth reminded Hanen why he hated all manticörs, large or small. A bite from a house cör could mangle a finger. What a full-sized one could do, he did not want to know. It let out a shriek that froze them all in place.

Searn fired a shot off with his crossbow. The monster ducked rapidly and the bolt barely missed its face. It made a single lunge toward the road and swatted out with a claw. Everyone jumped backwards. It was only a warning, but it was enough.

Chös moved separate from the others, his axe in hand. The long tail of the manticör, swishing back and forth, prevented him from making a move.

DEATHLESS BEAST

Searn reloaded his crossbow and Eunia took a step forward toward the beast, while Ozri matched step. He held both of his clubs in his hand. Hanen watched Aurín creep up the left, with Rallia to the right.

"We all need to attack at once," Hanen whispered harshly. He lifted an axe slowly, staring directly into the eyes of the monster.

It moved with wicked grace and struck like a lightning bolt, claws flying in several directions then spinning in a long arc. The first swing struck Eunia with the body of its tail, flinging her wide. The tail kept moving as the manticör turned back toward Hanen. The tip of the tail must have hit Chös as he cried out and crumpled to the ground.

Searn shouted, "Now!"

Hanen didn't even realize what he was doing as he drew back and threw his axe at the beast. It reared up as it swatted the flying object away, but it gave Searn the opening he needed. Another crossbow bolt flew, hitting home, burying itself deep into the ribcage of the creature. Aurín moved in quickly from one side, while Rallia seemed to move even faster from the other. Ozri charged forward, a club in each hand. The manticör crouched down on all fours and launched at Ozri, knocking the huge man flat out on the ground underneath it. Aurín had drawn a short sword, which he held out behind him, his own axe held out for defense. He struck out with his sword and scored a glancing hit on the manticör's foreleg. The sword came back covered in blood.

As the monster turned to its attacker, the deft Aurín leapt away and Rallia came in, swinging her staff in a large circle. The manticör's tail, which seemed to have a mind of its own, swung to find Rallia, who deflected it with a heavy swing. As she struck the bulbous stinger the monster wailed.

Searn walked up next to Hanen, another bolt loaded.

"We need to finish this quickly," he said, drawing up the crossbow. "Or it will hunt us from here to Birin."

He let the bolt loose. This one struck the beast in the eye. It screeched in pain, and began flailing wildly. It trampled over Ozri, and its tail began to strike out spasmadically.

Rallia was dancing around it, her staff spinning, as she tried to find a chance to move in. Aurín took swings as claws came close to him, but none struck home. The manticör stopped for a moment, seeing Ophedia standing near the road by herself, her club clenched in both hands. It suddenly lunged toward her.

Ymbrys dropped between the girl and the beast, his own tail snapping left, then right, distracting the creature as it followed the flipping end. The qavyl held his staff out in front of him and reached into a pouch with his other hand. The manticör snapped its mouth open and Ymbrys threw a powder into its face. It hissed and fell back, scratching at its own eyes. A few moments later, after snorting and snuffing its nose and mouth clear, it was now fully enraged.

Chös came to his feet, holding his belly and visibly pale.

Out of nowhere, the angry Eunia flew toward the beast, screaming wildly. The manticör visibly froze as she assailed it with her axe and wild screams. As the harpy continued her assault, the manticör fell back. It tried to bring its tail to bear, but Aurín stepped forward and with a gliding swipe, taking the tip of the tail clean off.

The monster panicked and rolled over onto its back. Eunia stepped up on top and began to chop the beast open like a rotten log. It stopped thrashing. Eunia stood atop it breathing heavily. She was covered in blood and scratches from manticör quills. She slowed her breath, as everyone stared at her with amazement and fear.

"Chös!" she cried, rushing to him as he collapsed to the ground.

Searn walked up to the form of Ozri and crouched down to check the man's breath.

"He's gone."

Ymbrys pulled Rallia and Aurín aside, instructing them to help him turn the creature over. He took out a hooked knife and began cutting off the long quills that came out of the run of hair along its spine.

Then he turned and said something under his breath to the two humans. They all three approached Eunia and Chös. Rallia and Aurín rushed to grab Eunia, pulling her away from Chös, who was now thrashing with seizures.

Ymbrys tore away the man's shirt, revealing a long, green, puss-filled cut. Taking quills one at a time, he forcefully stabbed them into the flesh around the wound.

"Ophedia?" he called. "You are to bring me my travel pack. Hanen? Get water to a boil. I need fresh, hot, wet cloth, constantly."

Ophedia brought the box, which Ymbrys opened, running a querying finger across several rows of vials and compartments. He lifted a little satchel and reached underneath to pull out a stick. He handed the stick to Ophedia.

"Hold that. When I say, put it into his mouth like a horse's bit."

Then he opened the little satchel made of a pliable but heavy leather. He took a pinch of powder from inside. He opened the mouth of the man and sprinkled it onto his tongue.

Hanen heard the qavyl counting off in his own language. He looked to the girl next to him. "Now, Ophedia."

She reached out to place the stick into Chös's mouth as the man suddenly clamped down on the stick, nearly breaking it in two as his eyes bulged. Drool began to fill his mouth. He arched his back as his face turned red. Then he fell back to the ground, out cold and breathing calmly.

"What was that?" Ophedia asked.

"The powder is waking-powder or yllith. It'll wake a sleeping auroch. But it can also drive someone mad enough to kill them. The stick is called calm-stick or as we call it dedin. It is soporific and calms someone enough to keep them from going mad. Together, they balance each other out. Either way, he's stabilized, if only for now—long enough for the quills to do their work."

He proceeded to replace the first quills with more. The blood around the puncture marks where he stabbed Chös had ceased to ooze green color and began to bleed red.

"Those quills draw poison?" Searn asked.

The qavyl nodded. "They draw out anything."

Searn turned to Rallia, who held down Eunia, still hysterical and fighting against them.

"Does Ozri have any family?" Searn asked.

"Not that I am aware of. He was Macenan, though," Rallia said as an afterthought. "We should build a pyre for him. Even better that we have the body of what killed him. I think they usually burn murder victims with their murderers."

Soon Eunia had calmed enough to watch Ymbrys administering his medicine with interest.

"Rallia," Hanen said. "Let's you, Aurín, Ophedia, and I prepare the pyre for Ozri."

"Wait until morning, Hanen."

Hanen looked up to realize it was now fully dark. They chose watches, though Ymbrys said it was unnecessary. He'd stay up with Chös. Eunia stayed with him, too.

Hanen woke early in the morning. Eunia had fallen asleep next to the fire. Ymbrys sat over Chös, who was not nearly as pale as the night before. The long gash on his belly had been cleanly sutured.

"How is he?" Hanen asked.

"The man will be just fine," Ymbrys said. "Once the quills did their work, I was able to cut away some dead flesh. It was only his skin, fortunately. His insides were not harmed, except by what toxins seeped in."

"So he will live?"

"I hope so. There is no way to know what kind of changes he'll undergo, though. These toxins are said to cause more than their fair share of mental instabilities in survivors."

Hanen walked to the other side of the fire and looked toward the rising sun. Searn was down by the pond dragging logs out of the grass by Ozri's pyre.

"This is going to slow us down, considerably," Searn said.

"Only a day or so," Hanen replied.

"You expect Chös to bounce back that fast?"

"No. But we're a day's walk to Amstonhotten. We'll take him there and find a place we can leave him."

"We'll lose Eunia, too," Searn replied.

"I expect so. Of all of them Aurín is the fastest, anyway. We might be able to make up for some lost time."

He walked back toward his tent, passing by the still bodies of Ozri and the manticör. The man's wounds looked much worse in daylight, and Ozri seemed much smaller than he had in life.

Rallia was gone when Hanen opened the tent, probably out to find wood for the pyre. Hanen packed up the tent and put it away in his bag, making sure everything was ready. Aurín had risen and started boiling water for breakfast.

Soon they had a breakfast of flattened, parched grains and a meager but serviceable pyre ready. They ate quickly and together moved the manticör onto the pile with Ozri's body on top of it.

Eunia stayed with Chös while the others stood around the pile. They remained silent while Searn lit the fire.

"To a fellow Black Sentinel. May he find the soul of his killer in the afterlife, and send it to the Ever-Night." Searn took a stick and cast it on top of the bodies. Each threw an item or two. Hanen took three lír that had come from Ozri's pouch and tossed them on to pay the three-eyed god Wyv to entreat with Ozri well.

While the fire burned hot they broke camp. At Searn's suggestion they didn't burn Ozri's Black Sentinel cloak, but instead used it to create a rig that would carry Chös the rest of the way to Amstonhotten.

"I'd like to help carry him," Ophedia said, approaching Hanen as he finished putting the litter together.

"It's going to be a long walk today," Hanen replied.

"I know. But I feel like I owe him. I might have saved him or Ozri if I had been braver."

Rallia was packing her things nearby. "That was the first time any one of us had faced a creature like that. If there is blame to bear it's something we all share."

They went through Ozri's possessions and divided them. The only thing of sentimental value was a small doll made of tied-up cloth.

"I had a doll like this when I was a child," Ophedia said. "They gave them out at orphanages."

"Were you an orphan?" Rallia asked.

She nodded. "I wasn't even left at the orphanage. I was taken there by a Nefer after she found me on the street, I guess. I don't even remember my mother. I went to Macena after Suel to find her. Not much good that did me."

"Orphanhood happens to the best of us," Searn said. "I turned out alright." He turned toward the pyre. "I'm going to collapse the fire. Looks like the worst is done."

He went over and kicked at the dying embers. Then he took a log they had left out and levered the whole pile down into the pond.

"I guess no one will be drinking from that water anytime soon," Aurín chuckled. "At least I hope not."

Ophedia and Rallia lifted Chös up onto their shoulders and began walking. Hanen carried Rallia's pack, while Aurín took what was left of Ozri's belongings to sell at market.

25

Mordaun Road

Ever forward, ever on, from falls to sea, ribbon'd Mordaun.

—DÜRANI PROVERB

They walked the day in relative silence. They came to the crossroads leading to Amstonhotten at midday and turned toward it. Within five miles the city appeared as the woods thinned.

They arrived well before dark, and found an innkeeper willing to try reviving Chös. They made the man comfortable in a room, and Hanen paid the man out of Ozri's money, which he was glad he had brought with him. They all took seats at a table in the inn. The serving girl brought them a standard meal, and they ate in silence.

Eunia spoke first. "I will not be continuing with you to Birin."

"I expected as much," Searn said.

"I intend to watch after Chös." She handed Hanen the money he had paid her.

"No," Hanen said. "Keep that. You may need it to pay for additional medical attention."

Then he took out two crowns from Ozri's purse and put them on the table.

She nodded, took the money back, and excused herself. They didn't see her again.

"Chös has found himself a good woman, if he survives," Aurín said.

"He will live," Ymbrys said. "He will not be the same, but he will live."

"Do you have anyone back in Œron?" Searn asked Aurín.

"No. My mother intended for me to marry the daughter of a butcher. She was caught buttering a baker's bread," he said with a light chuckle. "That is why I left home. I joined the Sentinels in Limae."

"Do you have anyone of note in Edi?" Ymbrys asked both Hanen and Rallia.

"I've been too busy with the Sentinels," Hanen said. "So it hasn't come up."

"I haven't given it much thought myself," Rallia added. "I'm pretty particular, so I doubt there would be a man who would put up with my oddities."

"Oddities?" Ymbrys asked.

"Rallia means peculiarities," Hanen said. "She expects everything to be very neatly ordered. All of her things are placed in just the right spot, or she gets up for half the night to reorder them."

Rallia blushed. "I just want what little I have in its proper place."

"It's true, she does only have a few possessions she calls her own," Hanen said. "In the last five years I think I can recall only three or four things Rallia sought out, sparing no expense."

"I'm not someone who needs much," Rallia confessed, "but I want control. A man who wants my time will need to live with very little, and know to keep everything in its place."

"As for me," Hanen said, "I don't need control. I'm always in control of what I'm doing. But I wouldn't mind being valued. Though not by just one person. I feel like I might come to resent it."

"You both sound foolish," Aurín said. "If someone comes to your bed, it's good enough. You'll learn to adapt to them, too. Life is all about change and compromise."

"I guess that means I'm not ready to marry, then. Because I'm not changing for anyone," Hanen said.

"Do you have a gydith?" Rallia asked Ymbrys.

"What's a gydith?" Ophedia asked.

Rallia looked over at Ophedia and opened her mouth, then

turned back to Ymbrys. "Perhaps you ought to explain."

"We do not marry in the qavylli culture. Instead, not long after we are born, we develop an attachment to others born around the same time. We grow up together, hunt together, and know each other better than our own families. Gydith means 'same-water' in your language. We live and die with our gydith."

He sat back, and then started. "Ah yes. You asked if I have one. I do not. The closest I have to a gydith is a cousin. I often consider him my gydith. But he passed out of my life long ago. What about you, young Ophedia?"

The girl turned red.

"She's young," Searn said. "Let's not pull her into conversations of men and bedrooms."

She blushed even redder, but then burst out, hot and mad.

"I'm more than capable of holding my own in the sack, you shunts!" She rose and stomped off up the stairs.

Searn rolled his eyes.

"Let's plan on leaving mid-morning," Hanen said, changing the subject. "We can get a couple of stints in before dark."

They made their way through the market slowly and were nearly at the gates when Aurín pulled them into a tavern and told them all to sit down at a table. He approached the tavernkeep and they exchanged words before he came and sat down.

"As it turns out," Aurín said, "Ozri's little knicknacks he had all over him were worth a bit more than we all expected."

He placed a nice bolt case in front of Searn, and a satchel of black spice seeds in front of Ymbrys. Then he pushed a package in front of Ophedia.

"Those dull red stones he had set in the medallion on his chest were some quality uncut rubies."

He turned to Rallia and pushed a small box across the table. "I found a knife sharpener who gave me this, in exchange for Ozri's silver belt."

Rallia opened the box, revealing a new razor blade with a horn handle.

"The knife he had on him was actually a well-crafted hrelgren blade. I found a hrelgren ink merchant who was very interested in it."

He pushed another box across the table to Hanen, sitting atop a wood-bound hrelgren style blank ledger. Hanen took out and admired the sealed ink phials and nodded his approval.

"These are all nice," Searn said. "But why give these all to us. You could have kept them for yourself."

"You told Ozri, Chös, Eunia, and myself, that whoever made it to Birin would get to split ten gold crowns. Seeing as how I'm all that's left, trading a dead man's belongings and giving the rest of you what comes of it not only seems right, it is the least I could do."

"An attitude like that ought to mean something to the Three-Eyed King," Ymbrys said.

"I should hope so," Aurín said, chuckling.

"Superstitions aside," Searn said, hefting the bolt case and realizing that it was also filled with new crossbolts, "thank you."

"What's in your package?" Rallia asked Ophedia.

Ophedia was peeking inside the packaging. She blushed, and looked bashfully at Aurín. "You were listening when I was talking to Eunia and Rallia."

"I hear lots of things," Aurín said. "Go try them on."

She got up from the table, asked the bartender for loan of a room, and disappeared.

Food and drink came to the table, and they dove in. Ophedia re-emerged, a huge smile on her face. Instead of the tight vest over a cheap and flimsy blouse, she now had on a loose and comfortable wool blouse of wine red. She was walking confidently and stepping around oddly.

"These stockings are so comfortable!" she said.

Aurín stood up and choked down his food.

"Apparently they're Boronii capricör wool, which is hard to come by. Especially these days."

"But six of them?" Ophedia said.

"And the blouse?"

"I'm going to be very warm," she said. "Thank you."

She circled the table, sat, and quickly downed a tankard.

Aurín sat, and gave a wink to Hanen and Rallia.

The road out of Amstonhotten followed the Mordaun River towards Birin, and a pleasant warmth sat on the hills and their backs as they continued their walk north. They could have taken up their old pace and marched, but Searn didn't seem to be in a hurry, so they took their time. The following day, a cool breeze gave them a good excuse to resume their pace, to keep warm and make good time.

Rallia ranged ahead of them as they neared a small town, to

find them a good inn.

"You know, I've never been to Birin," Hanen told Searn as the road turned from dirt to cobbles. "Up and down the road from Garrou to Edi, but I've never taken the time to go there. Even our old master never went there with us. Morriego a few times, as well as Setera and Nemen."

"But not Birin?" Searn said. "Remind me what business your master was in."

"He was a cheesemonger," Hanen said. "But in actuality, he moved precious goods for the wealthy, stashed in his cheese."

"He smuggled it?"

"It took me longer than it should have to catch on. We would roll into town and go to an inn, where some well-to-do lady would buy the cheapest cheese we had for a great deal more than they were worth."

"The cheapest cheese?" Searn said.

"Well, if a guard would stop us, or even the odd thief, they'd be quick to take the more expensive cheese from us, and while we'd put up a protest, we'd let them go. No one ever inspected any closer."

"That's smart."

"It was. Right before you met us, we were able to finish up with Master Verith's contracts, and it set us up quite nicely."

"And he had no family?"

"None mentioned in his ledgers. And he never spoke of anyone. There was a widow he often entertained in Deld. We made sure she got a nice gift from him."

As they came to the inn, Rallia was outside, a broad smile on her face.

"What's that face for?" Hanen said.

"I ran into someone I know. Come on in. The innkeeper is already bringing food to the table."

She led the way in and to a larger table at the back, where a figure sat. Her eyes were bound by cloth, and against the wall leaned a staff, atop which were mounted several rings. Her head was shaved, and the blue cowl that sat on her shoulders was pushed away from her face so she could eat the bread in her hands. There was a tray of tankards in the center of the table, full of dark brown ale.

"A Nifaran?" Hanen muttered.

"I met her at Diono's chapel on my way south," Rallia said. "I thought that since we were going to Birin, as she is, we could escort her into town, as a show of good faith, and to have an ally when we speak to the monks there."

"That's good thinking," Searn said. "Although, it's going to slow us down considerably."

"I'd be interested in knowing how a blind monk has managed to stay ahead of us until now, when she only had a two day's lead on us," Hanen said.

"Nefer Seriah?" Rallia said, touching the monk's shoulder. "I'd like to introduce you to my companions." She turned to the others. "This is Nefer Seriah Yaledít. We met as I was heading down to Edi."

Her frame was covered by a singular grey robe that fit well but allowed movement, and her eyes were bound by pale blue cloth.

"It's a pleasure to meet you all, and thank you for inviting me to join you for a meal," she said.

"You seem to have the wings of your goddess on your sandals," Ymbrys said.

"What do you mean?" Seriah asked.

"These Sentinels I've traveled north with set a good pace. If you met our acquaintance Rallia as she said, on her way to Edi, not three days later we came back to the same chapel. How do you, a humble, sight-bound monk, make so many hundred miles?"

"I suppose it is rather impossible, isn't it?" the monk said. "Two days after I left that chapel, I met with a Paladin riding north from Piedala. Pater Pellian Noss. He was riding north, and offered me a ride. He left me off in Amstonhotten a few days ago."

"Impressive, nonetheless," the qavyl said.

"While I'm perhaps a bit naïve to say so," the monk said, "I don't often meet many qavylli. But then, I'm also sight-bound. So perhaps I pass them by everyday and they don't speak with me. What are you doing so far north?"

"You'd be right to guess I'm an oddity. Though we're not so rare as to not come north. We just prefer our warmer southern climes."

"Master Veronia is a spice merchant," Searn interrupted. "We're escorting him to Birin. Perhaps you'd like to join us? It would ensure your safe arrival, and we'd be honored if you'd allow us."

"Generally, we prefer to travel slowly, so that people can approach us, and we can offer our services," she said. "But I do need to get back to Birin, and there have been several other monks along the road this near to the Capital."

"Then think nothing of it," Searn said, offering a big smile. "Hanen?" he said, indicating he speak with him.

Hanen got up from the table and walked over to the bar.

"I'm a little disappointed," Searn said.

"Why?" Hanen said. "Because Rallia asked her to join us?"

"I understood the entrepreneurial spirit you had when you invited the qavyl. It rankles me a bit that Rallia overstepped her bounds and invited another person to slow us down."

"Rallia and I are equal partners," Hanen said. "You know she doesn't offer many opinions, nor complain about her lot. So when she does do something like this, younger sister or not, I listen. She's rarely wrong."

"So you're not doing this just to entertain her?"

"No," Hanen said. "I trust Rallia's gut more than anyone else in the world. If she tells me to trust someone, I do. If she has qualms about something, she'll say so, and I know to turn around and walk the other way."

"If that's the case, then I do, too," Searn said. "I just wanted to hear that from your own mouth."

Hanen watched Searn turn to the barkeep, and watched his face, to see if he'd shift countenance. He didn't. Searn asked the barkeep for another tray of drinks and waited while the man filled it up and returned with the tray in his arms.

"Now come on. If we're going to go at a slower pace, then there is nothing stopping us from diving deep into these tankards and that ham the barmaid just dropped onto the table."

26

St. Rämmon

A shadow is simply a place that light has not yet been brought to.

—BORONII SAYING

Waglÿsaor had not been built upon the sea, but was hidden from view behind a group of sharp crags. You could not see it from the water, nor could you see it from the trade road that ran from Garrou along the sea toward the jarldoms of Boroni. In fact, if you didn't read the signs on the road, you could pass it and travel into Boroni without knowing you had passed it at all.

The road branched to the north in two directions. One led off to the left toward Boroni, and the other would take them to their destination. The paladinial carts took a hard right and began to circle around the mountains that rose directly up on their left, while the ocean soon came into view below on their right.

Wet ocean tang hung in the air as mist, intermingling with wet drizzle that fell from volatile gray skies, promising soon to rust them in place.

It was a long and treacherous road that led around the edge of the mountains, with the sea crashing against the cliffs below. The carriages just barely fit. Rocks, recently fallen from above, were strewn across the road, forcing them to steer the wagon wheels around them. All was slick with rainwater.

Jined Brazstein rode atop his sleipnir. His tower gorget, obscuring his chin, threatened to fill with water and drown him. His hammer, held at attention, became heavier and heavier, giving him cramps in muscles that had never hurt before. His heavy brow was the only thing that kept the rain that ran down his bald head out of his eyes.

The Prima Pater, usually so jovial, was sullen and on edge. With him rode the now entirely silent Pater Minoris Gui, returning to his own Fortress of St. Rämmon, his failure to stop the Bortali conflict single-handedly written across his face.

Amal Yollis rode not far ahead of Jined. Even he was grumbling in misery. "I pray the Fortress of St. Rämmon is warm. If they don't have a hearth, I might throw myself off this cliff."

The silent twins, Loïc and Cävian rode behind Jined. They continually sighed in their discomfort.

Jined had nearly admitted his own defeat. He had spent the last three weeks on the road from Garrou asking around regarding the teachings of the long-missing blind Paladins, but found nothing. If the fortress had a library, perhaps it would have an answer. If it didn't, he intended to ask the Prima Pater himself. He had requested a chance to meet with him, but the meeting had been pushed back by the Prima Pater's seneschal several times.

They came around a sharp bend. Ahead, Jined thought he saw a light, slowly blinking, continually, rhythmically. He heard someone shout, "The fortress of the sailor Paladin, St. Rämmon!"

The black slate stone fortress, topped with a blinking lighthouse, promised sailors in the treacherous Lupinfang Sea safety, and, to a Paladin of the Hammer, a warm hearth and a bed for the night.

It was larger than a bastion, but smaller than a citadel, housing sixty Paladins. There was no outer wall, but the black fortress rose up directly out of the rock and seemed to grow into the mountain itself. Doors opened. Ruddy light from recesses along the corridor that led into the monastery guttered, begging to be given new air. Jined passed by alcoves to see torches wavering in a way that seemed to speak of their reticence to provide light to anyone save themselves.

They came into a courtyard, more a hall, not exposed to the sky above. The Paladins were shown where to take their mounts.

They were glad to see fresh hay in the stables, saving them the trouble of needing to feed their own mounts. The sleipnirs looked just as relieved to be left alone.

Local Paladins escorted the line of long, weary Paladins and Paladames deep into the heart of the mountain. The Paladames were led directly toward the natural hot springs further in the mountain, while the Paladins were shown the cells where they could find respite while awaiting their turn to bathe.

Jined took out the book he had borrowed from the bastion in Garrou. He continued to run his fingers over the unknown script. Each letter was strange and block-like, made up of individual lines, some short, some long. No curves.

A deep bell rang. Jined put the book back into his satchel and made his way to the hot baths. Arriving, he found there were multiple pools, each large enough for a few men at once. He found one not being used and slipped out of his robe and into the hot water. He almost sobbed out a cry of weariness as his pain faded away. He had to catch himself twice before slipping under the surface.

Two men shuffled in and slipped in next to him. Jined rose to leave when he noticed the older of the two was Pater Segundus Gallahan Pír. His assistant, the Primus Aeger, sat silently next to him.

"I shall let you have this pool," Jined said as he began to leave.

"Nonsense," the old Paladin said, "take your place, Brazstein."

Jined gratefully slipped back in.

"Don't feel any need to rush back to your room, either. I just came from a meeting with the Prima Pater. You'll hear soon enough. We've all been given the rest of the day and tomorrow to do as we please. We've been long enough on the road."

Jined sighed in relief to hear it and slipped deeply into the water.

He closed his eyes and dozed for a time. The other two seemed to be sitting in silence, but when Jined opened his eyes he realized they were speaking to one another in the silent vow's hand language.

"Do you speak the silent language, Brazstein?" the Pater Segundus said.

"I do not, but it is something I feel I must learn."

"What prevents you from learning it? Do you study something else?"

"That is interesting that you should ask," Jined said. "I am in the midst of a quandary. Having the opinion of two scholars might be exactly what I need."

"I am always happy to help with scholarly pursuits."

"Well, I came across a book in the library at the Garrou Bastion. It's a mystery I can't seem to unravel."

"I'm familiar with all the great books. What is this one entitled?"
"Deeper Faith."
The smile on Segundus Pír's face disappeared.
"It doesn't have any written words in it, just raised lines," Jined continued, "and I feel the need to translate it."
"You found a copy of Deeper Faith?"
"Yes."
"I must see this book."

Gallahan stood and wiped himself down with a towel, then pulled his robe over his shoulders. He looked back at Jined and Aeger. "Well? Are you coming?"

Jined moved quickly back to his room with the two scribes now in tow. He slipped inside and brought the book out. Gallahan took it from him, his hands shaking. He felt the cover, and opened it, feeling the first page. He fell back against the wall and began to sob as he crumpled to the floor. Aeger rushed to his side, but was pushed back.

"I had given up hope of ever finding this book. For thirty years I have sought it."

"What is it, exactly?" Jined asked.

"Let us find the fortress's library; we'll have better light there."

They walked through the fortress in silent anticipation and came to the library. It was about the same size as the one in Garrou. Aeger began lighting candles. It had no windows and cloth hung on the walls between bookshelves.

They took the center table and gathered around it. Gallahan touched his fingers to the symbols.

"Hear now the rites of deeper faith, taught by St. Ikhail to Sternovis the Silent and Ferruce Kalida the Blind. Let this be written in the ancient script of the two brothers in arms. Let only those scholarly enough to decipher it, learn these rites."

He stopped and looked up, opening his eyes. His fingers had not touched more than a single line of text.

Aeger sat with an astonished look on his face.

"Here, Aeger, touch the lines, slowly, tell me what you feel."

Aeger felt the symbols one at a time. After five symbols, he went back and touched them again, more slowly. Then he threw his hands up and began signing animatedly. Gallahan simply nodded, a huge grin plastered across his face.

"I don't understand," Jined said, "that was a large body of text to contain in a single line."

"Let me explain. Feel this here." He moved Jined's fingers to feel a word. "This symbol is a single word for 'brother'. Do you know the silent word for brother?"

It was one of the first symbols taught. Jined nodded and made the symbol with his hand. Gallahan and Aeger did the same. "Now feel the word again."

Jined touched it, and it dawned on him. It was the same symbol. The lines equated to fingers. It was the same language as that of the Silent Brothers.

"This language was designed for the Blind and Silent to communicate to one another. Back when there was a sixth vow, those two vows were very deeply aligned with one another."

Aeger continued to animatedly sign, more to himself now, it seemed.

"Aeger is excited because before today, this was a myth. You just discovered something we've speculated on for centuries."

"I don't feel I did anything," Jined said, "but, if you can help me translate this for reading, I would be grateful."

"Brother Brazstein, I would be glad to give you the text. May I have this for a day or so?"

"Please do. If I were to learn the silent language, who should I ask to tutor me? I think it's apparent I need to learn sooner rather than later."

"Ask your fellow guardsmen. Loïc and Cävian are quite good, I've been told. Guards they may be, but they are also scholars."

The following day, he awoke long after daybreak with a panicked start before remembering he had the day to himself.

He dressed in a robe and gorget and left to find food. The storm was still blowing outside, and threatened to tear off the curtains that were bolted over the stone window frames. It left the place cold and drafty.

He found the refectory where the provisioners had left out bread and cold stew. A few members of the Entourage were sitting and eating, including the twins. Across the hall he saw Paladins from the fortress eating by themselves.

"May I sit here?" Jined asked.

Loïc nodded, and stared at Jined, his eyes demanding he say something.

"What?" Jined asked. Cävian was now looking at him, too. "Ah. The news has spread?"

They both nodded.

"Well, did the news also spread that I really need to learn your silent language?"

Loïc rolled his eyes, then nodded and began to gesture in simple signals so he would understand. Yes. You. Learn.

"Can I ask the two of you to teach me?"

They both shrugged. Cävian signed, Tomorrow. Today off.

Jined didn't know what to do with himself. He spent hours walking the halls and familiarizing himself with the place. For a fortress, it was highly defensible, even though it was not intended for war, but instead a sign to the people, offering protection. As a lighthouse, too, it provided protection on the sea itself.

As the day wore on, though, St. Rämmon took on a different light. The face of the fortress, exposed to the elements, was made of black granite. The windows were slits, and wind continually howled through them. The torches recessed in the walls cast ruddy orange light that flickered in the moving air. The remainder of the monastery was cut back into the mountain itself. There was no natural light, so it was perpetually night. The torches further in the mountain were less affected by the winds outside, due to the maze-like corridors.

Chanting echoed eerily through solemn halls. Paladins of St. Rämmon wore their hoods over their heads and walked past in pairs, eyeing the Paladins of the entourage with suspicion. In between each torch alcove the halls were cold and damp.

Eventually, Jined found his way back to the library, which was no easy task. When he arrived at the door, people spoke excitedly within. The scratch of what sounded like hundreds of quills was unceasing. In the center of the room, both Pater Segundus Guess and the Prima Pater stood on either side of Pater Segundus Pír, who spoke animatedly.

"Years, Dorian!" he shouted. "A scribe at Ammar Citadel in Ormach had a single page from this, and it was so faded, the imprints were practically unintelligible. That was thirty years ago!"

"I understand the importance of this. You've explained it all before when you asked my permission to conduct a pilgrimage to Ikhala."

"I still resent you not letting me go," he grumbled.

"Old friend, if you had gone you'd likely be dead now and someone else would be Pater Segundus."

Jined was now fully in the room and stood by the door.

"Were we not all given the day off?" Jined asked as Nichal Guess approached him.

"Yes, but every scribe from the entourage volunteered to do this today. Those from the fortress were conscripted."

Gallahan looked up and saw him there.

"Brother Brazstein!" He moved as quickly as his eighty-five-year-old frame could manage and pulled Jined toward the center. "Prima Pater, it was Brother Brazstein who discovered the text in Garrou and brought it with him. We owe him a great debt."

"Do we owe you a great debt, Brother Excelsior?" the Prima Pater asked.

"Prima Pater," Jined said, "I am but the messenger. Grissone led my hand to find it, because of something someone said to me at St. Hamul. To him let the debt be owed."

Dorian nodded his approval of Jined's comment.

"Prima Pater, you'll find I have a scheduled appointment with you to discuss this discovery. However, as I have found my answers in Pater Segundus Pír, I shall not need you to keep the appointment."

"Nonsense," Dorian said, smiling, "we should keep it, and when the time comes I shall gladly give you a meeting, at which point we can discuss anything you like."

"Thank you Prima Pater."

Jined looked at the scribes. Each had several sheets of paper and worked wildly.

"What are they doing, Pater Segundus?"

"I have been dictating the text of the book, page by page, and they are now copying their work. It is a small book. It may result in perhaps a prayer book's worth of text. Once we're done, we'll have twenty-five or more copies which we can bind and send to the scriptorium bastions. They'll make copies for themselves before passing them along. As I promised, you'll receive a copy of the text yourself."

"I'd like to hear the text read," Dorian pondered aloud.

"Shall we arrange something?" Gallahan asked.

"Yes. Let's give Pater Minoris Gui something to do; he's been under a lot of pressure from me. Nichal, please see that he plans a nightly reading after the meal."

Nichal saluted and left.

Dorian moved from station to station, looking over the scholars' shoulders and nodding approval before eventually leaving.

That evening at dinner they announced the reading. Most ate

quickly and made their way to the now-crowded chapel to listen. Jined took a seat in the middle.

The text had been written as a summary of theological proverbs by the silent and blind founders.

> "If you wish to serve the haughty, humble yourself.
> If you seek to protect the hardened, be pliable."

Jined left renewed after listening to the first two translated pages of the text.

The following morning, Jined was assigned to guard outside the Prima Pater's temporary office with Loïc. When no one was around to see them drop their guard Loïc pointed at things such as walls, torches, parts of his face, and made hand signals for Jined to copy.

Pater Gui arrived at one point, which divided Jined's attention away from learning the silent language, as the Prima Pater began to interview Gui.

Regardless, Jined felt he was starting to add a few words to his vocabulary, and he learned from his eavesdropping that Bortali was refusing the importation of Boronii goods through Bortali lands by enforcing gouging tariffs. The Boronii were still shipping west into Mahndür, and then down into Œron, but the costs to ship through Bortali into Düran and beyond were hurting the southern countries and vilifying the Boronii.

"You understand," Dorian was saying, "that wars break out all the time. And we, the Paladins of the Hammer, do what we can to remedy the situations as they arrive. What I am most disappointed in, is that you didn't warn us; you thought you could take care of a multi-national emergency on your own. We are part of a larger organization for a reason—so we can assist one another."

It was silent in the room for a long while.

"What would you have me do?" Pater Gui whimpered.

Jined heard the Prima Pater scoff.

"Gui, you and I have been travel companions for weeks. It feels like longer. Truth be told, I've lost count of the days. In all that time, I have given you your space, given you time to think and ponder on your error. I am of the Vow of Prayer. It teaches us to be good listeners and to be patient. I have listened, and I have passed the edge of my patience.

"You have yet to make an apology. I would wager a guess that you have yet to ask for forgiveness from Grissone. No. Don't drop to your knees now. It is too late. It is an empty plea if you think I will watch you grovel now. You're a Pater Minoris, for Grissone's sake! I should not have had to do this. I should not be taking you to the Pillory." The Prima Pater paused for some time in silence. "You shall be sent to Pariantür. You're going to be sentenced to the Fortress of Durance, along with the other penitents there."

Jined heard Gui begin to sob. He was blubbering something.

"You've...you've never been to Pariantür?"

"I was...an acolyte at Ammar."

"How did you make Pater Minoris having never pilgrimaged to Pariantür?! You know what? Never mind. That's an entirely different problem. I knew there was a reason Grissone asked that I travel through the Northern Scapes. You've enlightened me, Gui. For that, I thank you. Nichal?"

Jined heard the Pater Segundus grunt.

"I want him escorted back quietly. Let's send two."

"I would choose Brazstein," Nichal said.

Jined's heart sank in his chest.

"No. His journey with us is not yet finished. I think I'll send Hiram. It's time we sent someone of rank back to Pariantür to make some preparations."

Nichal came out, glanced at Jined and Loïc, and left.

Loïc gestured to Jined. The most he caught was the word *change*.

Jined signaled back, *Change?*

Loïc thought for a moment. *Big change.*

Jined nodded.

Not long after that, Pater Minoris Hiram van Höllebon arrived. He was Pariantür's chaplain, and the Prima Pater's choice to become the Pater Segundus of the Vow of Prayer when Dorian passed away. He was the Prima Pater's disciple, and his word often held great weight when he spoke, which was little. Adjutant Jurgon Upona arrived soon after and set up to record van Höllebon's orders. They discussed for some time before settling on Brother Excelsior Arrat, a provisioner whose health had not fared well in the cold climate.

Someone came to the door and looked out. Jined found himself looking at the head of Dorian Mür sticking out of the doorframe.

"Ah. Brazstein. And Cävian? No. Loïc. Please escort Sarren Gui to his quarters."

Dorian turned to reenter the room, then turned back. "Also, I have no doubt you've both heard much of what has been said here today. I ask that neither of you say a word about it." He looked at

Loïc for a moment and chuckled. "Of course I know I can rely on you to not speak, Brother Loïc. Perhaps you could not share the information with anyone else, words or otherwise?"

Jined and Loïc escorted the newly dubbed penitent Gui to his cell. At some point, the Prima Pater had taken his cordons from him. It marked him as no longer having any rank. Jined had never heard of such a thing ever happening—certainly not to such a high-ranking Paladin.

When Jined and Loïc returned, they had been replaced by Amal Yollis and Valér Queton.

"The Prima Pater left with Brother Cävian and Pater Segundus Guess to pay a visit to the city," Amal said.

Jined turned to leave, but Loïc put a hand on his shoulder. *Now we learn.*

They found a room near the lighthouse tower with several large windows. Loïc began pointing to features in the landscape nearby and showing him the words.

Jined had always considered himself a decent learner. Remembering the words was not the problem now, it was his fat fingers trying to make the shapes. He became increasingly frustrated, and could tell that Loïc's own patience was being tested.

"I think that's enough for the day," Jined said.

Loïc nodded and signed something Jined did not understand. Loïc pointed out over the sea. They spotted an odd flock of creatures harassing some smaller sea birds. From a distance, Jined thought they looked like wyloths—nasty little simians with wings for arms, but those were too small to ever gain proper flight. They usually leapt and glided above the ground, harassing animals, sleipnirs, and men. These were in full-flight and larger.

"What are those?" Jined asked.

Loïc signed a word. Jined stared at it and turned back to the creatures.

"Those are saverns." A Paladin who was looking to be about his business, heading to man the lighthouse, had stopped and looked with them toward the open sea. "Larger than those common nuisances, wyloths, but not as big as the wyverns of the far south. Just as nasty, though. Watch, they live in the cliffs above us. You'll get to see them return to their roost."

The creatures circled for some time before turning their attention back toward the mountain, flying toward it. They got closer and began picking at one another. They had long mouths and manes. One opened its mouth wide, like a serpent, and screamed at another. Their arms were leathery wings, and their hind legs bent forward and back, ending with feet that resembled hands. Their long tails whipped around behind them. They were certainly nastier looking than the small wyloths that hunted across the plains.

Everyone had been harassed by a wyloth at least once in their life. Jined couldn't imagine being bullied by something three times larger. They flew straight at the lighthouse above them, screaming in rage at the tower before disappearing up into the lofty heights of the shale mountain.

The bell pealed and counted off the hour. Jined looked to see that the light of the sun was dimming. Dinner was approaching. They had been running the lesson for over four hours. He made his way on his own, Loïc falling back to take his own time. By dinner, the Prima Pater had not returned, but he had sent back fresh food from the market.

They ate their fill and filed into the chapel once more to listen to the next translated excerpt from Deeper Faith. This time it spoke of readying your mind through meditation on the words of Grissone, and by serving others. Lesser Vows were mentioned, similar to penitentiary vows, suggesting that they be taken not as punishments, but as voluntary prohibitions to ready oneself. It was the talk of everyone as the evening ended. Jined overheard Pater Segundus Pír mention something about how this may be the earliest historical reference to the Lesser Vows and how they had been bastardized into the modern "philosophies."

Jined considered these calls of faith from the book, and felt a nudge at his heart. He was reminded, too, of the final words the Paladin had said, regarding the rose.

"She sees now a rose whose petals wilt.
    She sees now a vine that has been cut.
        Prepare, then, a hedge of thorns.
    And be vigilant as a dwov watches over her nest."

He would need to speak to the Paladames soon, if not on the morrow, but it could wait. The nudge on his heart told him it could wait.

27

Lesser Vows

Thy bones infused with faith shall stand firm. For just as the horde of blood washed over us and stood we there upon that rock, so too shall thy rock be found to stand upon. Make thyself a bastion upon a rock such as that was. For there, Pariantür stands as witness and proclamation of that fateful time.

—GOSPEL OF ST. IKHAIL 22:5

The next morning, Jined awoke to a flurry of activity. Cävian came and woke him. *Duty. Now.*

Jined rose, dressed, and made his way to the chapel. There, the Prima Pater, always calm, always jovial, was pacing the center, fuming. Both Pater Segundii looked on. None looked like they had slept.

"What kind of a fool do they take me for? How much ground have we lost due to Gui's foolishness?! First that fool of a King Vorso more than wasted my time, and now Duke Ergis is putting rocks in the mill and calling it grain."

Everybody watched him silently. Gallahan Pír stepped forward. Dorian spun to look at him.

"Prima Pater. You have an audience. Can we sit down and discuss this?"

"Very well. Everyone of Primus or higher stays. The rest of you, leave. Guards, man the doors. I don't want anyone but you eavesdropping."

Jined and the other guards left and took their posts down the halls that surrounded the room. Jined was assigned a side door to himself, in view of the twins at the next door. Jined was able to hear what was said, though the way the twins signed to one another it seemed as though he was the only one who might actually be able to pick anything up.

The leadership on the other side of the door, by Jined's reckoning, would number ten. He could hear them moving chairs and benches around into a council of sorts. Everyone worked in whispers. Then, they all sat. Pater Segundus Pír opened the meeting.

"Aeger, you will act as secretary and record the proceedings. All others bear witness to the meeting. Let it be titled the Rämmon Council, Hrelgren Imperial Year 2225."

Then, he proceeded to name off those present.

"Let me first begin by saying that I am proud of each and every one of you," Dorian spoke softly, more like his usual self. "I personally asked each of you here for a reason, and you have fulfilled my hopes and dreams admirably. Klamm, Yunt, Polun, you have seamlessly taken care of our finances and food. I greatly appreciate it. Gallahan, your work, as always, is perfect, and the discovery of this holy book, hidden right under our noses, may very well justify the whole trip. Nichal, your guards have performed impeccably, and against the vül, most notably.

"Primus Cautese, we could not have made this trip without your preparations. Your ability to work between nations is the reason you are the Primus of Internal Affairs. Let it be known, I hold nothing against you in this situation. Secrets kept from you were kept from all of us. Had we even the slightest inkling of what had gone on here, I would have sent you ahead months ago. As it were, we've all walked into what is most certainly a war zone, and we were ambushed in the political arena. Let me explain, and I will keep it short."

Several chuckled at this.

"Bortali and Boroni are on the verge of war. Bortali has plenty of exports, but in a bid to strengthen their coffers, they raised importation taxes. It seems the jarls of Boroni would have none of it, and cut down on exports into Bortali until they lower the taxes, sparking a fire of anger on both sides. It seems we're on the verge of another Hraldor-Temblin level conflict. We must staunch the blood flow from this metaphorical wound before further injury can be caused.

"The problem is, the country of Bortali is practically a nation of city-states. Each city controls its own surrounding area, and not much further. The wilds here are primeval. We might have seen a bit of that, had we traveled our originally intended route. As it was, we had to follow events through word of mouth, and that word is the vül are growing out of control. Men who live in the wilds, allied it seems to those foul creatures of Kos-Yran, are beginning to act up. And thanks to the poor and uneducated moves of our local Paladins here, our entire order is compromised in the eyes of the people.

"Thus, as a result, I have decided we will be enforcing a redistribution. Regardless of their track record, every Paladin in Bortali will be sent to Pariantür, and the Paladins from other places, most likely from Pariantür itself, will be sent out to replace them.

"Gallahan, I ask you to begin preparing Letters of Passage. We'll need approximately one hundred. Their first destination will be to arrive at the Citadel of St. Hamul. There, temporary guardians from the citadel will be sent out while awaiting those from Pariantür to arrive. I intend to send a message back to Pariantür before the Paladins we're sending back can arrive. When we visit the Crysalas temple at Precipice, the Matriarch Superioris can convey a message between the Oracle there and the Oracle near Pariantür."

There was a long silence while the orders settled in.

"Prima Pater," Nichal said, "that will leave the Northern Scapes, which you've said are on the verge of war, without any protection from us."

"I intend to proffer a deal or two with the jarls. That should help. I only hope they are more reasonable."

"Prima Pater, if I may," came the airy, oratorial voice of Beltran Cautese. "I request to stay in these lands to help with the turnover, and the development of an alliance, however temporary."

"I expect that is what will happen," Dorian said. "However, I won't have you stay here. I need you to travel with us at least to Donig. You can get a feel for the political climate and have a better chance at brokering peace. Primus Glynn is already working in Garrou to establish friendship with the king. We'll need that if we are to make any headway."

"We need to open the entourage coffers for this." Primus Dikun Polun had a tight, dry voice, like a coin purse that had never been opened.

"We will ask the Paladins being sent here to bring gold, and I also plan to use the money from the local coffers to pay. While I hold Penitent Gui as a primary contributor to the problems here, I hold all the ranking Paladins stationed in these lands at fault. Anyone could have told us."

Jined heard a commotion from down the hall near the front door to the room. A knock came to the main door.

"Nichal, see who feels the need to interrupt us."

The door creaked and then shut.

"It's the Paladins from St. Hamul," Nichal announced. "They've arrived!"

"Very well. Guards, open the doors."

Jined gave a sigh of relief and opened his.

Through the main doors walked Primus Jamis Zoumerik, the man who had brought Jined into the folds of Pariantür in the first place. Dane Marric and Etienne Oren stood beside him, along with twenty other Paladins.

The Prima Pater rose from his seat at the table. As he came around to the edge of the two stairs that led up to the platform, Zoumerik dropped to his knee. The Paladins behind him did the same.

"Prima Pater Dorian Mür," Zoumerik said, "you have called and we have answered. Our hammers are yours."

"Thank you, Primus Zoumerik. I am glad you have arrived so quickly. Was the ride hard?"

"We traveled through Nemen, Düran, and up through the Tremelar pass to reach you. Nothing could keep us from you. Your two messengers," he gestured to Dane and Etienne, "are to be commended. They arrived ready to fall over dead, and yet they were more than willing to journey back with us."

Dorian came down and took Zoumerik's hand. "Grissone blessed your trip."

Zoumerik simply nodded. Looking around he said, "I hope I wasn't interrupting an important meeting?"

"No. I had said enough, and you and I have much to speak of." Dorian turned to the rest. "We all have our duties to perform. Let us be about them."

Pater Segundus Pír approached Jined. "Brother Brazstein, if you will come to the library tomorrow evening after the reading, I expect to have something for you."

He said nothing more, though it excited Jined. He turned to

leave, and noticed among the twenty Paladins the one who had led him to find the book in the first place. He pushed his way toward him.

"Brother Paladin," he said.

The Paladin nodded back. "The way was long, and it is longer still."

"Another verse?" Jined's concentration was broken. His intention to tell him of the discovery would, it seemed, have to wait. "Quatrodox 19:17—'Long may be the road, but every step defines the one before, and gives purpose to what comes next.'"

The Paladin nodded. "Know ye the steps of faith?"

"Ah. Ikhail's Testimony. The next line is…'Choose the way. Take the vow. Draw from Hope. Seek Grissone.'"

"What we seek is found. What we seek is seen."

"Brother Paladin," Jined said, "you are a fascinating mystery. You know the scriptures so well. May I ask a question? Will you answer in truth?"

The Paladin nodded.

"You gave me the scripture about seeking deeper faith. Grissone led me directly to the book."

"His ways are lofty and they always lead to the truth."

"Yes. Oh. That is from the Quatrodox as well. Now, what did you hope I would learn from that book? Or how did Grissone lead you to guide me to the book? What do you suppose he intended for me to learn from it?"

"Ikhail spoke unto Grissone and asked him his will, and from the sky came a bright light. And Ikhail saw the way. For it was Holy."

The Paladin turned and began to walk away.

"Brother Paladin, what is your name," Jined called after him.

The Paladin turned around and winked. "Aquila-Malleus 54:8."

Before dinner, Nichal gathered the guards together. They all stood in an antechamber of the chapel.

"The Prima Pater asked that I inform you that we are leaving in three days' time. So please make sure your armor is polished and your gear is packed. Otherwise, you'll not really be needed unless requested. Do not consider these days to be used for idleness."

Both evenings' readings of Deeper Faith prescribed the study of scripture, time spent praying, and singing hymns. The second evening ended with the beginning of a list of rarely spoken-of Lesser Vows. Jined found himself distracted, watching as Dane

Marric ate up the text. Etienne now sat with him, taking his own copious notes. As Jined turned his attention back, Gallahan Pír was finishing up the reading.

"Speak then in scripture only, drawing yourself closer to the words of Grissone," Gallahan read.

Jined immediately thought of the Paladin, whose name he still did not know.

"Or let thy hair grow out, but only as a hermit, for this will show a bad appearance, and it is a Vow of Secret Service to Faith."

The idea of hermitage intrigued Jined. Growing up, he heard of hermits of Aben, but never of Grissoni ones.

"Be one of service, accepting any request made of you, so you may be humbled. And lastly, isolate yourself, so that you may center yourself on the truths of Grissone."

After the reading, Jined did as he was instructed and went to the library. There, Gallahan sat alone, working over a sheet of parchment and a booklet.

"Brother Brazstein," he said, not looking up, "please, take a seat."

Jined took one at a drafting desk. A page there was half complete. Others nearby looked identical.

"Does the translation proceed well?" Jined asked.

"It does. I apologize, Brother. Please give me just a few more minutes of quiet. I am almost done with my task."

Gallahan took the page and moved over to another table.

"Come and assist me, Brother Brazstein."

Gallahan placed a stack of pages upon the desk and leafed through them, nodding. He reached for a large leather hammer and began to pound the stack of pages. After a while, he took the stack, moved to a stool, and took a seat. Placing the pages up against tall rods of what seemed like a bleached and waxed leather, he instructed Jined to hold the pages in place so they wouldn't slip. Pulling out a needle and thread, he began sewing through the pages.

"I'm tired, Jined," Gallahan said as he finished his work, "but proud of what I've accomplished. Your book is done. Take a look over at the table by the window."

A package sat there. Jined took it and brought it back to the Pater Segundus.

"I have been working to translate ahead of the others. You are to receive the first bound copy, and this one I am working on now will go to the Prima Pater."

"Thank you, Pater Segundus." Jined held the book, running his hand over the cover. It was decorated with a blue dye. He lifted the new leather to his nose and breathed deeply.

"Do be gentle with it, especially for the next week as the glue sets."

"I will. I cannot thank you enough." He paused for a moment, carefully leafing through the book, and came to the page read during the reading earlier.

"Pater Segundus? The reading today, it spoke about the 'Lesser Vows' as we often call them."

"Yes. From them we drew both the penitentiary vows and the philosophies."

"There are a few I didn't know existed."

"None were a surprise to me. But then, I'm well-versed in all the great books. Each major vow tends to adopt one or another."

"I'm curious about two of them."

"Oh? Thinking of taking a Lesser Vow, are you?"

"Well, yes. I feel Grissone drew me to the book for a reason, not only for the title, but for its meaning: to draw me to a deeper faith."

"And what is it you wish to attain with this deeper faith? Do you find your faith lacking? Have you not performed miracles?"

"Is it not the nature of faith to always be lacking and ever drawing nearer to it?"

"Well said."

"And no, I have never performed a miracle. But I don't feel as though I am lacking for it. I am as astonished every time I see one as I was the first time."

"Very well. What vows were you curious about?"

"Well, the first is more curiosity than interest."

"You are going to ask about the hairy hermits."

"Yes. Does anyone still practice it?"

"Interestingly enough, yes. The Blind Paladins often adopted it as a Lesser Vow. It's why we lost the last Blind Pater Segundus; he went off on a hermitage and never returned. More recently, after the Protectorate Wars, many left to the mountains together to form hairy hermitages, although they were not blind. I have known perhaps only two Paladins in my lifetime who took the vow since then."

"That is interesting. Thank you."

"And what is the other Lesser Vow?"

"The Vow of Compliance," Jined said.

"Ah. Yes. That is an interesting one. What did you take it to mean?"

"Well, I only have the passage read tonight to go off of: accept any request."

"Yes. It's an interesting one and we often try to dissuade anyone from it, because it is not only very hard to withstand, but also, it is a vow one must keep secret or others will abuse it and ask much of you."

"What is entailed?"

"Exactly what you said. Someone asks something of you, and you are vowed to not refuse, unless it is immoral. If they ask you to carry things, you would say yes. Even if they ask you to give them food, you must."

"That is rather harsh, isn't it?"

"Yes, but no harsher than the rigidity of those of Chastity, who take on the philosophy of the Chaste Mind and refuse contact with any member of the opposite gender."

"I would like to take the vow. It feels right. Grissone asked me to take a step into deeper faith."

"Perhaps you should read the entirety of the book first?"

"I could, but if the entire book is intended to develop a deeper faith, then why not take as many steps as I can?"

"That sounds reasonable enough. As your superior, I can bear witness, and I shall keep it secret from all but the Prima Pater."

Jined dropped to one knee.

"Brother Excelsior Jined Brazstein, do you swear to take on a Vow of Service for the time of one month?"

"I swear."

"Then let no request of you, within moral reasoning, be denied. You are so vowed."

"So be it." Jined rose and clasped hands with the older Paladin. "Thank you, Pater Segundus."

"No. Thank you, Jined. Young Paladins like you give me hope that we shall continue to thrive as an order. Stay true to the faith."

Jined saluted and left. Dane Marric was approaching the door.

"Good evening, Brother Brazstein," he said.

"Good evening, Dane. The trip went well for you, it would seem."

"It did. It did. The chance to get away for a time and just

concentrate on my faith with Grissone was reinvigorating. Brother Etienne Oren was a worthy companion."

"Very well," Jined said, turning to leave.

"Brother Brazstein," Dane said, stopping him. "I was going to deliver this letter to Pater Segundus Nichal Guess, but if I might make a request of you to do so, I would be grateful."

Jined thought over the work he had to do, and polishing he needed to accomplish, as the weather had started forming rust on his armor. That, and he would have preferred to not help Dane with anything. He looked back to Dane's still extended hand and recalled his new vow.

"Very well, I shall deliver it."

Dane smiled a smug look and handed him the letter. It bore a seal he did not recognize.

He delivered the letter with little thought and went back to his room, and began the long process of polishing his armor, keeping at it well into the night.

28

Disrepair

My lord, please reconsider my request. We uncovered the hidden temple, best described as a coven, and captured ten women. Through dark means eight of them escaped. The remaining two were soon let go before I could question them, due to connections with your esteemed mother's household. I fear they have spread lies from the top of society down to the bottom. If women are given the freedom to do as they see fit, they may plot to topple us from our pantheon-given authority. Please allow me to continue my investigation and root out further hidden vaults of the heretical Crysalas.

— LETTER FROM LORD GRAVVA OF WAGLŸSAOR TO DUKE YORGON, EXECUTED THE FOLLOWING YEAR FOR COLLUDING WITH VÜL TRIBES AND HAVING MULTIPLE WIVES IN SEVERAL BORTALI CITIES

The road to St. Rämmon had been long and tiring. The usually stoic Paladins had resorted to incessant grumbling, and the sisters were no better. Katiam was relieved to hear that they would be escorted to the baths St. Rämmon was famous for as the Paladins saw to the sleipnirs.

They dismounted and walked single file behind the Matriarch as they made their way deep into the mountain. As they came to the entrance to the baths, the servants had disappeared.

"You have until the bell tolls," Sister Upona said. "Then you will follow Captain Smith as we make our way to the Crysalas Societas Vault in Waglÿsaor."

They quickly filed in, stripped down to their under gowns, and slipped into the water. Any other day and they might have chatted idly. The weeks of travel had not been kind. All soaked in silence.

The bell chimed and a collective groan came from the sisterhood.

They rose from the water and slipped into clean peasant frocks. They took up their armor, bundled into packs, and followed Captain Smith through the back halls of St. Rämmon.

"Move quickly," Captain Smith said.

Alongside her walked the now permanently morose Astrid Glass, and one of the newest members of their entourage, young Little Maeda, who might have been more cheerful than Astrid ever was before she lost her brother, Killian.

They walked one-by-one past the kitchens bustling with dinner preparations and came to a set of stairs. They took a downward spiral leading far under the monastery, a cold draft blowing over them from below. They came to the bottom to find Esenath standing with another woman. The hall opened out into the dark sky beyond, with ocean waves beating against the cliffs. The woman held a rope in her hands; the other end ran through a ring set into the ceiling.

"Where are we?" Little Maeda asked.

"You are below the commodes that let out onto the cliff face," Esenath shouted through the rain that splattered around them in the exposed arch.

"You will need to trust us," the other woman shouted as Katiam approached. "Are you afraid of heights?"

Katiam shook her head. "Not particularly. Why?"

"Good, though you'll still likely scream. You can put a rag in your mouth if you need to."

They tied the rope to Katiam's belt and checked that it was secure.

"Katiam," Esenath said, her face wet with rain. "You'll need to jump."

"I'm sorry, jump?!"

"Yes. It's the only way to take the secret path."

Katiam walked to the edge. "I don't know if I can..."

Esenath didn't wait, she shoved Katiam out the door. She fell ten feet before the rope went taut and she swung back to slam against the cliff. Except instead of hitting the wall, she kept going. Sets of arms grabbed her, stopping her from going any farther. She stood shakily, looking out into the rain, the rope rising up into the sky. She turned hesitantly to see two other women smiling broadly at her.

"That was exciting, no?" one of them asked.

Katiam couldn't bring herself to smile, still reeling from her fall.

Instructed to wait, soon Astrid came down from above. She did not panic, keeping the same dead look on her face as before. The two of them continued down the hallway. A squeal of fear and excitement shot down the hall behind them as Little Maeda came to their side of the path.

Katiam looked back to see her shaking, but with a look of glee plastered across her face. She rushed to join them, wiping her soaked face and hair with a hand.

"That was fun," she said.

Katiam shook her head. "I hope we don't have to do that again."

They moved quietly through the tunnels and came out in a large cavern-like opening. The Matriarch waited there with another Paladame and her scribes.

Esenath soon joined them, completing their numbers.

"This is the Abbess Krinna," the Matriarch said, introducing a woman with strong arms and a high hairline. "She has a Crysalas Societas Vault sponsored by the local alewives. We'll be staying at their vault for the next few days. Then we will eventually meet with the tallow-wives."

"And what of the flower-wives?" Little Maeda asked.

"It is unlikely you will be allowed to visit their vault," the abbess said. "They are quite secretive. Their vault was almost discovered by the duke of Waglÿsaor fifteen years ago. They are very distrusting now."

"How long do you expect it will take us to reach your vault, Abbess Krinna?" the Matriarch asked.

"It is perhaps an hour's walk."

"Then let us go. I am tired and should like a good night's sleep before we review your mission here."

It was an extensive set of tunnels. The countless halls and moldering double doors led to side chambers just out of view, indicating just how large the place was. Perhaps it once housed a whole city. It made Katiam wonder more about the history of Waglÿsaor, and how people could forget about what lay beneath them.

The Abbess stopped them as they came to a space. Only their

candles lit the calm, breezeless dark.

"Move slowly and make no sounds until after we pass through this next space. Noise made here is rumored to travel into some homes up above, and we'd rather not alert anyone to the presence of this place."

They moved slowly across the floor. Katiam was reminded of the old writings that spoke of the pogroms that had forced the sisterhood into hiding centuries ago. Perhaps tunnels under cities like these were what first hid them. Perhaps a whole community of women once existed down here. Now the tradition continued, but in a much different environment—a sisterhood aimed at hiding the downtrodden and those harmed by ones who should love their wives, sisters, mothers, daughters.

They came to a large door. The abbess approached and tapped lightly on the brass plate in the center. It opened. Not with a boom, but in silence. They walked into a vault built just like the one in Garrou. The walls of this one were lined with barrels.

There was no great crowd of women assembled and visiting in the middle of the night. They were guided down a side hall and shown beds. Katiam gladly obliged, setting her pack down on the floor and falling into the bed. She and her companion, who would sleep in the bed next to her, did not speak nor light a candle. She wasn't even sure who shared the room with her. They both fell asleep in the comfortable, pitch-black darkness.

There was no call to wake, so Katiam wasn't sure how long she had slept. She only knew that she felt more rested than she had in weeks. She sat up and tried to see if the sister in the other bed was still asleep. She finally heard a long, deep breath. She felt around for her boots, pulled them on, and went to the door, coming out into the hall. She lit an extra candle stacked in one of the alcoves and went in search of the kitchen to prepare an easy breakfast for the Matriarch, who would likely sleep for several hours still.

Eventually they assembled. By the reckoning of the abbess, they were meeting at midday. All sat in the pew benches of the chapel of Crysania. A stained glass rose window, set with blush-pink glass, was back-lit by candles. It was one of the simpler chapels Katiam had seen. The Matriarch was given the abbess's seat at the front, while the hostess took a simple wooden chair next to her.

"It has been a hard couple of months," Abbess Krinna said. "As you no doubt know, Waglÿsaor is built on the trade of others. The city's biggest trade is the moving of goods, carting them into and out of Boroni. Thus, the embargo has hurt. Even more so since the city needs the imports of others to survive. Some of the goods are more readily available from our neighbors across the border than from nearby villages, to be honest."

"And this has cost you money in the sale of ale?" the Matriarch asked.

"No. Financially we are doing better than usual. The men have nothing better to do now than drink. But that means they drink too much—spend too much. We've had to try to reduce how much we are serving, since the men get violent when they are bored and drunk, but they are also going too quickly through their coin. It has caused the women of the city to seek alternate means of providing for their families."

Katiam startled as Captain Sigri Smith scoffed loudly. The Matriarch also seemed to understand and was shaking her head in sorrowful disappointment.

"This is not the worst that has happened, though," the Abbess continued.

The Matriarch looked up.

"The city has also been hit by a blinding malady. It most often affects children, but others have been struck by it. It hit Boroni last winter and then spread here."

"What are the symptoms?"

"Some of our physicians are calling it Day-Blind. It causes a dimming of the vision. Actually, that is not the best way to describe it. Blurring, perhaps. In light it is worse, causing a washing out of the world into whiteness. Those who suffer from it are more comfortable in darkness, and they seem to be able to see as well as anyone else at night. During the day they are very blind."

"How many have come under the effects?"

"I have seen perhaps three dozen individuals who have suffered the effects. But that could mean hundreds are suffering from it, if not more."

"What have you heard from the other vaults?"

"We speak with the other vaults regularly. Well, I should say, we receive word from the flower-wives, though they do not openly communicate with us. The tallow-wives are much more communicative."

"And do each of you interact with specific levels of society? In Garrou this is the case."

"No. The city is fairly uniform. Yes, there are levels of society, there always are, but almost everyone lives alongside one another."

"I expect that we shall be staying here for a time," the Matriarch said. "Please send messages to the other vaults. I should like to visit the tallow-wives in three days. And if the flower-wives wish to meet us, they are welcome to seek us out."

Over the course of the three days in the vault they reviewed the finances of the alewives, who were doing even better than they had reported. The Paladames under Sigri Smith reviewed their safety procedures. Fedelmina and Sabine Upona looked over their finances, and the rest of them served those who came to seek refuge.

"We'll be visiting the tallow-wives," the Matriarch informed them during an evening meeting. "They are not connected to the underground tunnels, so we'll be making our way through the city. The abbess has warned us to be cautious and move quickly. Those not seen to be about their business are often accosted by guards who have nothing better to do."

They left at dawn the following day. Katiam walked arm-in-arm with Astrid Glass, who, as usual, walked solemnly with little remark. The streets were empty of people as the sun rose behind the mountains that ringed the city. A few candles burned in windows but did little to warm the air. A few women stepped out of homes, holding bundles in their arms. From one of the windows a man peeked out and watched one walk away, calling out with lewd remarks. Another woman passed them, glancing up once, then back down. Her face was dark with shame and tired from no sleep. She had painted her eyes, now smudged with tears. The second woman they passed stole a glance at Katiam and Astrid, though her face was full of anger rather than shame. She too carried a bundle of clothes under her arms.

"Astrid?" Katiam asked. "I usually expect housewives to be about their business this early, but not to take a single set of clothes to laundry."

"They aren't going to do laundry," Astrid said, "and they aren't about their business. They're finished with their business, and they're headed home, with yesterday's clothes under their arms."

"What are they doing away from home this early in the morning?" It dawned on Katiam what Astrid meant. Her ears began to burn. "Is...is that what the Abbess meant by the women here seeking other means?"

Astrid nodded.

"That's awful!"

"That's what happens," Astrid said. "Our father came to Pariantür from a mining town in Mahndür. When the mine failed, and the men waited for new mines to open, the women sold themselves to provide for the children. My father was a product of that sin. He came to become a Paladin, but ended up a glazier providing for Pariantür instead."

Katiam shook her head. Her heart broke each time another door opened. Far too many did. Far too many women stepped out into the streets with shame, anger, or deadness in their eyes.

They passed away from the streets filled with homes and walked into a district filled with workshops and warehouses. A large stone building stood at the edge of a wide square. It was derelict, though Katiam could see signs of life moving in the alleys nearby. Inside the open front door she saw a figure who stepped out—Sigri Smith—waving for them to approach.

Katiam urged Astrid to turn toward the building.

"That is not where we're going," Astrid said.

"I know, but Captain Smith is signaling us."

They walked toward the edifice. The stone was pink sandstone, with large glass windows, three stories high. They walked up the three steps to the door. Captain Smith had already disappeared into the darkness. They came into the entryway. All decorations had been removed or vandalized. The captain stood off to one side with Sabine Upona.

"Sister Borreau, Sister Glass," Sigri Smith said.

"What are we doing here, Captain?" Astrid asked. "This isn't where we were told to go."

"No. I stopped here because I remember this place from my childhood. I was raised in Waglÿsaor, after all."

"What is this place?" Katiam asked.

"It was once the Bortali Maritime Academy. It was moved to Garrou twenty years ago. Now it's just an empty shell for vagrants, prostitutes, and drunkards." She pointed the lantern in her hand off toward a corner where several people slept huddled next to one another. "Come. I'd like to see how far it has fallen into disrepair."

"Captain," Katiam said, "we should continue on to meet up with the Matriarch. They'll be worried."

"We won't tarry long."

They moved down the halls. The smell of bread arose, and Katiam remembered they had not yet eaten.

"How well do you know this building?" Sister Upona asked.

"Well enough," Captain Smith said. "My father forged fittings for the academy."

"If the place is derelict, why do we smell bread?"

"I wondered the same thing."

They came to an empty doorframe leading into the servant's halls. The smell of bread was overwhelming. Coming around a corner, the kitchen opened up before them.

There were twenty children within. Some sat huddled together against the walls. Half of them had cloth tied around their eyes. They shielded their eyes from the lantern light. Next to the bread oven, three older girls worked dough into loaves. The oldest, perhaps more a woman than a girl, moved bread into the oven with a paddle. Another girl nudged her and she spun about, wielding the paddle menacingly.

"Out! This is our kitchen, you can't have it. And put that lantern out!"

Sigri lifted her free hand as a sign of peace.

"Please," the tall sister said. "We mean no harm."

A child came out of nowhere, snatched the lantern out of Sigri's hand, and blew out the candle within. The place went dark. Only the dull glow of the oven lit the room.

Katiam heard a rush of movement and was just able to make out the paddle held under the chin of Sigri Smith.

"I said, 'get out.'"

"And I said," Sigri had a tone of firm finality in her voice, "I mean no harm. Put the bread paddle down. I'm a Paladame."

"I'm sure you are," the girl said. "Doesn't mean you have business here."

"No, it doesn't. I would know why you are baking bread in the dark."

"The light hurts most of our eyes."

"They must be Day-Blind," Sister Upona whispered.

"And you're watching out for each other?" Sigri asked.

"None of your business, woman," the girl said.

"We'll be on our way then," Sigri said, "come along sisters."

They left behind the smell of bread and took a turn. They came to a break in the wall, and Sigri, tall enough to look through the crack, stopped and watched for a long moment.

"She's feeding the children. The blind are feeding the blind."

"She was blind, too?" Upona asked.

"Yes. Though as the abbess said, they can see a bit in the dark." She turned and continued down the hall. "Come on."

They came to a long row of smaller rooms. Some of the rooms still had beds within, marking them as former dormitories of the now-defunct academy. A man snuck out of a room up ahead, still trying to pull his trousers on. He saw them and bolted. Sigri took a glance into the room he had come from and took off after the man with long-legged strides.

He shouted out as they both tumbled to the ground. Sigri stood and pulled the man up.

"I swear I didn't know she had a madam!"

"What?" Sigri asked.

"I'll pay, I'll pay!" He reached in and pulled out a handful of coins. "I swear, I thought the girls here were on their own. I'm sorry madam!"

Sigri slapped the money out of his hands. She looked back at the others and indicated they investigate. Katiam followed Upona and Astrid into the room. A girl no older than fifteen sat on the bed. As they entered, she pulled her knees up to her chin.

"Girl," Upona said, sitting down on the bed next to her. The girl flinched. "Don't be afraid. We will help you. We're with the Crysalas."

"I didn't know what else to do!" the girl cried, throwing herself into Sabine's arms, sobbing.

They calmed the girl down, and offered her a shawl, leading her into the hallway. The man was gone, but Sigri's knuckles were red with fresh scrapes.

"We need to take this girl to the vault," Sabine said.

"No! I can't. I have to feed my daughter." The girl was pulling away from Sabine.

"Come with us, and we will retrieve and keep your daughter safe, too."

29

Sister Baker

Make trench upon wood and check palm to water for proper coolness.

Pour out contents, first gently, then roughly, then strive against the dough that forms. Knead in the Keep from the day prior.

If a flat bread is needed for travel, do not knead in the Keep, but save for another day in a jar.

Beat well, while singing the song "Crysania's Tears."

Place in a wooden bowl, covered by cloth, until the midday sun passes over and then turn. Let rise until morn, taking out a palmful of Keep.

Bake until ready.

—*QUEEN OF ŒRON'S BAKERIE*

They arrived at the tallow warehouse built into one of the mountain faces that rose up out of the city, much like the Fortress of St. Rämmon. It had several upper levels, though the majority of it descended into the earth, hiding multiple secret levels dedicated to the Crysalas Vault.

They found the Matriarch sitting with the abbess in front of a fire in the vault.

"Ah, Captain Smith," she said as they entered, "I wondered where you had gone."

"Matriarch," Sigri Smith said. She walked up and knelt down

beside her. "Matriarch, what Abbess Krinna said is more true than we first thought."

"What about, child?"

"The women of the city cannot provide for their families and have turned to selling themselves. The blinding malady is leaving countless children blind."

"What do you propose we do, Captain?" the Matriarch said, her hands folded across her.

"We still have some of the gold from the vül."

"It is true. But we cannot just throw money at the problem. It will be spent too fast by husbands that will question where it came from in the first place."

"The Maritime Academy is abandoned," Sigri said. "It could be purchased by the sisters, and we could do something with it."

"Such as?"

Sigri fell silent.

"Matriarch," Fedelmina said, "as we went over the numbers, I saw that between the three vaults of the city there are a great number of physicians among the sisters."

"I noticed that, too," the Matriarch said.

"A hospital!" Sigri said.

"And would that help?" the Matriarch asked.

"The women who need work could be taught to nurse people back to health," Sabine Upona added.

"I would see it done," Sigri said, "but I would need help."

"You would leave us?" the Matriarch asked.

"Waglÿsaor is my hometown. If this must be done, then who better than I? I could protect the women who come there."

"The men of the city would not take to a woman beating them senseless every time one of them comes seeking their wife."

"No, perhaps not. But I would like you to consider leaving me here."

"I would stay and help, also," Fedelmina said. "I could see the hospital manages its money well to pay the women who work for it."

"Very well," the Matriarch said, "let us consider this. I should like to see this academy. But only after we are done here at the tallow-wives' vault."

The next morning, Katiam was awoken early by a summons from the Matriarch.

She walked into the Matriarch's room. Maeda Mür was sitting

up in bed reviewing a ledger.

"It's practically a mutiny," the Matriarch said as she walked in.

"What's a mutiny, Auntie?"

"Sigri, and now several others want to stay and start this hospital."

"Auntie, it's for the best," Katiam said.

Sigri had spent her time working with Fedelmina, discussing what her vision for the hospital might be. Katiam had tried not to show interest, but she was losing her will to hide it.

"You're being very quiet," the Matriarch said, watching Katiam prepare a plate of breakfast for her. Katiam placed the tinctures and balms in their respective spots and turned back to the Matriarch.

"What was that, Auntie?" she looked up to see the Matriarch staring at her quizzically.

"I said you're being very quiet. You're thinking of the hospital, too."

Katiam nodded slowly.

"Give me the plate, girl," the Matriarch said. "I'm hungry."

"It's a good idea," Katiam said. "With winter setting in, it could take a full year for the Nifarans to act and take on an orphanage that might form under them for those suffering from Day-Blind. It would be an opportunity for the Crysalas to help in the Paladins' effort to stifle the war."

"And if war can't be helped?"

"Then a hospital in a town like this is exactly what is needed. Perhaps I could stay and help. I'm qualified to help the elderly, and I could learn how to care for others on the job."

"No."

Katiam looked up.

"You will attend to me. I need you by my side. Perhaps on the way home we can discuss it. I'd rather you stay with me, for now."

Katiam nodded in defeat.

"We'll be visiting this academy today. I've eaten enough. Take it away."

"After you've had your medicine."

"I took my medicine," the old lady said.

"No you didn't. You may be the Matriarch and my auntie, but I'm your physician. If you're not going to let me stay and work at this hospital, you'll do what I say as your doctor and take your medicine."

"Well," the Matriarch said, with a smile. "You're as snippy as I was at your age after a spat with Dorian. But I suppose I deserve it. Come here, child."

Katiam came and stood next to her.

"Sit," Maeda patted the bed.

"Katiam," she sighed, "you're the daughter I never had. I can't let you go so easily. I love you."

"I love you too, Auntie, and I understand. But please know that I feel inadequate without training from the college, and without a certain purpose serving the downtrodden, as we are called to do."

"I know, Katiam. I know."

Katiam rose. "Now take your medicine so we can get you dressed."

The Matriarch grumbled and did as she was told.

They soon stood outside the Maritime Academy. The Matriarch's arm in Katiam's.

"It's certainly impressive," she said.

"Sigri grew up here and had been inside it as a girl. I think she recalled how grand it was then, and wants to restore it."

"I know. She has not stopped talking about it. I intend to fuel that passion."

They started to walk and the Matriarch stopped, looking to her left. A Paladin with the cordons of a Primus was approaching with two other Paladins riding alongside him. With the street clothes the women wore, they were unrecognizable to the Paladin, nor did Katiam recognize the man.

"Brother," Maeda called as he rode up. He was a handsome Paladin, in the beginning of his later years.

"Good day, lady," he said. "How may I serve you?"

"First, you can come down off that mount."

The Paladin looked a little startled, but did as he was told.

"How is my husband?"

"Your husband?"

"Yes, the Prima Pater, Dorian Mür."

"Ma'am, the Prima Pater has a wife, and she is off on her own mission, I believe."

"And yet here I stand before you. I am she."

The Primus looked at Katiam, who nodded and took out a small silver rose from her satchel as proof.

"Matriarch, I apologize that I didn't recognize you. How could I, though? We have not met."

"I didn't think so. You came with the delegation from St. Hamul, then? Last night?"

"You are well informed."

"Yes, I am. And your name, Primus?"

"Zoumerik. Primus Zoumerik."

"Ah, yes. Dorian has spoken of you. Come along then, I'll need you to escort us today."

"I'm familiarizing myself with the town, as I'll be assigned here for a time."

"Good. Then you're exactly who I need with me today."

The Matriarch started walking with Primus Zoumerik hesitantly following behind. He sent his companions off to find a place to tie off their horses, and then offered the old woman his arm as they walked up the steps and into the building. Sigri stood in the large lobby and waved them over. She saw Primus Zoumerik and nodded curtly.

"Matriarch, please allow me to show you around."

The Matriarch took Sigri's arm and they began the tour. Zoumerik walked alongside Katiam.

"What is happening?" he asked her.

Katiam summarized the discussion from the past several days.

"I see," Zoumerik said as she finished. "It won't work."

"Why is that?"

"There are few trades in Bortali that allow women to run things. Physicians are not one of them."

Katiam didn't respond. She felt slightly offended, and also disheartened that Sigri's dream might not be a reality.

"Of course," Zoumerik said, "if the Fortress of St. Rämmon sponsored it, the city would be more likely to accept the idea."

The Primus's two companions returned and were immediately sent off again to buy food for the day. As they proceeded through the building, they found no men seeking the companionship of women, but orphans running every which way, and those struck with Day-Blind hiding in shadows.

"What would your role be?" Zoumerik asked Sigri as they sat on the stairs and ate bread and cheese provided by Zoumerik's men.

"I would administrate. And I would also defend against those that would cause harm."

"You mean to wear your armor? As a Paladame?"

"Yes. It would send a message."

"Those are bold words, Sigri," the Matriarch said, "the men of the city may not take it well."

"They would take it well enough if she was flanked by Paladins," Zoumerik added, "even more so if she was seen in public with the leader of the fortress-monastery."

"This is true," the Matriarch conceded.

"Let us walk and discuss our hospital then," Zoumerik said, taking Sigri's arm, and walking off down the hall.

"I think they've made up their mind," Maeda said. "I'll have little say from here on out."

"Is Primus Zoumerik the new leader of the monastery?" Katiam asked.

"Dorian shared with me that he intended to have him sent here to make him so, but I don't know if that has happened yet."

They came to the hall leading to the kitchen.

"Matriarch, it might not be a good idea to go further on our own."

"Nonsense. There are orphans in the kitchen, are there not? I can smell the lingering scent of bread on the air."

She forged ahead, pulling Katiam with her. They came around the corner and looked into the kitchen. Katiam could make out some of the children sitting huddled together in a corner. One of the older girls was speaking in hushed tones to the little ones. Katiam could hear her teaching them their letters. As they approached, the girl looked up, and continued to scratch in the black ash she had spread on the floor. After she finished her lesson she looked up.

"Can I make you some bread, granny?" she said. "The oven is still hot from earlier."

The Matriarch smiled and took a seat.

"Why are you here, granny?" she said. "Don't you have any family? Can't your grand-daughter take care of you?"

Katiam opened her mouth to protest, but fell silent as Maeda squeezed her arm.

"We do just fine. But I heard a rumor you make excellent bread, and I had to taste it for myself. Bread is a gift from the gods."

"It is a gift from my own hands, and the people we had to take the grain from." She tore dough away from a large mass not yet risen and began to knead it into shape—deftly folding it into a braid.

"You don't have to steal, you know."

"Of course we have to. No one will care for us. We're worthless and unwanted." She placed the dough onto a paddle, moved over to the oven, and pushed it in.

"Are you a baker's daughter?"

"What does it matter?"

"I've not seen someone your age able to prepare a dough so quickly."

"Yes, well, you'll have to wait a while. The oven is cooler, it will take longer to bake, and it may not rise much, since I didn't give it any time."

"Bread is bread."

"Bread is not just bread," the girl said matter-of-factly. "Flour and water mixed together and thrown over heat is not bread. It's not even food. A bread must be made with skill and love."

They stood there in silence. Another girl, no older than ten walked up.

"Mama Baker," the girl said.

"What is it, Lelah?"

"Jorn found out Kleren is having a shipment delivered tonight."

"Very well. Tell the others we'll make a grain run after sunset."

The girl nodded and ran off.

After long minutes in silence the baker took the bread out and placed it on the table. She began fanning it with a towel.

"Why are you here, granny?"

"I will tell you once you give me bread. Tell me why you are here?"

"Because it's safe. And it's dark. We Moon-Eyes don't do well in the daylight."

"Why is that?"

"Because we're cursed by the Judge who has brought Noccitan to us."

"That's a dark thought," the Matriarch said.

"It's true."

"It is not true. If I have learned anything in this life, it is that suffering happens. When all is done, we stand before Wyv, and he decides if we go to Lomïn, the Ever-Day, or stay in Noccitan, the Ever-Night."

"But why?"

"Let us eat bread," the Matriarch said.

The girl handed the loaf to the old lady. She held it, crunched it in her hands, smelled deeply of the freshly baked flour, and held it up.

"You see in the dark places, Wyv-Thüm. See this girl, who has served an old lady. And my Mistress, the Life-Mother Crysania, make sure your brother sees this, too."

She broke the bread and gave the girl a piece, then gave a piece to Katiam, and kept the last piece for herself.

The smell of the bread filled Katiam's nose, and as she bit into the dense piece it dissolved. It was the most pleasant piece of flat bread she had ever tasted. There was some unknown herb within it that took her to a place she could not name.

"Mama Baker, they call you?" the Matriarch asked.

"Yes, now who are you? That you dare call out the name of the Judge, and to call upon the Life-Mother?"

"This is the most wonderful bread I have ever tasted, Mama Baker. It is a blessing to these lost children that it is they who eat it every day. Yet I feel sorry for the rest of the city who has not tasted it."

"Who are you?"

"Why does it matter who I am?"

"Because I fear you. I fear you are going to take this all away from me, somehow."

"Do not listen to that small voice," the Matriarch said. "It is a lie. Perhaps from Achanerüt himself."

"Stop calling down the names of the gods," Mama Baker said.

"I am more able to call upon them because I have the authority to keep them at bay. Does Sakharn haunt your dreams? Do you fear that perhaps Nifara shall come and take your charges away? Your bread keeps her away. Shall I tell Kos-Yran to stay back, so that his Madness does not fall upon you and leave your mind as blind as your eyes?"

"Stop it. Stop it! You will call down their wrath! You will take all of this away from me, from my children!"

The other children in the room had begun to cry.

"I am not going to take this away from you, child," the Matriarch said, standing up. She held out a hand toward Mama Baker. "I want to give you all of this. I can make this kitchen yours. The breads you make will bring life to the dying and happiness to the sick."

"Who are you? Are you the Life-Mother?" Mama Baker was on her knees now, holding up her hands in a plea. "Please don't take this away."

"I am not Crysania. I'm the next best thing. I am her High

Priestess, the Matriarch Superioris. I would make you Sister Baker. You will make bread here for the hospital we intend to turn this building into. You will have an unending supply of grain and you will never go hungry again."

"I will only agree to this," Mama Baker said hesitantly, "if the Moon-Eyes are my only assistants."

"Agreed," the Matriarch said, helping the girl to her feet.

The Matriarch clutched at her chest suddenly and made a grimace, followed by a smile. She nodded.

"Our prayer has been heard. It seems you need to begin making bread. Much bread. Crysania says that Grissone will need it tomorrow."

30

Day of Bread

Persevere. Fight on. For by your sweat shall your legacy continue to be watered as a flower.

— ANVIL OF FAITH 26:3

The black slate roofs over the white-painted houses and shops of Waglÿsaor stretched out in the distance as the Prima Pater and his guards came to one of the highest points in the city. They looked down on their destination—a city square, with a jagged, sky-fallen slab of iron, that was the namesake of the city. The entourage almoner Stevan Filip, was up ahead on foot, distributing coins to the destitute who seemed to proliferate the place. Near Stevan, the herald Amal Yollis and the standard bearer Valér Queton kept watch, the presence of the standard of Grissone stating this mission was official, providing help to the poor where the duke and his people refused to.

Jined rode barely awake in his saddle, having spent the evening, well into the early hours, polishing his armor, followed by helping clean up a mess at the request of a baker looking for anyone awake, after he burned the day's bread.

The Paladames had not yet returned from their own mission into the city, but as Nichal explained, this was to be expected. They had received a message from the Matriarch to meet them at the city center.

As they approached the wide space, Jined could see a group of people forming up and watching their arrival.

"It seems the word has spread, Prima Pater," Nichal said.

"I expected this may happen," Dorian replied.

They came out of the tight confines of the side streets into the large square. The massive, red-stained slab in the center stood at a steep angle, lodged in the ground, and stank of rust.

A few groups of people went about their normal business, while others moved closer, perhaps wondering why so many Paladins marched together.

"Loïc, Cävian," the Prima Pater said, "please do as we discussed."

Both twins nodded, splitting up and moving along the run of shops that circled the square. They each came to a different shop with a sign for bread hanging out front, and disappeared within.

"Have faith!" Amal called.

The herald had a knack for his role, and he could make his voice heard even on the windiest battlefield. Jined suspected it was a god-ordained miracle, though not one that Jined had ever heard performed in the past.

"Have faith! Grissonc shall not forget the forgotten. He shall feed the weary and give them strength."

People began to gather closer in a small crowd of perhaps fifty. From various side streets Jined saw more poor begin to appear, hobbling across the cobblestones. Loïc appeared from the bakery with his arms full of bread loaves. Behind him, apprentices, the baker's wife, and finally the baker himself, appeared, each carrying the same. His sleipnir followed him as he approached the almoner.

"Guards, dismount, and help," Nichal commanded.

Jined got down, took half of what Loïc had in his arms, and came to stand behind the almoner.

"Bring your mind, hungry for the wisdom of faith," Amal said, "and be fed."

The almoner took a loaf of bread, as long as a forearm, and tore it in three. He walked up to those in the front of the crowd and gave each piece away.

"Go and find ways to do the same," the almoner said to each person as they took the bread.

An energy rose in the square as people realized what was happening. They soon began forming a breadline, taking from the almoner piece by piece. Cävian soon came out with bread from his bakery. Jined saw Nichal speaking with one of the bakers, and the baker's own boy took off running from the square.

The people stood alongside one another. Men, women, children, the poor, the workers. All were speaking to one another in hushed tones, but those who had received bread stood off to the side, talking more animatedly with one another—the act of kindness changing their countenances.

A group of ten men appeared at the back of the crowd. They all wore a faded blue set of clothes made of thick material. Jined had seen a few dressed likewise cleaning the streets with sweeps and shovels. There may have been a large number of poor throughout the city, but Jined could tell the city took pride in keeping itself clean.

The men watched for a time, then pushed their way through the crowd and came to the front, standing at the beginning of the single-file line.

Jined frowned, but his hands were full. He thought to go and tell them to stand back and wait their turn.

Dane didn't hesitate. He shoved the bread he held into Etienne's arms and marched up to them. Dane stood a head shorter than their leader, but looked up at the man without fear. Jined could only hear the tones of the words they spoke to one another. Nichal was growing tense, and opened his mouth to speak.

The men suddenly parted. They did not step aside—they parted. Dane had his hands out, and had moved two men bodily out of the way. The rest were moved simultaneously. An open walkway was created as the men stumbled to the ground. A man stood at the end of the opening. He had a crutch under his left arm, and no leg below. He wore the tattered remains of a military uniform and had a basket held over his back by a sorry piece of rope. Dane walked up to the man and offered him his arm.

They walked to the front of the line together. The men in blue did not open their mouths, but Jined could feel anger rising by their stance.

Dane took a loaf from Etienne and offered the entire thing to the war veteran.

"Grissone protect you. You have already served those less than you."

The man looked up at Dane with tears in his eyes.

"Thank you, Brother," he replied before hobbling off.

"Have you no dignity left?" Dane directed his comment at the men in blue. "The city does not help its own poor and unclean, yet the streets are washed, paid for by coin from the duke, taken from the people.

"'Clean your hearts and then your bodies,' Clio Grissoni 64:9. You dare to pass by a man who has done more than you will ever do. He has fought your enemies so you could continue to sweep your streets. Have you not been paid enough gold to buy your own bread?"

The men looked at their feet.

"The Prima Pater has promised that all will receive bread, and yet you push and shove, and deny it to those who should first be served."

Dane took two loaves from Loïc and held them up. Then he looked at a child. "Are you sick?"

The child shook its head.

"Do you know someone who is?"

The child nodded.

"Then take this loaf and go and share it with them."

The child took the bread and ran off.

"You," he pointed to a woman holding a child in her arms, "take this. No matter your sins, all should have bread. All should share in the grains given by the gods themselves."

He indicated Etienne give her a loaf.

"There." He pointed over the heads of the crowd. A group of people huddled together, cloth tied over their eyes, suffering some form of blinding malady.

"Who shall help them forward so they need not walk alone in the dark?"

Several immediately offered their arms and began to guide the blind to the front.

"Humanity is a brotherhood. Return to your god, Grissone. Serve one another, and strengthen your faith."

He turned back to Loïc and Cävian. "Brothers, pray the prayer of abundance."

"Brother Marric," Nichal said, "that blessing has not been answered in centuries."

"That is because it has not been needed," Marric said. He had a determination Jined had never seen in him.

Nichal looked at the Prima Pater. Dorian nodded.

The twins began signing a phrase over and over again. Jined picked out a few words, and soon recognized the prayer shortly before Nichal and Dorian began mouthing it. Dane began to speak it aloud, and everyone else joined in.

"Our god and creator, your power upon us. Anka, your visage shine down. Strength of the hammer, Pariantür, bestow our wish. Abundance. Abundance. Abundance."

The sunlight broke through the clouds in response and fell upon Dane. Five Paladins appeared from a side street. At the front rode Primus Zoumerik. He saw the Prima Pater and smiled. Driving forward, the crowd parted to make way. One of them led a cart pulled by an auroch. Jined recognized the Paladin as the one who spoke in verse. The cart was filled to overflowing with more bread brought, perhaps, from another end of the city.

An excitement rose in the crowd, and they smiled. They began taking the bread and sharing it amongst themselves.

"This is a day of bread," Zoumerik said, pulling his sleipnir next to the Prima Pater's. "Your wife has asked I meet you here and take you to her. She has much to share with you. The kitchen they took over spent all of today making this bread, saying you would need it."

Dorian laughed. "It seems Grissone has been speaking with his mother and seeing the future. It is well met that you have come, Primus Zoumerik. Let us ride together and discuss the future of St. Rämmon and your role here."

The Prima Pater ordered Nichal to stay with the almoner, standard bearer, and Dane to help continue to distribute the bread. Zoumerik instructed the Paladins he had ridden with to stay as well.

Jined, Etienne, and the twins followed behind the Prima Pater and Primus Zoumerik.

"First off," the Prima Pater started, "I'd like to thank you again for coming from St. Hamul when I called."

"And as I said the past few times you thanked me—it is my pleasure."

They both laughed.

"I think this breadline," the Prima Pater continued, "is an example of what needs to happen under your leadership. The order has lost clout in Bortali, and I need you to reestablish it, if only through the feeding of the people here."

"I will endeavor to do so."

"If Eraim Glynn is to harvest a peacetime in Garrou, I need you to be the farmer, preparing the soil."

"That is a good analogy," Zoumerik said.

"What do you need from me?" Dorian asked.

"I want to take back Samul Haly, who accompanied you when you left St. Hamul. He's a good administrator, and I will trust him to run things smoothly while I'm away from St. Rämmon."

"I'm glad to hear you'll be active and not idle, stuck in that black fortress."

"I will. And so I will also ask that you leave your almoner, Stevan Filip. He has just established himself as a face of the charity we will be performing. That being said, I also want Dane Marric."

"I will grant you all of your requests save for keeping Brother Marric here. I believe he has some maturing to do. Perhaps when I am done in Mahn Fulhar, I can send him to you. But I'd like to see him mature a bit more first."

"Is something wrong with his faith?" the Primus asked. "He was a good companion on the road from St. Hamul."

"He has great faith. A far too blind faith at times, but faith," Dorian paused. "What I'm referring to is his unbridled loathing of women. It sets a bad example for those under him, and it verges on getting him in trouble."

"You think he might fall into the sin he fears?"

"Precisely the opposite. I've seen men like him become a tinder that lights the sparks of persecution. I will not have the goddess-ordained Crysalas Integritas coming under fire from someone who should be their ally."

"Perhaps staying here would be good for him then, separating him from those he deems offensive."

"I have considered that. But I'd like to keep him near so I can watch his growth, so he can see the sisters acting upon their own faith. That said, what else will you need?"

"We had discussed my needing more coin to run things. I know you will be able to arrange something, but I may need more than you first believed."

"And why is that?"

"Because I need the money to finance the endeavor your wife has undertaken. I'll act as the sponsor for it, with your blessing, of course."

"I'll be interested in seeing what she's been up to. You won't need my blessing, of course, because I'm promoting you to Pater

Minoris."

He handed Zoumerik a wooden box, who opened it and pulled out gold cordons.

"You honor me, Prima Pater."

"I can't have you running a fortress as a Primus. Go ahead and put those on. We'll conduct an official ceremony tonight at St. Rämmon."

Zoumerik affixed the cordons and put his old ones into the box, setting it into his satchel.

"We're almost there," Pater Zoumerik said. "There is much work to do, but by winter solstice we should have it up and running."

Jined found a quiet walkway at the back of St. Rämmon fortress and walked in silence, hoping for one last moment to himself before they left for his home country of Boroni the next day. Another Paladin was approaching, walking along, reciting something to himself. Jined didn't recognize him with the spray from the ocean and the mist rising off the turf below. The figure came out of the obscurity. It was the Paladin who had no name.

"You always seem to find me alone," Jined said.

"The Anka's sight is far-reaching. The grace of Grissone deeper still."

"I looked up the verse you mentioned, Aquila-Malleus 54:8. And it left me with yet another quandary. Let me see. 'Be then a hammer. Not of war but of peace.'"

The Paladin nodded.

"I had asked you your name, and you gave me that verse. So, I suppose you are Brother Hammer?"

Again, the Paladin nodded.

"You're a mystery."

"Listen now my brother, for peril marks the path." Brother Hammer began to walk away into the mist. "Seek to grow deeper still. There is only one way, and you know what it must be in your heart of hearts." The mist obscured him, and he disappeared.

It was no verse Jined knew, and so he knew that meant an even greater truth must be in it.

He turned and made his way toward the refectory, where the

twins sat eating together. They made him sign more often than speak when he was with them. Jined fumbled his way through communicating with only gestures as they corrected him in the nuances of their language. Loïc was not the patient teacher that Cävian was, but he was more thorough. Eventually, Loïc got fed up with the lesson and left, leaving Jined and Cävian to work on his lessons.

What vows have Silence? Jined asked.

Vows? Cävian asked.

I understand that each vow has Lesser Vows taken to strengthen oneself. Chastity has Chaste Mind and Upward Path.

Yes. Cävian signed. *We take Service and also Pure Silence.*

Jined nodded. It answered what he wanted to know. The Lesser Vow of Service was a philosophy of the silent. *Have you?* Jined asked.

No. But brother follows one.

It made sense to Jined. Loïc was always compliant. It put his nature into an entirely different perspective.

He thanked Cävian for his time and began to leave the refectory to check that his pack was ready for the road.

"Brother Brazstein."

Jined stopped in his step. He did not wish to turn around. He had expected Dane to take the opportunity to find another chore for him. It was becoming a daily thing. Jined reluctantly turned and saw Dane sitting with Etienne, who had a cowed look on his face. Others were beside them too, with Dane as the center of attention. How he had amassed a following was beyond Jined's comprehension.

"Brother Brazstein, I just finished with these. We all did. Would you take them to the kitchen?"

Jined walked forward and began to collect the plates that sat in front of them.

"When you're done, return here."

Jined turned to walk away with them. He was halfway to the kitchen when Dane spoke again.

"Bring back a spare loaf of bread from our excursion to the city when you come."

Jined stepped into the kitchen. The provisioners had taken over the kitchen to ensure the feeding went well.

"What can I do for you, Brother Brazstein?" one of them asked.

"A loaf of bread, if you'll allow me."

"Help yourself." He pointed over to the wall where a line of loaves waited.

Jined walked over and picked one up. There was a cup of melted butter next to them. Jined could hear the laughter of Dane in the other room. He took the butter and reached out to the spices nearby, taking a heavy spoonful of salt, and several other spices, dumping them into the butter. He split the loaf with a knife and poured the contents of the cup into the bread and closed up the loaf. He walked up to Dane and placed it in front of him.

"Brother Brazstein, you are such a good servant. Grissone must be very proud of you. I'm sure you've performed plenty of miracles yourself."

Jined stood there stoically.

Dane laughed and began tearing pieces off and doling them out. He negligently tore a bit off and stuffed it in his mouth. Immediately his face contorted. "What did you do?!" He shouted at Jined. He began spitting the bread out.

"'A bitter bread is all that comes from a priest that kneads gossip into his proverbs,' Anvil of Faith 89:3."

Dane stood up. "Vow Breaker," he hissed, "and Faithless!"

Jined turned and walked out while Dane continued to hurl insults at him. His ears burned, and he felt ashamed, because he knew Dane was right. He had broken his Vow of Service. He arrived at his room and checked his pack, while he awaited the inevitable.

It came an hour later. Etienne entered their cell.

"Brother Brazstein, you're to report to the Prima Pater."

Jined walked with as much stoicism as he could muster and arrived at the office door. Inside sat the Prima Pater and both Pater Segundii.

"You may leave," Dorian said.

Jurgon Upona rose, and from a seat Jined had not seen, Dane Marric rose and left with him.

As he passed, he smiled at Jined. "See you at the Pillory."

"Close the door behind you, Brother Brazstein," the Prima Pater said.

Jined did so.

"Take a seat and account for yourself."

Jined sighed. "Prima Pater, please allow me to apologize for my actions."

"I don't want an apology, Jined, I want your account of events."

"Prima Pater, I took a vow in the sight of Pater Segundus Pír, a Vow of Service. And I broke it today."

"I see. Why? Why did you break it?"

"Well, it seems Brother Marric heard me take the vow, and has made use of it since that day. Today I couldn't take it anymore. He pressed too hard and I did something terrible."

"Which was?"

"I poured butter into the loaf of bread he asked for. I mixed in who knows what spices and a large helping of salt, too."

The three men burst out laughing.

"That's it?" the Prima Pater continued to laugh. "Marric stormed in here apoplectic about having caught you breaking your vow. I was afraid this was going to be much more dire than I thought."

"I did break the vow I made, though," Jined said.

Dorian waved his hand dismissively. "I'm not particularly worried about that. We can give you a little wrist slap for it. It will make you humble and Marric will feel satisfied. How much longer are you on this vow?"

"Three weeks perhaps."

"Very well. We'll also keep the two of you away from one another. I don't need this circling out of hand any more than it already has."

"When would you like to exact my punishment?"

"We'll do it on the road one evening. Now please hurry along, I have other pressing matters to deal with before we leave."

Jined left with a wave of relief running over him. He walked past Dane, who was loitering in a recessed bench along the wall. He watched Jined walk by standing tall, a look of suspicion plastered across his face.

31

Interludes

Jined avoided speaking to anyone as they prepared to leave St. Rämmon. Everyone stood in the antechamber by the stables and waited. The Paladames suddenly emerged from a side hall. None had recalled them coming back to the fortress, and the Paladins looked at one another questioningly, wondering just how they were able to come and go so easily.

A few were missing from their original company, including Captain Sigri Smith and the taller Fedelmina Barba—a Paladame the Matriarch Superioris had given much attention to regarding the finances of her church.

The Prima Pater appeared with the two Pater Segundii, accompanied by the newly promoted Pater Minoris Zoumerik. Pater Segundus Pír's assistant, Primus Aeger came in behind them, and moved to join the other scribes.

"If I may have your attention," Dorian said. "It is a welcome sight to see each of you eager to see the road once again. We have a long journey through the pass into Boroni, and I should like to think that there will be nothing hanging over us as we go. Unfortunately, this means we must first conduct some rather unpleasant business. I feel it best that we do it now, rather than later, and get our issues out of the way so we can better enjoy the trip as a whole."

Adjutant Upona brought out a chair for the Prima Pater to sit on.

"We have the unfortunate responsibility to conduct a Pillory tonight for Brother Jined Brazstein."

Jined stepped forward, bowed his head, and folded his hands before him.

"Shall I go and fetch a pillory?" Pater Minoris Zoumerik asked.

"No need, we'll make do."

Loïc and Cävian both came forward at Pater Segundus Guess's signal and unhooked Jined's hammer from his chain and together held the other end. Jined dropped to his knees and held his hammer before him.

"A Paladin's vow is a sacred oath of allegiance to Grissone," Dorian said. "A Lesser Vow, while not as necessary to the faith, is still a vow made and must be adhered to. The reason philosophies have risen around Lesser Vows and the rules of each vow is because they do indeed draw us closer to our faith. It is important to note, though, that this is why the Lesser Vows are usually reserved for punishment.

"There are no 'vows' taken in a philosophy. Taking a vow, outside of a punishment, is often discouraged for this very reason. For if you do not take a vow, but still follow the laws, you can still draw closer to faith. Brother Brazstein took a Lesser Vow several days ago—the Vow of Service. Yesterday, he broke that vow in favor of insulting someone who had asked him a simple request. Excelsior Dane Marric, please step forward."

Dane marched abruptly to the front, a smug look on his face.

"Please state the request you made of Brother Brazstein."

"Excelsior Brazstein was asked to fetch a loaf of bread for me. When he returned, the bread contained vast amounts of butter, salt, and other spices. It was inedible. It was insulting. And it was wasteful."

Most of the company began to chuckle. The Prima Pater forced down a laugh himself, and raised a fist, silencing the congregation.

"Excelsior Marric. Were you aware of the vow Brother Brazstein had taken?"

"Prima Pater, I don't understand what that means."

"Did you know?"

"I was…vaguely aware of it."

"You were aware or you weren't. Do not lie to me."

"Yes."

"And how many other requests had you made of Brother Brazstein over the past week?"

"No more than I might at any other time."

The Prima Pater scanned out into the darkness. "How many

brothers here were informed to make requests of Brother Brazstein? Please step into the light."

Slowly but surely several Paladins stepped into view, looks of shame on their faces.

"Very well. It seems we also have another punishment to give. Dane Marric, you have caused another brother to stumble. It is the same as if someone had provided you a whore with which to break your own Vow of Chastity. You will resume the Lesser Vow of asceticism which was prescribed to you at St. Hamul, effective for three months this time."

Dane was about to speak, but the Prima Pater waved a dismissive hand.

"Brother Brazstein. This brings us to the punishment we must visit on you. You understand the slight."

"I do, Prima Pater."

"You will also have your vow extended. However, I consider your Lesser Vow of Service severed. You may select for yourself another Lesser Vow. Once you have selected it, I will designate the length the vow will take place." The Prima Pater lifted his head toward the ceiling. "Let us pray that Grissone guides your decision.

"Grissone, God of Faith. Guide now our brother Jined Brazstein. He desires a deeper faith from you. Let this time of penance be one of your hand on his shoulder, guiding him. Your will be done here."

Jined looked up. He saw only the Prima Pater before him, the dimly torchlit room seemed to close about him, drawing attention to one brother in the throng of Paladins and Paladames—Brother Hammer, who nodded to him. A nudge on Jined's heart told him what he must do.

Jined spoke more clearly than he ever had. His voice resonated off the walls and back to him.

"Prima Pater, I disavow all worldly goods. I deny myself possessions of any kind. From this day forth all that I am owed shall go to my next of kin or to the involuntarily impoverished. I take, therefore, the Vow of Poverty, effective immediately and without end."

The Prima Pater stared at Jined in astonishment, while Brother Hammer nodded his approval. A bright light flashed over Jined, and when the light cleared, everyone wiped their eyes to adjust to seeing again in the torchlight.

Brother Hammer had vanished once more.

The Prima Pater stepped forward and put his hand on Jined's shoulder.

"Never in my time as a Paladin has someone taken a second full vow, Brother Adjutant."

Jined looked down. His cordons had miraculously turned from green to white, and a second vow bead sat next to the other. Grissone himself had willed he take the second vow and be given the rank. Jined realized the weight of the words he had spoken, and he fell to his hands, his hammer clattering to the ground next to him as Paladins crowded in to see the miracle.

The monk had proven good company and afforded him the excuse to travel north that he had been looking for. He left her off at Amstonhotten and from there rode the sleipnir west as hard as he could. That he had been given a such a fresh mount was the first bit of bad luck he had run into. No matter how hard he pushed the creature, it never seemed to weary. It would not validate his story if the beast of burden did not at least work up a lather.

He arrived at the Mordaun waterfall, and the sleipnir fought hard on the reins to get a drink. He knew then that he was finally pushing the creature to its limits. In the distance, he could see the walls of the city, and the bell tower of the paladinial fortress.

As he neared the walls, a bell sounded off from the fortress. The sleipnir knew the sound and suddenly fell into line, knowing that fresh water and hay were not far off.

Wyloths watched his approach from the walls, hooping and hollering. He had never seen so many in one place. He shook his head free of the distraction and settled himself in the saddle to appear even more exhausted than he felt. The Bulwark, the paladinial fortress of Birin, stoically sat in the large square, only a few merchants still hawking their wares nearby. A Paladin stood outside the gate, watching him approach.

"Pater Minoris," the Paladin called out.

"Noss. Of Piedala," he said, dismounting the handing the other man his reins.

"This sleipnir has been ridden near to death," the Paladin said.

"And it is urgent I speak to your Pater Minoris."

"I'll see to your mount then."

Pater Noss rushed to the inner entry to the fortress, and through the halls he had traveled less than a year before to the office of the Pater Minoris. He did not knock.

"What is the meaning—," the other Pater Minoris said, turning to see who had barged in. "Pater Noss!"

"Pater Didus Koel, I just rode hard from The Aerie. They are calling for your aid!"

"What do you mean?" Koel asked as he moved to the sideboard and poured Noss a tankard of small mead. "What are you doing so far from Piedala?"

"While it is of little consequence, I have been traveling these last three months to visit with several colleagues. While I was visiting the Aerie, though, the unexpected happened."

He stopped and took a long pull on the mead. The tension in the room went taut.

"Vül, a large army of them, have assembled not far from Haven. Pater Gladen asked I ride to you and ask for aid."

"Vül?" Koel asked. "They've not formed up into more than raiding parties in decades."

"Regardless, it's happened."

"How large a force?"

"Large enough to frighten the great warrior Pater Minoris Jakis Gladen."

"How many Paladins is he requesting?"

"All of you."

Koel looked up from his seat, incredulity across his face.

"He can't be serious."

"He has sent other riders to other fortresses. But yours is the only one almost entirely made up of soldiers."

"Save our cooks, and a few scholars."

"And I don't doubt their services would be useful for preparing missives if this is to be a drawn out campaign."

"I answer to St. Hamul. Not the Aerie."

"And yet, he asks for you anyway. I will ride to St. Hamul from here, and tell them what has transpired. And I shall take full responsibility for this. Gladen needs your force."

"Then I shall answer," Pater Koel said with a dark smile. "It has been a long time since I've seen battle. It will be good to raise the hammer against the enemies of man."

"How long will it take you to prepare?"

"There will be communiques to prepare for the Nifarans and nearby bastions."

"I'm riding south toward Piedala. I'll stop at bastions along the way to spread the word. Give me lease of your office. I'll see your missives are sent. You worry about leaving, and ride to the Aerie's aid."

Koel opened a drawer, took out a brass seal, and handed it over.

"If you'll do that, I've got three hundred Paladins to ready for war."

"Prim...Pater Minoris Zoumerik," the Adjutant said as he poked his head into the office.

"Yes, Brother Pyle," Pater Zoumerik said, smiling.

"That may take some getting used to," Brother Pyle said.

"I imagine so."

"There is a Primus Aeger here to see you."

"See him in."

"He has taken the Vow of Silence. Will you require a translator?"

"I would not have made Primus if I could not understand the hand signals of a Silent Brother."

"Of course, Pater," the Adjutant said.

"I imagine it's nearing the evening meal," Zoumerik said. "Why don't you go down ahead of me? I'm sure I can find my own way."

Brother Pyle nodded and left the room. A moment later, quiet Primus Aeger shuffled in.

"Greetings, Primus Aeger," Zoumerik said, rising. "Why don't you drop the bar on the door there?"

Aeger nodded, and did so before turning back to Zoumerik.

"Greetings, Dusk," Aeger said out loud.

Zoumerik nodded. "Likewise, Cup. It has been a long time."

"Indeed it has. Five years, in fact."

"Will you take a seat?" Zoumerik motioned for the man to take the chair across from him as he poured strong red wine for both of them.

"Has it been five years?" Aeger said.

"Yes, it has."

They both sipped their wine for a time.

"I suppose," Aeger said, "you already know most of what I have to say."

"I do, but coming from you will mean so much more."

"Do you still have Master Talon's shadebook in your possession?"

"I do."

"Then you also know that it is my turn to carry him for a time."

Zoumerik shook his head seriously. "I can't part with him just yet."

"Why is that?" Aeger asked.

"The two of us are working through a problem, and I need his insight."

"Into what, Brother?"

"Creation of a living shadebook."

"A living shadebook?" Aeger said, his eyes bulging. "That would be very dangerous! Even if it was possible, the risk would be too great."

"But it has been done," Zoumerik said.

"By whom?"

"I am not at liberty to say."

"I know whom you speak of," Aeger said, a smile toying at the edge of his mouth, "and what if I told you that I expect to meet that individual in Mahn Fulhar?"

"I would ask who it is, to confirm both of our suspicions."

"To echo you, 'I am not at liberty to say.'"

Zoumerik sat back and sighed. "I need to know. What good does being the highest member in the Mystery of the Feather do, if I can't perform this task?"

"I will send word on how to achieve this, if you would part with the master's shadebook."

"There is another reason I can't give his shadebook to you," Zoumerik said as he refilled the other man's drink.

"What would that be?"

"You would have two master shadebooks in your company. That would be dangerous."

"What are you talking about?"

"I gave an unassuming member of your company a shadebook to deliver to the brotherhood in Mahn Fulhar."

"What brother would that be? What master shadebook?"

"The shadebook of Veil."

"Why? Why would you move that shade? Veil was dangerous in life, and more so as a shade."

"I know. But I needed to move it along. He and Master Talon don't get along when they're in the same library."

"And who holds the shadebook?"

"One of your guards. Brazstein is his name."

"He's loyal enough," Aeger nodded. "The book will be delivered, if Veil doesn't live up to his name and just see he's carried about for the next decade."

"It's worth the risk. The brotherhood in Mahn Fulhar has been asking for a shadebook for some time anyway."

"Speaking of Brazstein," Aeger said, finishing his cup and holding up a hand to keep Zoumerik from pouring him any more, "did you hear what he uncovered in Garrou?"

"Discovery of the written silent language?"

"Yes. It changes everything, and we'll need to explicitly inform all members of the brotherhood."

"No need to tell those under Vanguard's sway, however."

Aeger cocked an eyebrow. "Why is that?"

"I think he's turning away from the cause and forming his own. It might make things difficult for us, but if we were to keep that information from him, he might expose himself and ruin some of his own plans."

"Very well," Aeger said.

"Was there anything else?" Zoumerik asked, pouring himself another glass.

"Well," Aeger said, "we've known each other a long time."

"This is true."

"So I should like to think that we can trust one another."

"As much as any member of the brotherhood can."

"Then will you tell me what news you have of the other two branches? Of the Piedala sect? Or what you believe Vanguard is up to?"

"I will tell you what you wish to know if you'll tell me who holds the title of Fidelity."

"No need to worry about Fidelity. He was returned to Pariantür with the hapless fool you had stationed up here to run things into the earth."

"Then he is not part of the equation anymore?"

"Not this equation, anyway," Aeger said.

"Yes, not this equation. The problem of Pariantür remains a separate part of the plan."

"Indeed. Now, what can you tell me of Bell and Vanguard?"

"Well," Zoumerik said, "you are aware of the Prima Pater's charge to seek the Dread Plate, lost after the Protectorate Wars?"

"Of course. Vanguard is currently the most senior member of the Mysteries of the Plate, seeking it out, still—after all these decades."

"Correct. Bell and I believe he has it in his possession, and will no doubt have another tool for our brotherhood to use to tear the order down from within, if he doesn't already have it at his command."

A knock came to the door.

"Don your Vow of Silence again," Zoumerik said. "It's time to see the Prima Pater and his entourage off to Boroni."

PART 4

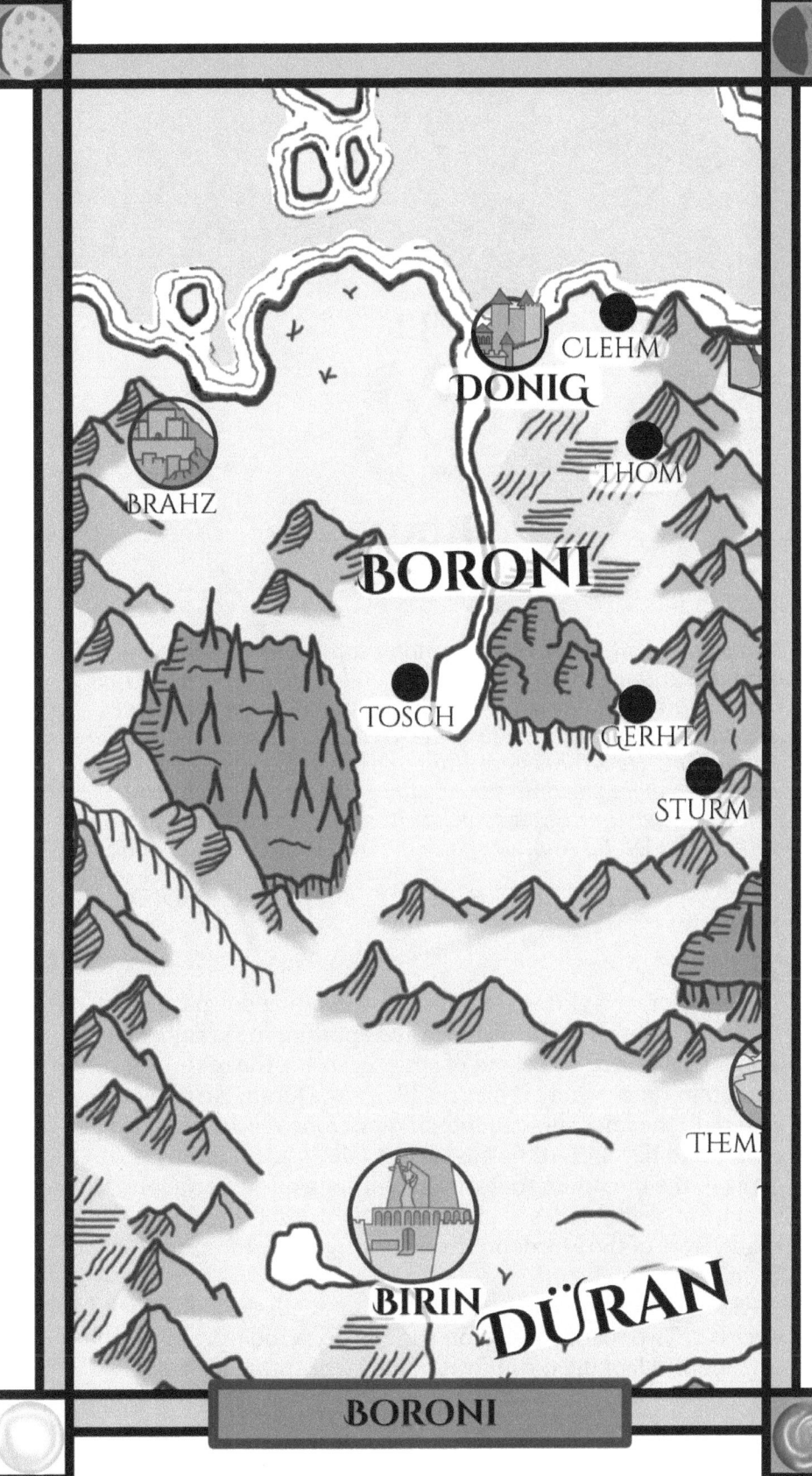

32

BIRIN

Minderone and Sinderone, the mountain brothers. They say there once was a third, Ämmarone, but it collapsed between the two that remained. Some say there was no third mountain. That Ämmarone was indeed one of the great Gigantes of Wyv-Thüm, Ämma-Tor. He left his home and walked away to the north and east. Now there sits only two vast holes where his feet were planted. Over time Sinderone has diminished, collapsing into one of the holes left by Ämmarone. Minderone continues to stand tall.

—A NATURAL HISTORY OF THE ABEI MOUNTAINS

A silver vein glittered in the sun, cascading down the mountains in the distance and splitting the granite face. It terminated in a cloud of spray covering the roots of the Abei mountain range where it met the plains of Düran. Far above the waterfall, the imposing mountain Minderone reached up into the clouds and beyond. At the base of the falls, under the mist that clung to the mountain roots, Lake Mordaun glinted as a long blue streak for several miles in either direction, and formed the headwaters of the Mordaun River, cutting a line toward the city of Birin.

Hanen stood above the Mordaun Scar, a hill through which the river cut. Two roads rose up on either side, wandering along the cliffside and looking down toward the large sprawling city.

The jumbled capital looked like a child's toy, cast aside and shattered upon hard clay earth. There was no plan to the city. Random buildings cast shadows on their neighbors. Small hovels and even luxurious inns clung to the outer walls, while outlying collections of homes and trade buildings sprinkled the large valley. Perhaps they had been built away from the wall to avoid city taxation, yet the growth of the city threatened to overtake and consume them eventually, as seen by the gap in the eastern wall, where masons placed new foundations around a well and the village around it.

Though Hanen had hoped to make it in sixteen days, it had taken eighteen, and the weariness settled heavily upon his shoulders. Searn didn't seem upset by their loss of time, but Hanen still felt like he had failed the Sentinel captain.

"What are you muttering about?" Rallia asked.

"I wasn't muttering."

"You were. When you're tired your thoughts come out in mutterings."

Hanen shook his head. "I'm just wondering if we couldn't have gotten here sooner. If we could have been farther along, would Ozri still be alive?"

"Or would we have met Ymbrys or Nefer Yaledít?"

"At the cost of Ozri's life, I don't know that meeting a qavyl and a monk is a fair trade."

"Not a fair trade at all," Rallia said. "But it just feels like fate."

"I don't like that idea."

"Why not?"

"The stories of those that seek to improve themselves are usually unseated by the gods or fate."

"Those same stories have the hero worrying that is the case. So by that logic, stop worrying, which you do too much."

At the monk's pace it took several hours to reach the gate, which stood open and sparsely protected by a smattering of guards.

"Has Birin never been threatened?" Hanen said. "The gates appear unused, as though they've never been closed."

"They say there is little crime here," Aurín replied. "But if you knew your soul was taken to Noccitan by the goddess that protects this city, would you ever commit a crime in front of her?"

"That would make sense," Searn said. "If you believed such things. It doesn't stop crime from occurring here, though. You just need to know where to look."

"What does that mean?" Ymbrys asked.

"It means that while brigands and raiders don't touch the city, the king of Düran still allows illicit trade to occur. But don't think he doesn't benefit from it. By allowing it to occur, it limits crime in the nearby area. Towns farther out can't claim such safety."

They passed under the gate. Two identical statues of Nifara stood guard. In one arm she held a staff. In her other hand she held out a pair of scales. A wyloth sat in the scale bowl, working to open a nut with its teeth. It looked at Hanen and then dropped the nut, scampering away. The flow of people into the city pulled them in alongside the current of others leaving.

In Edi City, the streets either dropped down directly toward the sea, or circled a hill. Here, Hanen's sense of direction disappeared. They squeezed their way through the crowds, who paid them little heed, with the blind monk blindly leading them on. As they continued on, Hanen could see the streets widening, curving less, and all leading toward a single location.

The street they walked along emptied into a central plaza in the center of Birin. On the west side the palace of Düran stood squat and nondescript. Important-looking officials in black robes filed in and out. A few merchants were attempting to sell their wares until soldiers came and shoved them off toward the broad north-running street, which ran away from the plaza filled to overflowing with stalls. Opposite the palace, on the east side of the plaza, the Templum of Nifara loomed above all else.

A long wall ran along the street, separating the Templum from the city. Seriah led them through the first threshold. As at the main gates of the city, two statues of Nifara stood guard. Once within the walls, the façade of the Templum loomed above them. Three doors led into its face. Upon the lintel above the doors stood a statuary of ten figures, sculpted to look like monks of Nifara, each with their own symbology—all that is but the tenth statue, which was incomplete—made of rough-hewn stone. A tall central tower of brick rose from the Templum, and attached to this tower, acting as a buttress but also supported by the tower, was a seventy-foot tall statue of Nifara overlooking the city.

In most images of the gods, each was depicted with three pairs of wings, or at least a semblance of them. On Nifara, these took the form of an enormous set of balanced scales that rose from her shoulders. The other set of wings were upon her heels, giving her speedy flight for traveling to and fro, from both Lomïn, the Ever-

Day, and Noccitan, the Ever-Night, as well as between the gods; for daily she journeyed into the underworld to speak to Wyv for the souls that had passed on.

Chin lifted high, her sculpted, imperious, and slender shoulders almost visibly held the weight of the entirety of the world's collective souls. The sun glinted off her marble eyes and flashed, seeming to look down upon Hanen for the briefest of moments, acknowledging that she had seen him there.

They stood inside the courtyard with couriers constantly coming and going. Sight-bound monks entered and exited, some with assistants dressed in the same robes offering their arms to the unseeing ones. These did not have cloth across their eyes.

"Thank you for joining me on the road," Seriah said, turning to face them. "It was nice to have no interruptions, and be in pleasant company."

"I would ask that you tell those you know of our service and cordiality," Searn said with a bow. He took her hand in his. "I hope to speak to members of your order to offer a similar service, soon. A word from one of their own would be welcome."

"I doubt there are many that would take my word over another's. If given the opportunity, though, I'll do just that. Thank you, good sir VcTurrcs."

Searn motioned for them all to come with him over against a wall.

"Does this seem to be a good place to fulfill our contract, Ymbrys?" Searn asked the tall qavyl.

"It does. I thank you all for the splendid trip, despite its little misadventure with the manticör." Ymbrys turned to Aurín. "You are a consummate cook. Thank you for sharing with me." Aurín bowed to Ymbrys, who handed him a small pouch of some spice.

"Searn, thank you for your conversation. If you seek the gods, they will find you."

Searn chuckled and took the qavyl's hand.

Hanen could see that Searn wasn't smiling, though.

"Ophedia, even I can see your beauty, and I am not a human, who might appreciate it even more. Don't squander it."

Ophedia blushed.

"Rallia Clouw, I see a greatness in you. Your prowess in battle is growing. I don't doubt you are capable of defeating even the greatest of foes. Do not cease to strive to be worthy."

Lastly, he turned to Hanen and put a hand on his shoulder.

"Continue to seek your path, Hanen Clouw. You'll see me again."

Hanen expected the qavyl to say more, and felt let down when he hadn't.

The qavyl set his pack down and came up with a heavy leather coin pouch, which he handed to Hanen. Then he waved over his shoulder as he walked away, his staff kicking out ahead of him every few strides.

"Now," Searn said, turning away from the qavyl. "Let's talk."

He pulled them all in closer.

"We have a lot to deal with here. And we need to not give a show of force. That means that Aurín, I need you and Ophedia to go and make some connections for us. Please stay away from the Templum until I send for you. That will, however, require that I do something first." He pulled out a bundle and thrust it at Ophedia. "Welcome to the Sentinels, girl."

Ophedia was stunned in silence.

"Aurín, how many contacts do you have here?"

"A few. I'm sure they'll know more themselves."

"I want a list of ten Sentinels ready to go if we call. I also need you to hand deliver this message to a man by the name of Norin Laud." He handed Aurín a sealed letter.

Ophedia opened the package and pulled out a black cloak, quickly placing it over her shoulders. She practically danced out into the street with Aurín following.

"Now, Hanen and Rallia," Searn said. "I offered you equal shares in this mission, because I know what you're capable of. For the most part, though, I need you to keep your mouths shut here at the Templum. I have a plan to make this mission go off without a hitch, and it relies on me doing my bit."

"What do you want us to do then?" Hanen asked.

"Watch and learn. The monks can't see us, but their assistants can. They'll tell their superiors what we say and do."

He looked toward the entrance. "Are you ready?"

Hanen nodded and Rallia followed.

They approached the doors that led from the courtyard into the halls of the Templum. The ground in front of the doors was a single bronze plate. As they stepped onto the metal, they all three caught themselves as the ground moved slightly. It tinkled with thousands of tiny bells with each step. Across from them, beside the door, a monk sat upon a carved stool, leaning forward on his staff.

"Greetings in the name of our most holy virgin goddess, Nifara!" he said as he stood.

"Hello, Holy Nefer!" Searn said, jovially. He walked up and muttered something to the monk, who nodded as he listened.

"That's rather irregular," he said, "but we do accept guests. They just never ask to speak with the assembly. I can submit a request, I suppose."

The monk reached into his satchel and pulled out several sticks with notches along them. "You say we have three guests? May I give you all a blessing?"

He handed a stick to each of them.

"This stick you now hold is a rod of residency. You shall keep it on you. If a member of our order asks, produce it for them. If they should question it still, you send them to me, Beliga Mann. We are always happy to house those in need, but just as the scales balance, so too shall you provide us your labor for your time here. You've no doubt noticed that we are all blind here, and must use our hospitality to find those that would do what we cannot."

The doors opened when the monk pounded his staff on the brass floor, and all the hidden bells jingled beneath them in a clamor.

They entered the first hall, filled to overflowing with the echoing whispered murmurs of the countless monks conversing. Across from them a single large door stood closed. Other doors led off in different directions. A young boy dressed like the other Nifarans approached and held out a hand. When the three of them just stared at him, he pointed at the sticks in their hands. Hanen handed his to the boy, who felt up along the notches, nodded, and indicated they follow.

They took a hallway, leaving the whispering silence.

"Thank you for not talking," the boy said. "I hate having to shush guests in the Hall. I'm supposed to take new guests to their rooms, and then have you report for help in the arboretum."

He led them to a room with four beds, where they dropped their cloaks and packs. The boy hurried them along to a large orchard garden at the back of the complex. He introduced them to a gardener not dressed as a monk.

"I'm Kap," he said. "You working for lodgings, too? Follow me."

They walked down a long row of trees covered heavily in green apples and came to several shorter plants with reddened fruit.

"You'll be picking these trees clean until the dinner bell rings," he said, and left them without another word.

A man and wife, who bragged to every newcomer that they went out of their way to help with the harvest each year, showed them the trick of twisting the fruit free of the branches, and they soon got down to the hot, dusty work, sneaking a sample or two for themselves. After an hour or so, the bell for dinner rang. The workers shuffled off towards a dining hall set for them, unsurprisingly, with apple-filled breads and well-cured ham slathered in applesauce. The beer was weak, but free, so Hanen didn't complain.

"The roads to the north have become more dangerous?" Searn was asking another.

"Well of course they have, what with Bortali keeping us all from getting our goods into and out of the jarldoms of Boroni. If they're not at war already, then it's coming."

The man speaking was older, and carried himself as a soldier who had seen time on the march. Searn hunched his shoulders forward, matching his posture, putting the man across from him at ease. Others leaned in, too, matching the two of them.

"I heard that Bortali soldiers are deserting and picking up brigandry. With winter coming soon, they'll all come here looking for work or to steal what can't be bought. I just wish they'd a'gone over to Limae sooner. Leave us honest folk alone."

"Never hurts to hire a Sentinel," Searn said.

"Coin Cloaks? They're always asking for more money than they're worth."

"Doesn't stop you from paying money to Paladins whenever they ask for coin," Searn said. "You ever stop to think about how much you've given them in your lifetime?"

The man went silent and finally shook his head. "Money to a Paladin helps those who can't even come here and work for the monks in their yards."

"Honestly," Rallia said, "I don't have a problem with the Paladins, as you seem to, Searn."

Searn snapped a look at Rallia, who missed the cue.

"My own grandfather was one," Rallia continued. "My mother and father—Hanen and I share the same father—ran a soup kitchen that ran off Paladin coin."

Hanen gave Rallia's arm a tight squeeze. "Rallia, Searn asked us to keep our peace."

Rallia bit her lip, and gave Searn an apologetic, embarrassed look.

As the long dinner of conversation ended, they shuffled to their own rooms. Hanen, Rallia, and Searn took to their beds and fell asleep easily.

Hanen woke with a start as a procession of monks walked down the hallways shaking clackers and banging hollow rods of wood to wake other monks and guests. While they could hear guests groaning in other rooms, Rallia sat up quickly before Searn and Hanen did the same. As they stepped out into the hall, a group of monks shuffled along with their hands on each other's shoulders, making their way to the council hall for the morning prayer.

Searn indicated that they follow the monks, who stopped once they came to the main hall. They stood outside the closed doors and waited. Searn soon excused himself and disappeared, leaving Hanen and Rallia to wait in silence.

After about an hour, Searn reappeared with their cloaks in his hands. "They've agreed to see us shortly."

A few minutes later, the large doors opened and the three of them stepped in.

Hanen looked around the steep council chamber. Five tiers rose immediately over a small speaking area about thirty feet in diameter. A vast majority of the chairs sat empty.

At the top of the room, a dais alcove held three monks. The oldest of the three had a quaint smile and next to him stood a tall and muscular man. In the second seat sat a middle-aged woman. On the lower levels, monks sat on benches, attended to by younger boys and girls who were not yet sight-bound scribbling away with styluses on ledgers.

The muscular monk on the dais banged a heavy iron staff on the stone to command the council's attention.

"All present," he said in a loud, booming voice, "acknowledge that the Templum Session on this date, the 6th of Anqyl, in the Imperial Year 2225 is attended. Archimandrite Pell Maran presiding."

All monks and their attendants rose, and in near-perfect unison they struck the ground with their staffs three times.

The old Archimandrite stood and placed his hands on the edge of the dais. "Very well. Be seated. We shall begin."

The middle-aged woman who sat nearby then said in a loud and clear voice, "Gregor Hans. Will you please present the first report?"

Gregor Hans called their road companion, Seriah Yaledít, down from her place. She came to the center of the room and tapped the marble to mark that she was ready.

The woman on the dais leaned forward and said, "Seriah Yaledít, you shall give your report. I, Kerei Lant, shall act as witness to your testimony."

Seriah detailed her journey to the south-east, to Temblin, where she had acted as go-between for a small orphanage and the neighborhood constable. She had interceded for the underrepresented orphanage and had, in order to lock in the orphanage's claim on the fatherless of the city, taken the deed onto the burden of the Templum.

Kerei Lant smiled. "Another orphanage, Seriah? This is becoming a habit."

"No child should be without the protection of those who have love to give."

"Well put. Proceed."

She spoke of the long path she had taken home, then made mention of the Sentinels she had met, first at a chapel, then Amstonhotten, and finally, gave a kind report.

"Thank you, Nefer Yaledít," Kerei Lant said. "We will have your testimony recorded."

This continued for several hours, while Hanen listened to monk after monk report on the lands they had traveled to, and the justice they had served. An assistant motioned that Searn would be next. He stood up at the edge of the speaking area.

"We will now hear Searn VeTurres, of the Black Sentinels."

Rallia jabbed Hanen in the ribs and pointed toward Seriah, who had a look of surprise on her face.

"I doubt she realized we were in the room when she gave her report," Rallia said, smiling.

Searn stepped up onto the stage. He took a long moment of silence and turned to look around at those who watched, and, more importantly, those who listened.

"Holy Nefers!" Searn started. "I am Searn VeTurres, a member of the prestigious Black Sentinels. Though mercenary, we strive to provide protection to travelers on roads, and even protect people in their own homes. We are not rabble looking to make an easy coin, but work hard to provide a service that others cannot, due to the fact that we are organized and because we strive to be the best."

"We know who the Black Sentinels are, VeTurres," Gregor

Hans, the tall monk on the dais, said, interrupting him. "Please proceed with why you are here today."

"As you must very likely know by now, the Prima Pater of the Paladins of the Hammer has come from Pariantür, and even now travels across the Northern Scapes."

There was no reaction.

"I see that you have not yet sent high-ranking members of your organization to meet with the Prima Pater. My assumption is that the onset of winter, fast approaching, might keep you from doing so until spring, at which time, the Prima Pater may be heading back to the east, to not return again for another decade. I would like to offer my services, and the services of the Black Sentinels, to escort those willing to make the journey north at this time."

"And why," Archimandrite Pell Maran said, "should we not simply wait until spring to go and seek him out?"

"For one, because spring in the mountains is volatile," Searn said. "Yes, winter can come quickly, but if prepared, one can still make the passes to Mahndür safely. And secondly, because your bonds of allegiance with Pariantür are strong, almost as strong as their bond with the Paladames of the Rose."

"And lastly," Gregor Hans interrupted, "because you hope a prestigious contract such as this will vault you into a position of high rank with the Black Sentinels."

Searn did not respond to this.

"You are nothing but a greedy Coin Cloak, looking to use our own eagerness to meet up with our fellow faithful for your own gain."

"Gregor," the Archimandrite said, silencing him. "Let the man speak. Please proceed, and you, Sentinel, may even defend yourself against this accusation if you wish."

"Thank you, Archimandrite Maran. I will do just that. First, let me assuage your fears. I do not suggest this for my own personal gain. What I do, I do for the good of the Black Sentinels.

"I traveled for over a month to arrive here, two weeks just from Edi City to Birin, in hopes to find that you had not yet left, and I discover you have indeed not. I have traveled here because I have something greater to offer you. Allegiance. I am not a lowly Black Sentinel. I am not even a captain of the Black Sentinels. You are speaking to Searn VeTurres, the Master and Commander of the Black Sentinel Council in Limae."

33

Filthy King

What living prison he curses them with? That those who bring him worship must suffer as he. Kos-Yran is cruel. Yet for that we are grateful. For those he raises up are destined only to fall under a curse of their own doing. I recall a man who survived battle with the Dry Walker, Glyth-Dormak. He told me the blood in his veins dried up as the vül approached, not a hair on his body, nor an ounce of meat on his bones. He was famine incarnate. Even the river fled from him as he stepped down into the cut upon the land. And yet, try as he might, the Dry Walker could not drink for himself a single drop.

—OLD STORYTELLER IN ZHIGAVA

Rallia gasped beside Hanen, and Hanen almost did the same. Finally, the room fell to whispering. Gregor Hans' staff struck flagstone, silencing the congregation.

"This does change things," Pell Maran said. "You are not offering a simple escort. You wish to put your good name, and the name of your organization, to use. By escorting us to the Paladins, you feel as though you'll validate yourselves to them."

"As you say," Searn responded.

"Well then, I say I shall discuss with my colleagues for a time, and we shall seek you out when we have a decision."

Searn bowed and led the Clouws out. They returned to their

room in silence.

Rallia sat down on the bed, while Hanen leaned against the back wall. Searn stood by the door.

"I apologize that I didn't tell you," Searn said.

"You're our leader?" Hanen asked. "As in, the head of the Sentinels?"

"I am."

"I didn't even know there was a leader," Rallia said.

"I knew you outranked us; you carry a crossbow. But I've never met anyone with higher rank," Hanen said.

"After the rank of captain with a crossbow, the commanders carry a long axe. I happen to carry the double-bladed axe which puts me at a rank above the six men and women who hold the rank of commander. Though I don't keep the battle-axe with me. It's cumbersome. I leave that in Haven."

"What does it mean?" Rallia asked. "For us, I mean."

"Mean?" Searn laughed. "Nothing. I'm still a Black Sentinel. I just take a higher pay for contracts and pay less in dues."

"What does that mean for this mission? We can't still split this three ways," Hanen said.

"We can," Searn said, "but at the same time, I still have one more trick up my sleeve for the monks if they say no."

"What's that?"

"We need this assignment. So I plan on offering to do this free of charge. It will launch the Black Sentinels into an organization equal to the Paladins and the monks."

"But with no god at the head of the organization."

"Precisely. I think you're starting to understand what I have been saying this whole trip now."

A knock came on the door. Hanen answered.

"The Archimandrite Pell Maran has agreed to see you tomorrow evening. You are free to come and go as you please from your room." The messenger left as quickly as he had come.

"Looks like we have the rest of the day," Searn said. "Shall we go find some food? I'll buy."

As they came out into the courtyard, Aurín was across the space accosting an acolyte.

"I need you to give a message to one of your guests!" he was nearly shouting. "It's urgent!"

"Tell him yourself," Searn said.

Aurín looked up, relief flooding his face. It fell over the acolyte's face, too, who took the opportunity to disappear.

"Oh good. Searn, Clouws. There's a problem."

"Not here!" Searn hissed.

Aurín nodded, and they all walked out into the city square. Searn continued to walk until they were standing near the middle, far away from everyone else.

"What made you think it was alright to return to the Templum and try to interrupt me? We're in the middle of ingratiating ourselves to the monks and you're causing trouble."

"No, I'm not the one causing trouble. This is not a laughing matter. Hanen, Rallia, it's Ghoré Dziony causing the trouble."

"Ghoré?" Hanen asked.

"He's out?" Rallia hissed. "Escaped?"

"Who is Ghoré?" Searn asked.

"A Sentinel," Hanen said. "We sent him to the authorities when he baited wyloths to harass our caravan in order to drum up respect for the Sentinels."

"So not very smart then?"

"No. We had prepared a message to send to Sentinel headquarters in Haven, to have it reported that we took his cloak from him."

"Come on. Let's go find this man."

"He's not hard to find," Aurín said as he began to walk. "The other Sentinels have been talking about him and say so."

"Is there somewhere the Sentinels gather in town?" Searn asked.

"Yes. There's an inn owned by a Sentinel too old to take on any more contracts. He still has his cloak, though."

"That would be Uré Long," Searn said. "He pays his dues from the tavern proceeds. I don't think he's taken a contract in over ten years, but plenty of contracts get signed at his inn."

"From there they say it's not hard to find Ghoré."

"What do you mean?" Rallia asked.

"You'll see."

They left the main square and walked down the straightest thoroughfare in the city running west. Merchants lined the side of the road, hawking their wares. Green-skinned hrelgrens had booths intermingled with the human vendors, selling foreign goods. Several qavylli, all wearing nearly matching clothes, had a series of booths lined up together, shaded by fine silks. Hanen felt a pull to slow down and look, but Searn forged ahead.

As they walked farther and farther, people became fewer and far between, and the road became more cluttered with debris. Beggars held out hands. An old lady sat with two children, each with cloths tied loosely over their eyes, their hands blocking what little light reached them in the shade.

The buildings in the poor district were older than anything else. They were made of stark granite slabs stacked upon each other. As they neared the western edge of the city, the streets once more became cleaner and wealthier.

They came to a courtyard-like square. There were only a small handful of people there, and they moved quickly to make themselves scarce. Across the cobblestone a large edifice rose, made of the same granite covered with a coating of green moss. All of the walls, parapets, and inner buildings seemed to rise together in angles that fed into the shape of a singular dome.

"What is that?" Rallia asked, pointing to the complex.

"The Bulwark," Searn said. "A Paladin fortress."

"It looks empty," Hanen said. The gates were shut and the walls were unmanned.

"Rumor is that it is empty," Aurín replied. "The Paladins are said to have just up and left in the middle of the night, riding toward Limae a few days ago."

Aurín took them down a side road to a cul-de-sac belonging to a single inn that had been coated with plaster under granite eaves.

"That's it. Oldest Inn, it's called."

They walked up to the door. A wyloth was perched on a roof nearby. It screeched at them, and disappeared.

Searn walked in ahead of the others. The inn was busy. Perhaps ten Sentinels sat intermingled with other clientele. The man behind the bar was old and grizzled. Above the bar a Sentinel's cloak was pinned open. It looked like a black bird outstretched on the wall like a trophy.

"Uré," Searn said, sitting at the bar.

"' Ullo captain," the barkeep said. "I haven't seen you through here in a year or two."

"True. Got any Limaean Common?"

"Nope. Only Limaean Strong."

"Fine. For all of us." Searn indicated to the Clouws and Aurín.

Ophedia was sitting at a table playing cards with two other Sentinels. She saw them, folded her hand, and came over to sit next to them, too.

"Girl, too?" the barkeep asked.

Searn nodded.

"We heard there's been trouble with a man who was once a Sentinel. Ghoré Dziony?" Hanen asked.

"Ah. You mean the Wyloth King? Sure. He's been causing trouble all this last week. A couple of the boys tried roughing him up when he tried to walk in here. His 'subjects' wrecked their faces something fierce. It took far too much work to get him out of here. I was cleaning up the mess they made for three days."

"What do you mean 'Wyloth King'?"

"That's what he called himself. Set himself up a little throne in a back alley not a week ago. Even the town guard won't do anything about him. They don't know what to do."

"What's this about?" Ophedia asked.

"A Sentinel we gave over to the authorities," Hanen said. "Sounds like maybe he went crazy."

"What should we do?" Rallia asked.

"Do?" Hanen replied. "Why should we do anything? We gave him over. He's not our problem any more."

"I'm going to go see what's going on," Rallia said, rising. "After all, I was responsible for him."

"Even if he was a backstabbing little shunt?" Hanen asked.

"Yes. Because it's the right thing to do."

Hanen sighed and stood, following Rallia to the door. Rallia looked up toward the roof edges at a wyloth. It scampered away, and Rallia took off south after it. Hanen tried to keep up. He heard the patter of boots behind him as Searn, Ophedia, and Aurín followed farther behind. As they continued, additional wyloths appeared overhead. Coming to a cross-street, Rallia stood in the middle and looked up at the nasty creatures. They began screeching at her in anger.

Hanen came and stood next to her.

"Which way?"

Rallia continued to look up and pointed. "Wyloths are peeling off that way."

They walked down the alleyway. The sky was nearly darkened with wyloths leaping overhead from roof edge to roof edge. They came to a corner and Rallia pulled up short. Hanen had both of his axes out. The others had their hands on their own weapons.

Rallia moved to turn the corner.

"Wait," Hanen said, "let me talk to him."

"Hello Hanen, Rallia," a voice snapped out from around the corner. "And Aurín too, it seems. Come, Come!"

Hanen took a deep breath and turned the corner. Ghoré sat on a pile of debris. Wyloths were everywhere. Hundreds of them sat on every surface. A few of them dropped out of the sky, flapping over Hanen's head, startling him. They had fruit in their hands, which they dropped in front of Ghoré. The man sat stark naked on the pile. He had gathered up a black material and wrapped it around his head, with a wyloth's skull set in the center of his forehead.

"What's going on here, Ghoré?" Hanen asked nervously.

"I should ask you the same thing, coming into my kingdom and seeking me out."

"We heard you were here and thought we might find out how the authorities treated you."

Ghoré laughed. There was a hint of hysteria in his voice. "They're gone now. I met someone on the road to Birin who showed me things I didn't even know I could do."

Hanen had slowly taken ten steps forward. With every step another wyloth came and landed within a foot or two of Ghoré, eyeing the usurpers.

"What did he show you?"

"How to be king. I could make my servants do as I command. I could even make my enemies my servants. My slaves."

"You mean these creatures?"

Ghoré smiled with glee. "Yes! Watch!"

He pointed to a wyloth and screeched at it. Then he whooped at a second one. The two wyloths turned on each other and lunged forward, tearing fur off each other's backs. They scratched and clawed at one another until they were both bloody and fell still.

Ghoré cackled. "See? I am king!"

"He's mad," Searn said.

"I am not mad," Ghoré said cooly. "I have been given a gift. A gift by the Gift-Giver."

"Nocc," Ophedia swore, spitting on the ground.

"You met Kos-Yran, huh?" Hanen asked dubiously.

Ghoré smiled. "He's been roaming around these parts looking for new servants. He said I could have what I wanted."

"At what cost?" Rallia asked.

"He told me there was no cost."

"There is always a cost," Rallia replied. "In all the old stories Kos-Yran always demands a cost."

DEATHLESS BEAST

"Ha!" Ghoré said. "Then I fooled him. He took nothing from me."

"Only his sanity," Searn muttered.

"I'm not mad!!" he screamed, then calming himself, said, "Who is this?"

"I'm Searn VeTurres," Searn said, stepping forward. "Head Commander of the Sentinels."

Ophedia and Aurín jerked their heads toward Searn in surprise. Hanen waved his own hand in dismissal, silencing them before they spoke.

"You brought a higher authority, Hanen? It seems you still have no spine. You can't take care of your own problems. That's fine. You can all suffer."

He pointed to Hanen. His arm seemed longer, and the flesh almost seemed to hang off his bones.

The wyloths all turned to look at Hanen. Their eyes looked empty, but their faces said otherwise. Ten of them lunged and loped down the alley toward them, soaring as they leapt. Rallia's staff came up in succession and took three out of the air. Hanen swatted two of them away, while the other Sentinels quickly batted the others down.

"What is your aim, Ghoré?" Hanen said.

"Aim? Revenge. For laughing at me. Mocking me. Chaining me up like some animal and shipping me off to a prison to rot."

"Torch?" Hanen muttered to Rallia.

Rallia nodded and turned away. Hanen heard a ripping sound.

"What is she doing?" Ghoré said. "I'm not through with you."

"You're not making any sense or getting to any point," Hanen said. "The city doesn't want you here. No one wants those wyloths here either. It's time for you to leave."

"I'm not leaving! I am giving you a choice. You can serve me. Or you can die."

"You're not going to hurt us," Hanen said.

Ghoré grinned. Then his lips peeled away into a wicked grin of teeth no longer wholly human. They were fangs—wyloth teeth. Standing, Hanen could make out between his legs a tail that hung as low as his knees. The loose skin on his arms was not as loose as he thought, but rather hung as flaps or a webbing.

Ghoré stepped down off the rubble pile, licking his moist lips and holding his hands far up above him in the air. His fingers didn't seem so long moments ago.

"I am the Wyloth King."

"Alright," Searn said. "This has gone far enough."

He raised his crossbow and pulled the trigger.

A wyloth dove in front of the bolt. It impaled the creature, and threw it backward into the arms of its king. Ghoré looked at the creature and then set it down on the cobblestone gently.

"Usurpers!" he screamed and lunged forward.

Rallia spun around, her staff now wrapped in cloth. She held a lit piece of tinder in her hand, and touched it to the cloth, which ignited.

Ghoré froze in his tracks and Rallia stepped forward.

"You were my responsibility," Rallia said. "I thought perhaps we had even come to an understanding before I turned you over. You admitted that it was wrong, what you did."

Ghoré took steps backward, away from the flame. The wyloths were going mad with frenzy and fear. Some made to flee, but the motion of Ghoré's hand stopped them huddling in their tracks.

"I said those things to shut you up, girl."

"You're not even human anymore," Rallia continued, "you sold your soul. I didn't really believe Kos-Yran could even be real until today. Now you make me wonder what other tales are true."

Ghoré stopped as his foot, more like a hand, touched his rubble throne. Rallia continued forward.

"Rallia!" Searn shouted. "Don't corner him!"

Ghoré's elongated arms snapped out, his fist meeting Rallia's jaw and spinning her around.

Ghoré dove past Rallia as she fell to the ground. The wyloths leapt with their king, descending upon the interlopers en masse.

All Hanen could do was flail his arms. He felt the creatures swarming over him, trying to scratch at anything they could get to. He rushed forward, trying to reach Rallia.

One scratched his ear. Another bit his leg. He lunged through an invisible wall, coming to a small space surrounding Rallia and her burning torch, where no wyloth dared approach. Hanen crouched low as wyloths spun and leapt overhead.

"Rallia, are you alright?" He reached out and took hold of the still-burning torch.

"My jaw hurts," Rallia said, "but it's not broken. We need to help the others."

Hanen nodded and stood. He held the torch out for Rallia.

Rallia shook her head. "You take the torch. I take the king."

DEATHLESS BEAST

Hanen handed Rallia his axes, then held out the firebrand. The wyloths would not get near. They pushed through and came to Ophedia, curled up on the ground under her cloak, screaming. Aurín was doing his best, but scratches covered his face. Searn wasn't visible. They spun around looking for him. Dead wyloths littered the entrance to the alley.

They each grabbed debris, quickly put together torches, and took off, following the trail of wyloth bodies.

They heard a strange sound up ahead, and as they came around the corner, another few downed wyloths lay where they fell. They looked slightly singed.

They ran farther and came to the central square in front of the paladinial fortress.

Ghoré stood now in the middle of the square. Wyloths clung to him like his own cloak that writhed upon wind and flesh, hundreds of eyes looking about in menace.

"I'll do it again," Searn said. "Don't make me. Leave now. And take your monsters."

"I do as I please. I am king."

"You're a bad mark for the Sentinels, is what you are. You'll mar the name I've worked so hard to build."

Searn glanced up and saw the others enter the square. He nodded and pulled out a bottle.

"I warned you," Searn said.

"You have no power! I have more power than you'll ever know!"

"How little you know, you sorry fool."

Searn threw the bottle at the foot of Ghoré, splattering the contents about.

"Hah! Beer!" Ghoré said.

The others approached from behind with lit torches.

Ghoré pointed out his gnarled hand. It seemed covered in a coarse orange fur that thickened each moment. The wyloths leapt off him, soaring through the air at Searn.

Rallia rushed forward, Hanen followed, and they put themselves between Ghoré and Searn. Some of the wyloths saw this and turned toward the Clouws, but froze, unable to approach the fire. Rallia tossed the torch toward Ghoré. It touched the strong beer and lit it with a smoldering, guttering flame. It wasn't much heat, but it was enough. Ghoré screeched and dove away. The hair on his arm and legs and tail easily lit. He ran away toward the fortress and leapt high up into the air, higher than any man should be able. The skin under his arms caught the wind and he was lifted, still screaming as the flame licked at his fur.

The wyloths in the area quickly lost their impulse to fight and fled after him as he flew off over the city and out into the northern sky.

Searn took his crossbow from Ophedia, who had retrieved it from the alley.

"That was, interesting," Searn said.

"That's an understatement," Hanen said. "What did you do back there that killed so many wyloths at once? Why don't you have a scratch on you."

"My pretty face is fairly important to the Black Sentinels. I kept it protected. And I had another bottle of Limaen Strong on me. It made a nice little splatter and flame when I lit it."

"I did not know you could do that with beer," Aurín said.

"Some beers. Limaen Strong for one." Searn looked up at the Bulwark. "I don't expect we'll see him again; especially if we head north. Wyloths don't like cold."

"He looked more like a savern than a wyloth at his size," Hanen said.

"True, but we just burnt off any hair that might keep that naked thing warm."

"Too bad he couldn't stay," Aurín said to Ophedia. "Maybe he'd have made you his queen."

The girl hit Aurín in the arm. Aurín winced in genuine pain.

"Woman! I wouldn't make you my own queen with a punch like that. Not unless I wanted to get hurt every day."

She punched him again, a smile on her face this time.

34

Amethyst City

Keep secret the vaults that protect us from harm.

Keep oath on the Dweol that guards what's to come.

Keep wary eye on Veld, where dreams and dark inspire.

Keep soul for life beyond where gods live and retire.

—ABBESS GHELLIVEN OF MAHN FULHAR

There was a marked difference between Bortali and the first valley of Boroni. Setting aside the black rocks and rainy weather of the dour city of Waglÿsaor, Katiam Borreau noticed there was a civilized greenness to Boroni not seen in the darkly forested country of Bortali.

She felt as though she was casting off the cloak meant to keep her warm from a coldness that she had not realized pervaded everything. The vül attack, the Crysalas Vaults in their perpetual darkness, the frustration at the walls of Garrou—all of it seemed to be yesterday's problems.

The entourage descended down the long slope from the pass into the meadows, kissed by the rays of the sun breaking through the clouds. Katiam rode alongside Esenath Chlöise, the master botanist that had joined their company at the College of

Thementhu.

Like Katiam and the other Paladames of the Crysalas Honoris, Esenath wore full armor over her robes. Each piece of the suit was fitted to her, and functional, but decorated with motifs of rose blossoms, leaves, and thorns. While most of the Paladames wore their hair cropped short, Esenath had shaved her head in the manner of those who had taken the Aspect of Cleanliness. Her dark Sidieratan skin was almost the same color as the brown robe of Charity that she wore.

Katiam pursued what she thought were simpler Aspects. She negligently touched the wooden mace of the Aspect of Peace at her side, setting her apart from the others, unwilling to raise a hand against another. A simple necklace of stylized thorns on her throat marked the dietary Aspect of St. Klare, and, while not as visible under her armor, the leather thongs which bound her sleeves—the Aspect of Dignity—was what she was most known for by the others.

The Matriarch Superioris, Maeda Mür, rode in the lead carriage. She leaned out the window to take in the view, her rose-bloom headdress off, and her thin white hair toyed with by the passing breeze. Though out of view, Katiam could hear the voice of the Matriarch's husband, the Prima Pater of the Paladins of the Hammer, speaking with her. Katiam had the privilege of calling them her great aunt and uncle, and acted as their physician, both when they were at home at Pariantür and now on the road.

The Paladames of the Rose were interspersed throughout the company, riding alongside and chatting with the Paladins of the Hammer. While the Paladames sat atop the faster riding sleipnirs, the Paladins rode specially bred six-legged war sleipnirs.

From that massive stock, the work sleipnirs of Ganthic had been bred. Their height kept the Paladins sitting well above the palfreys of the women. While the Paladame armor bore motifs of roses and thorns across their armor, the Paladins plates bore no symbols.

Instead, the Paladins held either at attention or across their laps the two-headed hammer that was their namesake. The hammers were chained to their belts by twenty-two links. The Paladins' chins were obscured by tall, tower gorgets, but their shaved heads were bared to the elements. The heavy leather beneath their armor creaked against the brightly polished metal.

Astrid Glass, the Paladame charged with the safety of the Matriarch, rode alongside the twin Paladins, Loïc and Cävian, chatting with them. Both had the sun-darkened skin of Seterans and spoke animatedly with their hands, having taken the life-long Vow of Silence. While Astrid did not speak with her hands, she followed what they were saying, and replied in speech. She did not smile. She had not smiled since her brother died at the hands of a vül attack on the company. Whatever Astrid said sent the brothers into a fit of silent laughter.

Nearby, another Paladin watched the three of them talk together with a look that rode the line between envy and contempt. Dane Marric was a burr in many a saddle. Katiam often found herself observing him and wondering what had separated him from the joy of community that the people of Pariantür had to offer.

Another Paladin rode up to him and said something from over his shoulder. Dane turned and scoffed, then urged his sleipnir forward to ride on ahead of the company. That revealed Jined Brazstein, who pulled up short to consider Dane as he rode away.

Jined had been the talk of everyone as they rode out of Waglÿsaor and through the pass. He had not been one Katiam had ever given much attention to, save that he often stood out like a sore thumb in any crowd—being taller and built like the war sleipnir he sat atop.

What had caused everyone to take note of him was that, unlike every other Paladin in the world of Kallattai, he wore two vow beads from his cordons across his breastplate. When taken to the Pillory by the Prima Pater for breaking a minor Vow he had taken, Jined had taken upon himself a second Vow. His god, Grissone, had divinely ordained the decision, changing the color of his cordons to white and adding the second vow bead in a flash of miraculous light.

Jined touched the satchel hanging from the side of his hip, and shook free whatever thought was distracting him, and urged his own mount back into a walk.

Shepherds goaded herds of capricör through the meadow with the help of scaled ynfalds, which were built heavier in Bortali than the sleeker ones used in Setera and out east near Pariantür. One of the younger shepherd boys had stopped by the side of the road to watch them pass, and kept a hand on the gray ynfald at his side.

Its head sat almost even with the boy's chest. The scales across its body were like a pinecone's scales, and had begun to grow in hefty fur between the scales for winter. It rustled in acknowledgment of their passing, but kept a close eye on the flock of white and black wooled capricör in the field, its long tongue flicking out of its pointed snout. One of the flock began to wander, and the ynfald, knowing its business before the boy could give the command, loped off to rein it back in.

Far off to the north, the sun rays caressed the Lupinfang Sea, just beyond the mauve city of Clehm. At first Katiam thought the city was an illusion. She had heard descriptions from others of the City of Amethyst. She thought it to be a descriptor of the dyes the city exported, but the closer they drew toward the walls of Clehm, the more she realized the truth of the city's nickname.

The gates were guarded by soldiers in a deep purple uniform that verged on black, the rocks the city was built from were a light mauve, and the people of the city took pride in their color, all wearing various forms of purple dyed clothing. Katiam's attention was abruptly pulled from the admiration of the city's dedication to the color by a scoff from Dane Marric, who rode next to her.

"Such vanity," he muttered to himself.

"People of Pariantür wear a light orange from the porumarian dyes collected there," she countered.

He gave her only a glance, but said nothing. His silence was not due to the Vow of Chastity he had taken, but the more stringent philosophy some of that Vow had taken, refusing to interact with women.

A younger man suddenly rushed out of the crowd toward them, wearing the trappings of nobility.

"Pantheon bless you!" he cried. "Do you come from Pariantür?"

Dane moved to put himself between the man and the carriages trundling through the streets.

"I'd ask you to stand back," Dane demanded.

"Pardon," the man said, "I am Ørzan Clemmbäkker, son of the Jarl of Clehm."

One of the carriages came to a halt, and the face of the head scribe, Pater Segundus Gallahan Pír, peeked out.

"You come from the house of Clehm to greet us?"

"Uh...," Ørzan faltered.

"Brother Marric," the Pater Segundus said, "please halt the entourage for a moment."

Dane pressed through the crowd to reach the front carriage, and it halted.

"Are we expected?"

"I heard my father speaking with one of our contacts from

Waglÿsaor about a rumor that an entourage of Paladins had been seen, who were not from St. Rämmon. But we did not know you were headed this way. I was out visiting an...acquaintance, and saw you enter the city."

"How long does it take to make it through the city to your father's home?"

"With the route you're taking," the boy said, considering where they stood, "an hour. The market will be full at this time."

"Then perhaps you ought to ride ahead and warn your father that the Prima Pater of the Paladins of the Hammer is approaching, and he'll have all of us as guests."

The boy's eyes started, and he dropped to his knee.

"I am not the Prima Pater. The best you can do for us is to take that message."

"I will. Thank you," Ørzan said, rising, and taking off into the crowd.

Gallahan descended from the carriage and walked past the other idle carriage to the Prima Pater's in the lead.

"How do they not know we were coming?!" Katiam heard the voice of the Prima Pater demand, followed by the calming tones of the Matriarch.

This had become a common theme since they entered Bortali. None seemed to know the Prima Pater's entourage was nearing, despite the entourage having sent messages ahead of time over the course of the past year in preparation for the journey.

The carriages lurched forward, and they came to the market, which was packed with people shopping through harvest-laden stalls.

Several merchants saw the Paladins and carriages and ignorantly began hawking their wares towards the nobles they thought remained hidden within.

As one merchant began to shout, others soon followed suit. Katiam couldn't help but laugh. The joy of people who did not seem to have a looming war with their neighbor hanging over them was a welcome relief compared to those she had seen and visited over the past weeks.

They made it through the market and the crowds thinned out. The street became easier to navigate, and led them toward a final street overlooking the sea, approaching the purple castle of the Clemmbäkkers.

Standing on the stairs that lead up to the entrance stood only four figures. The young man, Ørzan, stood next to a girl about the same age, her hair tied up in two heavy braids. The two of them wore light lilac outfits, while their parents wore rich velvets of deep purple. The jarl descended the stairs and dropped to one knee in front of the carriage. He had a straight red beard that descended to his chest with gold beads braided into it, each set with purple amethysts.

"Greetings to the Prima Pater of Pariantür!" he said from the ground. "I welcome you to my home."

The door to the carriage opened, and Prima Pater Dorian Mür stepped down. Most assumed him blessed by his god, to be able to move so agilely at his ancient age of ninety-five. He wore armor, motifed in multi-winged eagles. A red cape, slashed to resemble pinion feathers, hung down to his knees. From his belt a chain ran back to the carriage. His seneschal, Brother Adjutant Jurgon Upona, descended with the Prima Pater's scepter attached to the other end of the chain. It resembled a hammer, but was decidedly fashioned from two slabs of metal, suggesting two sets of wings, representing the god Grissone's twin-soul, the Anka. Jurgon handed the Prima Pater the scepter, and the old man took it in his arm.

"Thank you for the greeting," Dorian said sternly. "We met your son upon our arrival, and he seemed to indicate we were not expected."

"My son spoke the truth," Jarl Clemmbäkker said. "I have not heard a word of your coming. Regardless, I humbly welcome you."

Dorian indicated for the jarl to rise.

"Bygones," Dorian said. "Perhaps you can introduce us to your family, and we can move on with our day?"

The jarl's look of worry turned to a smile.

"Of course! I am Jarl Saedrick von Clemmbäkker."

He turned and motioned toward the three on the stairs. An elegant, auburn-haired woman came down the stairs, took her husband's hand, and curtsied.

"This is my wife, Frü Lerda Clemmbäkker, formerly of House Rodock."

"Our home welcomes you," the woman said. "Our son and daughter, Ørzan and Onelie, also welcome you."

The children, nearly adults, each gave a timid bow and curtsy.

"I see you have Paladames of the Rose riding with you," Lerda said.

The Prima Pater turned to the carriage and held out a hand.

"I am accompanied by my wife, the Matriarch Superioris of the church of Crysania."

As the Matriarch peeked out, her faux-armor made of blocked wool was struck by the light of the sun breaking through the clouds, and she looked like a cloud herself, of whites and grays. She worked her way down to the cobbles as the two noblewomen fell to their knees.

"Matriarch Superioris!" Lerda cried.

"Thank you," the old woman said, waving a hand for them to rise. "No need for all that. I'd like to talk to you about finding refreshment and rest."

"Of course," the lady said as her daughter helped her to her feet. "Please, bring the sisters with you."

Lerda turned to her husband. "I am going to retreat now, husband."

"Of course, Lerda," he said. "Give my regards."

"Please follow me," Lerda said, as she turned to walk around the side of the castle into the garden.

The Matriarch followed without giving a second thought to the Paladames. Sabine Upona, the Matriarch's assistant, motioned for Astrid to follow the Matriarch, as Sabine turned to Jurgon Upona, the Prima Pater's seneschal.

"We'll take care of the sleipnir," Jurgon said.

She touched her husband's elbow, then turned to go after Astrid. The other sisters followed after her in a line.

The garden was being cleaned for winter. At the back, against the stone wall, women were disappearing through a stone entryway and down a flight of stairs. There was no secret made of it. Candles set in small alcoves lit the way. The hushed voices of Katiam's companions echoed up the incline. As suddenly as they descended, they reached the bottom. One by one, they disappeared through a doorway into an antechamber, which was well-lit by hundreds of candles.

"It is astonishing that you've not known of our coming," the Matriarch was saying.

"Any number of things might have prevented our knowing," Frü Lerda said. "Regardless, you are here now. In the noble lands of the Boronii you are most welcome as our guest, and will want for nothing, least of all in my own home."

"I do not doubt it. I rather forgot how unsecretive the Vaults in

Boroni were."

"As you know, we have little to fear, for the traditions we keep among the women of the Northern Scapes."

"This may be true in your country, but not as much in the lands to the east of here."

"The women not encaged by the vulgarities of the Bortali men and the forest people are cowed and feared. They're more than welcome to come here and live more freely, or among the Isles of the Bronue."

"But they remain," the Matriarch said, "and we must respect that wish."

"Have you been long on the road?" the lady asked. "I assume you traveled by way of Waglÿsaor?"

"Three days' travel through the pass," the Matriarch said. "There was a rock slide that slowed us after the first night, but we managed."

"I'll speak to my husband about the rocks."

"Despite being at war with Bortali, you would clear the way?"

"Bortali may think they are at war with us, but I do not view it that way."

"And what does your husband say?"

"It matters little this day," she said. "Follow me, and we'll enjoy some tea, and you can tell me about your travels."

She led the way into another chamber, where candles behind a rosy glass lit the room. A handful of women moved about in white robes, wearing small circlets styled as black thorns. They moved about with wooden, steaming cups and handed them to the Paladames.

"By the mother and the thorn," they said as they gave the cups up, retreating suddenly.

The Matriarch and Frü Clemmbäkker spoke together for over an hour before a small bell jingled in the corner.

"Would you prefer to take your food here? Or join my husband and yours in the halls above?"

"I would be interested in rest, I think," the Matriarch said, "but I leave the choice to each of those who follow me."

Most chose to go and join the others, following the women in white robes and black thorns through a side door. The Matriarch, Sister Upona, and Katiam followed one of the servants upstairs to a room that had been prepared for the Matriarch. It was a small but amply furnished room of reds and purples. The attendant excused herself, leaving them to their privacy.

The Matriarch puttered about the room a bit, opening up the wardrobe, and touching cushions on seats, while Katiam and Sabine watched her go through her ritual. Then, the Matriarch walked over to the bed and sat down.

"Well?" the Matriarch asked.

"It was rather odd," Sabine said.

"What was? And how so?" the Matriarch asked.

"I usually expect to be whisked away," Sabine said. "That has become the norm for us as we arrive in a city. To be done so, so publicly?"

"Katiam?" the Matriarch asked.

"I do not recognize the black metal thorn crowns the women wore. Does it signify something?"

"It does. Both are good lines of query. I think it safe to say that the Bronuan Shieldmaidens have a strong following here in Boroni. Perhaps more here in Clehm than elsewhere, but time will tell."

"Shieldmaidens?" Katiam asked.

"When the Crysalas fled the pogroms and sought refuge at Pariantür, where did they come from?" the Matriarch asked.

"From all over. The women fled from every country."

"Every country? Or from many?"

Katiam gave her a look, and turned to open up her apothecary box and prepare the Matriarch's nightly medicine.

"Where did the women not flee from? Or better yet, where else did the Crysalas turn to for safety?"

"There was safety in Nemen, and in the far north of Mahn Fulhar."

"Correct. And where else?"

"There were few in the founding ledgers from Ikhala," Sabine said, "and from Nasun and Bronue."

"Why?"

"It is said the Ikhalans came from the stock of the far north, mixed with those Tambii who left their homeland, hence, their red hair. The same is said of the Bronuans—'happy to settle where the lands are harsh—'"

"'—and the women cheerful, despite the stark stones among which they lived,'" the Matriarch said, finishing the quote from her favorite playwright. "We shall know more tomorrow, but the martial tradition of the Bronuans in the middle of the Lupinfang is likely to be one adopted by the women of this city. Our own tradition is steeped in the lore of our mother goddess. They are steeped in the rigid will to fight for the right to enjoy their lives. It is a hope that seems lost in those of the Bortalians."

She scooted herself farther onto the bed and took the cup from Katiam.

"Now, let us seek sleep. I imagine Frü Clemmbäkker will want to see us early tomorrow morning, and we'll all likely need energy to keep up with her."

Katiam and Sabine turned to go and find their own room, in the adjacent chamber, where two beds had been prepared for them.

"Shieldmaidens?" Katiam asked.

"I'm not as up to date with my history of the Northern Scapes as I would like," Sabine said, "but I know we brought our own martial tradition to Pariantür when the Crysalas founded the Paladames. We aren't simply copying the brothers."

Katiam took out the Rotha pod from her satchel and held it in both hands as she finished readying herself for bed, thinking on the Shieldmaidens, and the abrupt nature of Frü Clemmbäkker and the women of her not-so-hidden vault. She hoped that morning didn't come too soon as the down pillow encased her face.

35

Shield and Blade

The garden requires care—water and fertilizer. And above all it requires light. But there is another tool with which to encourage a more healthy life: aggressively wielded pruning shears.

—SISTER VERIDA NEINSHUSS ON

THE GARDEN OF THE SOUL

As the Matriarch had guessed, Frü Lerda had ten sleipnirs saddled and ready for them in the morning. Katiam had the courtesy to say nothing of it until the Matriarch had swallowed her last bite of food. Save for the servants, who had been up to tend the fires, there were few in the dining hall to join them. The bread and honey served to them was fresh, and a few extra rolls found their way into Katiam's satchel, tucked alongside the Rotha.

Astrid Glass took the lead with Lerda's daughter, Onelie, while Esenath and the others rode behind the Matriarch and Frü Lerda. They chatted about the harvest and the successful lambing season from the previous year. They came out of the southern gate of the town and continued down the road that kept the slope of the mountains to their left, and long, now-empty fields to their right.

"I had not realized what a breadbasket Clehm was," the Matriarch commented.

"We're very proud of it. We are near enough to Donig, and have the eastern jarls to our south, situated to help us defend the border."

"You've read the intention of my statement well," the Matriarch said. "Our focus these last few weeks has been solely on the remedy of the situation here in the north. I have lived through war. I do not wish that on anyone."

"Wars do happen," Lerda said, "and while I do not expect the threats made by King Vorso to amount to much, I can say this—he'll not find an idle people in the Boronii."

"That is not my worry," the Matriarch said. "My worry is that Vorso will act rashly and strike at the heart of your people."

"If he does that, he'll find cold hearts of steel, ready to meet him."

"How did it start?"

"How did what start?"

"The animosity between Bortali and Boroni?"

"Long before you or I," Lerda said.

"That's a long time ago," the Matriarch said. "I'm nearly a century old."

"If you know your history, you know how Boroni formed. We and Bortali were once the same people. Except our country was pushed to the edge of 'proper' Bortali society, designated only as farmers and lumberjacks. We were meant to provide for the king's table, and to make the table he sat at. Yet, we were taxed relentlessly, starved of the very food and wood we brought from field and forest, and sold back the metal mined from our own ground with what coin we had left.

"There were the six barons, who stood up together, hoarding metals for several seasons, reporting back loss to the king. Over one harsh winter they forged the armaments for starving men, and in the spring the Boronii made their stand. And when Bronue sailed to our aid, the king had no recourse. At the end of that summer, at our threat of razing our own fields just before harvest, he gave us our freedom. We had plenty to eat, but the people of the east grew restless, and series of rebellions harassed the king for decades while our people thrived."

"And now?"

"Today, the Bortali are united in their hatred of our success and happiness. In the last decade, the mines of Brahz have struck affluent veins of iron, while Gerht has found silver, causing an influx of miners from other countries to migrate here. The Bortali have watched jealously; they are reliant on the leasing of Nemen mines for their own precious metals."

"They do not move on Nemen."

"They will, if envy takes hold of their throats. But their animosity and jealousy ties to our shared history. So they've pushed to harm us by our trade with the southern nations. You know that there are several passes into Bortali. To the south, the border we share with Düran and a bit of Limae is marked by a pass that can only be accessed by entering a stretch of forest legally claimed by the Bortali.

"We've long paid dues to pass through there, and they've avoided building anything more than border houses there for two reasons—to avoid cutting down the forest, marking it as theirs, and to keep the Üterk appeased. The wild men of the forest mark that wood as sacred."

"Could you not export through Mahndür, and then down to Düran?"

"We can. But export duties through Mahndür, and Limae force our prices up in Düran. Düran can pay those prices for our steel, but those further afield? Could not Hraldor use our steel in their vigilance against the Tambii?"

"And so you're forced to outlast Bortali."

"We can. And in all honesty, we will continue to trade with Mahndür, and others around the Lupinfang, and our steel will sell. But not to Bortali. Should the vül could rise up from their own forests, and march from their cursed dens to the east, threatening to raze Bortali to the ground, Bortali will find they have not Boronii steel to defend themselves with."

"Those are dark words," the Matriarch said.

"They are fair words," Lerda said.

They came over a hill and looked down into a small forest that filled a deep vale. The ten women cantered down the road that led into the peaceful serenity of the well-cared-for woods. The ground cover and bushes had all been removed and Katiam could see hundreds of yards through the tall trees only just starting to turn. There was a gradual shift from the deciduous to the evergreen, and the scent of pine suddenly filled the senses. She found herself touching the satchel, reminded of the scent of the Rotha hidden at her side.

The evergreens were suddenly a dense mass to be passed

through, and the sleipnirs fell into line, moving through the verdant canyon and out the other side into a large parkway that spread out before them.

Katiam was not prepared for the sight that awaited her. The Matriarch pulled up to a stop, and Katiam heard Astrid gasp in surprise. The estate sat in a steep bowl, with vineyards running up the sides. Women tended the vines, gathering up the fruit to take to a nearby winepress. To call the cluster of buildings in the center a complex did it no justice. It was a Crysalas Convent of old, out of the legends and tales told by the sisters. Much of it was crafted of newer stone, but the layout, in the rose-like pattern of petals, was obvious.

"What foolishness," the Matriarch said. "What utterly beautiful foolishness."

Katiam looked to see a broad smile on the Matriarch's face.

"What do you mean, Auntie?"

"To have found and rebuilt one of the convents of old. If this place was discovered by those that wish us harm... I can't imagine what those who might seek our order's demise might think."

"Perhaps the world is changing," Upona offered. "Perhaps a time is coming when our order can live in the light, instead of the darkness."

"That may be true, child," the Matriarch said, "but are we ready? Darkness hates light and winter hates spring."

"Spring arrives regardless."

Despite her critique, the old woman urged her sleipnir into a walk with a smile plastered across her face. When they arrived at the gate to the manor house, an Abbess came to greet them. She wore the white robes of a full Crysalas Abbess, and had down her arms black iron thorn bracelets.

"Matriarch Superioris Mür," the Abbess said. "The Vinegrove Convent welcomes you. I am Abbess Tashi Vell."

Sister Upona leaned in and whispered something to the Matriarch.

"You report to the church under the Vintner's Guild from Donig," the Matriarch said.

"And from Gerht, and Tosch. It is best to spread out the value of our convent among many, and the many that we care for."

"I do not much like surprises," the old woman said, "but I find myself liking this one. What keeps this place secret from the prying eyes of men?"

"The forest you passed through is well guarded by our people. The community here thrives in its size and care for itself."

"How many women live here?"

"Officially? One hundred. But there are ten times that many that call this place home—women presumed dead or lost, and prostitutes escaping their life and no longer welcomed by their families."

"The Hospital of Waglÿsaor could learn lessons from a place like this," Sister Upona muttered.

"I've already thought of that," the Matriarch replied, turning back to the Abbess. Lerda Clemmbäkker stood at her side now.

"And what keeps the jarls from absorbing a place like this, or giving it to some lordling?"

"I think perhaps there is more you do not yet understand of the women of Boroni," Lerda said, "In short, the jarls only have the support of the people because the women gave it to them. The women of the Northern Scapes were once free and equal. When the ideas of the Morraneans invaded into Mahndür, and kindled across the north, we lost some of that. But the Bronuans and the Boronii never forgot. Thus, when the jarls shrugged off the shackles of the Bortalian Kings, we stood alongside them, at the price of yet more of our freedom. Were someone to seek to take this haven from us, the entire country's women would stand arm in arm to defend it."

"By sheer stubbornness?" the Matriarch said.

"By shield and by blade," the Abbess said.

Lerda and Onelie echoed her.

"What does the Convent want for?" the Matriarch asked as she followed the Abbess into her domain.

"Very little. Perhaps we should ask my other guests who have arrived. They may have things they need."

"Other guests?"

"You've come at an opportune time," Lerda said from behind the Matriarch. "You and your husband's entourage, I mean. You see, the jarls have called a council. The jarlwives of the south rode out ahead of their husbands, who are at this moment only a few days behind. I don't doubt my own husband will share this news with the Prima Pater, if he hasn't already. We're all making our way to Donig tomorrow, to prepare for a feast."

"A council of war, then?" the Matriarch asked.

"It may result in that," Lerda said, "but it is customary to join together during the harvest to discuss the winter. Then, we will meet again on the Solstice, in a council of jarls and their vassals, to elect a new duke, and to barter vassal towns for the coming year."

"Barter towns?" Sabine asked.

Lerda laughed. "They barter themselves. Many barons are made 'free of fealty' during the council. While each town usually stays loyal to the barons and jarl who are closest to them, some may provide their town's taxes and trade to another jarl's estate for a period of seven years. It is often a means to trade with a larger city, or to exchange trade goods between two towns that might not normally share wealth."

"It was started by two towns of Eberveld and Gustice," Lerda's daughter, Onelie, spoke up. "Eberveld was small but it had an extensive cooperage trade, not a rich trade in any city. Gustice produces wines that almost puts this Convent to shame. They allied with one another, with the sponsorship of Tosch—which sits nowhere near them—and the aged wines of that alliance have become legendary."

"Often," Lerda added, "it is done at the request of a jarl desiring trade with another jarl. in the end, all benefit from these seven-year trades. Our own council of women sees to that."

"What do you mean?" the Matriarch asked.

"The law of this land is practiced by women. We hold the annals and codices of case law. It is by our recommendation that the deals are made."

"And what benefit do the men receive by capitulating to this?" the Matriarch asked.

Lerda stopped and considered the old woman next to her.

"We bear their children without complaint," she said with a smile. "Is there not a satisfaction in seeing the next generation rise to continue our traditions?"

They came out into a courtyard, where several hundred women wearing the white robes of the convent encircled the two women in the center. It immediately brought to mind the sparring training of the Paladames at Pariantür. Even Katiam, being dedicated to the Aspect of Peace, had been trained in some grappling to defend herself.

The two women in the center each had a shield on their arm, and held a long, wooden club in their other hand. They wore a wide-rimmed helmet, their faces covered by a heavy leather mask. One stood nearly as tall as Captain Sigri Smith, but would have outweighed her in muscle. The other was smaller, and danced about lithely. Her black hair fell down her back in a single braid.

Katiam had seen fights like this before. The smaller one sought the other's fatigue as they circled one another. The taller woman gave testing swings of her faux-mace, and the smaller danced out of reach each time. They paused for a moment to consider one another and Katiam saw the smaller woman breathing heavily. She would make a move soon, or else risk reaching the end of her strength.

Katiam could just make out the eyes of the taller woman, who glanced over and saw the Matriarch standing in the entryway. The move she made was sudden, severe, and beautiful.

The smaller woman only had time to raise her weapon across her shield and brace for the impact of the taller woman closing the gap and shouldering her backwards. She stumbled back as she took the brunt of the charging woman's plank across her sword arm; she came down onto her back. The second swing brought the weapon down to stop a hair's breadth from the other woman's face.

The woman on the ground let her plank fall from her hand, and dropped her head back in defeat. The women cheered, but instead of reveling in her victory, the taller woman turned toward the Paladames and dropped to one knee.

The cheering died suddenly, and the others followed suit as they turned and saw who she bowed to.

The Matriarch gave a wave of her hand in acknowledgment and then motioned for them to rise.

"Greetings from Pariantür," the Matriarch said. "I am the Matriarch Superioris, head of the Crysalas Church, and we welcome our sister sect by the name of the goddess Crysania. By Bloom and Thorn."

"By Shield and Blade," the collected women said in unison.

The Matriarch smiled. "Now, I should like to meet and congratulate the victor."

The two women had taken their helmets off and stood beside one another. The taller woman had flaming red hair, and skin that verged on translucent.

"This is Toire Siobh," Frü Clemmbäkker said. "She has come as our guest from the Isles of Bronue Jinre. That alone was no mean feat."

"How so?"

"Donig has denied the Bronuans access to the ports of Boroni,"

Toire Siobh said, "for the fact that we have been suing for peace between Bortali and Boroni. I have been sent by my father, Rhi Barra of Œndin."

"And you're to join the women journeying to Donig? Will that not be conspicuous? You are astonishingly beautiful. I don't imagine anyone who knows you won't immediately recognize you," the Matriarch said.

"It is a fear of ours," the woman Toire defeated said, stepping forward. She was older than Katiam had expected, but certainly not yet fifty, with some gray hairs playing at the edge of her black hair. "But your own appearance in our country may provide the answer we seek."

She gave a deep bow to the Matriarch and stood. "I am Frü Gederin, wife of the High Duke Toschbrecht. If our guest, Toire Siobh, would come as one of your own Paladames, my usually very discerning and paranoid husband would be quick to overlook her."

"I will consider joining this subterfuge under two conditions," the Matriarch said, smiling.

"And those are?"

"That you provide me a seat at your council of women in Donig."

"Done," Gederin and Lerda said in unison.

"And that if you have a scrying bowl here, or in Donig, you grant me the use of it."

"We have one here, and would gladly make use of it," Abbess Vell said, "Although we are running short of our own rosebud crystals."

"We shall request that more be sent to you from the Oracle, of course."

"Then please follow me," the abbess said, turning to walk to the main building.

36

Distant Voices

Our protection of the helpless took root long before they tried to destroy our garden with fire. And thus the green returned, and it flourished.

—SAYINGS OF MATRIARCH DENSWYN

Luxuriously cushioned chairs sat in a circle under a flattened rotunda. A mirrored bowl sat on a marble pedestal in the center of the space. The Matriarch had taken her seat in a throne-like chair made of white wood and satin, and the women of the convent introduced themselves. Most were Boronii. The wives of the jarls from Thom, Gerht, and Sturm introduced themselves.

Astrid took a seat next to Katiam, across the room from the Matriarch, to allow the other women a chance to sit nearer to the Matriarch, who smiled serenely and listened as each woman gave their name and hometown.

"Abbess Venn," the Matriarch said loudly enough for most to hear, "the alewives of Bortali are saying their men are giving into drunkenness, more so during the rising conflict with your own country. Have you seen the same here?"

"No more than usual," the Abbess said.

"Bronue cannot say the same," Toire Siobh said.

"And why is that?"

"The northern Zhigavan have stumbled upon a new way to prepare stronger drink," the red-haired woman said. "It's become a bit of a novelty among my people; more so among the traders of Killark-Slione."

"And are you doing anything to combat this? Waglÿsaor has seen the men spend their money on drink, and the women forced to seek means elsewhere."

"You mean with their bodies," Toire scoffed.

The Matriarch shrugged in confirmation.

"My late mother and I have waged a war to rid our country of such an 'occupation'."

"And have you found yourself successful?"

"It long will be a battle," Toire said, "but even if it takes my own grandchildren's efforts to finally squash it, it will have been worth it."

"Matriarch Superioris," Sister Upona said, "all is ready."

All turned their attention to the center. Sabine Upona had placed a single rose-tinted crystal in the center of the mirrored bowl, filling the silvered basin with its color. The Matriarch waved her hand, and Upona took out a small silver hammer. She tapped the rim, sending a singing tone around the room. The bowl bloomed to life with a glow of ruddy pink light. The sound continued, and a voice hung in the air.

"Greetings? Greetings?" the distant voice called.

"Greetings, Sister Krena," Upona said speaking into the bowl.

"Sister Upona?" the voice replied. "Where are you speaking from?"

"We are in a vault in Boroni."

"And how does the Matriarch Superioris fare?"

"I am well," the old woman called out.

"We have much to say, with very little time," Sister Upona said. "The sisterhood here has a few Dweol-Petals left, and we do not wish to use up their entire supply."

"You took a great deal with you."

"Which we've been giving to the sisterhoods. They'll have need of it in the coming months."

"Why is that?"

"Bortali and Boroni are at war," the Matriarch said. "Well, nearly at war."

"What would you have us do?" the voice in the bowl said.

"Please send word down the valley to Pariantür. New sisters will be arriving from the college to replace those on the list they carry. I would ask you send with those who leave to attend the college a score of new Paladames, to bring additional relief to the vaults of Bortali. Have an additional twelve take the longer route through

Düran to Boroni, where they are to pass through the vaults to be under the authority of Abbess Vell."

"We shall see it done."

Katiam felt a tug at her belt and looked down to see the satchel at her side moving. She gasped and covered it with her arms, and then reached a tentative hand into the bag.

Her fingers graced the surface of the large Rotha pod, and it suddenly moved away from her touch. She scrambled to open the bag and look in, wondering if some creature, a wyloth, or their little cousin the fury, had snuck in to seek a treat and moved the Rotha away, finding nothing else within. She lifted it up and held it in both hands. As the voice of Sister Krena spoke, the subtle crystalline sound that reverberated along with it washed over Katiam, and the Rotha in her hands, which shook with each pulse. She lifted the pod and looked at it closer. A seam across its circumference had raised beneath the surface. Within, there was a subtle rattling, like a nut broken free within its shell.

"My husband also has a message for Pariantür. A more detailed message is to come when we reach the Green Grove Bastion in Mahndür, but in case that takes us longer than expected, St. Hamul is sending a large number of brothers from Boroni back to Pariantür, to be replaced by members of the brotherhood. He wanted me to at least convey that they were coming."

"We will make sure they expect their arrival. And we'll inform the Green Grove Bastion that you're to arrive within the month."

"Very well. By Rose and Thorn."

The voice of the Abbess Krina began to intone her reply but was suddenly interrupted by a cracking sound as the petal within the bowl expired and shattered.

The crystalline resonance stopped abruptly, and the pod in Katiam's hand no longer moved.

"They will send a message ahead of us to the Oracle in Mahndür, to deliver fresh Dweol petals to us at the Green Grove Bastion," Upona said.

"And I should hope," the Matriarch said, "that they'll bring enough that we can send some back to you, Abbess Venn."

Katiam continued staring at the Rotha.

"What was that?" Astrid asked.

"What was what?"

"The thing in your hand. It was moving."

"You saw it too?"

Astrid nodded.

"It's not moving now though," Katiam said.

"But what is it?"

"One of the sisters at the college gave it to me. It's some mysterious seed that has gone from person to person for centuries, and no one can figure out how to get it to bloom."

"Well," Astrid said, "it seems something made it move."

"But what?" Katiam said, considering the Rotha for a few moments more before putting it back into her satchel.

As they came out into the courtyard, a rider pulled her sleipnir up short.

"I come bearing a message for Frü Clemmbäkker and the Matriarch Superioris," the woman said.

"What is it, Aalla?" Lerda said, moving past the Matriarch.

"The Prima Pater left this morning with your husband, to begin the journey to Donig. He has asked the Matriarch Superioris to meet them on the road—you're to join when you're able."

"That wry wyloth beat me to it," Lerda laughed.

"What is so funny?" the Matriarch asked.

"My husband knows how long I can take to get ready when we leave to go anywhere. I had hoped to surprise him with a message that I had already left to go with the other jarlwives. It seems he played his hand to try to rush me out the door by going on without me."

She turned back to the messenger. "Have my ladies-in-waiting prepared everything?"

"They are awaiting your orders, yes. They have been preparing since you left this morning."

"Then return and tell them to meet me on the road. I'll join the Matriarch Superioris and her attendants, along with Frü Gerhtigan, Frü Sturmguard, and Frü Thommus.

"It seems," the Matriarch muttered to Astrid, Sabine, and Katiam, "we'll not be returning to Clehm. Did you bring everything you needed with you?"

"My apothecary case is still there," Katiam said.

"You need not worry about that," Frü Clemmbäkker said. "I'll make sure that anything your husband's people have forgotten to gather is brought in my own carriage. If you'd like to join me as I ride north, we can take our time, and make the men wait a bit, if they're so eager to make it to Donig."

As they rode out of the grove that hid the convent, Katiam was more than aware of people in the forest watching them, bows in their hands, though not drawn. The woman from Bronue Jinre, Toire Siobh, now wore full Paladame regalia, and answered to Astrid as a member of the Matriarch's personal guard. She looked the part, and several times Katiam forgot she rode with them incognito under Astrid's command.

Esenath pulled her sleipnir up next to Katiam as they fell back into their loose formation and came out onto the open road.

"What were you and Astrid talking about during the ceremony?"

"What?" Katiam replied.

"You had the Rotha pod in your hand. Astrid sat next to you, and she asked you something. And you looked confused."

"I thought a wyloth or a fury had climbed into my satchel, and I reached in to check, and to protect the pod."

"But there was no wyloth?"

"No. Only the Rotha."

"Those who have possessed it have thought odd things happened around it. Like a nagging obsession at the edge of your awareness."

"You speak from experience? Did that happen to you with the Rotha?"

"It happened with me with my book. I started dreaming in illustrated images. The colorful ink peeled back layers, and I was even able to know what was hidden behind petals of flowers I had not yet dissected. There were times during the year I spent working on it the hardest, where I swear I lived twice as long. I worked on it during the day and was immersed in the dream of it at night."

"That sounds dangerous. Like the stories of those who delve too deep in the Dreamworld of Sakharn."

Esenath gave her a sheepish look.

"That was a worry of mine as well, and so I visited the chapel at the college. The Abbess there advised me. She gave me a Dweol petal, and I had it worked into a necklace which I wore to sleep."

She smiled to herself, a memory playing on her lips. She glanced over at Katiam.

"The dreams got stronger after that. I think perhaps I was in the Veld."

Katiam frowned. "That's dangerous ground, Esenath."

"I had Crysania's protection, though. The edges of my vision glowed pink while I was there. It was a place of true inspiration, like the old tales—before the wife of the Judge faltered and her dream realm, the Veld, was poisoned. But it's there, Katiam. A place of idea."

"And nightmare."

"Yes," she said, clutching something under her blouse. "It can be a place of nightmare, too."

She took a deep breath and looked back at Katiam. "It has been over two years since I have had dreams like those. That Dweol charm I wore then, that I still wear, protected me, and perhaps still keeps me safe now."

She touched at her throat to check the strap, and smiled.

Frü Clemmbäkker led them on a road that kept hills between them and the sea for several hours. As dark began to fall, they entered a forested portion of the road, and she slowed her pace.

"With night fast approaching," Astrid Glass said, bringing her mount up next to Lerda and her daughter Onelie, "we ought to move faster, in hopes of finding shelter."

"Not through these woods, no," Lerda said. "There is an Üterk tribe who lives in the woods that stretch south from here. They do not take kindly to those who trespass without first making arrangements."

"Why is that? "The Matriarch asked. "I would think that being so close to your capital, the roads are safer than elsewhere."

"And you feel caution is best now?" Astrid asked.

"I do," Lerda said.

Astrid gave some quick orders to surround the ladies and the Matriarch.

They moved with purpose down the road, the clip clip-clop of their sleipnirs' six-shod hooves reverberating off the trees. In the dark, the glow of a fire near the road acted as a beacon.

Lerda hissed for Astrid, who continued to march forward.

"Sister Glass," Lerda then said, "we ought not to approach too boldly."

"I am charged with your safety," Astrid said. "As that is the case, you should trust me."

"I trust no one but myself on a dark road. And the sound of stringed instruments playing at that fire should give us further pause. The Üterk are known to play their instruments long into the night."

"A manticör seen is one that wants to be seen," Astrid said.

They came around a bend, and two figures sat at the fire. One tended a pot over the flames, and the other plucked at the strings of an ancient, many-stringed instrument.

"Pantheon bless you," Astrid said, not dismounting.

The figure holding the instrument stood up and approached. He had a massive jaw, with teeth his mouth seemed barely able to contain. He smiled around his teeth and ran a hand over his bald head.

"Now what would a unit of Paladames be doing out at this time of night?" he asked.

"We travel on our own business. And we would like to hope you and your people would grant us permission to pass through their forest."

"I can't rightly say this is my forest. Nor can my brother."

"You are not Üterk?"

"No, we are not Üterk. But we did run into a band of them earlier today. They were headed off to the south, for work to be found there in Tosch. My brother and I are traveling storytellers."

The second man stood up. He had a massive frame, though in the firelight, Katiam thought they were both built similarly. This brother though had a head covered in tall, wild hair, and a beard to match.

"We are on the road, trying to catch up with our entourage," Astrid said.

"If you're wandering after the Paladins of the Hammer that rode through, you're still a couple hours behind them."

"It's not likely you'll catch up with them before morning," the second brother grunted.

"Do we have enough to feed thirteen women?" the first brother said.

"I could make do," the second said.

"We really ought to be on our way," Astrid said.

The frigid breeze that wafted through the trees picked up.

"It looks like the night will continue to grow colder," the bald brother said. "Let us host you at our fire. We'll feed you, keep you lit by our fire, and perhaps we'll muster up a good story to tell you."

Astrid looked over her shoulder to the Matriarch, who gave a nod.

She dismounted, took out a purse of money, weighed it in her hand, and gave it to the storyteller.

"This ought the pay for your hospitality."

"I won't say no to coin. The gods gave it to the people, you know."

"I am not familiar with that tale," the Matriarch said, coming to sit by the fire.

"That might be a good one to tell," the brother said, looking to the other.

"What is your name?" the Matriarch asked.

"I am called Nair," the bald one said. "My brother here is Kash."

"And where do you hail from?" the Matriarch asked.

"We've walked many a land," Nair said.

"I do not doubt this," the Matriarch said. "Let us hear this story you've chosen to tell us, and hope that the gold given you is more than enough to pay for it and the food."

Katiam glanced at the Matriarch. The odd tone her aunt was using was out of place.

Nair laughed. "If you truly deem the story worthy, then we shall consider our debt even. Now, where to begin?"

"The gods, you said, gave coin to the people."

"Ah yes. The gods," Nair began.

It was within the City, that great and glorious city gifted to all by the crafter of civilization, Rionne, that there lived a man. On each day he rose, and each night he slept, and he took to following the sun up to top of the city, and to its sky-touching apex as the sun peaked the sky, and he would follow its trail, and mark its passing. And to the people around him, whether they be the people of Rionne, or the qavyl of Lae'Zeq, or his own men, he would declare to them the rising and setting of the sun.

Be it bread he needed, or pleasurable drink, when trade was asked, he gave that simple fact. 'I am he who charts the sun, to declare its rise and declare its fall. Know that it is so.'

There were, in those days, no seasons to mark change, nor cold to bring about winter. Many a year passed, and it was so. Qavyl offered insightful wisdom. The people of Rionne their crafts. Men bartered and traded. And the Sun-Caller, as he was known, did as he always did.

There was a time that came when every day, upon the setting of the sun, when Sun-Caller came to take his bread and drink daily from a woman who had plenty to give. For her ability to find fair trade was known, and all came to her to understand their worth by her knowledge. And every day Sun-Caller took from her a single loaf of bread and a cup of drink.

Be it her last loaf, or the first to come from the oven, Sun-

Caller declared it his. And she came to resent his appearance. For her day began before the rise of sun, and ended long after it set, and she had no time to leave her place and watch light bloom nor fade. And every day he came and told her it was so, without her observation.

One day Sun-Caller entered her place, and to her he gave the news.

"This morning the sun rose, and passed overhead, and I watched it set in the west."

"Why is it so?' She asked, placing the bread and drink before him.

"I do not know," the man said, "nor would I wish to know. I have only the purpose of seeing that it is so."

The following day he came in again.

"This morning the sun rose, and passed overhead, and I watched it set in the west."

"Have you asked it as it passed why it does so?"

"I do not know," the man replied, "nor would I wish to know. I have only the purpose of seeing it is so."

The following day Sun-Caller entered, and the woman held up her hand that he be silent.

"Why must I?" he said. "I come to offer the news of the sun, and take my bread and drink from you."

"Take is all you do," she said "what need have I to know the rising of the sun, if I should not see it myself? It has been years since I felt its touch on my skin. Had you something novel to tell, I might be willing, but this day, I am not."

"But I am here to tell you that the sun has risen, and it has set. I have given you now what you ought to know. And you must give me the food and drink that I need."

"You have need of bread. But I have no need of the sun."

Sun-Caller became angry and marched toward the door.

"I have given you news, and as you have not given me my bread nor drink, you are now in my debt."

Others came to know of this debt, and less people came to her table, distrusting her as one who did not fulfill a debt. Thus came two guests to her table she did not expect. The first was tall and elegant, clad in the color red itself. With him a companion, the armor upon his frame enrobed in a richer red still. She knew them when they entered, and fell to her face in respect.

"My lords, Lae'Zeq and Rionne. I am humbled by your

presence."

"We come to sup at your table," Lae'zeq spoke. The pages of his wings turned as he did.

"And to take drink from your cask," Rionne said. The robes that enfolded him were, in fact, his feathered black wings, for this was before he fell to despondency.

"To what honor do I owe your arrival?"

"We would ask what you would take from us in trade for bread and drink?" Lae'Zeq said, taking a stool at the counter as any mortal might.

"I gift you these things for the fact you honor me with your presence," she said.

"And what if we were to say we come on business for the Pantheon? To determine your fate?"

"I do not know what this means," she said, "and I do not fathom why you've come?"

"You live within my city," Rionne said. "It was my gift to all, a city by which civilization would be born."

"And for that, my Lord, I am at your disposal."

"My cous' called me to join him, for he values my wisdom," Lae'Zeq spoke. "And we would hear why so few now grace your table."

"For the rumor that I keep my debts unpaid."

"And is this so?"

"To one who comes in, I offer bread and drink, and I ask then a payment that befits the opening of my door to guests."

"And what of the Sun-Caller?"

"To him I owe him no debt," she said, "save the one he imagines."

"Tell us how this came to be?"

And thus she told them of the day, and days after, in which Sun-Caller told her his news, of sunrise and sunset, and how she came to no longer give him bread and drink.

"He provides something which all trade him for. Thus it is," Rionne said, "that the value of his goods are set."

"And yet," she countered, "he offered it when I told him I did not want it, then demanded I pay."

"Indeed. He did do this," Lae'Zeq said.

The two gods looked at one another for a time, and they spoke in a tongue the woman did not know. Finally, they turned to her.

"All people should have bread to eat and drink to quench their

DEATHLESS BEAST

thirst," Rionne said, "but it is only fair that it be given in fair trade for what one offers."

"But am I not at liberty to pass by a booth," the woman said, "that offers up a spoon for trade? Am I not allowed to pass by, having no need for a spoon? I do not see the sun, my life lived out by day and night in this hall."

"She is at liberty to do so," Lae'Zeq said.

"I think the solution then is this," Rionne said. "I shall gift another means of defining civilization. A means by which to measure value. Thus, I leave you this, in payment for your bread."

He placed upon the counter a round piece of red metal, stamped with bread.

"What is this?" She asked.

"What name do you go by?"

"I am Koyn," she said.

"Then let that be what it is called," Lae'Zeq said. "Let all who wish to buy your bread and drink pay you with these."

"And where shall they get them from?"

"I shall give them freely," Rionne said, "to those who wish to offer me trade."

"And my people too," Lae'Zeq said, "shall come to me, and give me their words to write down, in trade for coin."

"But what shall I do with this coin?"

"Trade it for what you will," Rionne said. "For its value will be known to all in coming days."

"But what if others come and stamp their own?"

"Trust in your fellow being to know its value, given by all to all."

"And what of Sun-Caller?"

"There may come a day when the sun changes its course, and he ought to find something else of value to give if that day comes. To sit idly and watch the sun is foolishness that leads only to blindness. He forges his own fate."

"And thus it was that the coin came to be," Nair said as the women finished their bowls of soup, given to them by his brother.

"And what is the purpose of the story?" Astrid asked. "I do not see the moral."

"I am but a humble teller of tales," Nair said. "Many have sought and found morals in stories like this. Perhaps you will find value greater than the coin you have paid."

"And for that, we would owe you an even greater debt than Sun-Caller owed to all he traded empty promises with," the Matriarch said.

She touched the arm of Sabine Upona. "Sister Upona, we paid for story, but not for the food, company, and moral. Will you please give our hosts another satchel of coin?"

Upona gave the old woman a look and then did as she was told.

"Why so generous a gift?" Nair said.

"I am not one to owe debts to strangers," the Matriarch said, "certainly not ones whom, I suspect, are greater than me."

"You are a very wise and powerful woman," Kash said, coming to stand next to his brother, "and you think us greater than you?"

"A king is no greater than the peasant who feeds him."

"And the peasant?"

"Born a simple peasant myself," the Matriarch said, "all are greater than me. But twelve are greater than all."

Nair smiled a toothy grin and took the coin from Upona, then turned back to tend their fire as the woman settled down for a rest.

37

Feast of Jarls

If you foolish Boronii should attempt to tear yourselves away from my grasp, I shall see to it that every one of you—man, woman, and child—perishes. First by sword, then by flame, followed by starvation, and lastly by personally escorting you to the Gates of Noccitan.

—KING BOSCH OF BORTALI

(Following this proclamation, the jarls who had not yet signed the proclamation of division immediately joined the cause, and war was declared by sundown the following day.)

Donig sat on a promontory overlooking the Lupinfang Sea. They saw the sea hours before they could see the city below, and it drew them ever onward. The Prima Pater and Matriarch rode alongside the Clemmbäkkers, along with the three other jarlwives. The night before, they had all stayed at an inn and sent a message on ahead that they'd be arriving not long after the sun had risen. The message had been received, as a battalion of soldiers spread out before the front of the city in formationed panoply made clear.

Each wore vivid blue long cloaks over their matching uniforms, a crossbow in their arms at attention. Standing at the front of the host, atop a large white sleipnir, sat the duke. Unlike most Boronii people, he had sun-beaten skin rather than pale white features, and his hair was pulled back in a long blonde braid.

His piercing blue eyes watched the Entourage as they

approached, his hand toying with his chest length and a full blonde beard. He wore the blue of the army, but his clothes were lined with full and fine capröta wool. Unlike tame capricör, their wild cousin, capröta, could only be found in the wild places of Boroni.

"Prima Pater Dorian Mür," the duke called as they rode up through the ranks of the army. "I am Ütol von Toschbrecht, High Duke of Boroni. Welcome to Donig."

Next to the duke sat another jarl in blue and white, this one short and squat, his beard adorned with many beads of gold, and bone. He wore a capröta hat to cover his bald head. As the Prima Pater and the High Duke spoke together, the shorter man fell in next to the Clemmbäkkers and jarlwives.

"While this was rather short notice," the shorter jarl said, "when your first messenger arrived to announce our new guests for the autumnal feast, my wife and Frü Toschbrecht have been working diligently to ensure all will be ready."

As the man spoke, he eyed the other nobles with a look of a kicked ynfald, eyes bulging for hope of their approval.

"Well met, Jarl Donigar," Jarl Clemmbäkker said. "Frü Sturmguard, how far behind us did you say you thought your husband?"

"If he and Jarl Gertigan had anything to say in the matter," the severe and gray-clad Frü Eleona Sturmguard said, "they'd be here already. I assume they are not, and thus, they'll likely be racing each other in by the day's end. Our timid companion, Frü Thommus will no doubt agree that her husband will keep up the pace."

Frü Helsbet Thommus blushed a crimson that off-set the yellow she wore.

"Actually," Jarl Donigar said timidly, "Jarl Thommus arrived in the middle of the night, by way of Tosch, his sleipnir halfway to Noccitan."

"Helsbet!" Frü Sturmguard said, pulling on her reins.

Frü Thommus blushed even redder, and her smile broadened.

"You heard us all placing those bets at the inn last night. Did you know?"

Frü Thommus gave a timid smile. "It was why I didn't place any myself. I thought it not fair."

Katiam saw Ørzan Clemmbäkker shake his head and reach out with a pouch to give to his sister, who lifted her own head with a smile. She turned and giggled with Frü Thommus' own daughter,

Gerta.

The city had streets of rounded cobblestone, and each building leaned out over the street in the same way the city hung out over the ocean. The smell of the sea breeze swept clean the scents of refuse coming from alleys, but the pleasant aromas from vendors, fresh fish, cheese, and breads, seemed untouched and wafted past them. In many places, the streets split around impressive taverns where workers moved large barrels in through back rooms.

The entourage passed through a short, ancient, stone archway. Katiam chuckled to herself as she watched Jined Brazstein, the tallest of the Paladins, duck to avoid an iron lantern that hung from the arch. She wasn't the only one who chuckled. They passed out from under the wall into a decidedly different inner town.

All of the buildings were kept in an older style that harkened back to the change of culture the jarlwives spoke of, when the Morraineans pushed their traditions on the other people of the Northern Scapes hundreds of years prior. The preserved inner city around the castle had signs announcing itself as Oldebyrg. Each shopkeep and vendor was dressed wealthily, and kept their area clean and cared for.

One baker stood with her wares on display, making no announcement save her presence. Her daughter held up a pair of loaves to the Matriarch as she passed by. Katiam watched the old woman smile and take from the girl the whitest loaf and blackest bread that Katiam had ever seen.

They came to the gate that led out of Oldebyrg and into the courtyard of Castle Stoneliht—a massive block-like structure with hundreds of slit windows looking down on the town. The castle almost glinted in the midday sun. The mortar used in its construction was said to contain crystals ground to dust, giving it its namesake.

"The bastion sits just within Stoneliht's courtyard," the High Duke said, turning to the Entourage. "If rumor is true, the Jarls Sturmguard and Gertigan are to arrive by nightfall, then I think it's safe to say the autumn feast will be held tonight. You are all, on course, invited."

The Paladins and their carriages began to trundle into the courtyard, and the Matriarch turned to Astrid to give her a quiet command. At Astrid's hand signal, the Paladames refrained from joining them.

As they watched the Paladins go, Katiam saw Jined's hand go

into his satchel again and pat it, and it reminded her to touch her own. The Rotha still sat there, unmoving.

"Frü Donigar," the Matriarch said to a woman who came out of the courtyard on foot.

"I would have you come and join me in the Oldebyrg Vault," the woman in green velvets said.

"We would be honored. We can refreshen ourselves from our trip there?"

The woman gave a bow. All of the nobles dismounted, and Astrid gave the signal for them to do the same.

"Do we need to ready ourselves in secret?" the Matriarch said.

"The Oldebyrg Vault is no secret," Frü Clemmbäkker offered.

"The things we learn each day," the Matriarch said.

"What the women of the world could learn from the likes of the Northern Scapes and Nemen," Esenath said, falling in next to Katiam.

"It is a different world," Katiam replied. "Even the Oracle near Pariantür is limited, and the path to find it kept a secret."

"Yet here the women are bold, and would even fight for their country."

They circled back through Oldebyrg and passed the gates leading down into the city. They came about the backside of the castle to an even older wall. Across a broad garden stood a small hill, surrounded by a mote of running water that disappeared off a cliff overlooking the sea. Atop the hill, in the form of an ancient bailey, but rebuilt in a much newer marble, stood the Vault of Donig. At first Katiam thought it might be a sepulcher, but caught the telltale signs of rose-colored glass and thorny vines climbing up a few white pillars.

"The City of Donig," Frü Donigar was saying, "more specifically Oldebyrg, grew up around the old mead hall that stood on this hill. It never fell to sieges by Morannean invaders. The Crysalas took it as gift of allegiance by a king of Old Bortali."

They walked across the long bridge to the foot of the hill as the jarlwife continued to give her history lesson.

"I've thought on the Rotha as we rode," Esenath muttered to Katiam as they walked together. "I was wondered if you'd let me try something."

"What's that?" Katiam asked, her hand going to her satchel.

Esenath gave her a wink, and turned to continue listening to the jarlwife speak.

They were shown rooms set in a deeper level, and were asked to meet back in the central chamber an hour later. Esenath indicated for Katiam to follow her, and they stepped out through the pillars to find a stone bench overlooking the sea.

"What is it, Esenath?" Katiam asked.

Esenath held out a hand to Katiam, and, turning it, dropped something into her palm. Katiam looked down and saw a pink crystal rose petal in a silver setting.

"I think you ought to keep this with the Rotha," Esenath offered.

"What do you think it would do?"

"I spoke with Astrid, and she thought she saw the Rotha move as someone spoke from the Scrying bowl. I wondered if it reacted to the Dweol petals."

"What would I do with this?"

"I don't know," Esenath said. "You've been charged with studying the Rotha. Perhaps you will think of something. But I don't have a need for the petal anymore, and I want to give it to you, to see if it will help you with your own study of the Rotha."

Katiam entered the feast hall with the Matriarch Superioris on her arm, who smiled broadly as she approached her husband. She dropped Katiam's arm in favor of his.

"Do enjoy yourself," she to Katiam. "I believe I can see a seat at the Clemmbäkker table next to Onelie."

Katiam turned to see the younger woman sitting at a purple table with her parents and brother. A few of the other girls had gathered near her and stood chatting, waiting for the feast to begin. Katiam walked over and took a seat across from her, between the red-headed Toire Siobh and one of the paladinial guard. The young-faced Etienne Oren looked over at her, startled, then turned back to listen to Dane Marric speaking next to him.

The door opened and ten guards marched in, tapping their halberds in unison. Everyone broke off their conversations and rushed to their seats as seven pairs of jarls and their wives emerged. Katiam knew all the women by sight now, save the tallest pair in red. They moved to tables in the same colors as the garb they wore and took their seats.

The Toschbrecht table had been placed a step higher than the others. Duke Ütol von Toschbrecht sat with the Prima Pater and the Matriarch Superioris sitting on either side of him, his wife seated next to the Matriarch. He wore a cloak of blue, but the velvet doublet he wore was the green of his hometown, Tosch.

He waited a few minutes as the other jarls settled in, and guests they had invited complimented them with small talk. Then he stood and the room went silent.

"This is a momentous day that shall go down in our annals. Gathered together are the jarls of our namesake, the Confederacy of Jarls. Welcome to our neighbors, the Brazsteins," he indicated to the red table.

Katiam noticed the two Paladins next to her immediately scan the room, their eyes falling on the yellow Thommus table, where Jined sat. He, in turn, stared at the red table. Katiam knew he had come from the Northern Scapes, but the consideration that he might be from a ruling family had not occurred to her.

"From Sturm, we welcome Ragnut von Sturmguard." The table in stark gray hit their empty mugs in a single report on their table.

"Our constant host, Jarl Klamen von Donigar of Donig." At a table in the blues of the army, the short bald man, with the long beard, nodded his head slowly and heavily, allowing all to recognize him.

The duke gestured next to Katiam's table, and then to a yellow table. "Saedrick von Clemmbäkker of Clehm, and Goreg von Thommüs from Thom, and of course, Serk von Gertigan of Gerht." He gestured to a table decorated in black. Those sitting there did not move, but looked about stoically.

The duke then walked around the table and approached some wooden barrels. Servants arrived with a tap and mallet. He took them in both of his hands.

"And now, I wish to extend our hospitality to the Prima Pater, Dorian Mür, who graces us with his presence tonight. We have prepared something special for you. These barrels are made of gospar wood; it is a soft pine from the mountains near my own city of Tosch. It is aged for over ten years before it is made into a barrel. The ale that was placed in these barrels over twenty years ago has awaited an occasion such as this. Just as the jarldoms were set to age for a time, and then built into the country we have become for a time, we are now ripe for drinking."

The duke placed the tap against the first barrel and struck it once, twice, thrice, and the tap sunk deep down into the wood. He handed the implements to a servant, took a gold chalice, and filled it with the first pouring. It was a golden, foamy ale that poured out over the top. Duke von Toschbrecht took the chalice and bore it to the Prima Pater. Dorian stood and lifted the chalice toward each of the seven jarls in turn, and then drank deeply. When he was done, his lips were covered in foam. He smiled, wiped the foam from his lips, and lifted the cup into the air.

Everyone cheered, and the place descended into a flurry of excitement. Servants quickly tapped the remaining barrels and began doling out the ale. Katiam took a heavy black loaf of bread from the center of the table, and as a flagon of mead passed by her, she put a healthy amount into her cup with water.

"Is that all you will have?" Onelie Clemmbäkker asked.

"I have chosen to limit what I am allowed to eat, as I've taken the Aspect of St. Klare."

"That is something my tutors have not been clear on," Onelie said. "My mother has had me read many of the holy texts. While I understand the Vows of the Paladins, it seems the Aspects are more fluid?"

"They can be just as stringent," Katiam said, "but the Vows the brothers take are, more often than not, taken as a means to cut them off from the thing they hold dearest, in order focus their reliance on Grissone."

"But the Aspects are not?"

"The Aspects we take are often aligned with the purity we wish to model, such as the Aspect of Dignity"

"Dignity?"

"Under the armor, I have my sleeves bound tight with leather thongs. This represents the Aspect of Dignity. I took it when I became the Matriarch Superioris' physician."

"And what function does the Aspect serve?"

"I take it upon myself to restore the dignity of the elderly."

"I don't understand. Such as helping fill the plate of someone too weak to?"

"Or helping them with private concerns that they would never themselves ask for help to do."

"I do not see the gilded rose on you," Onelie said.

"I have not taken the Vow of Virginity," Katiam said matter-of-factorily.

"Then there is someone at Pariantür?" Onelie asked, blushing.

"Oh no," Katiam said. "The vast majority of the sisters there are unmarried."

"Then why not take that Aspect? There are only a couple who came with you wearing the gilded rose, it seems."

"It isn't necessary. After all, we cannot be defined simply by whether we've been taken into the arms of someone else." Katiam could feel her own ears reddening.

"Isn't that the quickest route to purity?" Onelie asked. "That is what our mothers tell us."

"And that is something often debated among the Crysalas. That is why the Aspects are also grouped under the four branches. The Aspects of the Rose, such as Virginity, or Peace, as I have taken, are Aspects of Being. You are a virgin, or you are not. I have harmed another, or I have not. The other branches, such as the functional Aspects of the Root, or Aspects of the Leaf, which serve others to find the purity of their actions. It is the Aspects of the Thorn that are often hailed as far more pure than something like virginity."

"How many Aspects have you taken?" Onelie asked.

"Three," Katiam said.

She touched the wooden ornamental mace at her hip. "Peace, that I would not bring harm to another."

She turned her arm over and showed the leather straps holding her sleeve tight to her arm, words set into the surface. "Dignity, to restore through service the dignity of the elderly."

She touched the delicate necklace of silver rose thorns across her collar, and then pointed to the plate of food and said, "The Aspect of St. Klare is a strict, ascetic diet of water, bread, fruits and vegetables, and at times...," she leaned in conspiratorially, "bugs."

Onelie grimaced. "Really?"

"I only know a few sisters who like to eat them whole, to get a rise out of others. I usually only eat specially prepared ground-up meal, fried in an oil. But only if I need to."

"Sister Borreau," Etienne said at Katiam's left. She looked over with a smile still on her face. Etienne flushed red. "Er... My companion has asked that you refrain from speaking of such things."

"Your compan—" she said, leaning forward to look past Etienne.

Dane Marric sat rigidly staring forward, eating a similar piece of bread. She recalled the penitentiary Vow he had been given before they had left Waglÿsaor.

"If Brother Marric is uncomfortable with my talking about the

Diet of St. Klare, I was just about to move onto other things. I apologize."

"It is not the Aspect of St. Klare he refers to, but the subject of....purity."

"Purity? The focus of the Crysalas?"

"Of the, er, Gilded Rose."

"Virg...we weren't talking about that anymore," Katiam said.

"He also asked me to mention that he has been noticing how much time you spend watching Brother Brazstein, and that you ought not to do so."

"If he has spent so much time observing me," Katiam said, leaning forward so Dane could hear her, "in order to notice if I give any Paladin special attention, then perhaps he ought to watch his own Vow more carefully."

She turned in her seat towards Onelie, as Dane made choking sounds, and Etienne tried to calm him.

"What was that about?" Onelie said.

"Dane is a Paladin who has taken the Vow of Chastity. But, more specifically, he follows a philosophy that takes it to the extreme, avoiding even speaking to or associating with women."

"The Shieldmaidens might find that admirable."

"Do those who join the Shieldmaidens not marry, then?"

"Those that do, do so for the honor of their house, but lose some standing in the society."

"Your mother?"

"She wanted to be a Shieldmaiden. She even pushed me to take the Vows myself."

"But you're hesitant," Katiam said.

"I don't know if I could," she said.

"Because there is a boy?"

"Well, no," she said. "I'd have little choice in the matter if my father chose to arrange something that benefits the household. There are several lords whose sons would be a good alliance. I suppose I could learn to love them. I know I could. I've dreamt of it since I was a little girl, being the lady of a house."

"Then why are you torn?"

"As I've grown older, I've found those dreams waning. I just want to have the opportunity to have a choice in the matter. In my life."

"As have I," Katiam said.

38

INTERLUDES

"Archimandrite Pell," a tall and muscular monk of Nifara took the cup touched to his hand by the assistant and sipped the wine. "I think it's a foolish idea to put our lives into the hands of these Black Sentinels; I doubt they have our best interests in mind."

"I understand your wariness, Gregor," the old Archimandrite said, "but with the Bulwark eerily emptied of Paladins going who knows where, we find ourselves on our own. The Black Sentinels will assure no brigands of Limae seek to take our purse, since they themselves are based there."

"It is certainly a fear and suspicion that the Black Sentinels recruit from brigands of the mountain kingdom," Kerei Lant offered, "but that then gives me my own hesitations."

"And those are?"

"That the Sentinels have their hands in the politics of Limae. What if their goal is to hold us hostage, and extort the Paladins with our ransom?"

"What if's are not a concern of ours," Pell said. "We will leave very publicly. A negative outcome as you propose would reflect poorly on their organization."

"It sounds as though your mind is already made up," Kerei said.

"I admit, I am leaning that way."

"And you mean to go yourself?" Gregor asked.

"I do. I shall ask one of the Nine to come with us, as well. They should assure the blessing of Nifara on our journey."

"I should like to go with you as well," Gregor said.

"Afraid for my health, are you?"

"Afraid for your safety," Gregor replied.

"Then I'm to stay here and run the day-to-day of the Templum?" Kerei asked.

"That is what you already do," Gregor laughed.

Kerei scowled.

"While what Gregor said bears truth," Pell said, "I intended to take you with me."

"Archimandrite!" Kerei said. "We, the leadership, cannot all go."

"And why not? It will save a trip for the Prima Pater to come south and see us. We get the opportunity to go on a pilgrimage to the north."

"It is unprecedented," Gregor said.

"Which makes it all the more exciting."

"Leave the Templum without leadership," Kerei said.

"You know as well as I that that is not possible," Pell Maran said. "The Nine are always near. Even if we take one of them with us, there are eight who remain. I'm not sure who among them is out on their own pilgrimage right now, but they remain in constant communication with one another. I think we have little to fear."

"If you've decided all of this already," Kerei said, "then why even consult us?"

"Because I'd like you to decide to go with me, and come of your own volition."

"If you ask nicely, I will be obliged and honored to come."

"Very well," Pell laughed. "Kerei Lant, Gregor Hans, will you join me in both the selection of whom will attend me on a pilgrimage north to meet our brother churches, and will you add yourself to that number?"

"Even if it leads us to the gates of Noccitan, I will follow you," Gregor said.

"I will go, too," Kerei said, putting her own cup on a nearby table. "That also means I have much to prepare, and much to leave in the care of others."

She rose, took up her staff, and felt her way to the door.

A light frost covered the small valley. He tried to work his elongated fingers with a stick over the kindling he had gathered, and cried out in anguish as it snapped and gashed open his thumb. The long hairs that had miraculously grown across his body were now patchy and short from the singeing fire that had washed over him.

The sun was setting somewhere he could not see, and the coldness deepened around him. He stumbled across the floor of the valley towards the nearby rocks. In the dark he did not see the short slope, and fell in a roll down into the stream.

Hot tears were his only warmth as he scrabbled up out of the ice-cold water.

"Why?!" he raged at the sky. "Why have you done this to me?!"

A cold gray light could be seen moving through the trees.

"She comes to take my soul," he muttered, falling to his knees and waiting for death to approach. The puffs of his breath slowed in the cold air.

"What happened to you?" the Walker's voice said from the gray light.

Another figure walked with him, but stopped outside the circle of light he cast to watch from nearby.

"They destroyed me," Ghoré muttered.

He looked at the angry red skin across his elongated arms and fingers. The membrane that had formed under his arm had shriveled in the cold, and looked not unlike hardened leather.

"You destroyed me," he hissed at the Walker.

"Come now. No need to insult me. Tell me what happened."

"I was establishing my kingdom. They came, as you said they would, those usurpers. My people came to my aid, and I would have destroyed them, but that black cloak. It...consumed them."

"Fire will do that."

"You told me there was no cost!"

"You paid your price for the freedom from those shackles. You told me your story."

"And then you cursed me with this form!"

"You commanded that creature and it gave you the key. You are being prepared for something even greater. You are greater now than any man. What man has not dreamed to fly?"

"You have damned me!"

"You have damned yourself," the Walker said calmly. "Your actions are your own. I have given you great gifts. What you choose to do with them is upon your own soul."

Ghoré began to sob.

"You look cold. Command your lessers to come and warm you."

"They are all dead. If they did not die in the battle, they have died in the frosty climb to this valley."

"Rather foolish that you fled north then, isn't it? Yet you still have followers."

"Where?"

"You cannot feel them?"

Ghoré sniffled, and looked up and around. A pair of eyes observed him from a crag.

"They'll not accept you the way you look, however. We ought to see to it that you are a more regal monarch."

"You would have me pay another price."

The Walker laughed. "You have little left to give me."

"Because I am already damned."

"As you say."

"What would you gift to me?"

"I could make it so that She can never take your soul to Noccitan without first asking me for it."

"And in return?"

"Look upon me and see me in my glory. Worship me as they once did, when the world was new. Then I shall leave, and you will join those I have prepared for you in the cliffs above."

"And if I do not?"

"The cold will overtake you, and within an hour that feels itself like an eternity, you shall fall into the embrace of the goddess of Justice, and be taken to the court of the Three-Eyed King to be judged, and begin your penance in the Prison of Souls."

Ghoré clenched his chattering jaw and forced his eyes up at the light before him. In the midst, his eyes locked with the two that pierced out of that gray void. Around that face, a wreath of gray wisps, like the mane of some great beast, shone. A pelt hung across an emaciated frame, terminating in two powerful gauntlets crafted by no mortal. One was pitted with eons of rust and disrepair. The other bore small signs of corruption, but otherwise the gold in-laid upon its surface shown with an otherworldly light.

It was only for a moment that he looked upon the Walker and the gray light bathed over him, and into his innermost being. The baleful gaze scorched his soul and parched his mind. It was instantaneous and lasted for another moment. And then there was bliss. He stood not in a forest, but alongside the Walker at a place between the four worlds. Across the nothing, he could see verdant tendrils tying them all together. Then, in a fourth moment, they once more stood on solid ground.

Ghoré fell to his knees in worship.

"Kashir-Yran, y dosh mídosh!" he cried in the language his father had taught him.

"Again," the Walker said sternly.

Ghoré repeated it a second time, and then a third.

The hairs across his arms sprouted anew from his flesh in agonizing sensations. He laughed in relief as the cold completely left his body.

"Now rise, and go seek out your people," the Walker said.

Ghoré dared not look a second time. He rose to his feet, rejuvenated, and approached the wall of rocks nearby where he began to climb. He felt the gray light behind him watch him do so. He came up over the lip before the small cave.

Five creatures, smaller than man, with long, winged arms, crouched on rocks surrounding it, watching him tentatively. They had faces almost canine in nature, and beady eyes filled with distrust and anger.

"Saverns," Ghoré said to himself. "These will do even better than Wyloths."

He approached the hole and prepared to enter. The largest one dropped in front of him, and beat its chest, hooping in rage. The others followed suit.

Ghoré's own hand shot out and took the creature by the throat. He held it tight until it stopped moving. The others fell silent.

"Bring me wood for a fire," he ordered.

The other saverns' eyes glazed over, and they leapt from the cliff to obey his command.

He dragged the body of the largest savern down into the cave to prepare it for a feast—his first meal as the Deathless Beast.

PART 5

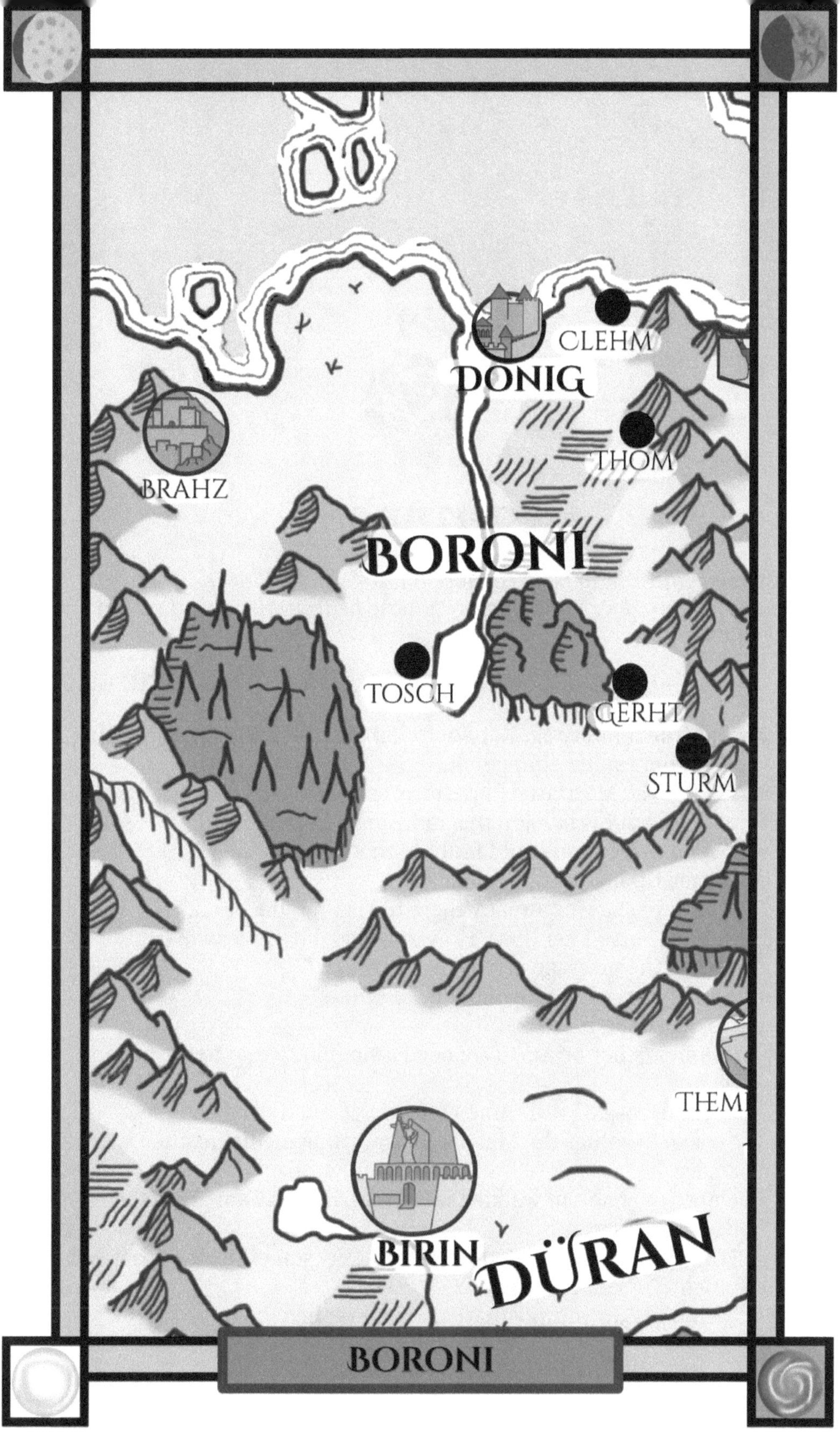
DONIG
CLEHM
THOM
BRAHZ
BORONI
TOSCH
GERHT
STURM
THEM
BIRIN
DÜRAN
BORONI

39

Positioning

Appearances may be deceiving, but to assume that the appearance does not convey what the bearer wishes is deceiving yourself.

—SISTER SUPERIORIS PAELLON OF THE THIRD ERA

The next morning, Katiam found several of the women sitting in the vault's dining hall.

"The Matriarch Superioris left with Astrid to visit the Prima Pater at his bastion this morning," Esenath said. "She said when you awoke you could find her there."

"Sister Upona went with her?"

"I believe she was already there to visit her husband."

Katiam pursed her lips. "How long ago did she leave?"

"When the message arrived an hour ago."

Katiam turned to one of the local sisters.

"Is there a stables here?"

She shook her head. "If we need a sleipnir, we go to the bastion to get one."

Esenath rose. "I can come with you, if you'd like."

"I have to gather the Matriarch's morning medicine, then we can leave."

Out of the habit of walking in secret pairs, Katiam and Esenath walked arm in arm.

"Did the Paladins seated next to you say something to upset you last night?" Esenath asked.

"What makes you say that?" Katiam replied.

"I saw your eyes roll at something Brother Oren said. And today you've been a bit more pensive."

"I was rolling my eyes at something Brother Marric asked Oren to say to me."

"And what was that?"

"Brother Marric was asking I refrain from watching Brother Brazstein so much."

"Have you been?"

"I don't think so," Katiam replied.

"I'm sure since he took his second Vow, we've all had our eye on Brother Brazstein more. It is not every day you see a miracle ordaining someone for a higher position."

Katiam nodded.

"Why did he seem so concerned?"

"Dane Marric is always concerned with the interactions between men and women," Katiam said.

"And he couldn't bother to tell you this himself?"

"For that same reason," Katiam said. "He observes the Chaste Mind philosophy."

"If he refuses interaction with us, why is he spending so much time watching us, and ensuring we're not interacting with other Paladins?"

"I'd say you should ask him," Katiam said, "but I doubt he'd give you the time of day."

Esenath laughed.

They came to the Stoneliht's courtyard and easily found the entrance to the bastion.

At the Primus' office, which the Prima Pater had been given the use of during their stay, Katiam could hear the Prima Pater speaking, and he did not sound happy.

"I am probably not welcome in there," Esenath said.

"I'm sure you can find a library somewhere?" Katiam offered.

"Good idea."

Katiam tapped lightly at the door, and Jined Brazstein stuck his head out.

"I've come with the Matriarch's morning medicine," she said.

He opened the door for her, and she moved in.

The Prima Pater paced in the center of the floor, while the two Pater Segundii and his own seneschal, Jurgon Upona sat next to his wife and the Matriarch.

"Are they each going to do this?" the Prima Pater asked. "If they think we're going to sit here all winter and wait for their proceedings, they're sorely mistaken."

Katiam circled the room to the serving board, took out a decanter, poured a splash, and then took out a phial of the Matriarch's medicine and stirred the contents into the drink. As she placed the phial back in her satchel, she pushed the Rotha to the side, up against the small satin pouch she had placed the pendant from Esenath in, making a note to consider having a smith fashion it into a bracelet so she could wear it.

Katiam took a seat next to the Matriarch and gave her the glass. The old woman took it from her and gave her a wan smile.

"Two of the jarls visited Dorian this morning," Maeda said. "Ragnut von Sturmguard appealed to Dorian to support him in the coming election so that he could put a stop to the conflict by bartering for peace with Bortali. Apparently, the other jarls have not been providing him the military support he needed, and he fears that Bortali will strike his city first. Then Jarl Klamen von Donigar came to ask not for Dorian to support him, but to suggest to the other jarls that they reelect Jarl Toschbrecht."

"And this has made Dorian mad?" Katiam asked.

"Dorian feared that traveling into Boroni would suggest to Bortali that he was throwing in support for the jarls. It seems the jarls think the same thing."

Another rap came at the door, and Jined let in both Jarl Clemmbäkker and Jarl Goreg von Thommus in yellow.

Dorian turned his back to the two of them and gave his wife a look, pleading her to pray for patience. Then he donned a smile and turned to greet the two men.

"Prima Pater," Jarl Thommus said, giving a deep bow. "I've come to you on urgent business, with my friend, Jarl Clemmbäkker."

Saedrick von Clemmbäkker smiled.

"I am interested in knowing why you've both come together," Dorian said, "rather than perhaps calling a meeting of the jarls, so you may each present questions and requests more publicly?"

"Are we not the first to visit you?"

"Given the conspiratorial nature of this morning," Dorian said, "it is not for me to say."

"We do not come here conspiratorially," Saedrick said. "We come here to discuss the future of our nation."

"Which perhaps would be better done in a council."

"If the jarls were not split as they are," Saedrick said, "that might be the case."

Dorian waved a hand. "Say your peace then."

"No one wants peace more than I," Saedrick said. "My friend Jarl Thommus believes that we may be able to sue for a better peace with Bortali by complying with Bortali's desire to close the border, and instead turn our attentions to other, better means of trade."

"Such as Bronue Jinre, Nasun, even Morraine," Goreg von Thommus said.

"So you would simply ignore Bortali," Dorian said, "and expect the trouble to go away?"

"Precisely," Saedrick said. "Let them burn their anger out."

"Prima Pater," Nichal Guess spoke up. "If I may?"

Dorian nodded.

"The Bortali embargo was not merely an act of spite. No nation with the hot-blooded nature Bortali shows waits two hundred years to act on their ire. Bortali did so in hopes that Boroni would react with a fight. Boroni has ships. I observed your docks here and in Clehm. Your nation is not a maritime one. Your hulls are shallow to combat rocky shores rather than enemy vessels."

"Rocky shores make up most of our coast, save my own harbor," Clemmbäkker said.

"Neither Clehm nor Thomm have access to woods. You would need to build a bigger trade fleet," Pater Segundus Pír said. "That would fall to Sturm or Tosch."

"Who both separately want more coin put into the war effort," Clemmbäkker said.

"As I understand it," Dorian said, "Sturm does not want war. He wants the means to protect his city and end the rising strife."

"Jarl Sturmguard is my friend," Thommus said, "but he treats his city as an island. He will, I do not doubt, push for election of himself as the High Duke, and use that to wrest the war effort to his aims. But, if he finds promises from Toschbrecht, he may instead turn his allegiance to him."

"You have not seemed worried about your own city," Dorian said to Saedrick.

"I am near enough to Donig that, should I be attacked, Toschbrecht and Donigar will come to my aid. We fear for our friend Jarl Sturmguard, that Toschbrecht will use him as a willing pawn, and sacrifice his city to unite our people."

"Why are you speaking with me on this, rather than with Sturmguard?"

"We merely wish to provide an uninterrupted proposal toward peace, for when you speak with the jarls tonight."

"What is tonight?" Dorian asked.

"Duke Toschbrecht sent messages to each of us, calling for a council. It mentioned you would be in attendance—to discuss the upcoming elections, as well as the war."

"Thank you," Dorian said. "I shall look forward to seeing you both there. Perhaps then you can present your proposal."

The two men smiled and left the room. Dorian walked to his chair and sat down, his head on his fist.

"Prima Pater?" Jurgon Upona muttered.

"Hmm?"

"You received no invite to the council meeting, as of yet."

"No. I don't expect I have."

"Perhaps we all ought to leave," the Matriarch Superioris said, preparing to rise, when another knock came to the door.

The door was opened to the broad smile of High Duke Ütol von Toschbrecht. "Good morning, Prima Pater," the duke said, giving a deep bow.

"Toschbrecht," Dorian said. He took a deep breath and rose from his seat, motioning for the Matriarch to sit back down.

"I understand you've had a few guests this morning," Toschbrecht said. "I feel rather embarrassed I was not able to make it here sooner. I had meant to deliver my invitation to you in person, to a council I've called with the other jarls."

"The news has preceded you, I'm afraid," Dorian said.

"I expected as much," Toschbrecht said.

"And now you're here to set things straight?"

"I imagine that you've come to understand that the position of the jarls is split in the support for the election of the next High Duke."

"And you'll note that I am not in a position to give my support to one or another," Dorian said. "I have come to this country in order to inspect my own holdings, and to sue for peace between you and your neighbor."

"I do not believe there is room for peace," Toschbrecht said.

"There is always room for peace."

"The Bortalians want nothing more than to reabsorb our nation into theirs."

"And if you turned your efforts elsewhere?" Dorian asked.

"You've been speaking with Clemmbäkker it seems. He would turn his own city into a port for a fleet. Do you know what that would do?"

"I have a feeling you're going to tell me."

"Bortali would either focus their war effort on destroying Sturmguard and the trees they would provide for the fleet, further enraging us, and then attack our ports before we could build, or realizing they had no one to battle with on this border, turn south to Nemen, and take from that mountain nation what they will."

"What makes you think they would refocus on Nemen?"

"Nemen has gold."

"But Nemen has allies, in Setera, and Düran."

"We thought we had allies in Düran ourselves, but they do not seem to want peace for us either. We stand alone."

"Bronue Jinre is not an ally?"

"The islands do not want what is best for us. They'd prefer we do nothing. That we turn in on ourselves and starve."

"Which is why you have closed your borders to them?"

"We have not closed our borders to Bronue, despite what Clemmbäkker might say."

"You are well informed," Dorian said.

"I'm the High Duke. I've held the position for over fifteen years. I am very well informed."

"Then perhaps," Dorian said, "you will, in the most concise manner possible, inform me. You seem to have no worries that you will retain your position."

Toschbrecht smiled. "I have the support of Donigar, that much I can count on. Clemmbäkker will do anything he can to wrest the power from me. He would have his own city made the center of Boronii culture. He will push to take the position himself, gaining support from Gerht, and Thomm. I have no doubt I can gain the vote of Sturm. He always votes in the way that will best keep things in Sturm normal."

"Which leaves Brahz," Dorian offered.

"I have little to worry about there," the High Duke said.

"Why is that?"

"I suppose a better question is why I would come and tell you this?" Toschbrecht said.

Dorian shrugged.

"I am telling you that I expect to continue to be the High Duke as a promise to you. I am going to continue doing all I can to make peace in the Northern Scapes."

"Except that you believe war is not only inevitable, it is the only course of action to achieve that peace."

"If it brings peace, I will march to war."

"I simply cannot condone this action," Dorian said.

"Then you are not for us, but against us? Are you siding with Bortali?"

Dorian leaned forward. "What made you think I was on anyone's side?"

"Paladins are the protectors of mankind," Toschbrecht said. "You are vowed to guard humanity, including against itself. If you are against war, then why have you not suggested you go back to Bortali and force them to agree to peace?"

"What do you think I was doing? I'm providing you the chance to rectify the situation on your own merit."

"You're not here to represent the Confederacy's interest. You would have our goods taxed by Bortali. That our ships are unable to out-trade Bronue. You would have us merely sit here and rot."

"I am here to represent peace, Duke Toschbrecht. That's what we represent. Peace by any means."

The duke rose and left without another word. Dorian sat in his chair in silence.

"Is everyone in this country so stubborn?" Dorian asked Jined Brazstein, who stood by the door.

"That's how I got this broken nose," Jined said. "Three times."

Dorian laughed heartily. "Thank you for that," he said through broken breaths.

There came a firm knock at the door.

"Come in," Dorian said.

The door opened toward Jined, who did not move. A tall, muscled figure entered and stood before the Prima Pater's desk. He dropped to one knee and bowed, then rose.

"Prima Pater, I am Jaegür von Brazstein. I am sorry I did not have the chance to visit before now."

"Are you also here to ask for my support to become High Duke?"

"I've held the position. I do not need to again; I have enough concerns of my own."

Dorian sighed with relief. "Then what concerns do you have?"

"Prima Pater, I'm not here to ask for any support. I come

humbly before you, as I am hoping you'll send a message for me, with your authority, to a member of your Order at Pariantür. I have a son there who has become a Paladin."

Katiam looked over at Jined, who watched in silence as the two men spoke. In fact, everyone's eyes darted back and forth from the jarl to Jined.

"My eldest son was offered the chance many years ago to face execution for the death of High Duke Toschbrecht's son, or become a Paladin. He chose the latter. It had been my assumption that when he did, his own inheritance would be forfeited. Instead, it is tied up in his position at Pariantür. His inheritance acts as his stipend to support him.

"With his lands tied up, it is breaking my treasury. We were forced, nearly at sword point, to take on the dead man's betrothed, since she bore my eldest son's seed in her womb, and give her to my younger son. To make matters worse, the bride price was considerable, considering the embarrassment this all created. Now I am forced to continually feed coin into an as-of-yet unpaid weregild of the dead man from my own coffers, unable to touch my son's inheritance."

"This is the leverage Toschbrecht has over you then," the Prima Pater said. "What are you asking of me, Jarl Brazstein?"

"I'm asking you to speak with my eldest son, Jined Brazstein. Please ask him to forfeit his claim on my lands, or else my entire family may become destitute, and the jarldom will pass to someone under the thumb of Toschbrecht. I understand his inheritance is meant to pay for his life as a Paladin, but it is killing my family lands."

"I'm afraid that won't be necessary, nor shall I be passing the message on."

"And why not?"

"Because you've already asked him. Brother Brazstein?" Dorian indicated toward Jined, who still stood at attention, but had tears welling in his eyes.

The jarl turned to see Jined standing there and staggered forward.

"My son! I did not know you were here. I thought you were half a world away!"

Jined broke his stance and fell forward to embrace his father for the first time in ten years.

"Father, I did not know the millstone of grief I had tied to you."

"Will you help, son?"

"I already have," Jined said. "I forfeited my inheritance as we entered Boroni, when I took on a second Vow—the Vow of Poverty. The lands are already yours."

The huge jarl broke into a new stream of sobs, now filled with joy.

40

Jarlwives

Let every day be a decision to thrive. Be what that day calls for. Seek to improve on the last. Make proud the thoughts of tomorrow.

—FROM THE BOOK OF SAYINGS

All eyes turned to the door as it cracked open and the head of one of the castle serving-women peeked in. The woman walked awkwardly around the edge of the room to stand nearby Frü Toschbrecht, next to the Matriarch Superioris. The collection of women, from jarlwives to servants, sat in three concentric circles in the council room of the vault in silence.

Toschbrecht waved her hand and the woman stepped forward. Sabine Upona scribbled away furiously into a small book next to Katiam.

"The council of jarls is convening," the servant said quietly.

Frü Toschbrecht nodded and took a deep breath. "Then we shall begin."

Unexpectedly, the Matriarch Superioris stood before the smaller-framed Gederin Toschbrecht could speak any further.

"My husband is as much a fan of long councils as the next elderly world leader," she said, "but having seen the irritation he's already showing at the thought of the meeting at which he is now in attendance, I am going to move quickly past tradition and ask us all to move to the topics at hand. If there is a necessary pretext that must be met for your own records, then those can be done when the jarl's council concludes."

"If that is what you wish, Matriarch Superioris," Frü Toschbrecht said. "Of course, today was going to be our vote on who would become the next head of our own council, so that whomever that is can take a proactive role in the decisions made today."

"The subject on which I wish to speak shall require that you all take a proactive role, and despite your own term as head of this council still in effect, Frü Toschbrecht, I shall ask that you respect the allegiance you have to Shield and Blade under the leadership of Rose and Thorn."

"You have our allegiance," Gederin answered.

"And our attention," Frü Lerda Clemmbäkker said.

"Very well," the Matriarch said. "First, let me verify the following: to what extent do the jarlwives operate alongside their husbands?"

"Can you be more specific?" Gederin asked.

"Do you command authority? Are you autonomous?"

"Very much so," Frü Clemmbäkker said, "to an extent that goes relatively unnoticed by the jarls."

"And were your actions to go into direct conflict with their decisions?"

"What they don't know will not hurt them."

"And, if your actions, in conflict with the jarls might otherwise be considered treasonous?"

"What is it exactly you're asking of us?" the yellow-clad Frü Thommus asked. "Surely you're not asking us to betray our homeland."

Maeda smiled. "I would not ask that much of you. I am gauging merely how much in opposition this council operates."

"You have stepped over many a boundary," Frü Toschbrecht said, "that spoken by any one of us would cause trouble."

"But as an old woman you would hear me out?" Maeda said smiling.

"As the head of all Crysalas Orders we would hear you out. Your husband is recognized as equal to other heads of state, and you would be recognized as such, yourself. We would hear you out."

"Very well," Maeda said, sitting down and sighing. "The Prima Pater Dorian Mür and I have come to the decision that the fate of this upcoming war may lie in your own hands. The king of Bortali wants it, and your husbands seem Nocc-bent on giving him what he wants. We plead with you to act in what power you have to prevent this from happening."

"And should our husbands decide otherwise?" Frü Clemmbäkker asked.

"That is why I have insisted we hold this council, to address this issue now, while they also come to their own decisions. Your actions, predetermined as they may be, shall also not constitute an act of insurrection."

"A wise course," Frü Toschbrecht said.

"Now, before we proceed," Maeda said, "will you consider all possibilities to prevent this war?"

Frü Toschbrecht looked around the room. "Are there any in opposition to this request?"

No one raised a finger.

Gederin Toschbrecht looked back to the Matriarch. "I think we can all safely say that we'd like to avoid a war."

"Then I should like to open the floor to your council, to discuss just what actions ought first to be taken in order to assure lasting peace."

The room grew silent and still.

"Have not one of you spoken with your husbands? Has no one raised potential options, even in the sacred trust of the bedroom?"

Again, silence reigned.

Maeda folded her hands. "Let us sit then, in silence, and consider."

"Auntie Maeda already suggested they go and speak with Captain Smith in Waglÿsaor," Katiam muttered to Sister Upona. "Could that not be the best tactic?"

"How so?" Upona muttered back.

"Have you something to suggest?" the Matriarch said, turning to give Katiam the room's attention.

Katiam's ears burned red as all eyes fell on her.

"I know you are not one for public speaking," Maeda said, "but I should like to hear what you have to say."

Katiam felt a blanket of terror sweep over her, and her vision snapped to a single narrow tunnel.

"Katiam," Upona said, placing a hand on hers, "you can do it. Tell us what you said to me and what you mean."

Katiam felt a cup being pressed into her hand. She lifted it and took a sip of the cold water.

"The Waglÿsaor Hospital," she blurted out.

"What of it?" Upona goaded her on.

"Matriarch Superioris," Katiam continued, "you have already suggested that the Shieldmaidens make contact with Sister Smith and work together to ensure the Hospital is safely accomplishing its mission."

The Matriarch held up a hand for Katiam to pause and turned to the circles of women.

"In the city of Waglÿsaor we came upon a derelict naval academy. Having left the head of my personal guard there, one Sister-Captain Sigri Smith, we intend to turn that old academy into a hospital. It is to employ those women who might prefer to sell their bodies over starvation. It is established publicly, under the patronage of the Fortress of St. Rämmon, which sits adjacent to the city."

She waved for Katiam to continue.

"Could not the alliance between the Shieldmaidens and the Order of the Rose be more formally established, with the Hospital as a joint effort?"

"In what way?"

"Is it not the common practice to treat hospitals and churches as places of refuge in times of war?"

There was a general murmur of agreement.

"If the Shieldmaidens journeyed there under the pretense of supporting the hospital, it would flourish."

"How would it improve the situation leading two nations to war?"

"If I may," Frü Toschbrecht said.

The Matriarch waved acknowledgment.

"If we were to work with the hospital openly," Toschbrecht said, "it would effectively declare that the Rose, the Hammer, and the Shield all condemn the war, and establish the city of Waglÿsaor as a safe city. Even if the war proceeded, it would also ensure that the northern pass between the nations is secure. If either nation marched against the city, it would escalate the war to encompass other nations, forcing them to act in response to what would be considered by most a war crime."

"But that would also mean that Sturm is the central target," Frü Sturmguard said.

"I think we can all agree that many of our husbands planned to make Sturm the central theater for the war, no matter the outcome," Toschbrecht replied.

"Your husbands," Frü Sturmguard said. "But our city does not ask for war to be waged on our doorstep. What peace shall I have, knowing that the children of my own city are endangered?"

"The jarls currently argue over who will be the next Duke," the Matriarch said. "It comes down to whether Sturm or Clehm is the focus of the war. If you take one out, then the other becomes the obvious theater for a unified plan."

"Which would also mean that the vote is made with a clearer head," Frü Clemmbäkker said as she stood. "My husband has long coveted the title of Duke. I shall not make pretenses—I would enjoy the affluence that provides me and my son as future jarl. Were we to take this action, establishing hard peace in the north, changing the focus of the imminent war towards Sturm, it might even swing the council to vote Jarl Sturm in as Duke."

She walked across the room and took up Frü Sturmguard's hands in hers. "And that would not be such a bad thing for the next few years. Sturm has never held the title. It might help my own husband and Jarl Toschbrecht to make some sort of peace. Crysania knows that even our own friendship has not been enough to persuade our husbands to make their own peace."

"If we are to do this," a quiet voice said from across the room.

All eyes turned to the black-clad Frü Vünhilde Gertigan.

"Then we cannot do so with Frü Toschbrecht as the head of our council."

"Please elaborate," the Matriarch said as others began to murmur again.

"I mean this as no disrespect," Vünhilde said, "but with Jarl Toschbrecht as the current Duke, and his wife as head of the council, it would seem that this is a decision coming down from Tosch. We are due to elect a new leader of the Boronii Shieldmaidens. We ought to do so immediately, to better consolidate this decision."

"I think it obvious who it should be," Frü Clemmbäkker said.

No one said anything.

"If Sturm is to be the focus of the war, then their neighbor, Gerht, ought to hold the keys to the other half of the kingdom via Frü Gertigan as head of our order. Establishing peace in the north through a formal alliance with the Order of the Rose will also constitute acts of proper leadership before the Ducal title is even moved."

"That seems reasonable," the Matriarch said. "Is there a formal way to go about the transfer of power in this election?"

"We need only cast a vote. Is there anyone who also wishes to put their name forward for the leadership of the order for the next three years?"

No one raised their hand.

"Then the vote will take place between the current leader Frü Toschbrecht, and Frü Gertigan."

"In the meantime, shall we establish a plan to contact the hospital in Waglÿsaor?" the Matriarch asked.

"We have to send representatives immediately."

"From both Shieldmaidens and by order of the Matriarch," Upona said.

"I think it's safe to send me," the tall, red-headed Toire Siobh from Bronue said. "I am a foreigner, so I can go with little danger to myself. And it will constitute an act of peace from my own father in the Isles of Bronue Jinre."

"Very well. A group of medically trained sisters can accompany you," Frü Toschbrecht said.

"We ought to send others under my orders as well," the Matriarch said. "To ensure that this does not seem an act of espionage."

The Matriarch scanned the room, falling on each of the woman from her company. Katiam thought perhaps she would send Astrid or Esenath. Her eyes locked with Katiam, and a hope-filled up in her, thinking this might be the opportunity she had awaited, a journey back first to Waglÿsaor and then to the college of Nemen.

"I will go," a voice piped up.

The Matriarch gave a look of apology to Katiam and turned back to see who spoke.

Onelie Clemmbäkker stood up next to her own mother, who looked up at her daughter in horror.

"You are not a member of my order," the Matriarch said.

"But I would be," Onelie said.

"We have not discussed this," Frü Clemmbäkker said.

"I would hear your reasoning," the Matriarch said. "All here are equal. And if you have the courage to stand and state your claim, then you can be afforded the opportunity to defend it."

Onelie's mother closed her mouth and sat back, arms folded.

"As the daughter of a jarl, my life is one of sacrifice. One day, I will be called to marry for alliance rather than for love. So why not provide myself as sacrifice to help bring about peace in these times of war?"

"How would you leaving your family and nation provide peace?" her mother muttered.

"If I were to take Vows, not as a Shieldmaiden, but under the Order of the Rose, I could change my name, thus protecting myself from the Bortalians."

"Your father would not stand for it. He would not allow you to go to Bortali."

"He will not know where I go. Only that I have left with the Order of the Rose, perhaps to Mahndür."

"Yet you would secretly go to Waglÿsaor," the Matriarch said.

"As a secret hostage, yes."

"Hostage?" the Matriarch asked.

"It is an old practice," Frü Toschbrecht said. "Sons were often sent to live under the patronage of potential enemies. Should the father declare war, or ally against the host, then their son's life was forfeit. The same is said of women sent to marry potential allies or enemies."

"Should my own father find out later that I am indeed in Bortali, it might also ensure he commits assets to the war he might otherwise be hesitant to give."

"Matriarch Superioris, please do not take my daughter from me."

"I am in no position to forbid someone from joining my order," the Matriarch said. "However, if you and your daughter wish to join me and my company on the road to Brahz and then to the borders of Mahndür, then you will have plenty of time to discuss the possibility, and for another alternative to assert itself."

The council proceeded for several hours, and before the end they formally elected Frü Gertigan as the new leader of the council. Katiam followed the Matriarch to her chambers.

"Sister Glass," the Matriarch said to Astrid as they arrived at the door. "I should like no interruptions tonight. Although I expect I'll receive a message from my husband early tomorrow. At that time, please let Sister Upona know, so she can wake me to attend."

Astrid nodded and closed the door behind them as they entered.

"What arrangements shall I make for tomorrow?" Sister Upona asked.

"If it is not tomorrow, then the day after, we shall be leaving for the city of Brahz, with the Brazsteins. We'll need to make arrangements for Onelie Clemmbäkker to join our order."

"You were quick to accept her offer," Katiam said as she poured the Matriarch's medicine into a glass of wine.

"She was the only woman there willing to do so. Any one of them could have offered themselves in her place, but she had the backbone. She is choosing the honorable course, and I would respect that."

"And, of course," Upona said, bringing the blanket over to the Matriarch as she sat before the fire, "that's the kind of girl you want in our order."

"She will have plenty of time to change her mind, of course," the Matriarch said. "It is very unlikely we are able to cross the border from Brahz. Their coastal road is said to be notoriously dangerous."

"What happens then?" Katiam asked. "If I may ask."

"After we conduct our business here, we will travel south through Tosch, and through the pass west of there. I think it will be there that Onelie will make her final decision, and be secreted away to Waglÿsaor."

"And even then," Upona added, "she won't take her final Vows for a year or two. Perhaps if the war is stopped, or ends before then, she may at that time decide not to go through with it."

"That is something I will speak to her mother on," the Matriarch said. "We'll do nothing to dissuade her if she chooses to begin down the path. But her mother will either hold onto the hope that her daughter will return to her, or, and I expect this will be more likely, she will become her strongest advocate and patron."

The older woman took the glass from Katiam. "I think I'll sit here a while before I retire. I'll ring for you, Sabine, when I'm ready."

Katiam and Sabine walked to the door together.

"She seems content," Katiam said.

"Onelie standing up for herself was a minor victory for her, but I think she's more proud of you."

Katiam stopped and looked at Sabine, and back across the room to the Matriarch.

Sabine opened the door and they both entered the hall.

"When you speak up, and when you make decisions, like that time you ordered out the council of Sister Superiorii who were pressuring her to finance their project in Sidierata."

"They have been haranguing her for days, and it was ruining her sleep."

"Yes, but you ordered them out as her doctor and great niece."

"She still sided with them in the end."

"She might not have, if you had not stepped in. She enjoys seeing you take command."

"I'm no leader."

"Nor do you have to be," Sabine said, "but it reminds her that you are your own person, and that you don't live in her shadow. It was much the same with me when I put my foot down in order to marry Jurgon. Only with you, she truly considers you a daughter."

Katiam excused herself as she came to the door of her own room, and went inside the small, one bed cell. She sat down on the edge of the bed, a smile on her face.

41

Brahz

Hatred is a cold steel pin that strengthens the spine and poisons the blood.

—MINU THE GENTLE

If Waglÿsaor was hewn from the black rock it sprang from, then the city of Brahz and the castle that loomed over it had attached itself to the mountain heights in order to enjoy its view. Katiam patted the discouraged-looking sleipnir she sat atop as it considered the climb it was facing. Every street and every home had been fashioned to look out over the long slope to the blue Lupinfang Sea to the north. As in Clehm, the city wore its colors. Red banners and pennants flew from nearly every home, and tradesmen appeared at the doors to their shops and homes to watch the procession of Brazstein nobility, Paladins, and Paladames as they made their winding way up through the city.

The city founders had chosen white marble for their castle and each hall and building jutting from the face of the darker rock of the mountains. When the view above her didn't hold her attention, green orchards and gardens leading to the sea did. And when that didn't, she watched Jined.

The newly adorned Brother Adjutant had remained silent for the trip from Donig to Brahz, riding openly in secret, while his family tried their best to ignore that the disgraced son accompanied them. Katiam had caught glimpses of him watching them, and vice versa. Now, in the city of his birth, his smile had broadened, and the sights, sounds, and smells brought happiness to him that had long lay dormant.

After crossing back several times, they finally arrived at the portal that led first through the gate built into a stone outcropping, then over a causeway, and finally into a stable yard.

Jarl Brazstein dismounted and helped his wife from her own sleipnir. He led the way for the Prima Pater and Matriarch to join him, while his son took over the stabling of the collected group. There were few servants in attendance, no doubt due to the meager money the jarl commanded. The paladinial provisioners were shown the way to the kitchen, where they offered to cook a meal. The guards moved under the command of Pater Segundus Guess and Jined to light fires in hearths. All was done in a stoic resolve.

Jurgon Upona appeared after a time, as the entourage gathered in a great hall. Jined had taken a seat near the hearth.

"Jined," Jurgon said, "the Prima Pater requests your presence."

Then the seneschal turned to Katiam. "You are also requested. The Matriarch is tired, but hopes you can give her something to ward off fatigue."

Katiam nodded, and walked alongside Jined behind Jurgon.

Jurgon came to a hall and looked both ways, turned around by the new castle.

"To the right," Jined said, "if we're going to my father's study."

Jurgon nodded and led them in that direction.

They came to a large double door, held open and guarded by the twins, Loïc and Cävian.

Within, the Prima Pater and Matriarch had been provided seats near the head of the long table, with the jarl and his wife on either side.

Their son, Arthoss, sat next to his father. Beside him sat his wife Ketiva and their son, Avett. Jined's sister, Mari, who had married into another home in Brahz, had taken Lerda and Onelie Clemmbäkker to her private home as guests.

Everyone glanced up as Jurgon Upona escorted Jined and Katiam in, and both Arthoss and Ketiva quickly looked away, but their son, a heavily built boy of ten, gawked at Jined as he entered and came to stand at the other end of the table.

"Brother Adjutant Jined Brazstein," the Prima Pater said, standing.

Katiam slunk around the side of the room to the sideboard. She opened up her smaller medicine purse, took out a phial of ground kyllyt nut, and mixed a pinch into some wine. She then began to walk across the room to give it the Matriarch.

"We have concluded preparation of the paperwork, forfeiting your birthright back to your father, Jarl Brazstein."

Jined nodded his acknowledgement.

"It is not legally required for you to be here," Dorian said. "After all, you relinquished it to Pariantür when you took the second Vow. However, Jarl Brazstein and myself agree that having you formally sign a Boronii legal document will put him in a better position."

Jined nodded again.

"Would you care to come to this end of the table to sign the paperwork?"

Jined did not move. Katiam thought she saw tears welling up in his eyes.

"May I be given the opportunity to speak?" Jined asked.

The Prima Pater looked to the jarl, who nodded, a sad look in his own eyes.

"I have brought more disgrace to my family than I could know," Jined began. "For that, I owe an apology, and beg forgiveness from all here. I fled to join the Paladins out of shame, and the fear of losing my life. Through time, my pride led me to believe that what I had done was the honorable thing. I had no idea that my actions would continue to rupture the wound caused by my foolish actions as a younger man. For that, I make no excuse.

"Father, I apologize for the loss of dignity I have caused, and for betraying the house of Brazstein in an act of murder against the house of Tosch."

He turned to his mother. "Frü Brazstein. Mother. Please accept my apologies for the shame I brought you all the years of my life, by squandering my existence and noble birthright that you gave me.

"I know that Mari does not wish to see me. I don't doubt that her marriage was one of gain for the house of Brazstein, just as mine might have been. I pray to Grissone that she is blessed.

"Arthoss, my brother," he said, turning to the man next to their father, "I apologize for the burden I put upon you. I do not doubt you will make a better jarl than I would have been, but it still saddens me that it came by a path of shame.

"Most importantly," Jined said, turning to Arthoss' wife. "I beg the greatest forgiveness from you, Ketiva."

The woman did not look up, but Arthoss took the woman's hand in his.

"I could say my nature got the best of me that night. I could blame others. I could say that it was not my fault, that I pushed the Duke's son to his death. I will not do that. My pride and open arrogance destroyed your life. For that, I will always have a shadow of regret over me. So, I beg your forgiveness most of all, and I hope that you have found some joy in the life you live amongst the Brazsteins. Even if you do not forgive me, know that I shall always pray to Grissone that you are blessed, that your children are blessed, and that you will be blessed by my actions today."

He strode across the room, took the quill from the ink, and signed his name next to his father's and the Prima Pater's.

"Goodbye," he said. "And Grissone bless you all."

He turned and strode from the room.

"Well," Dorian said after a time, "I think perhaps that finalizes the proceedings."

"Thank you," Jarl Brazstein said. "I've said it before, but this takes a great burden from my shoulders."

"Given what I've read in the document, too, you'll now be able to open long-closed mines."

"Which should be a great source of income to us," the jarl said, "providing work to many."

"And I should hope too, a source of healing," the Prima Pater said as he rose. "Let us leave the Brazsteins to their privacy."

He took his wife's hand and helped her from her seat, and they both walked to the door.

Katiam glanced back into the room as she followed the others out. Frü Brazstein was crying, and tears streamed down her husband's face. But the sobbing that came from the room was one of relief, rather than sorrow. And none cried harder than Ketiva, the woman Jined Brazstein had killed for and left pregnant with the boy his own brother now raised.

The meal that night was filling, but eaten in relative quiet, though there was a tension that verged on excitement as the evening wore on.

The following day started full of bustling excitement as the Brazsteins marshaled the reestablishment of their leadership of the castle and city. Merchants and young men and women who sought to work for the jarl came in droves, and few were turned away. The coffers of the Brazsteins had, for the first time in nearly ten years, been opened.

"I should like to visit the market," the Matriarch said as Katiam entered with a midday plate of food.

"I can go find Sabine," Katiam said, "and arrange that."

"I gave her the day to spend with her husband," Maeda said. "They've gone down to the sea."

"Shall I tell sister Glass, then?"

"She left with several Paladins and a local guide to gauge the coastal road into Mahn Fulhar. You can escort me."

The Matriarch rose and opened up a wardrobe, pulling out fur-lined cloaks.

"Disguise, Auntie?"

"Warmth," Maeda said, handing one to her. "And disguise," she added with a wink.

Katiam gave the older woman her arm, and they made their way through the castle to the gate, which stood open as drovers and newly re-hired servants came and went.

"I'm not entirely sure which way to go."

"We have plenty of hours to both get lost and find our way again."

They came to the first switchback. Looking out from the wall, the city spread below them in tiers. The market took up a large square three tiers down, with streets leading off to the left and right, and multiple stairs leading down and away. A single set of stairs cut down through the layers.

"That was easy enough," the Matriarch said. "Looks like the Brazsteins wanted easy access for themselves and their servants to reach the market."

"Was there something in particular you are looking for, Auntie?"

"Nothing in particular. It's been some time since you and I had time together, and it seems like a good day to do so."

Katiam smiled and gave the Matriarch's arm a squeeze.

"How is your study of the Rotha?"

"There has been little change," Katiam said.

"But there has been some?"

"At the grove near Clehm, something happened. A raised seam appeared around the edge."

"That is interesting. What has Esenath said of it?"

"We've not nearly had enough time to speak of it," Katiam said.
"It is probably a good idea to do so soon."
"Why?"
"Winter is fast approaching, and I doubt the cold will be a benefit to the seed."

"Speaking of winter," Katiam said, "do you think we'll make it to Mahn Fulhar before it sets in?"

"I doubt it," the Matriarch said. "It's expected we'll not be able to take the coastal road. Rock falls often block the path, especially in winter, and the seas are too rough to take this time of year."

"So we'll go south?"

"It is expected to add several weeks of travel."

They came to the bottom of the long stairs, and Katiam moved them to a nearby bench for Maeda to catch her breath. It reminded her of the many stairs of Pariantür. The Matriarch never complained, but never relished the idea of a set of stairs, no matter the length.

"It appears we're not the only ones out and about today," the Matriarch said, pointing to several Paladins moving through the crowded market.

Pater Segundus Nichal Guess moved quietly through the people, with Jined Brazstein and Dane Marric on his right and left and three of the entourage provisioners, along with the purser, behind them. One of them stopped at a merchant selling sacks of ground seeds and began haggling with them, while another stopped a few stalls down to negotiate over baskets of dried fruit.

"It appears we'll be eating more porridge on the road," the Matriarch said.

"That is not a bad thing," Katiam replied.

"Spoken as an optimist and a follower of St. Klare."

"Spoken as your physician."

"Come, let me join them," the Matriarch said, beginning to rise.

As she did so a commotion arose, and Katiam turned to see a group of men pushing their way through the crowds.

"Brazstein," the man in front said. He was well-built, but dressed in clothes well past their prime. He sported a chest-length, scraggly beard. The men with him didn't look much better.

Jined took a step forward, but did not tighten his grip on the hammer in his hands.

"What seems to be the trouble?" he asked.

"You are," the man replied. "I demand weregild from you."

"What offense am I to have caused? Who makes this accusation?"

"Loeren Gott."

"Loeren?" Jined said, a smile creeping across his face. "It has been too long!"

"Don't attempt to supplicate me," Loeren said. "Those days I called you friend are long behind us."

"It's been ten years," Jined said.

"What hope or happiness have I had since that day, when your actions cost me my trade?"

"I don't understand," Jined said. "You're a blacksmith, or I assume so. You were about to make journeyman when I left."

"When you left and the mines closed, my master," he looked around to the men with him, "many masters no longer had work. Only those who serviced the larger mines remained. The rest were forced to take meager work, or leave."

"The mines are reopening," Jined said. "There will be work."

"Ten years," the man said, his eyes brimming with tears of anger. "I've been starving for ten years."

"Has not the city provided? My father has sold off much to ensure the poor eat, and that legal weregilds were paid."

"I would not take a handout from your family if I was on the brink of death."

"Yet here you are, demanding the handout of blood-gold."

"I want a pound of gold, or a pound of flesh. And these men want it too."

"That's a request I cannot grant," Jined said. "I'm sorry if my actions have led you to this state. I hope you were not deprived of loved ones."

"I never married, for none would have a beggar."

"There is work now," Jined said. "Tomorrow brings hope."

"Don't speak to me of hope."

"You came to fight," Dane said, stepping up next to Jined. "The words you speak only strive to strengthen your own spine."

"What?" Loeren asked.

"You never intended to let Brazstein walk away from this, so you gathered men to back you up, and had only the intention of assaulting a group of seven Paladins. Go ahead. Brandish your tools and weapons. Try and fight Paladins who train to fight and kill—those set aside by the Prima Pater of Pariantür to kill his enemies and guard his holdings."

Loeren looked over his shoulder as a few of the men lost their spine and ran to leave.

Jined took a step forward. The group of men took a step back, but Loeren stood his ground. Jined placed a hand on his shoulder.

"I do not seek a fight with an old friend, no matter the offense I may have caused him. Had I gold to give you, I would. But I have given up all worldly possessions."

Loeren looked up at the taller Jined. Katiam saw his fists clench on the smith's hammer. He moved suddenly, the hammer swinging into the breastplate of the larger Paladin with a dull clank. Jined stood to his full height, and let the man take several blows out on him. Each hitting soundly where leather and steel protected.

"That is enough," the commanding voice of Nichal Guess said.

Loeren stopped swinging, and Jined turned to Nichal.

"You have made your claim," Nichal said. "The Brother Adjutant here has even attempted to supplicate you, but I've heard enough, and you've now outstepped the law. An unwed man has many an opportunity before him, even at your age. You have never sought work away from your hometown? Never considered service to a god?"

Loeren looked down in shame.

"It is your pride that starved you. Now the jarl's opened the mines, and you seek instead to end your life and career by assaulting a holy Paladin."

He turned to Dane. "Brother Marric. You nor I are scribes, but is it not true that a man who attacks a Paladin of the Hammer forfeits his fealty, and becomes an indentured servant of Pariantür?"

"What?!" Loeren cried out.

The rest of the men who had come with him dissipated.

"Pater Segundus," Jined said, "I would prefer that we grant him some leniency."

"Please," Loeren said, dropping to his knees. "I ask you not do this."

Nichal motioned for the man to rise.

"Your hatred is a festering disease," Nichal said. "If you do not seek to cleanse the anger in your heart over the actions of a man from ten years ago, it will eat you alive."

Loeren gave Jined a look, and then in shame, turned to stare at the cobbles.

"I believe we have enough from the market," Nichal said, turning toward the stairs by which the Matriarch stood. He recognized her, and smiled. The Paladins with him followed, leaving Loeren standing in the middle of the empty space of the market. A few moments later, business proceeded as usual.

"Matriarch Superioris," Nichal said as he approached. "Sister Borreau," he said, nodding his head.

"Well negotiated," the Matriarch said.

"You saw that?"

"Indeed. I have not heard someone invoke the Indentured Servitude scripts in many a decade."

"If ever," Nichal said, laughing. "They were, after all, in a parable. Not in doctrinal scripture."

"Still," the Matriarch said, "it seems to have dissolved the conflict."

"Indeed. May we walk you back to the castle?"

"We've only just arrived," Maeda said. "I've still to look around."

Nichal pointed to where the conflict had taken place, then moved his finger back, counting ten stalls. "About there," he said, "is an ointner. You ought to see what Porumarian oils go for out here."

"They are much sought after."

"Perhaps Pariantür's coffers could use with selling it ourselves and directly."

"It was discussed at one point," Maeda said, "but we decided to let the peasants under our protection collect, prepare, and sell, to their own benefit."

"I've so long lived under the Vow of Poverty, I don't much understand, nor care to, the workings of coin and coffer."

"No need to admonish yourself, Nichal," she said, placing a hand on his arm. "It is a wise thought. Merely one considered before."

Nichal smiled faintly, then turned to the stairs with the others behind him. Katiam and Maeda watched him ascend.

"It is a mystery no woman of Pariantür has made good on that man."

"He is married to his role," Katiam said.

"And he always has been," Maeda said. "It is what makes him one of the youngest Paladins to hold the role of Pater Segundus."

"Though not as young as the Prima Pater was."

"Times of war will do that," Maeda said. "Did you know he was twenty-three?"

"So you've said."

"That is younger than most men who take their Vows."

They turned toward the market and joined the lines of people walking by stall after stall.

"There are times he regrets that he was made Prima Pater only two years later, at the height of the Protectorate Wars. He was young, and the power did, at times, go to his head."

"Pariantür still stands, so he can't have messed too much up."

"No. He did a good job—does do a good job. I've had the privilege of watching him all this time. But we often wonder how different life might have been had the order not unanimously elected him."

"Was there another who might have?"

"Of course. Many of them died in the war. I might not have been made Matriarch Superioris twenty years later, either. Many whispered that I was only made so for being his wife."

"But we know that is not true."

"Maybe I'd have gone to a nearby oracle and become a servant of the Dweol."

"But you were married then."

"Yes. There are plenty who are married in Pariantür who might go for years not seeing one another. Dorian and I were blessed to have one another so close at hand. It is what allowed us to make it through the worst of times. Perhaps you will, one day. Only the pantheon can know."

"Auntie," Katiam said, blushing.

"Maybe after I'm gone," the Matriarch pressed. "You'll go to the college, and there you'll meet a bright young man, and you'll stay there and live out your life as a physician and a teacher."

"What makes you think that is what I want? To teach?"

"What do you want?"

"Choice," Katiam said.

"At times we must set aside our desire for choice," Maeda said, patting her arm, "but that doesn't mean we give it up forever. Tomorrow is a different day, and we always have the choice to accept that fact."

42

Forest Homes

Let the Vow chosen be a burden, a fast to draw thy attention. For as one draws closer to thy god, all worldly distractions shall only be a crashing wave.

—ST. RÄMMON'S LOG, ENTRY 75

It seemed as though Jined hadn't slept at all in the weeks since he'd taken the Vow of Poverty. He hadn't felt he owned much of anything as a Paladin, so taking on the Vow seemed such a small thing. But it quickly escalated when his father, a noble jarl, had practically fell to his knees to beg Jined to relinquish his land and titles. It was a meeting of joy and sorrow, mixed with bitterness made all the more real when he made his apologies to his entire family in the sight of the Prima Pater and the two Pater Segundii.

It was no relief to give up his inheritance, nor did it seem a burden. Yet, almost immediately, as the accolades he hadn't expected to receive died down, Nichal Guess, Pater Segundus of the same Vow, took him under wing. Jined quickly discovered there was much more that came with the Vow than he had initially expected. Paladins, he had not fully understood before, were paid a stipend for their work. Mostly their service to the Hammer was paid in food and lodging, and in the upkeep of their armor.

And so the first thing Jined had to do was turn over his armor and hammer for used ones. Both needed a great deal of maintenance to make suitable. Yet, they were not his. Yearly, he was told, he would trade in his set and be given another old set of armor in utter disrepair that he would be charged with working back into a serviceable set.

Secondly, he would not be paid in food, nor in lodging. Instead, he was required to put in additional time in service and responsibilities in order to make up for it. He had not realized how much extra work the Paladins who had already taken the Vow had done in their spare time. Some spent time at soup kitchens for the poor, or mending their brothers' robes. It exhausted him.

Lastly, by divine ordination, he had been made a Brother Adjutant. The white cordons that now sat across his armor marked him as such by a miraculous change. The herald, Amal Yollis, was relieved of guard duty, and reassigned as one of the Prima Pater's personal attendants. Jined became the Adjutant under Nichal and over the other guards. He was now responsible for the guard duty roster, in which he would also be included.

Nichal had provided him ample opportunity to lead, but was kind enough to take some of the burden on himself. After they left Brahz, nearly all of the training fetters were removed. Jined was on his own.

The coastal road, as expected, would remain impassable until it was cleared in the spring, so they took the road from Brahz to Tosch, from which they would take the pass west into Mahndür.

They said goodbye to Frü Clemmbäkker and her daughter as they left Brahz, but had been joined, as they always seemed to, by a new veiled sister, who rode with the red-headed Paladame Toire Siobh. Jined recalled the new Paladame's familial name, Siobh, as belonging to the family of rulers in the Isles of Bronue Jinre. While the jarls had often bandied about the Siobh name as untrusted in the lands of Boroni, Jined ignored them, given that the Matriarch and those who traveled with her had taken a liking to Tiore Siobh.

The city of Tosch appeared abruptly as they came out of a stretch of woods and looked down over the valley. Half the valley floor was filled with manicured forests, and the bustling city filled the rest of the space. Jined had forgotten just how large it was, nearly double the population of the capital of Donig. Yet, unlike the other Boronii cities, it never felt crowded. Instead, the gate, while well-guarded, gave little attention to the Prima Pater's entourage, and people moved at an easy pace.

The browns and greens of the people were intermixed with

accoutrements of autumnal colors, as the trees in surrounding parks had begun their change. The scents of harvest pies wafted from nearby homes and taverns, in preparation for some celebration, while tradesman continued their work, and watched the entourage go by, considering whether or not to hawk their wares.

They came to a forested area, and Nichal stopped to consider whether to lead the carriages through or around it. Jined saw tents and figures through the woods.

"It looks like the area is a campsite for Üterk," Jined said as he came up next to Nichal.

"Is that a problem?"

"Where their tents sit, their homes lie," Jined said. "Travel through an Üterk camp is never the best idea, especially if your goal is to move past and beyond to the passes."

Nichal nodded and guided the entourage around the forested parkway. As they circled, a unit of guards in green marched alongside black-cloaked Sentinels. At the center, High Duke Toschbrecht rode. He held a hand up and waved.

Nichal gave a salute.

"I'd have thought you were to take the coastal road," he called as he neared.

"It was the plan," Nichal said, "but it was deemed unsafe."

"I'm glad you thought my own town and the passes beyond safe then. I only wish I could accompany you."

"Other matters?" Nichal asked.

"A glut of Forest Folk," Toschbrecht said, eyeing the forest. "Always seems to happen right before winter. And a bit worse this year."

"Are they a problem?"

"They provide enough public nuisance that I will end up dealing with it all winter if I don't take care of the problem now."

"Seems inhospitable," Nichal muttered to Jined.

"Duke Toschbrecht," Dorian said, leaning from his carriage.

The Duke brought his mount around alongside him.

"Greetings Prima Pater. Was your trip to Brahz successful?"

"Very. Is the pass west usable?"

"No issues to report. Although, we could get an early snow up there. I'd not waste time making for it."

"You'd not be put off if we don't stop as your guests?"

"Not at all. As I mentioned to your guards, I have my hands full anyway."

"And hiring Black Sentinels, too?"

"A necessity, I'm afraid. They're capable, and you get what you pay for."

The Duke gave a signal and the guards and Black Sentinels turned and marched off into the park.

"What are they doing?" Dorian asked. "I hope you're not forcing those within to move."

"It is harvest festival time," the Duke said as he turned to smile at the older man. "All are welcome, but they must abide by the rules of my city."

Dorian gave a nod that neither approved nor condemned.

"As long as the law is abided by, I'll be in a good position to return to Donig for the elections."

"Have you ever been prevented from them?"

Toschbrecht gave a small laugh. "Never. It's part of what ensures I'm reelected. Nothing you need to worry yourself about. You'll be in Mahndür, and far away from any conflict here."

"We had best continue on our journey," Dorian said, and sat back into his carriage. Jined could hear him muttering his displeasure to his wife as they continued through the city. The guards were not being rough with people with obviously less means, but they weren't being kind, either. They eyed the entourage with thinly veiled irritation.

As they neared the gate, the entourage picked up the pace, happy to move free of the city boasting false joy in their celebration. Jined came to the gate first and guided his sleipnir to the side to count the entourage as they passed. The red-headed Bronuan Paladame and the new veiled sister had disappeared from their number. Jurgon Upona, seneschal to the Prima Pater, along with his wife Sabine Upona, assistant to the Matriarch Superioris, took up the rear.

"We arrived with two new Crysalas," Jined said. "I don't see them."

Sabine nodded, muttering something under her breath, eyeing the guards atop the gate. Jurgon made a motion to Jined to lead the way out of the gate. Jined did so, and the three of them rode several hundred yards before anyone spoke.

"Sister Siobh was on mission with us," Sabine said, "to escort the veiled sister to another location. She traveled to Tosch with us as a roundabout way to reach that destination."

"It is not my place to ask about the secrets of the Crysalas."

"And in this situation," Jurgon said, "I understand that deniability will have the best results for the Prima Pater."

Jined nodded, sure that whatever had occurred was by design, and protected some woman from violence or actions by some jealous man.

As they neared the mountains, the changing gospar trees gave way to needled evergreens, but even here they grew thick, and the large boulders strewn beside the narrow road as they climbed the mountains beckoned like the tombs in a tightly confined sepulcher.

The company rode in silence, the incline having even seen the scribes and the Prima Pater out of their carriages, to afford the draft sleipnirs an easier burden.

"It's a wonder Tosch hasn't better cared for this road," Nichal said.

"I imagine it goes hand in hand with their superstitions," Gallahan replied.

"And the supply and demand it creates for the wood they export," Nichal added.

"I thought it interesting so many of the forest people had come to work in town," Gallahan said. Looking around he saw Jined. "Is that a common occurrence as the weather turns?"

Jined shook his head. "There are always some Üterk in most towns. More so in Tosch. But I don't think it is related to the weather. There is an old saying about how the more Üterk you have, the greater your bad luck."

"Why do you think they bring bad luck?"

"I'm not suggesting they do, only repeating the saying. My father always told me that if Üterk starting showing up in town in groups, then it meant something bad was either about to happen, or something bad had happened that made them leave their forest homes."

"It could be they came over from Bortali," Nichal said, "to escape war."

"They looked settled, though," Jined said. "So I'd wager they were local clans."

"What drove them from their forest?" Gallahan asked.

There was a piercing, bestial scream from up ahead of the entourage.

Everyone froze in place, and the sleipnirs suddenly became restless.

The scream was met by another, farther off.

"That sounded like saverns," Jined said. "I saw a troupe of them at St. Rämmon. They're rock dwelling."

"Might mean we're nearing the heights and the proper pass," Nichal said.

"Come on Brazstein," he said, urging his mount forward.

Jined caught the glance of the twins and Dane, who joined them at the front of the group.

"Are we expecting trouble?" the Prima Pater asked as they passed him.

"Only taking precautions," Nichal said.

Fifty feet ahead they came to a side path, well-trodden, that led off to the south.

"Night is approaching," Nichal said. "Perhaps we should see if this leads anywhere helpful."

"Brother Marric," Jined said, "please go up this path with Cävian and call back if you find anything. Don't go far. We're not looking to go an hour out of the way."

"Loïc," Nichal said. "Please ride ahead a bit, and give us news of the road."

The three Paladins rode away. Jined looked up at the sky and realized just how deep the shadows were growing.

"I didn't think it had gotten so late," he said.

"I don't think it is," Nichal said. "The mountains are casting a deep shadow, and it's getting cold. It won't hurt to stop and catch our bearings before continuing our climb tomorrow."

They heard a quick whistle come from Dane and Cävian's direction, indicating they come, and that all was well.

"I'll ride up to Loïc and determine how tomorrow will go," Nichal said. "You see what Dane found and administrate the setting up of camp, if you find a good place on a slope this steep."

Jined took the path, which appeared wide enough for the carriages, and came out onto a flat cut away in the rock. A village had been constructed in the space, which looked out over the tops of trees to the forest below. There were mining shafts cut into the rocks in several places, and a fresh scree field had been dumped off the far end of the village. Fresh boughs decorated the lintels of the homes, indicating whoever lived here had not been gone long.

"Forest people?" a sister was saying nearby. Jined turned to see Astrid Glass talking to the botanist, Esenath as they entered the village.

"There are a couple clans I've done trading with in Nemen," Esenath said. "They decorated their homes, and their market stalls with boughs."

"If that's the case," Jined said, "then we need to be overly cautious. If they left anyone to watch over their village, they've already seen us, and will watch how we treat their village."

"Surely we can draw water from their well," Astrid said.

"If an Üterk thinks he has been cheated, he exacts revenge. It will not hurt us to leave them gifts for anything we take."

"That's rather superstitious of you," Astrid said.

"Practical," Jined said. "I had a cousin who took an Üterk for a wife in order to gain access to a stretch of forest belonging to her people. She died before she could produce a child, and suddenly everything went wrong for him. He couldn't keep workers. Half the trees got rot. He paid a weregild on the bride, even if her death was not his fault, and suddenly everything went right."

"No one has explained to me what a weregild is," Esenath said. "It is not a practice south of the mountains."

"It's a Man's Price. It can mean any number of things. If an accident befalls a man, and the fault can be put on anyone, then it is paid to the man—or his family, if he is dead. There are whole courts of law in the north that state the prices for various weregilds. I knew a man who stubbed his toe on a cobble and received a weregild paid to him by the local baron for the injury for the loss of a week's work."

"And that is what tied your family up?" Astrid asked.

Jined nodded. "Both for the death of the son of Duke Toschbrecht, and for his son's fiancé, whom I both impregnated and cheated out of the dowry she would have received marrying into the Toschbrecht family."

"Wouldn't she take some blame for that?"

"She might have," Jined said, "but the greater blame was brought against me. And my fleeing to become a Paladin rather than face the court and noose was considered an admittance of guilt."

"You did the right thing," Astrid said. "Giving up your birthright."

"But the question remains if that will ever be enough," Jined said.

The scream of a savern startled the three of them again, and it was quickly met by another.

There was a thunder of hooves as Nichal and Loïc burst into the space. The other sleipnirs were being unsaddled for the evening, and everyone looked to Nichal. The Prima Pater came out of an abandoned house, his wife next to him.

"Arms!" Nichal called.

"What is going on Nichal!"

Three figures shot over everyone's heads, and one dipped lower than the others, toying with the sleipnirs before shooting up into the dusky sky.

"We're not far from the top of the pass," Nichal called out, "but there is a troupe of saverns roosting there, and on the lookout. They decided we were targets to pick on."

Five more saverns, all smaller than even the slightest sister, with wingspans longer than a sleipnir, shot overhead, and this time drew tighter and tighter circles around the group, pulling in together toward the well at the center of the clifftop village.

"I have never heard of saverns doing something like this," the botanist Esenath said.

"They and their little cousins, the wyloths and furies, do this to their prey," Dane said from nearby.

One of the winged creatures suddenly fell upon one of the provisioners. The older Paladin flailed about, screaming against the claws and fangs, as the long-mawed creature tried to tear him apart. Amal Yollis, the herald, stepped up and kicked the creature to the ground, where Astrid and another Paladame fell to beat the creature down.

Suddenly, out of the clouds of wings overhead a figure dropped to the ground. It stood much larger than the saverns, and upright like a man. Unlike the canine face of the savern, this creature's face, while elongated, bore the semblance of a person, and the light of the torches playing in its eyes glinted with intelligence.

Jined raised his hammer, and moved to run at the creature, but it held up its taloned wing, signaling for him to wait. Jined stopped.

"I come with a message," the figure said.

The Prima Pater pushed through the group, a torch in his hand. The figure shied away but did not flee. In the torchlight Jined could see it was a man, yet something new. He stood stark naked. Long fur clung to his body, and his fingers had elongated to accommodate the wings his arms had become.

"What are you?" Dorian asked. "And from whom do you deliver your message?"

DEATHLESS BEAST

"My master knows what you have done to his champion, Gar-Talosh, and he has decided that for your action, a price must be paid."

"I do not answer to your master," Dorian said, "and you ought to tell him to take it up with my own god."

"It will be settled on the mortal plane," the creature said.

"What name do you go by?" Dorian asked.

"Gho... The Deathless King."

"I've not heard of you," Dorian said. "You must be newly in the service of your god."

"You'll not live to see as many days as I will, and shall be forgotten," the creature said, "but I will be remembered. The Walker has foretold it."

"Even he does not know the days to come. Nor can he foretell your living or dying. But I can tell you this. If I die this day or next, I will stand by my master's side in the end. But you will be shackled next to yours, in eternal durance in Noccitan."

The creature roared its fury and leapt up into the sky even as the countless saverns dropped from the sky to attack.

The twins had hunting bows from which they shot arrows into the air, while Dane batted the creatures out of the way to reach Dorian, who had three of them on his shoulders trying to pull his armor off of him.

Jined leapt into action alongside Dane and Nichal, who struggled against the creatures to pull the Prima Pater toward one of the carriages. The Paladames already had the Matriarch Superioris sequestered. Jined felt the crunch of brittle bones as he stepped over the bodies of fallen saverns, pushing the Prima Pater forward in the dark, while batting blindly at the sky to wave off more attackers. The provisioners were trying to light more torches, but the black cloud of fluttering, slashing wings obscured the light.

"Grissone," Jined muttered, "help me stand against the darkness."

There was a sudden flash of light that pulsed from his hammer, illuminating everything around him.

The saverns screeched in terror. A few near the ground fell in shock, struggling to rise back into the air. The Paladins took the opportunity and rushed forward to smash their wings, ensuring they could not flee and return later.

It was a sudden and visceral victory, but hollow, as torches were passed around in the silence of night, and men and women examined each other for gashes and torn hair.

"What was that thing?" the Matriarch said, coming down from the protection of the carriage and approaching her husband.

"It is like in the Protectorate Wars, when they first started. Do you remember?"

"A new champion of one of the dark gods showing up every time we turned around," Gallahan said.

"I forgot that you saw the Wars first-hand," Nichal said.

"I was squire to Dorian in those days," Gallahan said, "before I took my final Vow."

"Do you remember fighting that thing that commanded dræks?" he said to the Prima Pater.

"We never found him after he fled," Dorian said, "but it's not beyond the power of Kos-Yran to grant that kind of command—dominion over creatures."

"He was the Walker and the Gift-Giver, even before he fell," the Matriarch said. "But the gifts always come with a curse."

"Self-loathing being the greatest of each curse, I don't doubt," Dorian said as he took a seat and let Katiam nurse a scratch on his scalp with a wince.

Jined looked up towards the mountains, where the red light of Norlok backlit the figure of the Deathless King as he raged at the sky and the Paladins bustling about the corpses of his followers.

43

Dead Pass

Silence. Friend and enemy to all.

—NASUNI PROVERB

Ten monks shuffled along the road, each identically dressed in tight, gray robes. A matching blue sash was tied across their middles, and a heavy cowl of the same color sat on their shoulders, obscuring their mouths. Across their eyes they wore a blue blinder, the only features of their clean-shaven heads, voluntarily taking from them their sight. They walked with the aid of a tall staff in their hands, upon which a single ring, from which hung several others, tinkled with each stride with a jin, jin, jin.

Four Black Sentinels walked alongside them—the only four the leaders of the Monks of Nifara had allowed. At the head walked Searn VeTurres, Master and Commander of the Black Sentinel organization, and next to him walked the young Ophedia del Ishé. Her hood was back, her black hair falling loosely over her shoulders. In the sun, a glint of red could be seen in her hair.

Behind the monks walked the Clouws. Hanen Clouw, the elder by four years, and as many inches taller, kept his peaked black hood off his own head in the sun, his contracts unable to see him anyway. His black hair was tied loosely up on top of his head, trying desperately to free itself from a leather thong. Next to him walked his younger sister, the stoic Rallia, who walked with a short staff in her hand, a Sentinel banded club mounted to each end.

Searn left Ophedia out front and stepped off the road to let the monks pass, then fell in beside Hanen.

"How long, would you say, to the pass?" Hanen asked.

"We'll travel north to where the borders of Düran, Limae, and Bortali meet," Searn said. "The pass there is well-guarded by all three nations. It marks a major trade point, and passes below a steep road to the city of Haven in Limae."

"The headquarters for the Sentinels is there, is it not?"

The question came from, Seriah Yaledít, one of the young monks the leader chose to take with them.

"Yes, Nefer," Searn said. "We'll be able to gauge the travel conditions in the north from there. The weather in Mahndür is almost always different than in Düran. We will be very welcomed, and we can resupply from there."

"Where do you suppose we'll rendezvous with the Paladins?" Rallia asked.

"I couldn't say. But from Haven, if we need to travel into the Boroni jarldoms, we can. I suspect we'll be chasing after them in Mahndür, though."

By the end of the day, they were walking along a road parallel to the mountains. Trees climbed up the boulder fields that made up the ridge. Hanen could tell he wasn't actually seeing the tops of the mountains, but just a glimpse of a lower lip. He wondered if many had ever ventured to their heights.

"You should see Düran from up there," Searn said.

"You're a mind reader now?" Hanen asked.

"I've seen that look before. You're thinking about climbing. It's best in summer."

"Do many live up there?"

"The pastures might be good for herds, but there's a lot of wild animals living on those heights. For the most part they stay away from people, unless they get hungry."

"Farmers then?"

"Trappers and hunters, that's about it. The exotic animals fetch a good price; some even more so alive."

"Such as?"

"Griffins, for one. There are several aeries of those majestic creatures. I met a man once who said he had ridden one. I guess I should say he tackled one, and it took him for a glide before throwing him off. He was obsessed with taming them."

They came to an inn that night. It was small, with room enough for the monks. The Sentinels stayed in the common room, finding their own corners to sleep in.

The road continued easily. Inns were spaced evenly on the road, with individual travelers moving their wares up and down the continent.

They were four days out from Birin when a warm wind from the south washed over them. The leaves had turned a wash of colors higher up the mountainside. Snow had capped the very tops overnight, but as the day proceeded, even that began to melt and reveal slabs of granite. Searn walked at the front with the three leaders of the monks—the Archimandrite Pell Maran, Gregor Hans, and Kerei Lant.

"I fail to understand why charity is so important," Searn said.

"Charity is the greatest work anyone can perform for common man!" Gregor growled. "Why would you question it?"

"Gregor," Pell Maran said, quieting him. "The man asks a question. We will answer it in a way that satisfies him. Tell me, Commander VeTurres, what is the true question you wish to ask?"

"I am making light conversation, mind you," Searn started, "but why do the Holy Nefers provide charity? The other holy orders, too, for that matter. It seems that is one of their primary purposes."

"We have the time," the Archimandrite said, "and the money to give to those in need, and so we do. Just as we offer judgment for those who cannot find a way to receive judgement from their own courts, we help those who are not being helped."

"If you did not help so readily, perhaps the people would go out of their way to do so, instead of assuming you're going to do it."

"That is true. If we do not give, others would. But then, what kind of people would we be if we, among men, cannot give?"

"We do not give out of obligation," Kerei Lant offered, "we give because we can, and because we want to."

They walked in silence for a mile.

"Commander VeTurres, may I give you a challenge?" the Archimandrite asked.

"What's that?"

"Do not seek to find out why an order does good to others. Simply ask yourself how you can give. Things will sort themselves out as you do so. You will find a way to improve others, and yourself, at the same time."

"Archimandrite, I mean no disrespect. But I do not question

why they do good. I merely do not believe in good, nor in evil. I believe instead only in right and wrong. There are times when what some perceive as an evil may be good, and times a good may be an evil."

"That is an interesting observation. You are more than a simple bodyguard. You ask questions the sages have long debated. I do not think I can answer that flippantly. I shall consider what you say, and speak with you on the subject later."

Ahead, two men walked alongside a large bovine auroch pulling a heavy-laden cart. They shuffled down the middle of the road, looking downtrodden, passing through the middle of the monks and Sentinels, who parted for them. When they had fully passed, the cart stopped. Hanen looked over his shoulder just as the canvas across the top began to flutter and uncover five men, who leapt out brandishing swords and daggers.

One man stepped forward, holding a buckler in his off hand. They were dressed in browns, with heavy hoods to cover their faces from view.

"Time to pay up, Nefers!" he shouted.

Rallia stood at the ready. She turned, whipping her cloak from her shoulder onto the ground, her heavy staff hefted up onto her shoulder.

"No need to be brave, girlie," one of the other brigands said. "Your monks here can pay up, and we'll be on our way."

"Ha!" Ophedia laughed as she came to stand next to Rallia. "You talk tall for a fool."

The little man she spoke to stepped forward. "Who are you calling a fool?"

"I think it's apparent you are the fool," Rallia said. "I think she was more pointing out how short you are."

The man gripped his sword tighter and growled.

"You ought to get your little mutt back on his chain," Ophedia called to the apparent leader. "He might get kicked."

Hanen and Searn had pushed their way up next to Ophedia.

"Did your mother feed you along with ynfalds?" Ophedia continued. "That's all that can account for your ugliness. That, or your father was an ynfald himself."

The man rushed toward Ophedia in a rage. Hanen barely caught Rallia's movement as the heavy staff came off her shoulder and spun out, almost taking Searn in the backside of the head. It reached out the four feet to where the man stood and took him in the ear, laying him out cold.

The first strike brought mayhem. Rallia got a second swing in, under the jaw of another man before the third bowled her over, pinning her to the ground, trying to shove a knife through her chest.

Searn stepped forward and gave the man a boot as he loosed a crossbow bolt into another.

Ophedia rushed forward and thrust her club into the chest of one man, knocking the wind out of him. She pressed him forward toward the wagon, and then Rallia spun her staff, whipping it across the top of the wagon and clipping the crown of the man's head.

Hanen took a step back as the leader walked up to him, swinging with the buckler. Hanen swung against him, lodging his axe in the wood. The man tore the axe out of Hanen's hand and swung with a short sword of his own. Hanen dove out of the way, and the leader walked past him, directly toward Pell Maran.

"Time to visit the Judge, old man!" The man screamed.

Gregor Hans stepped in front and reached out with large arms to engulf the thief, taking him down to the ground. As they fell together, the sword pushed through Gregor and out his back, covered in blood. The assistants, not sight-bound, began to scream in mass hysteria.

Gregor was not dead, though. He held onto the bandit, closing his hands around the bandit's throat and squeezing slowly, crushing the man's windpipe. Hanen could hear Gregor whisper harshly into the dead man's ears, "Let us visit the Judge together. I suspect you won't fare as well as I."

Hanen scrambled up, and began to herd the monks together, letting them know it would be fine, even if he didn't believe it himself. The attackers were down, some groaning, some unconscious. Only the leader was visibly dead.

Pell Maran asked to be led to the side of Gregor. He knelt down and felt the big man's frame. His finger touched the sword sticking out of his friend. He pulled his hand back with a hiss, and sucked on his finger.

"You have given so many sacrifices for Nifara, and now you have sentenced a man to death with your last breath. May she guide you quickly to her own house. Wait for me there. I shall look forward to our conversations."

He pulled the binding from Gregor's milky white eyes. "So you may see the goddess when she comes for you."

The mourning wail of the monks rose in crescendo.

"Hanen," Rallia said, "let's move the body of the monk to the cart. Ophedia, get some rope out. Are you good with knots? We drag the outlaws with us to the next inn."

"Archimandrite," Searn said, loud enough for everyone to hear him. "These brigands attacked holy men and women. They are, by all intents of the local law, dead men. I will give you a moment to deliver last rites to them, after which I will execute those that live." Searn said so with an authoritative sincerity.

"Commander," Pell Maran said, "you do not have the authority to take the lives of these men into your own hands."

"I do." Searn said. "The contract the Black Sentinels signed with the country of Düran allows us to exact punishments befitting crimes. Roadside brigandry is an offense only paid for by death."

"We shall see to the last rites," Pell Maran said hesitantly.

The monks sobbed openly as they moved from body to body, whispering through gritted teeth the words they had long practiced. Searn walked up to each bandit, and once the monks had completed their work, slit their throats.

One held up a hand and began to scream incoherently at Searn. He turned and tried to crawl away, frantically trying to rise to his feet. Searn drew out his crossbow, raised it, and shot the man in the back.

"This is why I said we needed more Black Sentinels," Searn shouted angrily. "A show of more Sentinels would have given these bandits second thoughts about taking advantage of us."

He turned to Rallia.

"Clouw, I want you to march back to Birin. Bring ten Sentinels back with you. We'll continue at the same speed we have been traveling. We're still a week away from the pass. I need you and the others back before then. Understood?"

Rallia nodded.

Hanen walked up to his sister. "Are you rested up?"

"Yeah. We're about thirty leagues out of Birin. I should be able to make it by some time tomorrow if I move fast."

"Don't kill yourself. If you make it by tomorrow night, and take a day to gather Sentinels by word of mouth, I bet you're back in five days tops. Get Sentinels that look like they'll remain in control. And," Hanen paused and pulled Rallia closer, "get Sentinels who you think won't be trouble like Thadar. Ones who won't cause trouble if we set up shop in Mahndür like we did in Edi."

Rallia nodded and grabbed her brother's arm. "Keep your head on your shoulders."

"And like I said, don't kill yourself."

Rallia took off at a jog back toward Birin.

"We need to move out," Searn said. The body of Gregor had been loaded into the bandit's wagon, a blanket laid over him. The bodies of brigands were dragged several hundred yards from the road. Carrion animals would take care of them soon enough. The monks were crying, albeit quietly to themselves.

The Nefer Seriah Yaledít walked nearby stoically. Her blindfold remained unstained by tears.

"Do you not mourn the passing of Gregor?" Hanen asked.

Searn now rode in the wagon, driving the auroch forward, while Ophedia walked silently alongside it.

"None of us mourn his passing. He is well-cared for by Nifara. But I do mourn."

"What do you mourn then?"

"The death of the brigands, executed without remorse, without a trial."

"They attacked us."

"Did they? They asked for our money. Perhaps we could have done so."

"Nefer... They were brigands. By law, their actions are punishable by death. If it had not been by our hands, it would have been by another authority."

"And what authority did your commander have? His own? By an organization not recognized by anyone as legitimate? You're just bodyguards for gods' sake. What right have you to be judge, jury, and executioner? We monks don't sentence people to death, and we're ordained by a goddess to judge fairly, honestly!"

Hanen sullenly watched her walk off. At least the monks now knew that the Sentinels were serious about their roles as bodyguards. It would be a long week without Rallia beside him and contracts who didn't care for, nor respect, their guards.

44

Fellow Dedicates

Pilgrims three came into view,

Paladin, monk, and friar.

Each curried his company.

First friar offered prayer.

Next monk a judgement fair.

—*THE TRAVELER*

The town of Mühndih and the bastion there offered a day's respite before they began their journey north. A breath of fresh air washed slowly over the entire company. In the evenings, Katiam bundled the Rotha pod up and kept it under her pillow to keep the cold from reaching it, and while they rode, when the sun warmed the earth, she brought it out and held it near her pommel horn. Nothing changed, but she liked to hope that maybe her love and care might bring it to bloom.

The evening of the second day out of Mühndih, they set up camp and dinner was just being served, when a sleipnir rode hard into their midst. The rider, a Black Sentinel in a peaked black cloak, rode with a monk of Nifara clinging to her back.

They were quickly escorted into the Prima Pater's tent, and within a few short minutes, the camp tension broke as Pater

DEATHLESS BEAST

Segundus Guess issued orders to ride south with the guard.

A few minutes later, two women emerged from the Prima Pater's tent. One was a blonde-haired Black Sentinel an inch or two taller than Katiam, with a short braid off the back of her head, and the sides of her head cleanly shaved. She wore her black cloak open, walking with a staff in her hand, and a banded club mounted to each end. Her blouse was immaculately white, which contrasted with the black trousers and boots she wore.

Next to her emerged the monk of Nifara, in a blue sash and cowl, with a shaved head and wearing a pale blue band over her eyes. She held her staff of order in one hand, and leaned on the Prima Pater's seneschal, Jurgon Upona, who kept a keen eye on the Sentinel's every move.

Katiam found herself watching the Sentinel as she moved from place to place, taking calm, deep breaths as she smiled, watching the Paladins and Crysalas go about their work. She soon settled at a fire. Katiam took a seat at the next fire over.

"I'm just glad we caught up with you," she was saying, "it's been a hard road from Edi to here."

"Edi?" a Paladin asked. "That's a long walk."

"Forced march," the Sentinel corrected. "A slower walk once we left Birin with the monks."

One of them offered the Sentinel a bowl of porridge. She took some with a smile and a thanks. "This tastes like home," she laughed.

"How so?" another asked.

"I was raised among Paladins."

"Yet you're a mercenary?"

"Yes. My mother was the daughter of a Paladin in Garrou. She married my father after acting as wet nurse for my brother. So, I was raised around Paladins—helping out in the soup kitchen."

"We just came from Garrou," one Paladin grumbled.

"Oh? How is Primus Derrig? He was assistant to my grandfather, Primus Brathe, when he was younger."

"Your grandfather is Jadsen Brathe?" It was Pater Segundus Pír speaking now. "I knew him when I was a young man."

"He was a good man," the Sentinel said.

"Yes. The best. Incorruptible, to say the least. Loyal, both to friends and to Grissone."

"It is a pleasure to be here," the Sentinel said. "I have been too long away from the company of Paladins."

The Monk of Nifara approached with her arm interlocked with Esenath, who brought her over to sit at the fire with Katiam.

"Tell us of your journey," Esenath said.

"I'm not sure where to start," the monk said.

Soon the monk, who introduced herself as Seriah Yaledít, began to detail their journey from Birin. Katiam listened as the monk explained the attack, and the after-effects on their Archimandrite. Esenath was nodding and glancing over at Katiam.

"As I said," Seriah continued, "when we were attacked, one of our leaders, Gregor Hans, was run through with a sword. As I understand it, Archimandrite Pell Maran cut himself on the blade when he leaned over to help Gregor. His finger quickly became infected, and we feared poison. He was delirious for days, but stayed alive. He is still not well after these three long weeks. We were marched through the pass, trying, perhaps, to catch up with you. We had just arrived in Mühndih when word came that you had recently passed through. The Black Sentinel, Rallia Clouw, agreed to ride north to meet you. I came to ensure you'd hear us out and not turn her away."

Esenath turned to Katiam. "Is there anything we can do for the Archimandrite when he arrives?"

"I will do what I can, but we have not seen the symptoms; there is little I can prepare for."

"Nefer Yaledít, do you know the symptoms?" Esenath asked.

"No. I have only heard what little was described to me. Even that was sparse. There was no time to talk as we pressed hard to meet with you here."

Two days later, just as the sky began to enter a gray and overcast twilight, Amal Yollis rode into camp, stationed a mile south to keep an eye out for the return of the guard.

Everyone made ready and came to stand alongside the road, to formally welcome their brothers and sisters of the dedicates of Nifara. Around the curve the standard of Grissone, carried by the aging standard bearer Valér Queton, appeared. Then half the guard, marching in formation. Perhaps ten men and women, all dressed in the cloaks and peaked hoods of the Black Sentinels, marched behind them. Two wagons came around the corner, the first was driven personally by Pater Segundus Guess, while the second, laden with supplies, was driven by two mercenaries.

Six Nifaran monks shuffled along behind the carts at a stately pace, then another ten Black Sentinels, and the remainder of the

DEATHLESS BEAST

Paladins took up the rear. The parade of people came up and stopped short before walking between those gathered.

The Pater Segundus and a black-clad mercenary on a sleipnir both dismounted. The monks gathered round the back of one of the carts. First, they helped down one of their number that looked as old as the Matriarch and her husband. He patted one of them with a smile on his face. Two of the black-cloaked Sentinels stepped forward with their leader and helped an old monk down from the back of the cart. He seemed only vaguely aware of his surroundings, and the three men had to help him walk down the corridor created by the entourage towards the Prima Pater and his wife.

Coming to stand before the two leaders of the churches, the old monk lifted his head and smiled, then bowed it again. The Black Sentinel, who was apparently their leader, said, "Most Holy and Distinguished Prima Pater of the Grissoni Church, and the Pure and Holy Matriarch Superioris of the Crysalas Integritas, I, Searn VeTurres, Master and Commander of the Black Sentinels, have to the best of my abilities delivered the Archimandrite of the Monks of Nifara to you. I pray you will look honorably upon us, and provide what help you can to the Archimandrite, poisoned by an assassin's blade."

The Prima Pater nodded, and several Paladins rushed forward, taking the Archimandrite from the Black Sentinels and carrying him into the Prima Pater's tent.

The Matriarch gestured for Katiam and Esenath to follow.

As they came into the tent, the Archimandrite was being laid out on a bed, having already slipped back into unconsciousness.

Katiam moved to his side and stripped his gray robe to his waist. His right arm was blue. It did not have the appearance of frostbite, but still appeared blue, as though he had placed his hand in a vat of dye and after days it had still not washed clean. It faded the further up his arm it went.

She turned to look at Esenath. "Beardfrost?"

Esenath nodded. "Well done, Katiam."

"And what is beardfrost?" the Prima Pater asked.

Esenath opened up one of the copies of her book, leafing through it. She came to a spread that showed a drawing of a plant, the stems below the flower drawn in blue, tiny hairs drawn along the leaves.

"Prima Pater," Esenath said, "beardfrost is a plant that blooms in the lowlands of Redot. Even in the hottest parts of summer it has fuzz growing on it that looks like frost. Its touch stings, and leaves the skin feeling cold. The apothecaries of Redot have learned to refine it into a venom that, when used, makes the victim feel icy and numb. Of course, it also turns their skin blue."

"What do you make of it?"

"The Archimandrite did not fully succumb. It obviously crept up his arm. Had it crept into his heart, he would have died. The blue will fade over time. However, I've heard recovery takes as long as a year. He'll have permanently lost the use of that arm. He will always be tired, and an invalid."

Katiam heard a sob and turned to see an older female monk standing in the doorway.

Esenath continued, "I suspect he will be awake at the most, for only a handful of hours a day. That is, after he has recovered."

The Matriarch escorted the other monk closer. "Please, Nefer, tell us your name."

"I am Kerei Lant. The Archimandrite, myself, and the late Gregor Hans are the ruling council of the Nifarans. It seems it falls to me to take leadership now."

"Very well," The Prima Pater said. "Once the Archimandrite awakes again, we'll discuss that. For now, I would like to hear your account of things. It bothers me that you felt you needed to hire mercenaries to escort you to find us. Where are the Paladins of the Bulwark Fortress in Birin?"

"We do not know, Prima Pater," she said. "Our message runners told us that the entirety of the Bulwark Paladins rode out toward Limae two weeks before we left. They had not returned. When this Searn VeTurres arrived, he made the point that we had to make quick time and leave to catch up with you before winter fully set in, or we never would."

"Perhaps he was right. Winter is fast approaching. If you had not caught up with us now, you would never have, until Mahn Fulhar. Still, did you not receive our message, requesting you join us in Mahn Fulhar? We sent it over a year ago."

"We did not. We heard that you had come to the continent, but, as you had not sent word, we assumed you would eventually make your way to visit us."

"That is a reasonable assumption. Except we did send messengers. This disturbs me."

The Prima Pater turned and left.

Over the course of the morning Kerei shared the events of their travels. Of the attack by bandits, the doubling and then tripling of the Black Sentinel guard, and the professional, albeit aggressive nature of Searn VeTurres. She kept her comments about the Sentinels curt. She would not speak ill of them, but she never came out and said she liked them. They were mercenaries. That was the fact. Why they needed validation by the heads of several churches did not make sense to her.

The Archimandrite came to for a time in the afternoon and ate. At one time all were excused, leaving Dorian, his wife, and the Archimandrite alone. When they came out, the Archimandrite joined them. He already looked better.

His voice cracked as he spoke, but those near, the monks most importantly, could hear him. "I feel weak, but I am doing well, and I am told I have made it through the worst. Please listen to what Dorian, the Prima Pater, has to announce." Pell Maran smiled, but slumped down onto a seat offered to him.

"My announcement is simple," the Prima Pater said, "the monks always have three leaders. One Archimandrite, and two councilors. Archimandrite Pell Maran has chosen to appoint Kerei Lant in his place, voluntarily stepping down to act as her councilor. If all here are in favor, she will become the temporary Archimandrite until she can return to Birin for a general election of her peers. As second councilor to the Archimandrite, he appoints the revered Cräg Narn. If all present agree, it is made truth."

The monks all nodded and bowed their heads in compliance.

The Prima Pater then stepped forward to address the rest of the congregation.

"We have made a rather regretful decision, though, that not everyone will agree with. Some of the sisters will be staying behind now with Pell Maran so that he can make the trip north at his own pace. The rest of us will continue on. It is regrettable that we must do this, but it is important that we reach Mahn Fulhar before winter makes travel nearly impossible.

"Lastly, we wish to address the Black Sentinels. Searn VeTurres, we thank you for your services rendered. You have completed your contract and are released from duty."

Searn stepped forward, two Sentinels behind him. One was the blonde Sentinel who had ridden into camp with the monk, and the other was taller, with scruffy black hair pulled up in a loose tail on his head.

"Prima Pater, thank you for your kind words. However, you will find that the contract we started with the Monks of Nifara does not conclude until we safely deliver them back to Birin. We are sworn to protect them as bodyguards throughout the winter and until they are returned. We thank you for thinking kindly to release us, but we are duty bound to continue. You will find us good company, and able camp fellows."

The Prima Pater turned to another Paladin, who was looking over a parchment sheet and nodding.

"Very well," he said with resolve, "we accept you into our camp. We leave at dawn."

45

Interlude

"I recall the late night walks you were known to take, when we were younger," the Paladin said, coming out of the woods and approaching a black-cloaked figure standing in the middle of the snowy plain. The two moons overhead cast eerie double shadows upon them both.

"You probably ought to have confirmed who I was before you spoke," the figure said. "What if I was someone else? Do you want someone to report you for breaking your Vow of Silence?"

The figure turned and looked at the Paladin.

"Shroud," the Paladin said. "I know your silhouette well enough. Frankly, I didn't expect you to come riding into camp."

"You've taken the mantle of Cup now that the old Cup is gone, yes?"

"Yes."

"They say that he died in his sleep. That is not the case, is it?"

"He almost succeeded at separating his shade from his body without it killing him."

"It is a difficult thing to do. Regardless, you were able to recover it afterwards?"

"I performed the preparation of his body for the catacombs myself. I collected his Shadequill and interred it into a book."

"Good. I'd hate to have lost his intellect, even if he wasn't as smart as you or I. How long ago was that?"

"Four years ago."

"I understand your company came through Boroni and Bortali.

Did you speak with Dusk?"

"Yes. He's made the rank of Pater Minoris, heading the fortress in Waglÿsaor."

"That will suit him. He'll bring many to the cause there, I suspect."

"Not until he can free himself of the distraction you've given him."

"What is that?"

"He said he knows you have made a living shade. And when I saw you ride into camp, I could tell yours was not with you. You finally accomplished what I taught you."

"This is true. Had your mentor succeeded, we three might be the only people in history to have done it. It has given me the perspective to accomplish so much more, no longer fettered as I was."

"Such as?"

"As you did not share what you had accomplished until you had proven to yourself it was so, I will share what I have done when the work is completed."

"Very well. I imagine we'll not have a chance to talk again until Mahn Fulhar."

"Until Mahn Fulhar," Shroud said.

Cup turned and walked away, back into his Vow.

Part 6

46

SOMETHING WRONG

The holy knight made offers three,

Safety, promise, accord.

He left the other two behind,

But found knight spoke no word.

Left he the knight at ford.

—THE TRAVELER

Hanen envied the Paladins their six-legged sleipnirs. The Prima Pater had convinced the monks to take the seats in the carriages, despite their tradition of walking, while the Paladins and Paladames rode alongside them. This left the Black Sentinels to walk on foot. He shouldn't have felt that way, but he did. The holy orders only furthered the implication that they were holier than those around them, holding their own morality above the rest.

Despite the incident with the roadside bandits, it had been going well. The head monk hadn't died, sleeping most days away in the carriage, and when rumor came that they were only a short ways behind the Paladins, Rallia and the monk Seriah had taken a sleipnir and rode ahead as heralds. The other Sentinels that had joined from Birin, and those that later came down from the home base city of Limae were stoic, and minded their manners.

None of the Sentinels would risk bad manners in front of those who would speak ill of them to the goddess, or might speak well or ill of them in the afterlife. Now the Paladins, ever holier than everyone else, dampened the mood of the Black Sentinels simply by looking down on them from atop their mounts.

The early snow that fell through the trees on the road to Bremüm lightly dusted the ground and made the tracking of fresh food easy. The Paladins adopted a simple schedule for the sake of the monks and their ailing Archimandrite. They did not travel long each day, setting up camp before dark each afternoon, providing more than enough time for the Black Sentinels to range out and bring back kills. There wasn't enough meat to feed the entire company of over seventy people, but it improved the stews the Paladin's provisioners prepared, and offered the Black Sentinels some ingratiation with their hosts.

At Bremüm, a smaller town with a thriving lumber trade, the Paladins, Paladames, and monks found their way to the local paladinial bastion. Hanen was glad to find a large enough tavern with the other Black Sentinels, away from the watchful gaze of the armored holy knights. It wasn't that he worried about himself; he didn't consider himself to be someone who strayed from any paths of morality. But the others around him needed time to be themselves.

It looked like most inns found in the northern countries. The common room was wide, encircled with benched tables, and a large hearth at one end.

Half of Hanen's tankard of ale was already empty. The rest of the Sentinels were already carousing, barmaids sitting on several of their laps. Ophedia had stepped down off a table, gasping for breath and red in the face from the jig the musicians by the hearth had just finished playing. Ophedia threw herself down on the bench next to him, winded. Searn sat nearby at a table of five others, laughing and smiling. Two more musicians had shown up and were preparing to join the first. It would get loud, and quickly.

Rallia dropped into place across from Hanen, a wooden chest in front of her. She opened the top and placed out four wooden cups then flipped the chest over, the open back engraved with squares.

"We haven't played a game of Edi-Foz since we left Edi City," she said.

"You two used to play that every time you came into the tavern in Suel," Ophedia said.

"Do you want to play?" Rallia replied.

DEATHLESS BEAST

Ophedia shook her head. "I've never gotten the hang of it."
Searn came over and sat next to Rallia.
"I'll play," he said, grabbing a wooden cup.
Ophedia rolled her eyes. "Alright. I'll play, but not for money."
"Just a friendly game," Rallia said, smiling.

Hanen took a cup himself, and the four of them poured out the contents, flat, glass beads, in front of them.

"You go first, Ophedia," Searn said, pointing to the white markers in front of her.

She took several of the markers and placed them down in one square near the middle.

"I thought you said you didn't know how to play?" Hanen said.

"Barely. Was that a good move?"

"It's an aggressive move," Rallia said, putting two yellows out near her own corner.

Round the four of them went, placing until the board was populated, and Ophedia took her first move, attacking into Hanen's quarter, removing a single piece.

"Now, we need to assign some lookouts," Searn said, splitting up a square of three pieces, to spread out across an invisible line between his quarter and Hanen's. "I don't trust the Paladins to keep to the agreement."

"You think they'll try to take off without us?" Hanen asked. He pulled his red pieces away from Searn, inviting the Sentinel Commander to come into his zone.

"I don't see why they wouldn't, if only as a test of our mettle. Might not even be in the next several weeks, but I don't want them getting away from us."

Rallia didn't move any pieces, and took advantage of her lull, adding extra pieces to several of her own territories. She looked up with a satisfied smile.

Ophedia continued to punch her way into Hanen's quarter, while Hanen continued to consolidate backward into himself. Searn didn't seem to have taken much of the bait, and continued to build up defense against Hanen's own area, while also keeping a watchful eye on Rallia, who continued to ignore the three of them, adding seemingly random pieces to her quarter.

The shift was sudden. Ophedia watched in sudden realization as Hanen's pieces, heavily built up along her outside flank, suddenly pierced her quarter, leaving her stretched and surrounded between Hanen and Searn. She looked at each of them, then to Rallia, who shrugged, her own army a bloated fortress. Searn watched the piercing invasion of Hanen's and Rallia's forces, boiling out into Ophedia's territories and his own.

Ophedia struggled as her own force was split into two, and she was pressed by all three. She was all but ousted from the game, allowed to continue only because Searn's own move was as savage as Hanen's turn on Ophedia.

His forces, now solidly controlling the middle of the board, began to expand each way as Hanen and Rallia pressed their forces into the periphery. Hanen and Rallia watched in horror as he did so.

There was a look of astonishment on Searn's face when all that remained of Ophedia's pieces made a last-ditch effort and attacked into Searn's territories. His response was swift and brutal, and she was quickly ousted from the game.

But he realized all too late that his efforts had left him controlling all of Ophedia's original territories, and none of his own. Hanen and Rallia together shared the rest of the board.

Searn began to laugh. "You both herded me into a false victory!"

Rallia gave a sheepish smile. "To be honest, we've tried this before, but against less experienced opponents it never works, because they end up making some other mistake and we complete the game with a victory."

"Do you mean no one wins?" Ophedia asked.

"It's a three-way tie," Searn said. "They used you to beat me into this position. I took the bait and took your territories, and they took all of mine. I have the strongest position. If either of them moves against me, they will lose."

"And if he attacked either of us," Rallia said, "he forfeits, as we both work together to defeat him, and push ourselves into a stalemate with each other."

"I don't understand," she replied.

"Basically," Hanen said, "this is a rare circumstance where if we proceed the game will go on until dawn. We've reached the point of maximum pieces, and no one can gain the upper hand."

"It's rare," Searn said, "but its rarity is very, very satisfying."

"You're not mad that they walked you into that trap?"

"Not at all," Searn said. "Disappointed I didn't win, sure, but the knowledge that these two play so well together makes me wonder what a one-on-one game with either of them would mean. You've played all your life, have you?"

Hanen nodded. "Our father taught us. And he said he learned from his grandfather. He never shared much about his grandfather, only that he was one of the best at Edi-Foz in the world."

"That's a bold statement."

"His grandfather was said to have learned it from Fozobaça himself."

"Your great-grandfather fought in the Protectorate Wars?" Searn asked.

"That is really all we know of him," Rallia said. "He was tutored by Fozobaça, and when our father would press him about whether he ever beat his own master, he avoided answering the question."

"He didn't," Searn said.

"How do you know?"

"Because I learned from Fozobaça's other student. He told me that no one ever beat Fozobaça when he brought the game from Edi to the Protectorate Wars, before his son, General Itream Fozobaça became the founder of the city that bears their name. But, his two students did, one time, accomplish what you just did—the False Victory."

Rallia rose.

"Where are you off to?" Hanen asked.

"I'm not that tired, and like you said, Searn, someone has to take first watch to ensure the Paladins don't leave without us."

"Good girl," Searn said.

"I don't think they will leave," Rallia replied. "But everyone here is probably in less of a condition to watch than I am."

She turned, took up her cloak and staff, and walked out of the inn.

"She has a deep sense of responsibility," Hanen said. "Got it from her mother."

"Oh? She had a different mother, right?"

"My father married a girl from one of the Üterk tribes from the Bortali forests. She died when I was born. They say I look just like her. He found a wet-nurse for me, Rallia's mother, the daughter of a Paladin. The Paladins paid off debts my father owed in return for him running their poor kitchen in Garrou, and marrying her."

"Where is your father now?"

"After he apprenticed us out he sort of disappeared. I'm not sure where he is. But I'm fine without him. He was unlucky."

"You and Rallia seem to have turned out alright. You certainly impressed me when I met you."

"I feel like that was just luck."

"No. It wasn't luck. You and your sister proceeded to set up a network on a highly trafficked road. Why was no one else doing it? Noccitan! Why haven't we Sentinels ever done anything on this scale before?"

"I wondered the same myself. But I'll admit, I thought to start the caravan because I wanted to find a way to fulfill contracts quicker—to rise faster through the ranks."

"Why?"

"Why what?"

"Why did you want to rise in the ranks?"

"I don't like owing anything to anyone. My father always owed someone something. Don't get me wrong. I'm grateful you gave us a place in the Sentinels. But I have always felt as though I owed you for giving us the opportunity."

"Well, consider any debt you owe me paid off. I'm grateful for you backing me up here."

"It seemed like a good idea at the time."

"What about now?"

"I think I understand what you're about, but I think we could also be getting ourselves in a bind with the Paladins. We're a thorn in their side right now. As you say, they'll want to get rid of us."

"You said yours and Rallia's grandfather was a Paladin?"

"Just Rallia's."

"I understand that. Still, perhaps you could pass this information on to a Paladin or two. Get friendly. It can't hurt us. In the meantime, we'll continue to hunt for food at night. Providing good meat for the company should continue to earn us plenty of favor."

The Paladins did not try to leave before the Sentinels joined them the next morning. Nor the one after that.

The road out of the forest continued to be a peaceful one. They entered the northeast plains of Mahndür. The wind drifted the light snow across the landscape, and the clouds above kept the sun from melting it away. The walk was not too cold, and the wild animals had not yet decided it was time to hide away for the winter. They neared the foothills of Crysania's Massif. The Paladins sent out a scouting party to go and meet with the bastion that was said to sit at the base of the mountain, guarding a steep and narrow climb to the top.

47

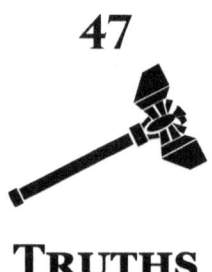

Truths

Are not all things from above? Did not Aben and Wyv stretch out their hands, empowered as they were by the Existence, and make our world of Kallattai? Our worship is to follow the instruction of our god. By our obedience our god gives glory to He That Is.

—SAYINGS OF ST. MACEN, BOOK OF SAGES

The arrival of the monks and mercenaries had been jarring to the entourage, but they had adapted, slowing their pace to accommodate the blind Nefers. They neared Crysania's Massif and began their approach to the Green Grove Bastion built up against the nearly unassailable slope into the massif, guarding the dangerous back passage to the top.

An eerily peaceful place, the sun barely reached the moss-covered ground through the dense Ebrw trees, and the stones of the tiered complex of buildings were soft and green with inches of mossy loam grown over their surfaces.

A Pater Minoris came out to great them, bowing humbly.

"Prima Pater Mür," he said, "welcome to my humble bastion."

"I have not had the chance to come here since I was a boy. It seems little has changed."

"I pray you consider that a good thing," the Pater Minoris said.

"There are fewer places I have ever experienced such a peace."

He turned and looked around at the grove.

"I recall the guesthouse to be large and accommodating.

Commander VeTurres, your Sentinels will find it very suitable, I should hope."

A Brother Primus stepped forward to guide the black-cloaked Sentinels away.

"Shall I show your company around? Or shall we first find you situated?"

"Let us see to the needs of the Nefers, and to that same purpose the rest of us."

The Pater Minoris gave a bow and turned to lead them into his bastion.

Jined accompanied Nichal, assigning cells to each Paladin. The Crysalas took the choir hall as their own, while the unused Infirmary became a common room for the Nefers.

"Let me show you to my own office," the Pater Minoris said.

"No need for that, Pater Minoris Averin," Dorian said, "perhaps the Chapter House might be of the same use to me."

"Very well," Averin said.

"I'm curious how a Pater Minoris bearing a bead of the Vow of Pacifism has only the one name, and to that, a name I recall from my own past."

Averin smiled. "My father and his father before him had the same name, and both had taken on the Vow of Silence. My grandfather served alongside you in the Protectorate Wars."

"And your mother did not think to give you a second name? Even her own?"

"My mother was a simple woman, of deep religious leanings. She preferred only to name me after my forefathers, devoted to Grissone as she was."

"Brother Averin," Dorian said with a smile, "was one of my closest boon companions. Tried to give his life for me on three occasions, but Nifara never came to take him from us, until he was the ripe old age of sixty."

"I was four when he passed away," the Pater Minoris said. "I've got ten more years to reach his age."

"May Grissone bless you to surpass your grandfather's ripe age," Dorian said.

"Thank you Prima Pater," Averin said. "Let me show you the Chapter House."

"For the size of the bastion," Gallahan muttered to Dorian, "I'm surprised this is not a fortress."

"As a place of peace and respite," Dorian said, "I think it's often

DEATHLESS BEAST

preferred to stay that way. It is no larger than it was when I came through here in pursuit of the girl who would one day be my wife."

"There are many rumors of how that came to be," Nichal said. "Although most consider the story to be hearsay."

"I've heard many of the rumors and stories surrounding that," Dorian said. "While they are mostly true, some of the more romantic portions are overblown. I didn't pursue her out of love. Her father asked me to chase her down and bring her back to the farm, on the promise that he would force her to be my wife. But Crysania had other plans for her, and Grissone for me."

The chapter house was also sizable, and probably once housed five times the thirty Paladins now stationed at the Green Grove Bastion.

"We hold Chapter every two days," Pater Minoris Averin said. "And we did so this morning. While I'd break tradition and call for a special Chapter tomorrow, perhaps given both your need of rest, and the considerable number of brothers here who have taken the Vow of Prayer, we might stick to our habits, and ask you to lead the chapter in two days?"

"I would be honored," Dorian said. "And I agree. I'd rather not upset the cart from my fellow Prayer Paladins."

Dorian turned to the company, the Pater Segundii, and their assistants.

"A day of rest tomorrow is a wise thing, I think. Please check that those under your command are well-situated, and then see to your own rest. I think I'd like to go for a walk with my wife in the grove now. No need for any of you to attend."

Nichal gave a salute and turned with Jined and the herald Amal Hollis to leave and find their own cells.

At dawn, Jined was awakened by the quiet rap of Etienne returning from the bathhouse.

"Pater Segundus Nichal has asked that you meet him in the chapter house," Etienne said.

Jined nodded and quickly pulled on his brown robe and gorget. His armor sat on the stand against the wall. He pulled his belt on to make sure his hammer hung comfortably, then proceeded through the haphazardly planned bastion.

Nichal sat near the front looking over a book on a stand. He glanced up and smiled at Jined as he approached.

"Take a seat, Brazstein," he said.

Nichal finished running his hand down the page he was

studying and nodded to himself as he closed it.

"The Matriarch Superioris has requested we stay here a week. Somehow a message was sent up the frigid mountain to their oracle, and she is awaiting a response. As it will be dangerous to travel to the oracle until spring, it is important that we wait here."

"This will put us well behind schedule."

"We're already behind schedule," Nichal said, "but the Prima Pater thinks this won't hurt anything."

"What can I do to be of assistance?"

"Nothing. I just wanted you to know. I do want you to go out and have a look through the grove, though. Two of the Black Sentinels were seen sneaking back to the guest lodge early this morning. They claim it is normal. They also say they saw a large nest of furies in the trees. Please verify this and look for signs of their truthfulness, or lack thereof."

"I will," Jined said. "If it was one of the Clouws, one of them is known to rise early."

"Very well. I'd still like you to go and look."

The ancient trees seemed to grow in planned lines, and each step on the loam was silent. He became aware of another figure walking parallel to him.

Jined stopped in his tracks, but did not turn sideways. He felt the figure approach from behind. Jined felt his heart begin to beat rapidly. He had awaited this meeting ever since he had taken his second Vow.

"Brother Hammer," Jined said, as he dropped to one knee and bowed his head.

The figure came around to stand in front of him. "Why do you bow, Brazstein?"

"Because you are no Paladin. I understand that now."

He could see only the figure's feet, and looking closely, saw that they might be perceived as boots, but indeed they were part of him.

"Look up now, Brazstein. No pretense. No speaking in scripture."

As Jined looked up, it was as though seeing Brother Hammer for the first time. The armor was embossed with lines of scripture written across it. It was in a language he did not know, yet seemed to understand, regardless. The hammer that hung on his hip was no hammer at all, but instead nothing hung there—a void that merely suggested a hammer. Jined's eyes came to the gorget and did not look further.

DEATHLESS BEAST

"I dare not look you in the eyes. I am not worthy."

"It is true. You are not worthy. But still, I allow you to look. Look at me."

A hand touched Jined's chin and lifted him to stand. Jined stood taller than him. Then, a finger lifted his chin, and he was forced to look into Brother Hammer's eyes.

His eyes were blindingly white, and the light of creation was in them. In a moment's flash he felt guilt fall away. His past was erased, and only the Jined of now stood there.

"Now you are made new."

"Grissone. My god," he said, as he fell once more to his knees, weeping.

"Rise and walk with me."

Jined stumbled to his feet, laughing and crying. "I'm... I'm sorry. It's overwhelming, being faced with the divine."

"I imagine it must be."

Jined gained control of himself, and laughing between sobs, said, "To think I've been talking to you like any other Paladin this whole time."

"That is how I prefer to talk to anyone who prays to me."

"I can only imagine you have something important to say to me," Jined said, "but I have to ask the question. Why me? Why not someone more worthy, such as the Prima Pater, or Nichal Guess?"

"Because you ask that question. Do not think I haven't appeared directly to Dorian. I have. It was many years ago, during the time you call the Protectorate Wars. And I have other plans for Nichal. I will visit him in due time. What is most important to me is that I visit you."

"Why? What's coming?"

"I don't know. I asked you to speak with the Paladames. Did you?"

"I have not been able to."

"Perhaps the second Vow contributes to this. Regardless, I suppose it may not be too late yet. Strive to do so. In the meantime, I have more important tasks for you. You must continue on the path of Deeper Faith."

"Further still?"

"There is no faith that is deep enough. Yes. I request of you a deeper faith. I cannot make of you what I wish if you do not submit. If you pray to me, I will answer. Not perhaps in word, but when I am elsewhere, I can still imbue a power in you."

"You speak of miracles?"

"I do."

"Not that I haven't seen them done, nor read of them in scripture, but miracles have not been part of my training."

"The so-called training in miracles is pointless. Either I answer a request, or I don't. But you, Jined Brazstein, I have chosen. If you have a need, I will answer it."

They walked along in silence for a stretch. Jined glanced over occasionally to see if he still walked alongside him.

"Why did you choose me, though? Of all the men in the world right now, why me? A murderer, an entitled son, and father of a bastard?"

"Why do I need a reason? I chose you. Stand up to the call I have made, and do as I command."

"Yes, my god. I will obey."

"Very good. It has been difficult for me to come and meet you since that day you took the second Vow. Or perhaps even since we first spoke at St. Hamul."

"Difficult?" Jined asked.

"Yes. I cannot explain why this is so, but something moves among your company. Something I cannot perceive. When you came to this glade I was encouraged. This is a holy place. Yet it feels defiled."

"By this thing that makes it hard for you to visit?"

"No," Grissone said. "Something else still."

Jined looked up and saw minuscule figures moving among the branches. A few turned and looked with taut faces, and smiled with bared fangs. They were furies, the smaller cousins to the wyloth, and the entire branch the furies clung to writhed. Hundreds, if not thousands of them swarmed across the branch and each other.

"That is not normal, is it?" Jined asked.

"Not usually. But the cold is coming," Grissone said. "I do not pay much attention to the creations of Wyv. When I am in a pensive mood, I much prefer to observe my own avian creations."

"They are not what causes your issue?" Jined asked.

"I'm not sure," Grissone said. "It's odd, I'm sure, for you to hear a god, such as I, speak this way."

"It is," Jined admitted. "I shall seek council with the Prima Pater."

"I may have to go and visit the Judge to see if he knows of this."

Grissone turned and touched Jined's forehead between the eyes.

DEATHLESS BEAST

"I will see what you see now, and I will answer you from afar if you call."

There was a flash of light, and Jined was left alone in the glade. He glanced up at the furies again, shuddered, and turned to go back to the bastion. A sense of awe sat over him, along with a sense of quiet dread.

As he approached the bastion, a pair of Paladames walked arm in arm with one another, empty buckets hanging from their other arms, toward a well. Jined watched them walk away, and thought to go immediately and find the Matriarch Superioris and tell her of the message Grissone had given him those months before at St. Hamul. He shook his head, not wishing to interrupt her own peace and quiet. He touched the satchel at his side and a shiver ran up his spine. The thought of going and speaking to her suddenly went away.

"Another time," Jined said dully.

"There is no other time," a wry voice said. Jined spun to see Dane slowly approaching.

"What?" Jined asked.

"Give no thought to the fragile sex," Dane said. "Nor give them your time, lest it become a bondage."

"I ought to take a look at what books you're reading," Jined said. "I fear the translations you and your sect of the Chaste Mind are studying are misleading."

"How dare you?" Dane sneered. "What I speak is scripture."

"I believe you are quoting Brother Brel Lorvad. His work was lost to the Ikhalans, and returned after the Protectorate Wars, of which there are several various translations, none of which agree. I read them when I was choosing my first Vow. And the verse you quote is only from one of the translations the rest disagree about."

"I've read them all. They do not disagree."

"The oldest of the translations reads,
    'Nor give over thought woman,
        'lest time spent pondering them becomes prison.'"

"In what way," Dane said, "is that different?"

"It does not forbid time spent in service to them. Paladins serve mankind. Women are, by definition, included in that."

"I believe that by serving man, we allow them to be greater and serve their own wives. It is not my responsibility, nor in my good conscience to serve them."

"Perhaps it would be best then, after this journey, that you find a way to avoid them altogether," Jined said. "Maybe in Mahn Fulhar, Nichal should assign you a task that ensures you never have to see another woman as long as you live."

"I should be so fortunate," Dane said with a sick-looking smile.

"Far be it from me to put you in a position where you might feel tempted," Jined chuckled.

"Tempted?" Dane scoffed. "Hardly."

"If you are not tempted, yet show so much contempt, why are you so hateful of them? It goes beyond reason. Beyond your Vow."

"My past is none of your concern. A second Vow, or new rank, does not preclude you to know me."

Jined held up his palms in defense. "I do not consider myself better than anyone. I only ask."

"Don't."

Jined nodded and watched the hate-filled Paladin march away, angrier than he was before.

48

Awakening

The path of Aben, the purity of Crysania, the wisdom of Lae'zeq, the faith of Grissone, the justice of Nifara, the cultivation of Kasne. The members of the White Pantheon seek the peace of all. Question your leaders if they speak in any way contrary.

—JANUL DORINSEN, PRIEST OF ABEN

BURNT AT STAKE IN ŒRON

Green Grove Bastion had been expecting them. The Paladins in attendance had already prepared their rooms and seen to their needs. The evening had been a quiet one, and the silence of the grove continued into the morning. The evening before, the Primus of the bastion had brought a small wooden box to present to the Matriarch. It contained a single crystal petal from the oracle in the mountains above. The Matriarch had used it to scry to the Crysalas temple. The return message was vague, conveying that they wait. And so, the Matriarch had asked that they wait.

"You have demanded very little," Katiam reminded the old lady. "If a woman of your age, and his wife besides, asks for a pause, in a country much less suited to late autumn travel than one of warmer climate, he can afford to oblige."

"Aren't you ornery today?" Maeda Mür said.

"I hate to see you fret," Katiam said.

"He could have left me at Pariantür in the first place."

"But he didn't."

"That's true, and I've made it this far. How many ninety-four-year-old women do you know who can make a trip of this length?"

"Ninety-five next week, Auntie."

"Is it really that soon?"

"I don't know any other women who have made it to ninety."

"Sister Perag."

Katiam looked at her quizzically.

"You said you didn't know any others who were ninety. She made it to one hundred and two."

"Then you have a ways to go to beat her."

The Matriarch moved the sheets and sat up on the side of the bed.

"Don't bother with the medicines today," she said, "I'm feeling good."

"Nonsense," Katiam said. "When you find time to rest is when sickness can most easily creep in. Drink this."

Maeda took the cup offered to her and hissed through the bitter taste. Then she stood up.

"Let us go and see this grove the others are talking about."

Once they were dressed, they walked towards the entrance to the bastion, only to be met by the Pater Segundus Nichal Guess.

"I'm afraid you will not be able to go out without an escort," he said.

"What is this nonsense, Nichal?" the Matriarch demanded.

"There seems to be an unusually large swarm of furies that have appeared in the grove. They haven't caused any real trouble. They're furies, though, so they might."

The Matriarch turned around, grumbling. "Come along, Katiam. Let's go find a place at least to set up a sitting room for the other sisters."

Four days later, Katiam prepared an afternoon meal for the Matriarch in the bastion's kitchen, before a knock came at the outer door. The Paladin provisioner by the hearth wiped his hands on his apron as he walked to answer it. A figure stepped in, bundled against the elements in fur, with a white veil over her face.

"I've come from the oracle with a package for the Matriarch," she said in a thick accent.

Katiam hurried over.

"Hello, I am Katiam Borreau. I'm an attendant to the Matriarch. Can I lead you to her?"

The veiled sister nodded, and Katiam led her through the complex.

The Matriarch looked up with a smile as they entered. Dorian seemed to be in a good mood, mirroring the look.

"You must be from the Oracle," the Matriarch said.

The girl in the veil almost floated across the room, kneeling before the old lady.

"I am Sister Elda Llon, and I was sent to deliver this to you." She delivered a small wooden box and offered it over to the Matriarch Superioris. A pink glow came from within as Maeda cracked the lid. She nodded. "When do they expect you to have delivered this?"

"The oracle is expecting to commune with you tomorrow at dawn."

"You have done well, Sister. You should rest now."

"Thank you, Matriarch Superioris."

"What is all this?" Dorian asked.

Maeda sat back in her chair, the wooden box now on her lap.

"Within this box is what we refer to as a sconce bud from the Dweol. It will allow me to speak with someone who sits in attendance at the bloom. I can convey information to the Oracle there. Then they can also send a message to the Oracle near Pariantür."

The Prima Pater stood and offered his hand to help his wife stand.

"I suppose I should leave you now, to speak with your sisters. Perhaps I'll go to the Archimandrite and see how he is doing."

He gave Katiam a nod, then left the room.

"Katiam, will you see to it that the sisters meet with me in the chapel at dawn?"

Katiam turned to the other door leading out into the room given over to the Crysalas. Sabine sat at a table with Esenath, looking through Esenath's botanical book. Katiam recognized the image of a plant root meant to encourage fertility. Sabine looked up, red-faced, as Katiam stopped several paces away.

"The Matriarch wishes us all to gather before dawn tomorrow. The Oracle delivered a sconce bud. We'll be able to speak with the Oracle atop the massif, as well as send messages to Pariantür."

Sabine rose, turning several pages in the book. "I'll make sure the others know."

"I was going to tell everyone. I'll leave you to what you were doing."

"I'm happy to," Sabine said, turning and leaving the room quickly.

Katiam watched her go.

"I take it you saw?" Esenath asked.

"Yes," Katiam said. "As a physician, she need not be embarrassed by me knowing. I won't bring it up."

"I think as her friend, almost her sister, it does embarrass, regardless."

"Do you think you will be able to help her?"

"There is no way to know until it works or doesn't. Have you kept the Rotha in a warm place?"

"Yes," Katiam said, patting the satchel at her side.

"It will be good to arrive in Mahn Fulhar, where you can provide it a more permanent place for observation."

Before dawn, Katiam arose and helped Maeda Mür through her morning routine in silence. They arrived at the chapel to a circle of women, yawning, but quiet.

Katiam sat next to the Matriarch Superioris, holding the Rotha in her lap, as she often did when the Crysalas met.

"My sisters," the Matriarch said, drawing their attention to her. "As we have arrived so late to Mahndür, we cannot make the journey to the Oracle at this time of year. Most certainly not from this side of Crysania's Massif. Thus, I sent a message to the Oracle above us, and we have been answered in the form of Sister Llon."

The veiled woman half rose and then sat in response.

"We meet here now, with a sconce bud brought down from above to this vale, a grove of trees planted by our own sisterhood before the pogroms, and cared for now by the Paladins of the bastion built here. It is fitting, then, that we shall commune with the oracle above by way of this bloom in the midst of this sacred place. We shall be prompt in our messages, but each shall have a moment to hold the bloom and ask what you will."

The Matriarch opened the wooden box held out by Sabine Upona. She pulled out a glowing piece of crystal formed into the shape of a rose bloom, which undulated faintly with light. Over time it would fade and the petals would drop off, each collected for use in various ceremonies in the sisterhood.

She held the crystal bud and kissed it. It seemed to bloom with more light.

"Oracle, are you attended? This is the Matriarch Superioris, Maeda Mür."

After a few long moments, a voice resonated from the rose, matched by the wavering of its light.

"Matriarch Superioris, the attendants of the Oracle hear you. Please speak your words."

The Matriarch smiled and looked at the women around her. "Let us proceed."

Each woman took the crystal in their hand in turn and spoke words into it. Esenath sent word to one of the women who had been sent to Pariantür from the college, providing words of encouragement, while Astrid sent a message to her parents, confirming to them that Killian had died. Finally, it came to Katiam. She took it cupped in her hands, and then paused. She put her hands down to rest over the Rotha. The pink glow of the bloom seemed to undulate erratically.

"Is something happening?" the voice from the crystal rose asked. "The Dweol is flashing with lights. Bands of light."

There was a pop that Katiam felt in her lap. She lifted the crystal only to find it was attached to the Rotha by a single vine. She took the Rotha in her other hand. The seam had cracked open, and a sinewy tendril had unfurled and writhed its way into and around the crystal bloom.

"Matriarch Superioris?" the voice asked again.

"Yes," Maeda said, with some awe in her voice. "I believe that concludes what we wished sent. We will see you again when we reach the Oracle, after we've been to Mahn Fulhar."

No more voices came from the rose, but all stared in awe, or had half risen to get a closer look. Esenath leaned over Astrid's lap to look closer.

"It opened?" she asked.

Four more tips were sticking out of the pod seam. It seemed not to move, but had completely bound itself into the crystal bloom. The light from the crystal began to fade, and small fissures had begun to form.

"I've never seen a bloom fade so fast," Sabine Upona said.

"It's as though the Rotha is taking strength from it," Esenath said.

"What do I do now?" Katiam asked, looking around. She held the two things now intertwined with one another, not sure how to even hold them.

"I don't think there is anything you can do," the Matriarch said. "We can find a better way to carry it, but I believe you've discovered how to make the Rotha grow. Now you can just watch what it does."

"I agree with the Matriarch Superioris," Esenath said. "I'll help you in any way that I can."

Katiam sat in her cell, the Rotha laid out on her blankets. It had done nothing more. Someone had brought straw from the barn, and Esenath had promised to bring soil and moss from the glade. She was scared to bury it in dirt, where she could not see it and care for it as she had.

"If you're just a seed, I have to treat you as such," Katiam said. "But why do I care? You're just a plant."

There was a skittering sound that came from the corner of the room by the straw. Katiam stood up and took hold of a broom. The small movement of the creature shooting along the wall caused Katiam to squeak. Then it leapt up onto the bedpost too easily. It looked up at Katiam with malice.

"You filthy little fury," she scolded, brandishing the broom. "Get out."

She swung the broom down on the post. It dove across the bed, opening its arms and gliding to the opposite end.

It hissed a squealing little noise and then leapt back again, soaring to the wall and clinging to the stone. It climbed up and to the ledge of the window. It looked back and scowled before jumping out. Its shadow streaked away, and was joined by another, then two more. Soon shadows flashed past the window, out of Katiam's view. She caught the sound of a scream, and recognized it as Esenath's.

Her breath caught in her chest. She took up the Rotha, placing it in her satchel before throwing the satchel over her shoulder, and ran out into the hall. Sabine Upona came flying out of her own room in a panic, swatting at her head. As she spun, Katiam caught sight of a pair of little wings as something clung to the back of her hair. Astrid came from her own room and took hold of Sabine and pushed her up against the wall, face first, and then reached up and took hold of the little fury in her gloved hand and pulled it away, bringing a tuft of hair with it and a startled scream from Sabine. She flung the creature against the other wall, and it fell still.

The three of them rushed down the hall and out the side entrance to the glade and froze in disgusted horror.

Thousands of creatures swarmed in the air, encircling a single figure in a whirlwind of wings. Katiam could not make out the person who stood there, flailing and trying to shake free the attackers, but the shovel in the freshly dug earth, next to a pot, and the screams of panic coming from the figure told Katiam it was Esenath.

A figure fell down through the trees and landed nearby. He had his back to the bastion, but stood stark naked. His back was covered in a coarse orange hair that ran a trail to the tail covered in the same fur. His legs seemed slightly elongated. Longer still were the arms. The hands could touch the ground, and the slender fingers had skin stretched between in crude wings.

"Savern?" Sister Llon said as she came out to stand with them.

In reply the creature turned and looked at them. He wore a crown of wyloth skulls, with another necklace of smaller skulls around his neck. It was no savern, but looked like some form of monstrous human made into a parody of man and wyloth. It was the creature that had attacked them in the mountains. The Deathless King.

"Enough!" the creature barked. The storm of wings that surrounded Esenath flew away to land on nearby branches, and she collapsed, panting.

"Sentinels," the creature said. It almost sounded like a question.

Esenath was covered in countless scratches and bites. Her eyes were puffy and couldn't focus on the creature standing over her.

"Get back," Astrid said. "Get the others back inside, and go and tell the Paladins. I will retrieve Esenath."

Katiam nodded and turned to start ushering the others inside. She watched as Astrid strode forward. Sister Llan walked alongside her in her furs and veil, as did Laugha Noccil, a veiled Paladame in full armor who had joined them in Mühndih. She had less to fear from the scratches. Katiam and Sabine moved to the door as the three of them retrieved Esenath and dragged her towards them.

"Take her to the infirmary," Katiam ordered. "Astrid. Please go to Pater Minoris Averin and see if he has any additional ointment stored away. Griefdark would be best."

49

FALLEN KING

The woodland speaks unto the trees:

Fall—for the ground must be covered.

And to the Skies: billow and drop your white.

　And Spring brings forth the flowers;

The trees gladly sing their beauty.

　And in summer they take in the fire of the sun.

—UNKNOWN QAVYLLI POET

"The others are starting to get argumentative again," Rallia said.

Hanen looked up. The Black Sentinels were spread out around the stable, lost in their own thoughts or looking around furtively. One of the new Sentinels who came down from Limae with Searn was nursing bite marks across the back of his neck.

They had been holed up for five days now. When they sent the Sentinel across the grounds to the bastion to ask for news, they had been assaulted by a cloud of pests, and had fallen back into the stables, but not before he saw a figure that seemed to walk naked and unscathed by the fury storm. The Paladins had sent no word. Either they had left without the Sentinels, or were themselves locked behind their own doors as they avoided the vermin plague.

DEATHLESS BEAST

"How long can we stay here?" Rallia asked.

"As long as we need to," Hanen said.

As if in reply, there came a knock at the door.

Nobody moved. They just looked looked up and stared.

Rallia turned and approached, reaching out tentatively. Then she paused. "State your name."

"Seriah Yaledít," the voice replied.

Rallia jerked the door open and pulled the girl in with as much force as she slammed the door shut behind her. She had her cowl pulled up over the top of her head, to either mask who she was or protect her from the furies.

"What are you...?" she said. Rallia shushed her and put her ear to the door. Then she turned to the monk. "How did you make it here without being harassed by the furies?"

"My order has been discussing it with the Prima Pater's entourage for over a day now. It seems they will not touch we Nifarans. This has led us to believe that the creature that seems to lead them is from Kos-Yran. The Mad Gift Giver has traditionally forbidden his people from harming Nifarans."

"Ghoré Dziony stated he met Kos-Yran," Hanen said to Rallia, stepping up to join them. "He was a Sentinel who escaped imprisonment several months ago."

"Why have you not come to tell us this?" Seriah asked.

"Because when one of us tries to leave the furies assault us."

"We assumed as much," Seriah said. She held out a package, which Rallia took from her. "Open it."

Rallia undid the bundle, revealing two Nifaran robes and cowls.

"What is this?" Rallia asked.

"The means for you to come to the bastion."

"Why?" Hanen asked.

"Because that creature out there, Ghoré Dziony you called him? He's been asking for the two of you and the Prima Pater wants to know why."

"How will these robes help us?" Rallia asked as she held up the blindfolds. "Neither of us can walk blindly."

"But I can," she offered. "If what we assume is correct holds true, the furies won't attack you if you look like a Nefer."

"You had best head out there," Searn said approaching the three of them. "Just make sure to come back with a plan. I'm not living out the rest of my life in a stable."

Hanen and Rallia pulled on the robes, and came back to the

entrance.

"Rallia," Seriah said. "Put your hand on my shoulder, and Hanen, you take your sister's."

Hanen put the cowl up over his head, then situated the blindfold across his eyes before finding Rallia's shoulder, which lurched forward as Seriah tugged them out into the vale. There was an eerie silence all around them. The smell of the mossy loam was tainted by an underlying fecal aroma. The silence was occasionally broken by a chirp or random screech. The air did not move, save for the occasional whip of wind as a fury fluttered past their heads, to which Hanen could not help but duck. The hundred yards to the bastion seemed to take half a day to reach, and his heart pounded in his chest.

When they reached the door, he heard it swing open. Someone took their arms and pulled them in. As Hanen took his own blindfold from his eyes, he saw Rallia remove hers with a gasp for breath, as though she'd held it the entire walk across in fear.

"Here is some water," a Paladin offered. It was the large Jined Brazstein. He held out two water skins, which Hanen took, and held the second out to his sister.

"Are you alright, Rallia?" Hanen asked.

Rallia nodded as she drank. "I did not like that. If one of those nasty things had landed on me while we walked in the dark, I'm not sure what I would have done."

"When you are composed," the Paladin next to them said, "I am to escort you to speak with our leaders."

They both followed the big man as he turned and began walking down the hall. They came to a set of double doors, standing open to the chapter house within. Members from all three holy orders sat grouped together near the front. The three Nifaran leaders sat on one side of the stage, with the Prima Pater and his wife, the Matriarch Superioris, on the other.

All but the Nifarans turned to watch the Clouws walk down the aisle. Rallia made a holy sign of Grissone, more out of habit than anything. Hanen kept his arms to his side, not sure what else to do with them.

"Welcome Clouws," the Prima Pater said. "Hanen and Rallia, I believe?"

Hanen nodded while Rallia smiled.

"I'm not sure what you were told, but do you understand that this creature outside has been asking for us to give you up?"

DEATHLESS BEAST

"If what we've heard is true, Ghoré Dziony is his name," Hanen said. "He was once a Black Sentinel."

"If you would be so kind as to explain more of this," the Matriarch said. "We should like to remedy the situation and be on our way to Mahn Fulhar, but it seems this forsaken storm of furies will not let us leave."

"As I said," Hanen began, "Ghoré was a Sentinel. He traveled with us on our caravan up and down the length of the continent, from Garrou to Edi, several times. But on this last trip south from Garrou, he took matters into his own hands. We placed him under arrest and delivered him to the Düran authorities."

"And what was it he did?" acting Archimandrite, Kerei Lant, asked.

"He used some sort of attractant to draw a wyloth infestation into our camp. He claims he had hoped that by then driving the wyloths away, the merchants we escorted would be ingratiated to us."

"Then what happened?" the Prima Pater said, rolling his eyes.

"I escorted him to Amstonhotten," Rallia offered. "There, I turned him over to the authorities to take to Birin. It was the last we expected to see of him."

"But it wasn't," the Prima Pater said.

"No," Hanen replied. "When we were in Birin we discovered he had escaped, and was living in a back alley, with hundreds of wyloths surrounding him, calling himself the Wyloth King. Along with Searn VeTurres, we went to confront him, and he admitted that he had been given a gift from the Gift-Giver––control over wyloths. In return he had also given up his humanity. He had grown a tail, and his arms elongated. By the time we had driven him and the wyloths off with fire, he leapt up into the air, the taut skin under his arms giving him the ability to fly. He flew off with licks of flame still scorching him."

"And now, we're here," the Prima Pater concluded.

"Now we're here."

The Prima Pater pursed his lips and sat back in his seat. His eyes rolled toward the sky in thought. He looked back at Hanen.

"What would you propose we do, Hanen Clouw?"

"Torches," Hanen said.

"Torches?"

"That is how we fought them off in Birin. I assume furies are just as afraid of torches as wyloths are."

"And may I ask why you haven't used torches yet? In the past five days, I mean."

"Prima Pater, our commander, Searn VeTurres, told you we needed very little. Because of this, we've had nothing but what we walked here with. This includes the five torches we had for the twenty of us Black Sentinels."

"Secondly," Rallia added, "the ancient grove here is likely flammable. The leaves started turning before we arrived."

"And a third thing," Hanen said, glancing over to Rallia, who chuckled. "There are too many furies. The Black Sentinels cannot handle this alone."

"It is always hard to ask for help," the old man said, "especially when you feel that the thing you face is your own fault. However, this was not your fault. You did not make this 'Wyloth King.' He made himself."

"We still feel like he is our responsibility, though," Rallia added.

"That may be the case," Dorian said, "but we will still offer our aid. The creature has been coming out to holler at the gates every few hours or so. I suspect he will be arriving again soon. Perhaps we will take the two of you out to meet him under armed guard. Nichal, see those preparations are made. The rest of the Paladins will form a second circle of torch bearers."

"Prima Pater," an older Paladin nearby said.

"Yes, Pater Segundus Pír?"

"The brothers who have taken the Vow of Pacifism cannot assist you with torches."

"But you can pray."

This seemed to satisfy the old man.

"And my Paladames?" the Matriarch asked.

"The guards will prepare to fight, and the other Paladins will form a ring of torches. Your sisters will keep torches lit and prepare to attend to wounds, if they should occur."

Maeda Mür scowled. "We will do more than that."

"I expect you will, but I do need your Paladames to meet those needs I spoke of. You can also oversee the Nifarans delivering torches to the Black Sentinels. That will need to happen immediately. Please convey the importance that when the battle begins, they charge from their stables, and form a flank. Past that, the sisters may do what they will."

The Matriarch was still scowling as she rose. The other women rose with her to leave. Hanen caught out of the corner of his eye the

Matriarch stopping at the door to speak to five women in full armor. They nodded and went a different direction than the others, along with a shorter, rounder girl who served as the Matriarch's personal physician.

"What do you mean for us? If you're going to escort us as offerings?" Rallia asked.

"You'll be under our protection," the Prima Pater said.

"That won't do us any good against the furies once the fighting starts," Hanen said.

"Then what would you have us do?"

"I don't know," Hanen replied. "I don't like that we're being walked out into the middle of a swarm of furies just to talk to a madman."

"No one is ever fully ready for a battle," the Prima Pater said. "All we can do is prepare, and when the fight starts, act according to the plan until that plan doesn't work anymore."

Everyone fell silent in their own thoughts for a long time until word came back from a sister that the Sentinels had been provided torches. Searn had conveyed that the Black Sentinels would act once the Paladins did.

The Prima Pater rose. "Let's prepare to face this Wyloth King."

Katiam moved excitedly around the room. She almost dropped a glass jar of griefdark ointment as she turned to apply it to Esenath's wounds. The girl was still irritable, but none of the bite marks showed any sign of serious infection.

"Then the Matriarch told the Paladames to damn the consequences and plan to go by another door to help the Paladins in the battle."

"And how will you help?" Esenath slurred. The medicine she had prescribed to herself, left her groggy, but dulled to the painful marks that covered her body.

"I don't know. The Matriarch thought I might come ask you if you knew anything about furies."

"I'm a botanist."

"Yes, but you're the only woman properly educated in the

physical sciences."

Esenath did not reply, but stared up at the ceiling. Katiam continued to apply the ointment.

"Has the Rotha done anything else?" Esenath asked.

"Done anything?" Katiam replied.

"Has it grown? Moved? Anything?"

"No," Katiam said. "Not that I can tell. The crystal bloom it's attached to has gone dull. I've been to the Oracle near Pariantür. The crystal buds on the wall have more life in them when nothing is happening than that one does now."

"Interesting," Esenath said. "Does it mean the Rotha is parasitic?"

Katiam scowled to herself. She shouldn't, but she felt offended that Esenath would call her Rotha a parasite. She took up the griefdark ointment on a gloved hand and began to apply it. A small portion of it touched her wrist, and she immediately felt the numbing beginning.

"Griefdark!" Katiam said.

"What?" Esenath asked.

"Griefdark," Katiam confirmed. "We could use griefdark on the furies."

"What do you mean?"

"I think we can use griefdark, mixed with ale or something else to stop the furies in their tracks. I need to go find the Matriarch."

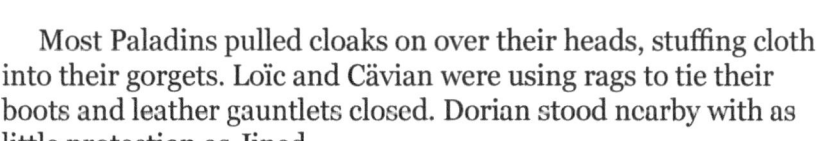

Most Paladins pulled cloaks on over their heads, stuffing cloth into their gorgets. Loïc and Cävian were using rags to tie their boots and leather gauntlets closed. Dorian stood nearby with as little protection as Jined.

"Prima Pater," Jined said, approaching the old man. "Would you like me to find you a cloak?"

"That is not necessary," Dorian said. "Grissone protects."

Jined nodded. "I was thinking the same thing."

The Paladin guards held their hammers in one hand and an unlit torch in the other.

The Paladins who had taken the Vow of Pacifism walked down

the line with a bucket of oil, dousing the top of each torch. The Prima Pater did not take one for himself. He turned to the standard bearer, Valér Queton. "My old friend, I ask you to stand outside the bastion, but I understand if you cannot go further with us."

"I will not cause harm, even to the smallest creature," Valér responded.

"I understand."

The Clouws approached. Both now wore their black cloaks over their shoulders, brought to them by the Nifaran monks. Rallia had a short staff in her hand, stout clubs mounted to each end. Of the two, she looked the strongest. Hanen, on the other hand, was gaunt, with scraggly black hair tied up on top of his head, with eyes that took in the whole situation with a degree of suspicion.

"We are ready," Rallia said.

"Very well," the Prima Pater replied.

"Prima Pater," Hanen said hesitantly. "Why are you doing this for us?"

"Doing what, exactly?"

"Helping us. It's been apparent you don't want the Sentinels along with you on this trip, yet you're risking your Paladins to help us."

"That is a good question," Dorian answered, "and one that has several answers. First, let me say, I have not been opposed to your company of Black Sentinels joining us. I have been opposed to your leader's personal reasons for doing so, but that does not reflect on you personally, only on him.

"Secondly, we Paladins are the protectors of mankind. This monster was sent from Kos-Yran. We will face it and we will fight alongside you, because your lives are in danger.

"But those are simple answers. There is a much more important reason I am helping you. That is because of who your father and grandfather were."

Hanen opened his mouth to speak, but Jined noticed Rallia elbow him into silence.

"Your grandfather was Primus Jadsen Brathe, who served in some capacity in Garrou for many years. His own son-in-law was your father, Marn Clouw. Our Pater Segundus Pír heard your name and recalled what information we gleaned while in Garrou. Did you know that Marn Clouw's service to the impoverished spent more money than any other mission in the entire continent?"

"I apologize for that," Rallia said.

The Prima Pater put up a hand, smiling. "No, please don't apologize. You misunderstand. He is to be commended. No mission has done more in serving humanity. And he wasn't even a Paladin."

"We have deep roots with the Paladins," Rallia added. "Our father's own grandfather was a Paladin."

"Oh, was he? What was his name?"

"I'm not sure," Rallia said. "He rarely mentioned it."

"Anyway," Dorian said, sighing, "I am doing this as repayment for what your father has done for the destitute. So let us meet this 'Wyloth King' and dethrone him. Open the gate."

Jined walked out front with Valér Queton, who immediately took a step to the side by the door and readied himself to close it once they had filed out.

When the Clouws stepped out of the bastion, the forest roared with a cacophony of shrill sounds. Each Paladin that passed through the door lit their torch by the lone scribe who stood by with a sconce of fire in his hand. The sun was starting to disappear behind the trees. A fury swooped overhead, then threw itself away as someone swung a torch at it. A few more tested their courage against the flames and failed.

A great gush of wind and shadow flew over their heads. It turned sharply into the air and then stopped, flapping its massive wings over them before it dropped the thirty feet to the ground. The forest behind the figure fell silent.

"I wondered if you would do as I asked," the creature said. His mouth, an elongated maw filled with fang-like teeth, made it harder for him to speak.

"What is it you want?" Hanen asked.

"I think that has been made abundantly clear," Ghoré said. "I want you. I want you to say that I was right."

"About what, Ghoré?" Hanen asked.

"About my bringing the wyloths to our camp to impress the merchants."

"You were wrong," Rallia said.

"Do you know what the punishment for poaching is in Düran?" Ghoré said. "Because that is what I was to be charged with. Naked exposure in the stocks for a week. Being treated as the lowest of the low. Treated as a vermin. Now I am the king of the vermin. King of the wyloth, the savern, and the fury."

"And I see you're as naked as you would be in the stocks, too," Hanen said.

"That does not matter to me anymore."

"We have discussed it," the Prima Pater said, "and I have decided that you will leave now."

The Wyloth King shot the old man a scowl. "No."

The Prima Pater waved a hand, and Jurgon Upona stepped forward, revealing the gold skull of Gold Eater.

Ghoré cringed back, his yard-long fingers crossed over his body.

Jined stepped out to stand beside the skull. He glanced over at Dorian, who gave him an approving look.

"Grissone, guide my hand," Jined muttered under his breath, "be my guide."

He raised his hammer in front of him as a faint glow began within the metal. It started to glow the faintest of blues, then grew brighter. He let out a startled laugh at the sight and then narrowed his eyes at the Wyloth King.

"You may be a chosen one of that dark god, but I was chosen by Grissone. I challenged Gar-Talosh. And today I challenge you!"

"You can all suffer if you won't give me what I want!"

Ghoré flapped his wings and leapt up into the air, screeching. The cacophony of the woods broke, and like a brown wave the small furies surged forward. They filtered around Jined, avoiding the light of his now brightly glowing hammer. The other Paladins held their torches up and formed a circle.

A battle cry rose to their left as almost twenty Black Sentinels charged out of their stable, torches in each hand. They dove into the swarm, their flashing flames catching the creatures alight, and smacking them away with wide, sweeping strokes.

A moment later, the cries of the Paladames came from their right. There were only five of them, but they held in their hands glass phials, which they threw in an arc across the swarm. The glass broke and a cloud of blue billowed out and then disappeared as it was absorbed by the furies. The women stopped in their tracks, and a moment later a large area of the cloud of winged creatures suddenly fell out of the air and onto the ground. The other furies fell back into the woods, startled.

"What was that?" the Prima Pater called out.

"Griefdark," a Paladame answered. "We're making more as we speak!"

Behind them, five more women rushed out and gave the women

each a flaming torch before retreating. The five armored Paladames now held a torch in one hand and a mace in the other, standing side by side with the Paladins.

The Black Sentinels looked eager to rush forward. A few of them were stepping on the little creatures who had no defense as they lay numb on the ground. One of the Sentinels began to dart out from the line.

"No!" their leader, Searn VeTurres, shouted. "Stay here in the clearing. No need to start a fire."

From the sky, the Wyloth King dove down and knocked the torch free from Searn's hand. It spun out and into one of the trees, catching the dry leaves easily. Ghoré Dziony flew away again, screeching out his satisfaction and rage. Searn took up his crossbow and shot wildly. Dropping it he took out his two hand axes and charging into the woods. One of the Black Sentinels ran off after him, while the others stopped and stared at the fire that was quickly spreading from branch to branch.

"I was hoping to avoid a fire," Dorian said, "but it looks like the gods have other plans."

"Bring axes!" Pater Segundus Guess shouted.

"We have three," a nearby Paladin said, "to cut up those branches that fall."

Nichal shot a look at the Prima Pater. "There is little we can do. The Sentinels have hand axes. Give them permission to cut down trees that have not yet caught. We can build trenches and throw water on the fire, but we will probably have to fall back to the shelter of the bastion and hope we survive the night."

"Prima Pater," Jined said. He was still holding his glowing hammer in his hand, looking at it in awe.

"Yes, Jined."

"What should I do?"

"Take the initiative. Go after the creature."

Jined nodded and turned to Loïc and Cävian. "Will you come with me?"

The twins nodded as they turned and charged into the woods alongside him.

50

Aspects

The green hills he walked upon,

Like mountains to the man

With no life to go back to

New vistas now open

Climb on, the road and wend.

—THE TRAVELER

Hanen raced to keep up with Rallia, who charged ahead into the woods in the direction Ghoré had flown as the torches lit the tree on fire. The others looked on in horror as the ancient grove began to burn. Bursts of light lit them from behind, and furies rained down on them in small spurts, having lost their courage and numbers to whatever the Paladames had splashed across the flood of vermin.

They came to a clearing, swatting at the small shadows that came every few moments, and looked around. Their only orientation came from the growing wall of flames and the cries of dismay from those trying to prevent it from spreading further.

"What do you want to do, Hanen?" Rallia shouted as she turned around, trying to decide which way to go.

"Leave," Hanen said. "We don't need to stay here. We could just leave."

"How can you say that?" Rallia asked. "The Prima Pater has

already sided with us. The least we can do is continue to help. Maybe Ghoré can be stopped before he causes any more damage."

"Then what? We continue marching forward so we end in Mahn Fulhar and not be paid?"

"If we leave we won't be paid either," Rallia said.

"Yes, but then we won't be stuck up north during the onset of winter."

"Either way, we need to decide now. Those trees are catching fast."

A gout of flames shot out as the winged form of Ghoré Dziony flew through the flame line and into the sky. He was looking to make his escape, when he swept over the two Clouws and reeled around. As he circled, he cackled and fell through the canopy to hit the ground in front of them. He stood tall, his wings unfurling around him.

"Looking to run away from your problems again, Clouws?" Ghoré scoffed.

"We were looking for you," Hanen said. He held up his hand. "Perhaps we can make a deal."

"No deal, Clouws. Only your death."

He flapped his wings at them, providing a gust of wind that his furies rode upon toward them. Rallia stepped out front and began to spin her staff in wide circles, deterring many of them. Hanen swung his torch in wide, slow arcs, but it seemed to no longer give the creatures hesitation. He dropped the torch onto the moss and drew another hand axe. The fire now lit the area easily. He could feel a bit of warmth coming toward them through the trees. He swung wildly at furies and pressed on towards Ghoré.

"I wish you could see what has happened to you," Hanen shouted, "what you've become!"

"I've become something greater!"

"You're a monster now," Hanen replied. "And you've become so by choice."

"I am a necessity," Ghoré said. "I tried to help you and your caravan, and you disgraced me."

"You disgraced yourself," Hanen corrected him.

A cry of rage came from behind the Wyloth King as Ophedia came charging out of the woods. She held a long plank of wood. As she neared, she swung it around, leveraging it from her shoulder. It glanced a long scratch across the membrane of Ghoré's wing.

The creature screamed in anger, but fell back. Ophedia

advanced, and Rallia lunged forward herself, her own weighted staff shooting out and hitting Ghoré in the shoulder blade. Pressed from both sides, Ghoré shot looks of anger at both and made to launch up into the air.

Hanen reached back and flung his axe at the monster. The blade spun in the air and caught the wing-flesh, slashing through.

Ghoré cried and leapt, his wing tearing open as he tried to gather wind. He spun in the air once and fell to the ground. The furies rushed from every direction and covered him in a writhing mass. Hanen, Rallia, and Ophedia watched in horror as the mass stood. Then, the bodies of the furies sloughed off his frame, falling dead to the ground. In the growing light of the burning forest, Ghoré looked healthier than before. His long wing spun out and struck Ophedia.

She cried out as she fell to the ground. Hanen could make out blood falling down her cut forehead and into her eyes.

"You see?" Ghoré said. "There is no point in trying to stop me."

"I see a very good reason, now," said a voice that came from next to Hanen's shoulder. Hanen startled and shrunk back with a shudder as coldness passed up his back. Where he came from, Hanen could not say, but the figure wore a thick black cloak that seemed to undulate.

"You again?" Ghoré said to the newcomer. "Why do you continue to hunt me? What have I done to you?"

Ghoré huddled back from them, taking several steps away.

"You have information I need," the figure said. As the figure moved forward, Hanen realized in the firelight that the blackness was seeping from the actual cloak the figure wore. At moments the black swept away like smoke in the wind, revealing a cloak of mail, except each link was the color of bleached bone, and rattled as the figure moved.

"What?" Ghoré said, panic rising in him. "What do you want to know?"

"How did you meet Kos-Yran?"

"Why? Which god are you? Or which god do you come from? The Deceiver?"

"No," the figure rasped. "I come from no god, but I intend to kill each of them in turn."

"I... don't know how to find the Gift Giver. He came to me. He had been with me for several days before I knew who he was."

The figure now stood in the middle of the glade. A tree twenty-five yards into the woods exploded flames. The dark figure turned in surprise, and the blackness on the cloak seemed to peel away, as though it wanted to escape the coming fire.

That moment of hesitation gave the Wyloth King all he needed. He screeched, and out of the nearby trees a new onslaught of furies pulsed across the glade toward the Clouws and the newly arrived ally.

In response, the darkness of the cloak seemed to open up into a net of blackness, the sound of rattling bones filling Hanen's ears. The furies hit the net and were flung away with soft little impacts on the loam.

The black figure stepped forward, undeterred by the creatures. He walked towards Ghoré, who took steps backward towards the dark tree line. He looked at Hanen, keeping a wary eye on the figure advancing on him. "This is all your doing! You could have let me be, and none of this would have ever happened! No promise from Kos-Yran, no bonding curse. No fire. No death enshrouded seeker hunting me."

The black figure now stood over the gibbering Wyloth King. He reached out with a hand and touched his shoulder. Ghoré screamed.

"The champion of a god. You're as close to a high priest as I'll ever lay my hands on for one of the Black Coterie. You might even complete the cloak."

"Stand down!" a low voice shouted. Hanen turned to see three Paladins step out into the clearing. Jined Brazstein stood between the twin Paladins who never spoke. In his hands, his hammer still glowed a soft blue.

The figure in the undulating black cloak turned to see the Paladins. He stood tall, as though ready to defy them, then visibly sighed. Then he turned and ran off into the woods.

"Ghoré Dziony, you are charged with endangering humanity."

"Ha!" Ghoré laughed nervously, relieved to be rid of the figure. "I answer to no one."

He opened his wings again to take flight. Jined Brazstein held out his glowing hammer.

"No more running, Dziony."

Hanen saw the Paladin take a single step forward, and he was suddenly next to the Wyloth King. His hammer came down on the creature's knee, and then came back up and took him under the jaw.

DEATHLESS BEAST

"You're a frail shade and a heretic," Jined growled.

The creature rolled over onto his back, holding an arm across his chest in defense.

"You're charged with protecting humanity!" Ghoré spat. "Yet you would kill me?"

He tried to back up across the ground, but Jined put a firm foot on his chest.

"You ceased being human long ago, when you made a promise to your dark god, binding yourself to him."

"Then what does that make you? Bound by your own god by Vows and chains?"

"It doesn't make me anything. I'm still just a servant."

"And I'm still a king," Ghoré said.

The flood of furies that came from every direction must have come from every corner of the continent. Their numbers were countless, and the sound of their screeches threatened to burst Hanen's ears.

Someone took hold of his arm and pulled him to the ground.

"Cover yourself!" Rallia shouted next to him.

The press of small bodies rushing towards king and Paladin went on for an eternity. The screeching continued long after the last fury flew past. Hanen peeked out from under his cloak, to see a writhing, screeching dome of brown where Jined had been standing over Ghoré.

The twin Paladins nearby clutched each other and looked at the mass with revulsion across their faces. Hanen saw they had crouched together over the form of Ophedia, who was now sitting up and staring blankly at the scene.

There was a moment of silence, then a glow came from inside the dome. It grew brighter and rays of light broke through the cracks between the bodies of the furies. The fire continued to burn across the forest, yet the light that formed inside the fury pile was brighter still.

The furies picked up their screeching once more, rising into a crescendo that met the scathing brightness, which seemed to hurt them as much as it hurt Hanen's eyes.

The light went dark for a single moment before there came a bright blue explosion. A wave of ash blew out from the center, and across the entire forest. Several of the nearby trees that were burning blew out like candles, although they still smoldered, and threatened to catch again. Jined stood in the center of the glade.

His armor had an afterglow that now faded slowly to nothing, along with the diminishing glow in the hammer in his hand.

All that remained of Ghoré Dziony was a pile of bones. Jined reached down and picked up the skull. There was nothing human about it anymore, and even without flesh clinging to it, it seemed to leer in anger.

The twin Paladins helped Ophedia to her feet and then came to stand in the middle as Hanen and Rallia looked at the skull in Jined's hands.

"What happened?" Ophedia asked.

"You charged out of nowhere," Rallia said with a smile. "You looked like Eunia when she climbed on top of the manticör."

"I didn't want the fear that froze me then to stop me now. It didn't work though."

"You're fine, though," Hanen said, "and Ghoré is gone."

"Where is Searn?" Rallia asked Ophedia.

"We took off into the woods together, to hunt for Ghoré, but then the flames rose and Searn said we had to get back to help put out the fire. Not long after that, he ran ahead, and I got lost."

"We need to get back to help those at the bastion," Jined said. "I just hope we're not too late to stop this fire."

51

Aftermath

18 The lamp lit your way,

and the watchers guided you,

19 But ye have faith, for when root rise up to hinder you,

   And bramble reach and cut you

20 When thorns seek your blood,

   And darkness cuts off all light,

21 You shall place your next step assuredly.

— THE QUATRODOX, #3, CANTO 47, 18-21

The forest blazed with light. Prayers sat on Jined's lips as he muttered for help and guidance. He raced on and watched as the distance between himself and the twins lengthened. Cävian had wrapped a loose cloth around the girl's head and held her hand as they ran to ensure she didn't trip, from either blood in her eyes or from lightheadedness. Loïc's hand moved quickly, reciting their own prayer for speed over and over again. Jined came to the edge of the forest just as the Clouws, the girl, and the twins disappeared into the bastion. The line of Sentinels had shovels in their hands or were using their axes to dig a trench side-by-side with Paladins and the sisters of the Crysalas.

    Dorian looked up, saw Jined standing there, and wiped his brow. He glanced up into the sky, nodding to himself. He turned down the line and shouted: "Paladins! To safety! Sentinels! Retreat to the bastion!"

A Black Sentinel next to Dorian stood and stretched his back out. He pulled the black cloak that he had tied around his face down and shouted. "You heard the Prima Pater! To the bastion!"

He ran up to Jined. It was the Sentinel Commander, Searn VeTurres. "We have tried to fight the flame long enough to see everyone out of the forest. There was a burst of light, and then some of the fire died down for a moment. Did the Clouws make it back? The girl?"

"If they were all you were waiting for, then we are all safe. Please take this and make sure that it goes to the bastion vault. The twins taking care of the girl will know where to take it."

Searn nodded and took the charred skull of Ghoré from Jined's hands, walking to the bastion. He and Dorian were the last to enter, save the old standard bearer, Valér Queton, who had not left his post. Jined turned and watched the forest burn. He turned back to the bastion and waved for them to go in without him. Dorian nodded and closed Jined outside.

"Grissone," Jined whispered.

The flames froze where they stood. A soft golden glow stood next to him.

"I have answered," Grissone said.

"You see what I see," Jined whispered.

"And I will command as you wish."

"Then please, end this destruction. This grove should not perish."

"This is the best that can happen for these trees, actually," Grissone said. "Their nuts will sprout best after a fire. If you tell the Paladins of this bastion that, then they can cut down the forest and plant it anew. They can plant its rows further out. They can sell this rare wood and make a fortune. In ten years' time this could be another paladinial fortress, built out to where the forest now stands."

"If that is your will."

"Yes," Grissone said. "One step at a time, I think."

"You saw all that I saw."

"Yes. The creature was a vile thing. But it is gone now."

"You also saw the figure who was facing that monster alongside the Clouws?"

"What figure?"

"If you saw through my eyes," Jined said, "then you must have. He wore a black cloak."

"All Sentinels wear black cloaks."

"This was different. Tendrils of black shadows whipped from it, like smoke. Like," his words faltered, and he felt sick, thinking about it.

"That is not something I know," Grissone said. "I know what you say is true, but I did not see it."

"Is that possible?" Jined asked.

"I do not know. I must think on this."

A moment later the air was sucked from Jined's lungs as Grissone left, and the flames simply ceased. There was no smoke in the air, but the crackle of wood cooling in the cloudless night gave Jined a momentary shiver as he turned and walked toward the bastion, disturbed that there were things his god did not know.

Katiam helped Esenath to her feet, and together they walked the halls to the door that led out into the grove. The blackened trees reached for the sky like hands clawing at the midday sun. A line of Sentinels, both men and women, laughed as they worked to chop down the trees under the supervision of an older Paladin.

"The fire stopped just shy of the last row of trees," Katiam said. "The Prima Pater gave the order to fell the entire grove, save those that did not burn, and the nuts are being gathered to plant beyond what was the grove in the spring. Jined Brazstein told the Prima Pater that the fire loosened them, and they will sprout now."

"How did he learn this?"

"His god told him."

"The knowledge of how to plant a Ebrw nut was lost with the planting of this grove," Esenath said. "The nuts do not come free of the tree without tearing them in half. Now they're just littering the floor of the forest. That answers another mystery almost as old as the Rotha."

Katiam fell silent and they walked out amongst the trees.

"Is the Rotha safe?" Esenath asked.

"What?" Katiam asked. Her hand shot to touch the satchel at

her side. It was still there. "Of course. I have it with me always."

"I think we ought to put it in soil."

"I do not wish to cover it up."

"It is covered now, sitting in your pouch. It needs nutrients to grow. You must give up sight of it so it can flourish. A seed planted is lost until it comes through the soil. We'll build a strong box, and keep it strapped to one of the carriages where the sun we ride under can touch the top and warm it."

"You know more of plants than I do," Katiam conceded.

"And you know physical ailments. I should like to return to my bed now. I'm tired. I need more griefdark ointment. Good thinking using the griefdark against the furies."

"It worked because they were so small. I'm just sorry it wasn't enough to stop the fire from happening in the first place."

"Yes," Esenath said, "but then a new forest couldn't be planted and a new chapter begin."

A knock came at the door. Rallia leapt to her feet and opened it, admitting Ophedia. She had a proper bandage over the cut on her forehead now, and she smiled.

"They say it might not even scar," she said.

"That's good," Rallia offered.

"I came to ask if you had seen Searn. Some of the Sentinels are asking to speak with him. They want to know what's next."

"What do you mean?"

"Most of them don't want to stick around to Mahn Fulhar, and want their pay so they can leave. I think the fire took the wind out of their sails."

"I haven't seen him since the doors to the bastion were shut."

She turned to leave. "I'll look elsewhere then."

"Are you going to stay on?" Rallia asked.

"No reason not to," she responded. "And you two are good company, even if bad things happen around you."

Rallia closed the door behind Ophedia.

"Are we bad luck?" Hanen asked.

"What do you mean?" Rallia replied.

"Bad things do seem to find us."

"No, I think life just happens around us. If we are going to protect people on the road again, after Mahn Fulhar, things are going to happen. We're far from unlucky. We can count only one person who has died under our watch."

"I suppose. Still, a lot does happen to us."

"We won't know if we lock ourselves away. Best to keep going."

"You mean so we can lock ourselves away in Mahn Fulhar?" Hanen asked.

"We'll have plenty to do, I'm sure. Though I suppose that depends on what we decide we're going to do."

"What do you mean?" Hanen asked.

"We haven't really talked about the plan for when we get to Mahn Fulhar."

Hanen sat silently for a long time. Rallia waited patiently.

"I think we spend the winter planning out another caravan. One from Mahn Fulhar to south Œron."

"That's what I thought you'd say," Rallia nodded.

"I'm going to go out for air," Hanen said.

"Just be back inside before it's fully dark. The Paladins want everyone kept safe from the last angry little furies still in the area."

Hanen nodded and walked out into the hall and then to the side door. The thought of sequestering himself in a strange city and planning out another caravan was growing on him. The thought of the Paladin stealing his opportunity to stop Ghoré by himself soured his mood. He stepped outside and pulled his hood up against the cold.

The smell of ash hung in the air as the light continued to fade behind the mountains that rose up directly behind the bastion. The claw-like hands of the blackened trees blinked in and out of view behind swirls of flurrying snow that now danced across the frosting ground. As he walked, Hanen felt his past slipping off his back, and the burden of the future settling squarely on his shoulders.

Epilogue

Searn raised the hammer a third time and brought it down on the hollow spike. It cleanly punched through the bone between the eye sockets. He put his foot against the skull and wrenched the piece of metal free. The plug of bone came free of the metal rod. He caught it in the air, held it up, and then turned to the dust-covered table. Sitting upon it was a long cloak made of bone-colored chainmail.

"What are you doing?" Ophedia asked from the doorway. Searn sighed and placed the circle of bone down.

"I had hoped to remain by myself, if you don't mind," he said.

"I've been looking all over for you. A few of the Sentinels are talking about leaving––not continuing on to Mahn Fulhar."

Searn turned and looked at the girl. A small smile played on the corner of his lips.

"I really don't care if they leave. I'll remember them when the time comes. Are you leaving, too?"

"I wasn't planning on it," she said. "What is that?"

She was pointing to the mail on the table and the new piece of bone next to it.

"I'm collecting something. A token."

"From that creature? Why? You weren't there when he was killed."

"Wasn't I?"

She walked over and touched the mail cloak. "How did someone even make this? Each link is solid."

"It's hard to do," Searn replied.

"You made this?"

He nodded.

"Why?"

"To kill the gods."

Ophedia let out a long laugh, and then let it die off when she realized he was serious.

"Why would you want that?"

"Because they toy with us. I discovered a way to make something that wasn't part of any of their plans. Not the gods of the White Pantheon, nor those beholden to the Deceiver."

"My finding out is not good for me, is it?" she said, shrinking away.

"I'm not going to hurt you. Others, I might. But not you."

"Why? You have a thing for young women?"

Searn chuckled. "It's not that."

She pursed her lips. "What does it do?"

"Let's find out," Searn said.

She joined him at the table. He took the hollow spike and pulled back his sleeve. He pushed on the piece of metal, which still had small bone shavings on it, and drew blood from the back of his wrist. His arm was covered in small scratches and scars.

"You do this every time?"

"No. Sometimes I was able to use the blood of the one I took it from, if it was fresh enough."

He then took up the single chain link and set it on his new cut until it was covered in blood. A blackness came up out of the minor laceration and covered the link. Then he lifted the link slowly, attached by the string of black on his arm.

"And that?" she asked.

"A portion of my shade. It's latching onto the tentative grip Ghoré's own shade still has with this world. It means Nifara has not yet come to claim him. We're not too late."

He placed it on the center of the cloak. The black of Searn's shade spread out from the single link to others and they seemed to shiver and make space for the new one. A moment later it subsided. The new link had joined with the others.

Searn sighed and took up the cloak tenderly, pulling it over himself.

Out of each circle small tendrils of black seeped out. A bigger one shot out of his chest. Searn wrapped his hands with the cloak edges and took hold of the thing like grabbing a hot pan with a woolen mitt.

"What is this?" a voice rasped from nowhere, yet all around them.

"Are you Ghoré Dziony? The Wyloth King?" Searn asked. His voice had dropped to a lower register, and it sounded as though he spoke through water.

"How? How dare you!"

"That's what I thought. Welcome."

"I still live?"

"If you can call it that."

"Then I am still his Deathless Beast," the voice said with some satisfaction.

"You are as close to a high priest of Kos-Yran as I can manage right now. I didn't trust the solid gold of that vül skull to do the trick. Now, let's see what you can do."

Searn let go of the shade, which began to scream in rage. The window high above the storage room burst open and a wave of furies flew in and swirled around Searn. They clung to him, shivering and screaming, then suddenly fell dead at his feet. A moment later and hundreds of small shade threads burst out from the bone mail, the faint screeches of furies hung on the air.

"Now go away," Searn said.

"I do as I please."

"No," Searn said to the shade of Ghoré Dziony, "you do as I please."

Searn took the cloak off his shoulders, and the blackness suddenly receded into the bones again.

"How did you do that?" Ophedia asked.

"I will tell you more, if you wish to know. Once we're in Mahn Fulhar. I am two links away from completing the cloak of bones. You can help me, but you will not hinder me."

"I won't tell," Ophedia said. "You're one of the first people to show me decency. You helped me out of that bind in Macena, and gave me something to do with myself."

"Good girl," Searn said. "Now, let's not speak of this again until I choose."

Ophedia nodded, and turned to leave. She closed the door, leaving him in the dark.

Searn pulled out a book and placed it on top of the cloak.

Opening it, he took out a quill and drew blood from his still bleeding wrist, and touched it to the book. The red disappeared. A line of words suddenly bloomed to life, the words screaming expletives across the page.

No need for that, Searn wrote on the page, the paper lapping the red up as he wrote it. *I take it you've recovered?*

I was out for a week after you did this to me, the words read, *but I still live. I've never been more uncomfortable.*

It's never comfortable, Searn wrote.

I'm not that far from you, the words said.

Oh?

I've been trailing you since your entered Mahndür, though my appearance would be an issue for the Prima Pater.

Then plan to come to Mahn Fulhar a week behind us. I want you to return the rest of my shade to me.

No words bloomed in response.

Vanguard has made his move, Searn wrote. *He absorbed the Paladins from Bulwark. I expect he'll be moving over the course of the winter to stake his claim over Mahndür.*

I'll find an inn by the water and send a message for where to find me. What will you do now?

I plan to break the Paladin leadership, Searn wrote. *Even if I have to murder the Prima Pater myself.*

The End

To be continued in

Volume Two of the

Kallattian Saga: **Bone Shroud**

GLOSSARY 1

DRAMATIS PERSONAE

HANEN CLOUW (*Ha-NEHN Khl-OW*) — A Black Sentinel mercenary and organizer of the Clouw Sentinel Merchant Detail. Hanen is a 1st Lieutenant in the Black Sentinels, and thus has earned his second hand axe.

RALLIA CLOUW (*Rah-LEEAH Khl-OW*) — Like her older brother Hanen, Rallia is a 1st Lieutenant in the Black Sentinels, though she prefers to carry a staff she had built with both of her clubs mounted on the ends. Rallia is also deft with a razor, and often shaves the heads and faces of fellow Black Sentinels.

JINED BRAZSTEIN (*Jih-NED BRADJ-steen*) — Rank of Brother Excelsior. Vow of Chastity. Son of Jarl Jaegür von Brazstein of Brazh, Jined left home to avoid execution for murdering a fellow prince of Boroni. Jined joined the Paladins of the Hammer as a Penitent, committing his life to Grissone, the god of Faith.

KATIAM BORREAU (*Kah-TEE-um Burr-OH*) — A Paladame of the Rose. Personal physician to the Matriarch Superioris and Prima Pater. Aspects of Peace, St. Klare, and Dignity.

SERIAH YALEDÍT (*Sur-EYE-uh Yah-leh-DEET*) — Monk of Nifara. She is known for often establishing orphanages in towns that have none.

AEGER (*A-gur*) — Paladin of the Hammer. Rank of Brother Primus. Vow of Silence. Scholar and assistant to Pater Segundus Gallahan Pír.

AMAL YOLLIS (*ah-MALL YAH-liss*) — Paladin of the Hammer. Rank of Brother Primus. Vow of Poverty. Herald.

ASTRID GLASS (*ASSS-trid GLASS*) — Paladame of the Rose. Aspects of Discretion, Compassion, and Honor.

AURÍN MATEAU (*AH-reen Ma-TOE*) — A Black Sentinel from Œron.

BELL (*Bell*) — A mysterious Paladin, member of the Motean sect.

BERMACH GELBLIHT (*BER-mak GEL-blight*) — Konig of Nemen.

CÄVIAN (*CAVE-ee-an*) — Paladin of the Hammer. Rank of Brother Excelsior. Vow of Silence. Twin of Loïc.

CHÖS TELMAR (*CHAHSS TEL-MAR*) — A Black Sentinel.

DANE MARRIC (*DAEN MARE-IK*) — Paladin of the Hammer. Rank of Brother Excelsior. Vow of Chastity.

DERRO ARITELO (*DER-roe AIR-ee-tell-OH*) — Nobleborn son of House Aritelo in Edi.

DORIAN MÜR (*DOOR-ee-an MEW-r*) — Prima Pater of the Paladins of the Hammer. Head of the Church of Grissone. Vow of Prayer. Became the youngest Prima Pater in history, elected almost unanimously during the Protectorate Wars. He still holds the title, seventy-five years later, at the ripe age of 95.

DUSK (*Dusk*) — A mysterious Paladin, member of the Motean sect.

EDDAL BARAÑO (*ed-DAHL Bar-ah-NYO*) — Nobleborn House Lord of House Baraño. This corpulent lord is a collector of vices, and the man every House Lord listens to when advice is given, but never trusts.

ERMANI WITTAL (*er-mon-EE VIT-ahl*) — Crysalas Societas Sister Superioris of the Flowerwive's Vault in Garrou.

ESENATH CHLOÏS (*AH-sen-OTH khl-oh-EES*) — Paladame of the Rose. Botanist. Sidieratan. Aspects of Cleanliness and Charity.

ETIENNE OREN (*eh-TEE-en OR-EN*) — Paladin of the Hammer. Rank of Brother Excelsior. Vow of Poverty. Brother Excelsior. Guard in the Prima Pater's Entourage.

EUNIA HALLA (*YOU-nee-ah HA-lah*) — A Black Sentinel

from southern Mahndür.

FATHER DIONO (*DIE-oh-no*) — Old priest of Aben from the Chapel near Suel in Düran.

FEDELMINA BARBA (*FE-dell-MEEN-ah BAR-bah*) — Paladame of the Rose. Aspects of Clarity and Peace.

GALLAHAN PÍR (*GAL-a-HAN PEER*) — Pater Segundus of the Paladins of the Hammer. Chief Librarian of Pariantür. Vow of Pacifism.

GELL SERITUE (*GELL SEHR-ih-too*) — Made House Lord of House Seritue in Edi after his father was killed. Does not trust any other House, and is very paranoid.

GAR-TALOSH (*GAHR tah-LOSH*) — Gold Eater. Cursed One of Kos-Yran. Head of the Vül Pack in Bortali.

GHORÉ DZIONY (*gor-EH zee-OH-NEE*) — Black Sentinel.

GOREG VON THOMMÜS (*GOR-eg von TOE-moos*) — Jarl of Thom in Boroni.

GREGOR HANS (*GREY-gor HANZ*) — Monk of Nifara. Councillor to the Archimandrite.

HIRAM VAN HÖLLEBON (*HI-ram van HOLE-eh-bahn*) — Paladin of the Hammer. Rank of Pater Minoris. Vow of Prayer. Chaplain of Pariantür.

JAEGÜR VON BRAZSTEIN (*YAY-goor von BRADJ-steen*) — Jarl of Brahz in Boroni.

JAMIS ZOUMERIK (*JAY-miss ZOO-mare-ick*) — Paladin of the Hammer. Rank of Brother Primus. Vow of Poverty.

JURGON UPONA (*YOOR-gahn Oo-POH-na*) — Paladin of the Hammer. Rank of Brother Primus. The Prima Pater's Seneschal. Husband of Sabine Upona. Vow of Prayer.

KASH (*CASH*) — A storyteller.

KEREI LANT (*KEE-REE LAN-t*) — Monk of Nifara. Councillor to the Archimandrite.

KILLIAN GLASS (*KILL-EE-AN GLASS*) — Paladin of the Hammer. Rank of Brother Excelsior. Vow of Poverty.

KLAMMEN VON DONIGAR (*KLA-men von DOE-nee-GAHR*) — Jarl of Donig in Boroni.

LERDA CLEMMBÄKKER (*LEHR-dah CLEM-bah-ker*) — Jarlwife of Clehm.

LOÏC (*Low-EEK*) — Paladin of the Hammer. Rank of Brother Excelsior. Vow of Silence. Twin of Cävian. From Setera.

LUTEA CALIMBRISE (*loo-TEE-ah Kal-ihm-BREE-SAY*) —

Paladame of the Rose. Aspects of Charity and Solemnity.

MAEDA MÜR (*MAY-dah MEW-r*) — Matriarch Superioris of the Paladames of the Rose. Head of the Crysalas Church. Wife to Dorian Mür, Prima Pater of the Paladins.

MAEDA SALNA (*MAY-dah SAHL-nah*) — Paladame of the Rose, "Little Maeda," Aspects of Virginity and Honor.

MALLA GELBLIHT (*MAH-lah GEL-blit*) — Queen of Nemen.

NAIR (*NAY-er*) — A storyteller.

NARAH WEVAN (*NA-rah WAY-vahn*) — Paladame of the Rose, Veiled Sister, Aspects of Silence, Sanctity, Solitude, and St. Klare.

NICHAL GUESS (*Nih-KAHL GESS*) — Pater Segundus of the Paladins of the Hammer. Castellan of Pariantür. Vow of Poverty.

ONELIE CLEMMBÄKKER (*OH-Neh-lee CLEM-bah-ker*) — Daughter of the Jarl of Clehm.

OPHEDIA DEL ISHÉ (*Oh-FEE-DEE-ah del EE-shay*) — A new Black Sentinel and apprentice to Searn VeTurres.

Ørzan CLEMMBÄKKER (*OR-zahn CLEM-bah-ker*) — Son of the Jarl of Clehm.

OZRI BAÇA (*OH-zree BAH-khah*) — A Black Sentinel.

PELL MARAN (*PELL MAH-RAN*) — Archimandrite of the Monks of Nifara.

PELLIAN NOSS (*PELL-ee-an NAH-ss*) — Paladin of the Hammer. Pater Minoris of the Piedala Fortress. Vow of Prayer.

RAGNUT VON STURMGUARD (*RAG-nut von Sch-TERM-gard*) — Jarl of Sturm in Boroni.

SABINE UPONA (sah-BEEN oo-POH-nah) — Paladame of the Rose. Assistant to the Matriarch Superioris. Aspects of Humility and Discretion.

SAEDRIK VON CLEMMBÄKKER (*SAY-drikh CLEM-bah-ker*) — Jarl of Clehm.

SAREN GUI (*SAYR-en g-WEE*) — Paladin of the Hammer. Pater Minoris of the Fortress of St. Rämmon. Vow of Pacifism.

SEARN VeTURRES (**SURN veh-TOOR-ez**) — Captain of the Black Sentinels.

SERK VON GEHRTIGAN (*SUR-kh von GAYR-tih-GHEN*) — Jarl of Gerht.

SHROUD (*Shroud*) — A mysterious disembodied voice who speaks through a Shadebook. Member of the Motean sect.

SIGRI SMITH (*SIH-gree SMITH*) — Captain of the Paladames of the Rose. Aspects of Virginity, Form, Function.

TERGON ARITELO (*TERR-gone Air-ee-TELL-oh*) — Lord of House Aritelo in Edi. Second son of the former House Lord.

THADAR SALISS (*THA-dahr SA-liss*) — Captain of the Black Sentinels.

TOIRE SIOBH (*tw-AHR shee-OHV*) — Shieldmaidens. Daughter of the Rhi of Bronue Jinre.

ÜTOL VON TOSBRECHT (*OO-tahl von TAH-sch-BREH-KT*) — Jarl of Tosch in Boroni.

VALÉR QUETON (*vah-LAIR keh-TAHN*) — Pater Minoris of the Paladins of the Hammer. Standard Bearer of Grissone. Vow of Pacifism.

VANGUARD (*VAN-gard*) — A mysterious Paladin, member of the Motean sect.

YMBRYS VERONIA (*IM-brees ver-OH-nee-ah*) — A qavyl spice merchant.

ZHANUR *BH* OBLIAU (*DJAH-noor beh ohb-LEE-aoo*) — A hrelgren merchant. At one time a Templar of the Third Responsibility.

GLOSSARY 2

PANTHEON OF KALLATTAI

The Existence — *Maker of All* and *He That Is*. The world of Kallattai came into being at his word: BEGIN. He made first the two brother gods, and then the two sisters as their wives. Power was granted to them, and through them all was created, and the Existence was worshiped.

ABEN (*A-benn*) — *High King in Lomïn, the Ever-Day*. Made from a white star. His way is the Path. His Gray Watchers hold lanterns to guide those that seek the Path. His tenets are an Arrow, pointing the way to the green fields of Lomïn. The Chalice raised symbolizes his first domain, the sea. And from those depths the Ancient Ones sing.

WYV-THÜM (*WIHV THOOM*) — *The Three-Eyed Judge in Noccitan, the Ever-Night*. Brother to Aben, and formed by the Existence from the well of a black star. When he descended to his Realm of Noccitan he donned the title Thüm, or Judge.

CRYSANIA (*Cri-SAH-nee-ah*) — *Life Mother, Purity Resplendent, and Seamstress of the Future Tapestry* is wife to Aben. Only she can untangle the knots caused by time and see what the future holds. Her people are those that seek to protect the Dweol, the World-Roses that speak directly to her and one another, providing the Crysalas Integritas a chance to glance, ever briefly, at the Future.

SAKHARN (*Sa-KAHRN*) — *Wife to Wyv, Shepherdess of the Veld*—the Dreamscape from which the impossible is dreamed and made fact. She is the goddess of the Improbable, for she impossibly birthed the Deceiver without her husband to sire him.

DEATHLESS BEAST

THE CHILDREN OF ABEN AND CRYSANIA

LAE'ZEQ (*Lay-ZEK*) — *Firstborn of Aben, god of Wisdom, Curious One.* His people, the qavylli, follow his path into the depths of knowledge, for upon his own pages he wrote the secrets of life. Long has he now sojourned, seeking an answer to the prophecy that ties his fate to the death of his closest friend.

GRISSONE-ANKA (*Gri-ZOHN AHN-kha*) — *Twin-Souled, god of Faith.* As Grissone came of age his soul was two. The Anka, who soars above all and sees all, is joined to him. He was the creator of man, who abandoned Grissone to worship many. Now his loyal followers are few: the Paladins who seek protection of the people who no longer follow their god.

NIFARA (*NEE-FA-rah*) — *The Virgin of Justice, Soul Messenger, Once-Betrothed, Future Healer.* She learned to step between worlds from her once-betrothed, Kos-Yran, before he fell. She bears now the responsibility of that now-mad god, escorting souls between worlds they were never meant to set foot upon. Justice is her only concern, as she attempts to balance the scales perfectly.

KASNE et TERRAL (*Kaz-NEH et Teh-RAHL*) — *Prince of the Forest, Toucher of Souls,* Youngest of Aben and Crysania, Kasne strode from the forests that he had created, his people, the Minotyr on his heels. And yet it was he who agreed to leave his own people to take the enslaving Gren under his command, and from them came the Hrelgrens, touched by his hand, and blessed with a command of peace.

THE CHILDREN OF WYV AND SAKHARN

RIONNE (*Rye-OWN*) — *Firstborn of Wyv and Sakharn, Creator of Civilization, the Arbiter, The Fallen Warrior*—fallen to ruin when he was deceived by Achanerüt. Driven mad, he slew his greatest creations, and turned his own people into a scourge of the sky.

KEA'RINOUL (*Kee-AH-rih-NOOL*) — *The Scarred One, He-Who-Was-Beautiful.* Kea'Rinoul abandoned his own people, the Goranc, for he had been a god of beauty, marred by his fallen brothers. It is said he is a god who bathes in the blood of his followers, the T'Akai, wracked with torment by his own visage.

KOS-YRAN (*KOSS-EE-RAHN*) — *The Mad Gift-Giver, Once-Walker-Between-Worlds, Kashir Two-Gloves, the Walker.* Yet now he is banished to wander, gifting curses to those that seek him out. His own people, the vül, though small in number, are an infestation upon the civilized, sowing mayhem and destruction wherever they call home.

ACHANERÜT (*AH-ken-er-OOT*) — *The Deceiver, The Weaver, The Thirteen-Limbed One, Fatherless.* His thirteen limbs sow lies and weave dissension. His eyes see far, and bring kings to their knees. All that is in ruin is his attribute. All that is built up fears that he shall tear it down. The machinations of his web cannot be understood, even by the gods.

GLOSSARY 3

BLACK SENTINELS

The Black Sentinels are a mercenary organization in which each individual seeks out their own bodyguard contracts, and pays dues back to the organization, thus allowing them to wear their trademark black, peak-hooded cloak. They carry various weapons to denote their rank, which equates to their pay grade, hidden under their cloaks to keep their ability concealed.

BANDED CLUB — Initiate to the Black Sentinels carry a single club.

BLACK CLOAK — Officially marks their entry in the organization.

2ND CLUB — Sergeant rank. Common rate for their service is a full silver Baro a day in the northern nations.

HAND AXE — Lieutenants can negotiate a higher pay, armed with a more lethal weapon.

2ND AXE — 1st Lieutenants have several clients willing to give them a good reference.

CROSSBOW — Only by being promoted by the upper echelons can a Black Sentinel become a Captain.

BATTLE AXE — Commanders are rarely seen away from the Black Sentinels headquarters in Limae.

GLOSSARY 4

PALADINS OF THE HAMMER

The Paladins are the followers of Grissone, god of Faith. Each Paladin takes on one of the five active Vows. (The sixth vow, Introspection, or Blindness, is no longer taken.) The Paladins were founded in the Hrelgren Imperial Year 1111, the same year the T'Akai first appeared, launching attacks into what is now the Protectorate of Pariantür, (simultaneously against the Hrelgren Empire and Qavylli Republic.) Heeding Grissone's call, the seven apostles founded the Order, and peoples from every nation came to help them build Pariantür to defend against the T'Akai incursion. Many of the men who survived the war stayed on at Pariantür, joining the Order.

VOWS OF THE PALADINS

VOW OF PRAYER — Those that adopt this Vow ground themselves in the memorization of scripture, making the conscious effort to speak their inner thoughts directly to their god.

VOW OF POVERTY — Paladins are supported via family stipend or by their own trade. Paladins who take this vow perform additional duty to pay for their room and board and they may not keep personal items.

VOW OF CHASTITY — Those that take this Vow are forbidden from marrying. Many avoid contact with members of the opposite sex entirely.

VOW OF PACIFISM — Paladins who take this Vow never raise their hammer against another, seeking peace by any other means.

VOW OF SILENCE — Brothers who take this Vow do not speak another word for the rest of their lives, instead communicating through their hands. These brothers also give up their surnames as their founder, Sternovis did.

VOW OF BLINDNESS — This Vow is no longer taken. Those that did bound their eyes away from the world.

HOLDINGS OF THE HAMMER

The Paladins live in communities of two or more brothers and their monasteries are scattered across the world, having different sizes and designations.

BASTIONS

A least two Paladins stationed at a bastion at any given time. Can be as high as twenty-five. Most major cities and towns have a bastion and many are raised at intervals along long stretches of road between cities.

FORTRESSES

Commanding local bastons, a fortress houses upward of one hundred Paladins.

CITADELS

There are four Citadels. Each commands a network of Fortresses and Bastions.

PARIANTÜR — Pariantür is the head of the entire order and acts as guardian over the eastern lands known as the Protectorate of the Hammer. Over half of the entire order is stationed there—over seven thousand Paladins. There is enough space to house over ten thousand Paladins if necessary. The Paladames have over three-thousand sisters stationed at Pariantür.

ST. HAMUL — This citadel holds sway over the Order in the eastern nations of Ganthic. Nearly five hundred brothers are stationed there.

THE AERIE — Located in the country of Limae, the Aerie has nearly four hundred brothers stationed there. Commands Northwestern Ganthic fortresses and bastions.

AMMAR — Located in Ormach, Ammar Citadel has over one thousand Paladins stationed there. While this citadel controls the fewest Fortresses and Bastions, it boasts one of the greatest human libraries outside of Pariantür.

ANDREW D MEREDITH

RANKS OF THE HAMMER

Those seeking admittance to the Order of the Hammer begin as either:

ACOLYTE — Individual who seeks out Pariantür to become a Paladin.

PENITENT — Individual who has chosen servitude over imprisonment or worse.

These lower level Acolytes and Penitents are grouped together and don brown robes and shaving their heads. They act as servants to the Hammer at Pariantür while learning to live as a Paladin.

ESTUDIATE — Having learned the Rule of St. Ikhail, Estudiates lives a life of routine and constant change as they are tested in various occupations over the course of a year. During this time they will review each Vow, and come to a decision regarding which Vow they will take. This decision marks their graduation to Neophyte.

NEOPHYTE — Having taken on a vow, the Neophyte begins study under a master in their chosen or assigned trade. They are given their hammer, which is chained to their belt by the twenty-two links, and they are given the Vow-Bead which will hang from their belt until they receive cordons.

    Vow of Chastity — Haloed Hammer
    Vow of Poverty — Stylized Pattern
    Vow of Silence — Tower
    Vow of Pacifism — Shield
    Vow of Prayer — Anka's Wing
    Vow of Blindness — Simple Band

PALADIN — When the Neophyte is given their armor, they are officially called a Paladin, but in name only. It is only if they proceed past this level that they will be considered a true Paladin by the Brotherhood. They have a single year to test as a Journeyman in their field if they wish to proceed. If they do not master their chosen profession, they will wait anywhere from five to ten years before being allowed to test once more.

BROTHER PALADIN — If deemed worthy, a Paladin is given the red cordons, marking them both a Master in their trade, and a Brother Paladin. Full member of the Brotherhood with full rights to vote on all matters. If leadership requires they move to a new trade, they will learn from and proceed through the same lessons and trials, however, nothing can take their rank of Brother Paladin from them.

BROTHER EXCELSIOR — Brother Excelsiors are the equivalent to a lieutenant, commanding brothers of lower rank, marked by green cordons. Quite often they are true experts or specialists in their assigned trade. A Brother Excelsior in the Smithy might be an expert at metal inlays. A baker might specialize in selecting and negotiating superior ingredients.

BROTHER ADJUTANT — Marked by white cordons, there is rarely more than a single Brother Adjutant in any occupation at a single location. They often fill vacant leadership roles when a higher rank is not present. This rank is also considered the first "true" leadership rank.

BROTHER PRIMUS — Leaders and masters, the black-cordoned Primus commands respect and authority. Primuses often hold the highest rank at Fortresses.

PATER MINORIS — A Paladin will rarely rise to this rank without there being a vacancy. Each Citadel is led by one, and many fortresses have a Pater Minoris stationed there as leader. There is a Pater Minoris representing each Vow stationed at Pariantür. Besides wearing gold cordons, their armor is also often adorned with symbology reflective of the long traditions of a Citadel. The five Pater Minorii stationed at Pariantür fill very important roles in the community.
- Pater Minoris of Prayer Hiram van Höllebon, Chaplain to Pariantür
- Pater Minoris of Poverty Mason Diggle, Keeper of Fealty
- Pater Minoris of Chastity Pol Dunkirk, Hospitaler
- Pater Minoris of Silence Daveth, Grandmaster Smith
- Pater Minoris of Pacifism Klous Girard, Groundskeeper

PATER SEGUNDUS — Under the Prima Pater rules a council of four Pater Segundii, each representing a different Vow. They are marked by blue cordons and their words hold nearly as much authority as the Prima Pater himself.
- Pater Segundus of Poverty Nichal Guess, Pariantür's Castellan
- Pater Segundus of Pacifism Gallahan Pír, Master Scribe
- Pater Segundus of Silence Athmor, Master Cellarer
- Pater Segundus of Chastity Agapius Emiro, Sacrist

PRIMA PATER — There is only one Prima Pater. A Prima Pater's armor is crafted to match the motifs and symbols of the founding saint of their Vow. When a Prima Pater's rank is passed on, one of the Pater Segundii under him will take on the role, donning armor of their own figurehead saint, thus ensuring that another Vow takes the helm.

GLOSSARY 5

THE CRYSALAS SOCIETAS

Followers of Crysania are known collectively as the Members of the Crysalas Societas. This includes women of the secret Vaults, known as the Crysalas Integritas, Paladames of the Rose known officially as the Crysalas Honoris, the Shieldmaidens of Boroni and Bronue, and several smaller factions of female qavylli and hrelgrens who have chosen to follow Crysania. All of these Societas meet in secret Vaults across the world of Kallattai, guarding prophecies gathered from the Dweol and each other.

Centuries ago, the Church of Aben long ago and went further into hiding. The majority of the Crysalas fled to Pariantür, where they formed the Crysalas Honoris, known as Paladame. This formation tricked down over time to changing the nature of the Crysalas Vaults to guarding women from predatory men and political leveraging.

ASPECTS OF PURITY

Across the entire organization members of the Crysalas take on Aspects of purity, rather than Vows as Paladins do. Some of these have been around since the foundation while others have developed over time. Most sisters take on an average of three Aspects, though some take on more. They are noted publicly by adornments, which creates a general customized look among the sisters who otherwise wear only white robes and headdresses. These Aspects fall into four categories:

BLOSSOM — Purity of Form
THORN — Purity of Choice
LEAF — Purity of Service
ROOT — Purity of Function

ASPECTS OF THE BLOSSOM

ASPECT OF CLEANLINESS — *(Shaven Head)* This Aspect focuses on a ritualistic and meticulous cleaning regimen.
ASPECT OF SILENCE — *(Veil)* Wears a veil over their face so they cannot be seen. They are not completely silent, talking in quiet whispers. Sisters of this aspect experience an aloneness that others naturally give them.
ASPECT OF VIRGINITY — *(Gilded Rose)* Women who select this Aspect are forbidden to marry. While most Crysalas do not marry, they are not forbidden from doing so as these sisters are.
ASPECT OF PEACE — *(Wooden Mace)* Sisters who take this Aspect vow to cause no harm to another.
ASPECT OF STRICTNESS — *(Solid Plate on Shoulder)* — Sisters who take this Aspect have no choice over their diet. They must eat what they are served, and may not leave any of it untouched, nor ask for more when the meal is concluded.

ASPECTS OF THE THORN

(It is often frowned upon that any sister take more than one Thorn Aspect, as each is known to be stringent and difficult.)
ASPECT OF SANCTITY — *(Gloves)* Sisters who take on the Aspect of Sanctity do not feel the touch of another save through their gloves.
ASPECT OF SOLITUDE — *(Fetter Hat)* The fetter hat is a very recognizable adornment. It forces the wearer to look towards their feet at all times.
ASPECT OF SOLEMNITY — *(Black Circlet)* One of the harder Aspects to master, the Aspect of Solemnity allows no outward emotion.
ASPECT OF PRESERVATION — *(Leaves—no roses on uniform)* Those who take this Aspect may not eat meat of any kind.
ASPECT OF ST. KLARE — *(Thorn Necklace)* This Aspect was developed when members of the Aspect of Preservation employed a work around for their abstinence from meat by excess drink. St. Klare developed a variant that was very ascetic, allowing the eating of only breads, insects, water, and certain fruits and vegetables.

ASPECTS OF THE LEAF

ASPECT OF DISCRETION — (*Rose Earrings*) This Aspect requires a sister to listen intently to others without interrupting.

ASPECT OF CHARITY — (*Brown Robe*) The Charitable Sisters are very often found matched with the Paladins who take on the Vow of Poverty.

ASPECT OF COMPASSION — (*Dwov Elbow Guards*) These sisters are required to serve those with needs that can be met.

ASPECT OF OBEDIENCE — (*Bell Earrings*) The Aspect of Obedience is not a slaving Aspect, but one that allows one to be congenial, and helpful as requested.

ASPECT OF DIGNITY — (*Bound Sleeves*) — Those sisters who practice this Aspect seek to restore the dignity of those that are ailing or are elderly.

ASPECTS OF THE ROOT

ASPECT OF HUMILITY — (*Heavy Boots*) — The menial, janitorial tasks of a sister of the Aspect of Humility keep the order continuing as they do what no one else wants.

ASPECT OF CLARITY — *(Scroll Front Cloth)* Those sisters with a knack for memory, or wish to develop such a gift take on this Aspect. They are constantly testing one another with the recitation of verse.

ASPECT OF HONOR — (*Thorn Spiked Mace*) Of all the Aspects, this is the most practiced among the Paladames at Pariantür. While they do not go out on patrol against the T'Akai, they act as guards at all the hidden Vaults across Ganthic.

ASPECT OF FORM — (*Plain Bracers*) The Aspect of Form practiced hand to hand techniques, to grapple and contain opponents.

ASPECT OF FUNCTION — (*Utility Belt*) Those that seek to master an art or craft will take on this Aspect and delve as deeply as they can into their art.

GLOSSARY 6

MONKS OF NIFARA

The Monastic Order of the Staff, or the Monks of Nifara as they are more commonly known, are perhaps the oldest religious organization on Kallattai, and make up the sole followers of Nifara. While the largest community of monks are humans, Nifarans can be found in every race on Kallattai. Their purpose is to offer judgment between two arguing parties. They rule fairly, impartially, and quickly. Some deem their judgments too harsh, but this is tempered by their consistency. When a monk of Nifara is addressed, the correct honorific in the lands of man is Nefer. This is said to be a very old title, dating back to an older name for Nifara, Nefereh. When a judgment is made, a stick is broken, and given to each side of the argument, in memoriam. Nine times a judgment has been made that was deemed world-shifting. When that occurred, the monk broke not a stick, but their staff. These nine are honored above all others, with statuary made in their likeness at the Templum of Nifara in Birin. While there are many myths surrounding the Nine Saints, the most interesting fact is that none of their tales reference how they died.

Afterword

There was a twelve-year-old boy. A kid who felt himself an outcast due to the Tourettes Syndrome that set him apart from others. It acted as a wall between potential friends, and filled him with a sense of longing: For new worlds. For magic. For griffins. For characters who felt as he did.

I can see myself reenacting scenes of caravans and mysterious dark figures as I dragged my siblings around our small back yard in that red wagon. As I climbed the apple tree, I imagined my ascent of dark towers, to fight darker wizards with nothing but the sword I had painted blue, powered by the rune I had painted on its pommel.

From those early imaginings, over twenty-five years ago, the world of Kallattai was born. Like that young boy, the early world of Kallattai was full of dreams, potential quests, and let's be honest, simple, basic, and underdeveloped stories. It took, as all things do, years to come to fruition. And now the harvest is here.

Hanen and Rallia, the most unchanged yet not the characters they started as, acted as our everyman (and woman) in Kallattai. Theirs was a normal life, now leading to adventure requiring, continually, that they choose to proceed.

In many ways, Jined has changed the most while remaining the same. He went from a two-dimensional, dense farmhand in an early draft, to the Paladin who had a lot to learn. That thrice-broken nose is symbolic to the changes his character has undergone. When I unshackled him from the original main character's plot in those early drafts and versions, and gave him his own, he flourished. He no longer took the side-seat. His was a tale just as important: follow the call of his god. It is Jined's chapters that come easiest to me, and yet, those are the ones I feel most anxious about, worried that Jined's story will go off the rails, and take me where I did not intend it to. And yet, every time I finish a chapter, I become introspective, and study the lessons he teaches me.

And then there is Katiam. None of the characters in the world of Kallattai has had more blood, sweat, and effort poured into them as she has. She may seem to most a simple physician, but there is more to Katiam and her tale than even I first knew when I started on the *Kallattian Saga*. While Jined has come to represent my sense of dignity found in facing your past actions, Katiam is the desire for choice. Her fate, she feels, has been chosen for her. (A constant theme in the series, if I'm honest.) Hers is the choice to flourish where she is planted.

I can't thank you enough for reaching this point—finishing *Deathless Beast* and starting your journey into the *Kallattian Saga*. But there is one more thing you could do for me. Could you take a moment to leave a review, or at least a handful of stars? That is the surest way to discovery. Perhaps you took a risk and read this book, but many others won't. Your spreading the word will provide a confidence that can't be expressed in any other way. So please, enable the next reader to join the path into the *Kallattian Saga*, and become a member of this, as of right now, very exclusive readership.

I have so much more in store for you, and can't wait to share it.

—Andrew D Meredith

ABOUT THE AUTHOR

Andrew D Meredith's journey has taken him to many fantastical places. From selling books in the wilds of western Washington to designing and publishing board games for *Fantasy Flight Games/Asmodee*. He's now committed to the quest he was called to so long ago: the telling of fantastical tales, and bringing to life underestimated characters willing to take on the responsibilities no one else will.

AndrewDMeredith.com

@AndrewDMth

www.ingramcontent.com/pod-product-compliance
Lightning Source LLC
LaVergne TN
LVHW041737060526
838201LV00046B/837